9X +/16 ✓ 1/21
(4 copies)

D0501851

BY DREW KARPYSHYN

STAR WARS

Star Wars: Darth Bane: Path of Destruction

Star Wars: Darth Bane: Rule of Two

Star Wars: Darth Bane: Dynasty of Evil

Star Wars: The Old Republic: Revan

Star Wars: The Old Republic: Annihilation

MASS EFFECT

Mass Effect: Revelation

Mass Effect: Ascension

Mass Effect: Retribution

TEMPLE HILL

Baldur's Gate II: Throne of Bhaal

Children
of Fire

Children of Fire

DREW KARPYSHYN

DEL REY

NEW YORK

Copyright © 2013 by Drew Karpyshyn

Published in the United States by Del Rey, an imprint of The Random House Publishing Group, a division of Random House, Inc., New York.

Del Rey and the House colophon are registered trademarks of Random House, Inc.

Library of Congress Cataloging-in-Publication Data
Karpyshyn, Drew.
Children of fire / Drew Karpyshyn.
pages cm
ISBN 978-0-345-54223-6 (hardback) — ISBN 978-0-345-54676-0 (ebook)
1. Fantasy fiction. I. Title.
PS3611.A7846C45 2013
813'.6—dc23
2013020337

Printed in the United States of America on acid-free paper

www.delreybooks.com

2 4 6 8 9 7 5 3 1

First Edition

Book design by Caroline Cunningham

To Jennifer,

my love and my life

Children
of Fire

Prologue

All things are born from fire. The flames of Chaos are the source of all life and all creation; the cause of all death and all destruction. The entirety of the mortal world was forged from the inferno of the Burning Sea, the Chaos shaped and bound by the power of the Old Gods to create an island of tranquility floating in an ocean of flame.

First came the plants and trees. Next came the fish of the oceans, then the birds of the air and the beasts of the land. Finally, the Old Gods created woman and man, and they spread out to populate the newly formed world.

But Chaos rebels against structure and order, and even the magic of a God cannot bind it forever. Nothing is eternal.

—SALIDARR, *founder and first Pontiff of the Order*

NOTHING LASTS FOREVER.

He knows this better than any. Elevated from the ranks of mortals by the Talismans; transformed by the infinite power of Chaos into a God himself . . . only to be cast down. For too long he has been imprisoned in this nether realm of smoke and shadow for the unforgivable sin of daring to challenge divine authority. But now the Old Gods are gone, and he alone remains.

Just as he is alone now, a single figure in a deserted, ashen plain:

dry, cracked earth beneath a gray and featureless sky. He stands before a fountain of white stone, a simple pedestal four feet high with a wide, deep bowl atop. He traces a clawed finger around the rim of the bowl, transcribing the final arcane figures of the ritual with the blood dripping from his nail . . . his blood, the blood of an Immortal. The offering will cripple him, leaving him weak and vulnerable as the magic feasts on his power. But it will give strength to his spell.

His is not the only blood that stains the fountain. A dozen of his followers, chosen from the descendants of those exiled with him, have died for this spell. He had hoped they would come without protest, giving up their own lives so that others might have a chance to escape this wasted land and return to the world their ancestors once knew. Not one was willing to make the sacrifice. But in this bleak nether realm his will is absolute, and those who were chosen for the ritual could not deny his claim. Their lifeblood now fills the fountain's bowl, their broken and shattered bones piled around the base of its pedestal.

The fountain trembles beneath his touch; the crimson pool quivers with the power of Chaos. Power enough to save him. Power enough to destroy him.

The lives of his followers hang in the balance with his own. Should the magic consume him, the denizens of this realm will tear one another apart to claim his barren throne. But they are mortal—what is life to them? How much more does an Immortal risk? He alone can understand the consequences of what he is doing; a calculated gamble; one he has no choice but to take.

For too long he has been forced to sit and watch, doing nothing, waiting in vain for the Legacy—the barrier that shields the mortal world from him and his followers—to crumble. Day by day, year by year, century by century he has slowly watched his power ebb, waiting for this last spell of the Old Gods to fade. But the magic of a God dies slowly. The Legacy is still strong, and now he himself is beginning to wither and die. The risk is great, but he can wait no longer.

Placing a scaled hand on either side of the bowl he tilts his head back to the empty sky and closes his eyes. Softly he begins to chant, mystic words meant to draw upon the power of Chaos, to channel it through his body and into the fountain.

He holds the gathering magic for as long as he is able, until the building power bursts forth in a rush of heat. The blood within the fountain seethes and boils. Thick bubbles burst with wet, sickly sounds, releasing clouds of crimson steam. The flesh of his palms begins to cook against the scorching stone of the fountain's bowl. Pointed teeth clenched, he endures the searing pain in silent agony as the color is burned away and the blood is transformed into clear, crystal water.

Only then does he let go, staggering back and gasping for breath as the waters quickly cool. His great leather wings twitching in anticipation, he watches as the bubbling surface of the fountain goes still, becoming a perfectly reflective pool. The ritual has begun.

He reaches up with one burned and blistered hand to clasp the fist-sized black stone that hangs from his neck. He has worn it for many years, dangling from a thin gold chain running through the tiny hole bored through its heart. Over the centuries he has kept it close, drawing patience and strength as he waited for this day that has finally arrived.

With a sharp tug he tears the stone free, oblivious to the bite of the chain digging into the flesh along the back of his neck before it snaps and slithers to the ground at his feet.

The stone is cold in his grasp, but quickly warms to his touch. Symbols are traced in blood across its smooth, dark surface: his blood. Runes from the Old Tongue, they represent the four aspects of everything he once was: wizard, warrior, prophet, king. Imbued with his divine essence, the stone is his seed. The spirit of his un-born child is trapped within . . . a child destined to tear down the Legacy.

Stepping forward he peers into the pool and sees the mortal world: a vision of a realm still tantalizingly beyond his grasp. Ignoring the pain of his mutilated palms he grips the dark stone tightly with both hands, raising it high above his head as he begins another chant.

The magic builds within him for a second time, the heat coursing through his veins yet again. The water in the fountain begins to bubble and boil once more. The tranquil vision of the mortal world disappears, replaced by the churning flames of the Chaos Sea.

The stone begins to pulse with heat; a steady rhythm that matches the beating of his own heart. His voice rises, his words channeling the power of the spell that will carry the stone across the Sea of Flame to touch the shores of the mortal world. There it will take root, and somewhere a child will be born. His child. A child born from the fires of Chaos.

His body begins to tremble from the strain; his words falter. And in that instant the Chaos breaks free. The stone explodes in his hands, tearing open the wounded flesh of his clawed fingers as it splits into quarters. He recoils with a scream to the empty sky as the pieces tumble from his grasp, disappearing beneath the surface without a ripple.

At their touch a roaring pillar of blue flame erupts from the pool. He hurls himself clear as the tower of fire engulfs the pedestal and the surrounding bones, utterly consuming them before vanishing a second later with a thunderous clap.

He lies huddled on the ground, panting, his wings folded over his head and back in an instinctive reaction to shield himself from the withering heat of the conflagration. Slowly the wings part and he peeks from beneath them at the scorched earth and small pile of black ash, a God humbled. Chaos cannot be contained; cannot be controlled.

Yet he senses that all is not lost. The stone was split, its essence fractured; but the four quarters were consumed by the fires of the spell. Stretching across the infinite breadth of the Chaos Sea, the effects will be muted and faint. Yet even those pebbles will send ripples to lap against the shores of the mortal world.

Not one child, but four, each touched by the power of his magic, each marked to be born in the flames of strife and suffering. Mortals imbued with the burning essence of a banished and forgotten God, their lives inevitably linked and intertwined. Even he cannot foresee their ultimate fate; salvation and destruction sit poised in perfect balance, the outcome is uncertain, his vision unclear.

Yet as he unfurls his wings and rises once more to his feet, he is certain of one thing: Chaos has been unleashed.

Chapter 1

AN UNSEEN BRANCH snaked through the darkness of the night to snag Nyra's ankle with dry wooden fingers. She toppled forward, her swollen belly making her awkward and clumsy. The heavy shawl wrapped about her shoulders tumbled to the ground as she thrust her hands out in front to break her fall.

She felt a sudden pain in her left wrist as her hands hit the unyielding frozen earth—sharp, but not severe. She struggled to her knees, her hands cradling her midsection, trying to comfort and console the unborn child in her womb. She whispered words of reassurance as she caressed her girth through the heavy wool of her winter dress, praying to the Old Gods and the New to feel the baby kick or squirm in protest at the unexpected fall.

Nothing. She stayed there on the cold earth, refusing to accept her child's lack of response. The chill of the night seeped up from the ground through her knees and into her weary thighs. The bite of the winter wind blew harsh against her cheeks and shoulders. But she wouldn't cry. Not yet. Not while she still had hope for her unborn child.

Slowly, she turned and reached back for the shawl she had brought to shield her from the night's cold. The Southlands rarely saw snow, but her village was no more than a few days' ride from the steppes of the Frozen East. Winter here had a sting the deep Southlands never felt.

She hefted the shawl and twirled it up and over her shoulders, noting a twinge in her left wrist as she did so. The unexpected pain made her grit her teeth. As best she could in the night's blackness she examined her injury.

Sprained, she decided at last. Only sprained.

With great effort she clambered to her feet, her hand instinctively dropping to her belly yet again. The child within remained still. Ignoring the cramping protest of her calves and thighs, the constant ache running through her back, and the knots in her neck and shoulders, she continued on her way.

She moved with greater care now. The crescent moon was obscured by the tangle of stark, bare branches overhead, and the forest cast disorienting shadows along the overgrown path she followed. But she knew it was more than that.

During the day the path would be easy to follow, worn flat by constant traffic from the nearby villages; kept clear by the constant passing of men and women coming to present their pleas. In the light of the sun, the path was simple enough for a rider on a sure-footed mount to safely traverse.

But the hag did not like visitors at night; her enchantments made the way more difficult than it should be. Chaos changed the route beneath the mantle of darkness. The earth became rough and uneven, the roots and limbs of the trees themselves grasped out to impede her progress.

Nyra had left her pony tied to a tree more than a mile back, knowing she would have to make the passage on foot. She pressed on; time was running short. She had no choice but to come under the cover of night, while her husband slept. In the twenty years since the Purge had ended, most of the laws against practicing magic had been repealed. But Gerrit still frowned upon those who possessed the Gift.

She didn't blame him. He was older than she was, old enough to remember the Purge. As a child he had watched the Order's public

executions; his earliest memories were of witches and heretics cry-
ing out as they burned at the stake. Times were different now.
Chaos magic was tolerated, though the Order still officially spoke
out against its dangers. And like most who lived in the Southlands,
Gerrit had no wish to do anything that might displease the Order.
He would have tried to talk her out of this.

"The baby has been healthy," he would argue. "We felt it kicking
and squirming inside you, eager to be born and full of life. The
times before it wasn't like this."

True, for a while. But shortly after the eighth moon of her pregnancy, the baby had grown still. Like the others. Gerrit didn't know.
She hadn't told him—and the Gods willing, she would never have to.

Nyra stumbled along, falling often. Her knees bruised and stiffened, her hands became red and raw from scraping over the frozen,
jagged ground with every tumble. Once she struck her jaw on a
jutting branch as she fell, splitting her lip and biting her tongue.
The taste of blood scared her; it reminded her of the blood of
birth. Too much blood, in her case. But she didn't spit it out. And
she didn't cry. She wouldn't let herself, not yet. Not while there
was still hope. Unconsciously, she passed a gentle hand over the
swell of her pregnancy.

After another mile she glimpsed the flicker of a small fire, just
beyond the crest of a knoll jutting up in the path. The way suddenly seemed to clear: The tripping roots melted into the now
smooth earth; the clutching branches retreated to a distance. The
icy air around her thawed with the warmth of the tempting fire,
carried forward on a whispering zephyr. Nyra crawled to the top
of the small but steep knoll, using her hands as much as her feet to
get her heavy, swollen form up and over the crest.

The other side was a gentle slope into a small clearing. In the
corner was a cramped cottage, little more than a wood-and-grass
hut. A campfire burned in the center of the clearing, well away
from the surrounding trees and the dry thatch of the tiny home.
The flames flickered blue and purple, then red and orange. Green
and yellow sparks popped and crackled within the unnatural blaze.

An old woman knelt by the fire, stirring the coals with a thin, crooked stick. She wore simple dark garments, heavy layers warding off whatever winter chill the fire could not keep at bay. Her hair was gray, her skin sallow. Beside her was a pile of small animal bones. Nyra hesitated, uncertain, until the witch looked up.

"Have you come all this way only to turn back now?" Gretchen the Hag asked. Her voice was a dry, raspy whisper.

Nyra slowly approached the strange flames until she stood across the fire, facing her withered host.

"Sit," the old woman instructed.

With great effort, Nyra lowered her bulk to the ground. She shifted her legs to try to get comfortable on the hard earth, but the effort was wasted.

"Speak," Gretchen ordered, oblivious to the pregnant woman's obvious physical discomfort. She poked the fire once more with the gnarled stick.

"I . . . I have come for my child," Nyra began.

"Another, or this one?" the old woman asked, jabbing her stick in the direction of Nyra's swollen belly.

"This one. There is no other. Twice my husband and I have tried, but both times the baby has been stillborn."

Gretchen snorted. "Stillborn. You mean dead. I cannot raise the dead."

It had been over a year since her last pregnancy, but still the hag's words stung. But she refused to let herself cry. Not for this child. Not yet.

"This baby is not dead. I felt it kicking on the night of the last full moon. The other pregnancies were different. I felt nothing but the weight of the child, like a cold stone in my belly."

Gretchen set her stick down and picked up a small bone from the pile at her side. Cracking it open with thin, twisted fingers she sucked the marrow out. She chewed and gnawed the two splintered ends with decayed stumps of teeth, making a squishing sound that twisted Nyra's face up in revulsion.

The witch picked up her stick and jabbed the fire with the tip,

then spit into the flames. There was a tiny shower of sparks in response, and a foul, rotting odor wafted up in a thin cloud of yellow
smoke.

"That was a fortnight ago," the hag declared, seeing the truth in
the flames. "The child is already dead within you. There is nothing
I can do. It will be born like the others: lifeless and cold."

Nyra wanted to scream her protest to this foul, bitter woman.
But hysterics would accomplish nothing. She took a deep breath
before speaking. "The child still lives within me. I know it."

"How?" Gretchen demanded. "Have you felt it move?"

A lie would be pointless here in the light of the enchanted fire.

"The child lives. I just know."

The hag nodded and laid her stick to the side to pick up another
tiny bone. As she cracked and chewed it, Nyra noticed that the
stick used to stir the embers was itself a long, thin animal bone,
blackened by years of smoke from the hag's fire.

Once more Gretchen spit into the fire. Again a shower of sparks,
but this time the rising smoke was blue. It smelled faintly of the
rich, pungent manure her husband used to spread on the fields.

"What have you brought me?"

Nyra reached down to the deep pocket at the front of her dress
and felt for the small leather pouch she had stuffed inside before
beginning her journey. It was awkward, fumbling around her stomach's girth to explore the pocket while sitting on the ground. For
a brief second she could not locate the pouch, and she feared it had
been lost during her stumbling journey up the path. Then her
fingers closed around the loop of drawstring. She pulled it out and
held it up for the hag to see.

Gretchen reached across the fire with eager hands to seize the
offering, undaunted by the heat rising up from the flames. She
snatched it from Nyra's grasp and poured the contents into her
wrinkled palm.

The small collection of coins and jewelry amounted to a substantial sum. Nyra's husband was not a rich man, but he was hard-
working and successful. And he loved to buy his wife beautiful and

interesting trinkets from the traveling merchants who passed through their small village. Before she had left her home this night, Nyra had selected the most valuable items from her collection, along with the small stash of gold coins she had saved up over the years.

"It's not enough," Gretchen declared after appraising the contents.

"I . . . I brought nothing else," Nyra stammered in surprise.

She had expected the cost of what she asked to be easily covered by the generous gift. The value of her offering exceeded two years' pay for a field hand working on their farm.

The hag eyed her with her milky orbs, a greedy gleam poking out from beneath the white of her cataracts. "Your ring."

Nyra recoiled, her hands clasping together over her wedding band as if she could hide it from the hag's greedy gaze. She had been hoping Gerrit would never miss the small stash of jewelry she had taken, but if she came back without the ring he had given her on their Union Day he would surely notice.

"No! My husband will ask what happened. He must not find out I have been here."

Gretchen shrugged. "The ring or nothing. That is the price of your child."

Nyra hated her, this wretched old woman who held the life of her unborn baby in her ugly, twisted hands. Slowly she removed her ring, struggling to get it over the bulging knuckle of her swollen finger. In a flash of spite she threw it at the hag with all the strength her weary arm could muster. The old woman's hand snatched it from the air with the speed of a striking serpent.

After examining the ring for a brief second the hag stuffed it into a hidden fold of her garments, along with the rest of the contents of the leather pouch. She tossed the pouch into the fire, where it was quickly consumed by the unnatural flames.

Reaching down Gretchen picked up another small bone and offered it to the young woman. Despite the fear in her breast Nyra reached out to accept it. She turned it over in her hands, trying to determine from what animal it must have come. The bone was thin and light, like a bird's. It was too large to be from any chicken she had seen.

As if reading her thoughts the hag said, "A young griffin. No more than a week or two old by the size. Not powerful, but powerful enough for this."

Nyra could do little but take the old woman at her word. She had never seen a griffin; no one had. No one living. Griffins had been extinct for centuries . . . if they had ever existed at all. Nyra wouldn't be surprised if Gretchen was lying to her about the origins of the bone.

"Break it," the hag instructed. "Suck the marrow, but do not swallow it. Chew it, gnaw the bone. Then spit it into the fire."

The bone was brittle and snapped easily in Nyra's grasp. She made a bitter face as the sour sting of the marrow burned the cut on her lip and the bite on her tongue. But she did as she was told, chewing and gnawing until the hag nodded her head in the direction of the flames.

Nyra spit, the gray of the bone mingling with the deep red of the blood still trickling from the injuries to her mouth. The fire flared with a bright orange heat so intense she had to turn her eyes away from the flash. When she looked back she could see a small gleaming white coal no larger than the size of her thumbnail in the center of the now blue-green flames.

"Take it," Gretchen commanded.

Nyra remembered the way the hag had earlier reached right across the magical fire without seeming to feel the heat. She thrust her hand into the flames and seized the white coal, then cried out in pain and surprise, yanking her arm back as the heat seared her flesh. But her fist remained clenched about her prize, which seemed to hold no heat at all.

Gretchen cackled as Nyra studied her burned hand. The skin was an angry red, and there were a few blisters from the heat. But nothing serious, nothing permanent. She felt tears welling up in her eyes: tears at the pain; tears at the cruelty of the hag; tears of fear and despair she had been denying herself ever since she realized the babe in her womb had gone still. But she would not cry. Not in front of this cackling old woman. Not now, when there was true hope for her baby. Nyra glared at the hag, and the evil laughter stopped.

"Swallow the coal. It will give you a healthy child with the coming of the next moon," the hag instructed. "But understand that there is yet a cost to be paid," she added under her breath.

Nyra didn't hear her . . . or at least pretended not to. Instead, she popped the small coal into her mouth. It burned with the salty warmth of life going down her throat. She gasped in surprise, then burst into tears of joy when she felt the baby give a sudden kick.

Two weeks later Nyra once again endured the agony of childbirth, soaked in a sheen of sweat. A cool cloth covered her forehead, but the room was hot; the midwife's assistant had piled the fire high to ward off the fading winter chill. The sticky warmth of blood coated the inside of her thighs, leaking out from between her legs . . . the same color as the moon in the sky the past three nights.

The Burning Moon, Nyra thought, panting in and out with short, quick breaths as she fought to control her contractions. *An ill omen.*

There was a sudden thrust of pain deep within her and she screamed aloud.

"Don't push!" the midwife yelled from down between her legs.

Nyra could hear the fear in her voice. She could feel hands down there; grasping, wiping, turning. She wanted Gerrit; wanted to feel his strong fingers enveloping her own, hear his whispered reassurance. But the women had sent him out partway through the birth.

One of the assistants rushed up to change the cloth on her head. She could see the horror on the teenage girl's face.

It's not always like this, Nyra tried to tell her. *There's not always this much blood, this much pain. It's not always like this—just for me.* But instead she screamed as she was ripped apart from the inside yet again.

"Now!" the midwife screamed, "Push now, Nyra!"

And she did, pushing even though she could feel herself being rent asunder. The world dissolved into a veil of blind suffering, and suddenly she understood the final warning of the hag in the woods. Now she knew the true toll exacted by the power of Chaos.

She heard the wailing cry of her son being born, the midwife's shouted, desperate orders, the hurried rush of the assistants to save the mother, and at last Nyra wept. Wept at what she had seen, at what she finally understood. Wept with joy and sorrow and terror at the price of her son's life, even as her world went dark and her own life oozed out between her legs in an ever-expanding pool of blood.

Chapter 2

THE BABY GIRL coughed once, spewing forth a ball of phlegm and blood that had blocked her breathing. She choked. She gasped. And then she began to cry. Her screams ripped through the heavy silence of the room at the back of the Golden Circlet, and Methodis muttered a quick prayer of thanks to the New Gods that the child had survived what the young, malnourished mother had not.

The little girl was strong; stronger than he would have imagined possible, given the circumstances of her birth. Had he believed in such things he might have called it a miracle . . . or a tragedy.

Her mother dead, the father unknown, the healer thought. *Only seconds old, and she's already alone in the world.*

He tied off the cord and handed the newborn to the terrified scullery girl who had been pressed into service as his assistant here in the back rooms of the pleasure-house. Like the dead mother, Methodis didn't recognize her. She must have been one of Luger's newest catches.

"Use the soft cloths to wipe the child clean," he explained slowly. "Be very gentle. Then wrap her in the blankets."

The wide-eyed girl nodded, gingerly taking the tiny baby's squirming form in her outstretched arms. She glanced down at the mother lying in a bed usually reserved for more carnal pursuits, then snatched her eyes away from the corpse's torn, bloodstained midsection.

"What about Ilana?" the serving girl asked in a trembling whisper.

Methodis wondered briefly if the serving girl had known the mother well. Had they perhaps been friends?

"Leave her to me. I will clean her up and arrange for a proper burial. After I speak with Luger."

Methodis made no effort to clean himself up before going to speak to the owner of the establishment. He wanted Luger to see everything: the blood smeared on the front of his smock, the gore covering his hands and arms all the way up to his elbows where he had reached in to rip the child free of the dying mother's womb. He left a crimson handprint on the handle of the door as he pulled it open.

Luger was leaning casually against the wall in the corridor beyond. His one good eye momentarily went wide, but otherwise he showed no reaction to the doctor's gruesome appearance. As always, the ugly scar and the empty socket staring back from the left side of Luger's face reminded Methodis of that night nearly two years ago when he had stitched the knife wound closed in this very same hallway. He had known better than to ask Luger about the fate of the customer who had inflicted the injury.

"I heard that baby crying, so I know it's alive," Luger said, then spit a wad of chewing leaf onto the floorboards. "Didn't think the whelp would live. Not being born under the Burning Moon."

For the past week the sky above Callastan had been dominated by a full moon the color of fresh blood, an incredibly rare phenomenon not seen since the days of the Purge over twenty years ago.

An old saying sprang unbidden into Methodis's mind. *Children born under the Burning Moon are touched by Chaos.* There were many, the doctor knew, who would consider the little girl cursed. *As if she doesn't have enough problems already.*

"How 'bout Ilana?" Luger demanded, interrupting the healer's thoughts. "How's she doing?"

Had Methodis been speaking with the scared serving girl in the back room he would have chosen his words to soften the blow. But he wasn't about to make the same effort with the pleasure-house's despicable owner. "She's dead."

"Dead? First the stupid wench gets herself pregnant, and then you let her die on me? You know how much she cost?"

Luger was no longer leaning against the wall, but was standing at full attention. His six-and-a-half-foot frame towered over the doctor's slight form.

"There is only so much I can do under these conditions," Methodis said, struggling to keep his voice calm and even. He knew the consequences of arousing Luger's temper. Yet remembering the bruises and welts covering the mother's body made his own anger difficult to control. "I am not trained to deliver a child in the back of a Callastan whorehouse."

"What the hell did I pay you for if you couldn't even save her? I ought to take what she cost out of your fee!" Luger spat once more on the floor and took a step forward, casting a dark shadow over the healer. "Gods' blood, I should be charging you for this visit! She was one of my best girls before she got herself swollen with that damn child!"

"You should have come for me sooner!" Methodis shot back, voice rising as his own rage bubbled over. "You waited too long. You let her bleed out. Trying to save yourself a few coins cost that girl her life!"

The healer took a defiant step forward, narrowing the distance between them to mere inches.

"Or maybe," Methodis added through clenched teeth, "you shouldn't have beaten a pregnant woman in the first place, you bastard!"

Luger moved so quickly that the smaller man didn't even have time to react. He scooped the healer up and slammed him against the wall, knocking the air from his lungs. He pressed his face in close enough for Methodis to smell his acrid breath and squinted his one good eye.

"Nobody talks that way to me in my house, little man."

He held the healer pinned to the wall for several seconds to emphasize his point, then released his grip and stepped back. Methodis dropped to one knee, gasping for breath. It was some time before he could stand upright again.

"You said the baby's gonna live?" Luger asked, as casually as two men making conversation in the market square. A fuse quick to fire, a mind quick to forget, they often said of Luger.

"The child will live, though I can't take credit for that. A little girl. She is a few weeks early, by the look of her. But she's a fighter. Don't worry, I'll take care of her."

"You?" Luger asked incredulously. "Why should you take her? I'll get a wet nurse to feed the brat, and I've got a dozen girls here to look after her."

The offer caught Methodis momentarily off guard. "You . . . you will raise this child? But why?"

"Because she's mine, damn it."

Methodis was stunned. The owner of a pleasure-house did not sleep with his girls. It simply wasn't done. It wasn't just bad business; it was seen as a sign of weakness. Luger's ruthless reputation was well known and hard-earned; the thought of him and one of his own girls was almost inconceivable.

"You're the father?" Methodis mumbled in confusion, still trying to wrap his head around the concept.

Luger gave a derisive snort.

"I'm not the father, you stupid dolt. I don't let my dick lead me around. No good can come of breeding my own whores! But I bought the mother, so the child is mine. I *own* her."

Suddenly it was all clear. Luger was the same vile and disgusting creature he had always been. At his core he was a businessman looking to recoup his expenses. To him the girl was an investment for the future. He had called the mother—Ilana—one of his best girls. No doubt he figured the daughter would take after her in beauty. In time she could earn as much as the mother in the back rooms of the whorehouse. More if Luger was depraved enough to rent her out before she reached her womanhood.

But for all the sins and vices widely available in the port city of Callastan slavery was still technically not legal. With the image of the babe struggling—and somehow succeeding—to draw her first painful breath outside the womb still fresh in his mind, Methodis made a sudden and rash decision.

"The body of the mother must be taken away for burial. The constables will be curious as to what happened to her."

Luger shrugged. "A hard childbirth under a cursed moon," he said by way of explanation. "If they don't buy that, I'll kick them a couple of coins to look the other way. Plenty of dead whores in this neighborhood."

"They will also ask about the child," Methodis pressed. "What happened to her; who plans to care for her? They might be curious as to why a man who is not the father claims ownership of the girl. Do you really want to tell them you bought Ilana?"

Smooth as silk a small knife appeared in Luger's hand. He rubbed the flat of the blade along his own chin as if in deep thought.

"Are you threatening me, Methodis? Do you really think you're so valuable to the people of this neighborhood that I won't kill you where you stand?"

The doctor chose his next words carefully.

"It's hard to find a healer willing to work in a district as close to the docks as this one. Before you kill me you better have a replacement in mind. You're not the only one who has a regular need of my services. The other tavern owners in the district might become very angry with you."

"Their anger can be soothed with silver," Luger countered, a dangerous glint in his eye.

"All this for one girl?" Methodis asked. "Think of the time and expense of raising her. Is it worth it? Hardly sound business."

An expression of uncertainty crept across Luger's face, though the knife continued to trace its menacing path across the stubble of his chin.

"And how will this look in the neighborhood?" Methodis added, playing his final card. "You claim you aren't the father, yet you seem unnaturally obsessed with this child. If you keep her there will be questions. Whispered rumors of how Luger couldn't keep his hands off one of his own girls."

Luger snarled and hurled his knife into the ground at the doctor's feet. "I don't lay with my own whores!"

Methodis glanced down at the blade embedded an inch deep in the wooden floorboard, still quivering from the force of the throw.

Looking up into Luger's one glaring eye he said, "I will take the mother's body away for burial. And I will take the child with me when I go."

"The little bitch is yours," Luger hissed as he turned away and stomped down the corridor.

The doctor breathed a sigh of relief before returning to the back room. Methodis was surprised to see that the child had stopped crying. The serving girl was gently rocking the babe back and forth in her arms, pointedly facing away from the mother's body on the bed.

At the sound of his approach the girl spoke. "You're going to take her away from all this? The baby, I mean? Take her somewhere safe?"

"You can hold her for a while longer," Methodis said gently. "I have to clean up the mother."

"She was from the Western Isles," the serving girl whispered. "Her name was Ilana. She told me it meant 'lucky.'"

Methodis nodded. He'd noticed his patient's olive skin and almond eyes when he'd first arrived to help birth the child.

In silence he cleaned the body and wrapped it in a funeral shroud so the authorities could take her. He removed his blood-soaked smock and rinsed his hands and arms clean in the basin.

The girl was still rocking the baby in the corner. He placed a hand on her shoulder, and she turned to face him. After the briefest hesitation she held the child out to him. "Have you . . . have you picked a name for her yet?"

"Sciithe," the doctor replied after a moment. "It means 'spirit' in the Old Tongue."

A hint of a smile passed over the serving girl's lips, though her eyes were moist with tears.

"She's got spirit, that's for sure. Good-bye, brave little darling." She did her best to wrap her tongue around the unfamiliar sound of the foreign name, but couldn't quite manage it. "Good-bye, Scythe."

Methodis didn't have the heart to correct her.

Chapter 3

ROLAND SAT NERVOUSLY, his large frame supported by a sturdy wooden chair outside Madam Wyndham's private quarters. From time to time he would shift his position by leaning forward, clenching and unclenching his heavily callused hands in helpless frustration.

For nearly ten years now he'd been working for Conrad Wyndham. In the beginning he'd been hired for his blade—a retired soldier to provide extra security for merchant caravans on the long trips to foreign lands. Over time, however, his employer had come to trust Roland with far greater responsibilities, such as supervising the manor staff, overseeing the stables, and securing the safety of the master's home and kin during his long absences on business.

Yet there was nothing Roland could have done to protect against this. Birthing was woman's work, and once he'd sent a servant to summon the midwife there was little else he could do but wait and worry.

The crimson orb that hung in the sky that night only fed his fears. He wasn't a superstitious man by nature, but sitting here helpless forced his mind to conjure up all the old wives' tales he heard over the years. *The Burning Moon's a harbinger of dark times. Withered crops. Two-headed calves. Plague and pestilence. Stillborn children.*

An hour ago he'd heard Madam Wyndham's screams of pain coming from the bedroom, each shriek causing his muscles to tighten involuntarily and his hand to twitch toward the short sword at his belt. He had thought nothing could be worse to bear than the sound of those screams . . . but he had been wrong.

The midwife must have given Madam Wyndham something to ease the pain, because the screams had changed to low moans before eventually stopping completely. In the ensuing silence Roland's mind had run wild, conjuring up terrifying images of everything that could have gone wrong. Several times he'd stood up and marched over to the door, determined to burst in just so he could know what was happening. Each time he'd stopped himself and returned to his chair, aware that any interference by him would only make the midwife's job harder.

When the door finally opened and the midwife emerged Roland leapt anxiously to his feet. She was a stout woman of middle age, with plain looks and a serious demeanor. Around the village it was said she had delivered over a hundred infants in her career. Roland could see that her apron was covered with blood, and the sober expression on her face confirmed his worst fears.

"I'm sorry," the midwife said in a low, steady voice. "The child was too weak. She's gone."

Roland sat back down heavily in his chair and leaned forward, clasping his head in his hands. Sir Wyndham would be back on the morrow's eve. How could Roland tell him that his daughter was dead?

With a deep breath and a shake of his head he managed to pull himself together enough to sit up straight. In a voice thick with grief he asked, "What of Madam Wyndham?"

"I gave her something for the pain. She's asleep now, but she will live," the midwife replied brusquely as she removed her stained apron and stuffed it into a thick leather satchel she had set by the bedroom door on her arrival. "But she will never birth again. The sickness that took her child has left her barren."

"The Burning Moon," Roland whispered, not even realizing he was speaking aloud. Even so, the midwife heard him and replied.

"Don't blame this on curses and magic," she muttered wearily. "Blame it on the fever."

Chagrined at his own foolishness, Roland nodded in acceptance of her more logical explanation. Celia Wyndham was not the first woman from the village to lose her child this month—not since the outbreak of pestilence had spread into their province. Yet this tragedy had still caught Roland unprepared. Some part of him had hoped that here in the manor they might be spared, as if illness and death would somehow recognize rank and privilege.

He watched silently as the midwife picked up her satchel and went back into the bedchamber, moving with a well-practiced efficiency. Through the half-opened door he could see her packing up the ointments, potions, and salves she had brought with her. It was bad luck for a man to touch the birthing medicines, so he made no move to help as she gathered up the vials, wrapping each one in cloth before placing it inside her satchel.

"What did Madam Wyndham say?" Roland finally called out to her, his sense of duty obligating him to shift his focus from the tragic death of his liege's daughter to the continued well-being of his wife. "What was her reaction when . . . when you told her."

"She doesn't know." The midwife's reply from the bedroom was distracted; she was concentrating on making sure she didn't leave any of her wares behind. "The pain was too great, she begged me for something to help her sleep through the birth. She won't awaken until the morn."

"Was it a difficult birth?" Roland asked, his brow furrowing.

"No worse than normal," she answered, emerging from the room and setting her satchel on the floor with a soft grunt. In her free arm she cradled a small bundle of clean white blankets. "Some women are strong, they can bear the pain. Others . . ." She trailed off with a shrug.

Celia Wyndham had a quick temper she would often unleash upon her servants, but she would never be mistaken for a strong woman. Her whole life she had been sheltered from the harsh realities of the world. Yet Roland was troubled that she hadn't even wanted to be awake for the birth of her first child.

He rose to his feet as the midwife crossed the room, extending the bundle out toward him: the child, wrapped in swaddling clothes.

"She might want to see the child when she wakes," the midwife explained.

The little girl had been cleaned, Roland noticed as he took the bundle from her. Yet her face was the color of ash; it was obvious she was dead. Staring down at the infant's corpse he felt compelled to ask another question. One he had no right to ask.

"I've heard the birth is more difficult if the mother cannot help," he began, choosing his words carefully.

The midwife nodded, then turned and walked slowly back over to her satchel to make a final accounting of the contents.

"Sometimes the mother can push or hold until I am ready," she admitted.

Satisfied that everything was safely packed away, she pulled the drawstrings shut and hoisted the bundle up over her meaty shoulder.

"Sometimes it can make a difference."

"But Madam Wyndham wanted to sleep," Roland muttered through clenched teeth. A moment later he added, "A mother should fight for her child!"

The midwife only shrugged, noncommittal. "Sometimes it makes no difference. I've seen the sickness take four children since the last moon. Two of the mothers died as well. If the madam had stayed awake to suffer through the birth she might be dead now, too. And it might not have saved the child in any case."

Somehow this offended Roland even more. "So it's all just chance? The whim of the Gods?"

The midwife's reply was matter-of-fact. "Life and death are intertwined." She sighed, weary from the night's long labor, tired of answering questions that had no real answer.

"The sickness takes some and spares others. There is no rhyme or reason. Four nights ago the fever took the smith's apprentice—as strong and strapping a lad as any in the village."

Roland had met the smith's apprentice; he knew she spoke the truth. But as he clutched the cold, gray child to his chest the midwife's simple wisdom offered no comfort.

"His wife is with child, too," he muttered, remembering a bit of gossip he'd heard from one of the chambermaids.

"That's the cruelest jape of all," the midwife countered, shifting from one foot to the other as she adjusted the weight of the satchel on her shoulder. She was clearly eager to be on her way, but she wasn't about to offend Roland by departing without proper leave. "Two nights ago the widow gave birth to a daughter. Then the fever took her, too."

Roland shook his head, numbed by the seemingly endless list of sorrow and suffering. "Another dead child."

"Not the child," the midwife answered, a hint of annoyance in her voice. "The mother. The mother died. The child survived." The midwife clucked her tongue. "Fate can be cruel. Not even a day old, and already an orphan.

"Most would say that child is cursed," she added, half under her breath. "It's a wonder I found anyone willing to take her in."

Roland stood before the door of the small, thatch-roofed hut. He was soaked from his journey; the hut had been built on the farthest edge of the town, and the rain of the midnight storm was coming down in heavy sheets. Still, Roland hesitated before knocking on the door. It wasn't the lateness of the hour that gave him pause; he suspected the woman inside would still be up—she was a creature of the night.

It was his own doubts that stayed his hand. This plan was madness . . . but he couldn't bear the thought of telling Sir Wyndham his child was dead. Gathering his resolve, he raised his fist and knocked hard upon the door. A minute later it swung open to reveal the small, slight form of Bella, the village witch-woman.

"Who comes to my door in the dead of night?" she demanded in a thin whisper, her ice-blue eyes squinting to see him through the darkness of the storm.

Roland knew her mostly by reputation. Bella rarely ventured from her home during the day, and living up at the manor house he'd never had reason or occasion to seek her aid before. He'd seen her once or twice on the streets, but never up close. He was surprised at how small she seemed without her cowl and walking staff: barely over five feet tall.

Some in town called her the white witch, and it wasn't hard to see why. She had long, silver hair, and her skin was so pale it looked as if she were carved from alabaster. Her plain features were creased with faint wrinkles, though the lines gave the impression of wisdom rather than age. She appeared to be in her early fifties, though if legends were true she was at least two decades older.

She carried a newborn infant, clutching the pink-skinned little girl hard against her chalky bosom with one wiry arm. The babe was naked, and Bella wore only a threadbare tunic, open at the top to expose her breast. The little girl in the witch's grasp sucked hungrily at the teat.

Roland didn't want to imagine what foul arts allowed the witch's breast to flow with milk. Suppressing a shudder at the sound of the babe's suckling, he pulled his gaze up to meet Bella's eye. Keeping his voice level he said, "I work for Sir Wyndham."

Bella pursed her lips together and her cold eyes narrowed. "Madam Wyndham, you mean." She made no effort to hider her contempt for Conrad's overly pious wife. "It's too late for her. Her child is dead, and I can do nothing to bring it back."

She tried to slam the door in his face, but Roland was too quick for her. Jamming it open with his foot he pushed his way inside.

"How do you know about that?" he demanded. "The midwife only delivered the child an hour ago!"

He was a tall man, thick through the chest and shoulders. He towered over Bella. But the tiny, silver-haired woman glared up at him unafraid before turning away and letting her free arm drop indifferently from the hut's door.

She headed to a small crib in the corner, glancing back over her shoulder to speak in a sinister whisper. "I see things. I know things. I have *power*."

"Then you know why I'm here," Roland said, ignoring the implied threat in her voice.

He followed her inside, closing the door behind him. The single room that made up the whole of the domicile was lit with a lone candle on a back wall near the crib. It kept the small hut warm, but most of the room was cast in dark shadow. He could just barely see shelves on the walls cluttered with numerous jars, and there was a small table piled with an assortment of bottles and vials in one corner. Things floated inside the glass, suspended in translucent fluids. In the gloom he couldn't make out enough detail to identify them . . . not that he would have wanted to anyway.

"I don't know why you're here," Bella admitted, speaking softly as she put the babe down in the crib and wrapped her in a soiled, stained blanket.

She laced up the front of her tunic before turning back to face him, much to Roland's relief.

"The things I see are not always clear," she explained. "Only death is always easy to understand."

"You knew Madam Wyndham's child would die?"

Bella nodded once.

"Why didn't you tell anyone?"

"Would she have listened to me?" she countered.

"You don't seem upset that a newborn is dead," Roland noted. He was angry, but he kept his voice quiet so as not to disturb the child.

"I had nothing to do with that!" she snapped, keeping her own voice low. "There is a plague upon this province. Children die!"

Her reaction was understandable. Bella was well respected in the town, but she was also feared, even by those she used her arcane powers to help. Celia Wyndham was a vocal supporter of the Order, and an outspoken critic of Bella and her ilk. It wasn't out of the question that she might try to blame her child's death on the witch-woman . . . if Madam Wyndham ever found out her child had died.

"I know how that child came to you," Roland said, getting to the heart of the matter with a slight nod toward the crib.

"And what of it?" Bella demanded, her voice defensive. "I offered to raise the child, teach her the ways of my craft."

"Why?" Roland wanted to know. "The child is cursed. Born under the Burning Moon."

Bella snorted. "Cursed? A word used by the fearful and ignorant! The child is blessed. She is *strong!*"

"She has the Gift?" Roland guessed, the pieces starting to fall into place.

The witch refused to answer his question. "Who else would take her in but me? Better to let her die an orphan?"

"The Order would have taken her."

Bella grinned at him, exposing pearly, too-perfect teeth. It was a joyless expression, a smile meant to mock him.

"You know what the Order does to children who have the Gift?" she asked, baiting him. "They take their eyes!"

It was true, in a fashion. The blind monks of the Order were a common enough sight across the Southlands. Yet it was also a lie. The Pilgrims were blessed with a mystical second sight that gave them complete awareness of the world around them; everyone knew they were not truly blind.

"And what will you take from this child?" Roland asked, his voice rising slightly.

He knew little about the ways of Chaos and magic, yet he feared the child might be used in some dark ritual, possibly to help the ageless woman keep the years at bay a little while longer.

"I mean this child no harm," Bella offered, as if sensing his thoughts. "She has power. Potential. But it will never be realized if she is given to the Order."

"I do not wish to turn her over to the Order," Roland assured her.

"The child is mine," Bella insisted one last time. "Nobody wanted her. I took her in. I won't give her up to the likes of Miss High and Mighty!" There was a long pause before she added, "Not without some type of . . . compensation."

By the time Roland returned to the manor the rain had stopped and the first faint light of dawn was coming up over the horizon, transforming the still-visible red moon to an eerie orange hue. Madam Wyndham was still asleep when he slipped into the room. The wet nurse—a sturdy, plain-looking young woman from one of the nearby farms who had given birth to her own child only a week ago—was waiting for him there.

She didn't say a word, simply took the little girl as Roland handed her over. She lifted the baby to her breast, and Roland released a breath he hadn't even known he was holding when the child began to nurse.

It was done. Only four people knew the truth—the wet nurse, the midwife, Bella, and Roland himself. And he'd done everything he could to ensure each woman's silence.

He'd made sure the young girl now holding the baby at her breast understood that she and her own newborn child would be well looked after as long as she kept her position at the manor. She was a smart, practical girl; he was confident she wouldn't risk that future by revealing their secret.

The midwife was even less likely to talk. He'd paid her to remove the body of Madam Wyndham's dead daughter, then paid her extra to keep silent. Besides, a woman whose livelihood depended on birthing had no reason to let people know she'd delivered another stillborn infant.

Bella was the only one he wasn't sure of. He'd offered her a very generous sum in exchange for the child and a vow never to speak of what had transpired, and he'd promised to steer Madam Wyndham's wrath away from the witch-woman and her work. He'd never heard of the white witch reneging on a deal with one of her clients, yet he couldn't bring himself to fully trust anyone who practiced the dark arts. So to seal the deal, he'd warned Bella that if she ever betrayed his trust he'd do everything in his power to bring the wrath of the Order down upon her.

The threat was mostly hollow, but the witch had accepted his offer. The money would have to come out of his own accounts; it was the only way to keep Sir Wyndham from asking questions. Roland wasn't a rich man, and Bella's price had been high. But looking down into the babe's brilliant green eyes, so vibrant and full of life as she suckled, he knew he'd made the right choice.

Chapter 4

A GUST OF wind leapt over the parapets and tore at the Queen's cape, fluttering it out from her shoulders. Here in the Northern capital of Ferlhame, protected by leagues of thick and ancient forest on every side, the winds were never fierce. Yet the evening breeze that swept over the high walls of the castle carried the dampness of a reluctantly fading Eastern winter, and the chill seeped down to her very core.

Rianna Avareen, the reigning Monarch over the Danaan people in her husband's absence, wrestled her cape back down and pulled it tight about her body, instinctively shielding her full belly and the unborn child within. She felt the baby kick inside her, as if in protest against the rush of cold air.

Soon, she thought, *very soon.*

Would her husband be home to see the birth of their firstborn child? Would the King ever return home again?

"My Queen, you will catch a chill."

She didn't need to turn to know who spoke; she recognized Drake's voice as well as her own. They had known each other almost twenty years, sharing their childhood: she a prophet and princess, betrothed to Llewellyn Avareen, firstborn son of the noble House of Avareen and heir to the Danaan throne; he the son of a decorated general who served in her father's armies, destined to one day lead the Queen's Personal Guard.

A chill is the least of my fears, she thought. Unbidden, her eyes turned up to the blood-red moon that hung in the sky above them. *The Burning Moon, a portent of Chaos.*

"There is no word from your scouts, Drake?" she asked, stubbornly pulling her gaze down to once more stare out over the castle walls.

"None, my Queen. Nor from the hawks."

Drake stepped forward to stand at her side and share her vigil . . . and to partly shield her from the wind, she noted. She wondered if it was intentional, or if he had done it simply on instinct bred from a lifetime of protecting and watching over her.

He was a tall man, thin but with broad shoulders. Like the Queen, he wore a cape to ward off the chill: a deep, rich green; the color of House Avareen. The garment set off the hue of his skin; like all the Danaan people, his greenish brown complexion reflected the blood of the forest that ran in his veins. His dark, shoulder-length hair flew out behind him with every gust of wind, wild and untamed.

Rianna's ladies-in-waiting often talked about how handsome Drake was, though she had known him far too long to think of him as anything but a friend. But she was glad to have a friend with her in this blackest of nights; she took some small comfort in his mere presence.

"We shouldn't worry," he assured her after a few moments of silence. "It's too soon to expect an answer from the King's party yet."

She nodded in mute acceptance. He was right, of course. The King and his company had left a full week ago. They had a large lead over the messenger hawks that had been sent after them three nights earlier in response to the Queen's dream.

The King is surrounded by nearly twenty mounted men, half armed with long, thin blades, the others with short but powerful bows. On either side rides a court sorcerer—one male, one female. A small army, all hunting a single foe.

The horses shy and rear, but are brought under control with soft yet firm words of command. The King signals to his wizards, and they begin to scan the forest for the beast. Their expressions fade to blank stares as they channel their power and cast out with their minds. Suddenly their faces twist into masks of terrible pain. The woman slumps forward in her saddle; the man cries out and falls from his mount.

The creature explodes from the nearby undergrowth with a terrible roar, a brutish monstrosity unfit to dwell in the natural world. The massive feline head spits searing venom, burning the flesh of rider and horse alike. The animals panic and several riders are thrown. In the carnage a volley of arrows are released only to shatter harmlessly against the thick, scaled hide of the monster's body.

And then the beast is upon them, battering them with bat-like wings, tearing at them with a lion's claws, savaging them with the jagged spikes of its twin tails as the vision is lost in an orgy of blood and screams.

"What did Andar call this creature?" she asked, struggling to push the memory of her dream aside by recalling the words of the High Sorcerer.

"A manticore, my Queen."

"And he is certain?"

"There is no way to be certain," Drake admitted. "But he has compared the reports with descriptions from the ancient texts."

There was a long silence, and the Queen felt the chill of the wind reaching down into her belly yet again. Once more her son kicked in response. The King had known their child was a son before he had left to destroy the abomination stalking the forest of his people, just as she had known. The Sight was strong in them both. They had decided to name him Vaaler.

"Andar tells me the manticore is one of the weaker Chaos Spawn," Drake said at last, hoping to bring her some reassurance.

"How could he possibly know?" Rianna wondered aloud.

"I . . . the ancient texts, no doubt . . . ," Drake stammered.

The Queen turned slowly to face him, a wan smile on her lips. "Drake, I know your words were words of comfort. But I am not a fool. For all his wisdom Andar knows as little about this beast as you or I."

Drake bowed his head in acknowledgment of the truth of her words.

"These are dark times," Rianna whispered, her gaze pointedly ignoring the ominous moon above them.

"We have seen dark times before," Drake replied. "We have survived them."

She knew he was referring to the Purge. Twenty years ago, when Rianna had been but a child, the Order—self-proclaimed guardians of the Southlands—had declared war on the wielders of Chaos. Nazir, the Order's bloodthirsty Pontiff, proclaimed the practice of magic to be a crime punishable by death. And, as had happened so many times before in the history of the Southlands, the Seven Capitals bowed meekly before the Pontiff's will.

Court mages were stripped of their positions as guides and advisers, replaced by Seers sent out from the black walls of the Monastery. Those who still dared to dabble in what had suddenly become the forbidden arts—wizards, witches, traveling conjurers—were seized and charged with the crime of sorcery. Anyone even suspected of having Chaos in their blood fled or faced imprisonment without trial. Any citizens foolish enough to protest the atrocities of the Purge were branded as heretics and suffered a similar fate.

Within a year the so-called purification of the Southlands was all but complete. Those who practiced magic had renounced their ways or disappeared into hiding. Hundreds had been executed by the legions of fanatical monks who served the Pontiff. Nazir's own loyal followers were strategically placed in every royal court, the power behind the throne in each of the Seven Capitals.

The Danaan kingdom had prepared itself for battle, certain Nazir would now turn his army of monks against the heathens of the Great Forest. The power of Chaos flowed freely in the blood of the Danaan monarchy; surely the Order would see their entire nation as an affront that must be destroyed. But the atrocities of the Purge never reached the Great Forest. They barely even left the Southlands.

In the Free Cities of the North people dared to speak out against the Order. Those who lived on the borders of the Great Forest bowed down to no one, not even the Pontiff. For a year the armies of the Order lay siege to the walled towns, with little success. Faced with their fierce independence and steadfast refusal to accept his will, Nazir had two choices: drive the entire Southlands into battle against the united armies of all the Free Cities, or end his holy war.

The Order's influence in the Seven Capitals was greater than it had been in three hundred years. The wizards and mages of the royal courts had been scattered and forced to live as outcasts, bereft of their former political power. The Order had little left to gain and much to lose, and in the end the Pontiff chose the path of appeasement.

To placate the Free Cities the brutal laws restricting Chaos wielders were relaxed. Two years after it had begun the Purge was over, though within the courts of the Seven Capitals the Order's Seers kept their recently appointed positions of power. That fact alone was enough to make the Danaan kingdom wary.

Over the past two decades an uneasy peace had settled over the Southlands. Magic was tolerated, but only grudgingly. Briar witches and traveling magicians could once again practice their arts in the open, though they were often shunned or feared by the common folk. And for Chaos wielders there was always the threat of retribution, the ever-present fear of being executed for heresy should they overstep their bounds and interfere with the business of the Order.

Rianna knew all this despite never having visited any of the Southern lands. In fact, she had never even met anyone who was not of her own people. Outsiders were forbidden on pain of death from entering the Great Forest, but the Free Cities eagerly welcomed the steady stream of merchants, diplomats, and explorers pouring forth from the Danaan kingdom. Among these adventurous subjects were a number of spies and agents of the Danaan throne, providing a constant flow of information about their neighbors to the south.

"The winds are cold up here, my Queen," Drake murmured, gently interrupting her thoughts. "You should retire to the castle."

Accepting his offered hand, Rianna let him escort her along the battlements to the nearest tower. Drake was right: They had survived the Purge. But it was not the armies of the Southlands that terrified Rianna these nights. The true threat lay far to the north, at the very edges of the world. A monster that had not been seen in centuries had reappeared, waking from some ancient slumber to terrorize the mortal world once again.

"I should never have let him go," she said as they reached the bottom of the tower stairs.

"You could not have stopped him," Drake replied, opening the door that led out into the courtyard between the castle walls and the enormous, hundred-room stone mansion that served as the residence for the royal family.

"The signs, the visions of our prophets, my own dreams . . . it was too dangerous. I should have begged him to stay."

"It would not have helped. He would have gone no matter what you said."

As they crossed the courtyard she admitted to herself that Drake was right. Her husband had the Sight, just as she did. His visions had shown him a terrible future, one where the Legacy had fallen and armies of Chaos Spawn were unleashed upon the world.

When scouts first brought reports of the manticore, the King knew what he had to do. If Llewellyn was to lead his people safely through the coming war he would need to understand the enemy they faced. The historical chronicles were not enough; the King would have to see the manticore for himself.

Rianna had understood and accepted all this. But that was before she had the dream in which she saw her husband's death. And by then he and his entourage were already four days gone.

The reached the doors of the royal quarters without further conversation. Lost in thoughts of her husband and what fate might befall him, Rianna barely noticed the soldiers standing guard at the entrance. But years of practice compelled her to wave her hand in a gesture of acknowledgment as they tilted their heads down at her passing in a silent show of respect.

She paused once she was inside the building, uncertain where she should go now that she was safely away from the wind. In truth she was content to simply stand in the entrance hall and let the hearth-warmed air of the great castle envelop her. Drake gently took her by the arm and led her through the corridors and rooms, then up the stairs to her private chambers.

"You must preserve your strength for the birth of your heir. You should sleep, my Queen."

There was no arguing with Drake on this point. She had spent far too much time the past few nights pacing the castle walls worrying about her husband. The strain was made even greater by her pregnancy. Yet even exhausted as she was, she knew rest would not come easily.

"How can I sleep? I cannot bear to face the dream of my husband's death night after night."

"Your dream shows only a possible future. One of many. It is a vision of what may be, not what will be. Perhaps the hawks will reach the King in time."

The Queen smiled, amused at Drake's efforts to explain the Sight to her, of all people. "You sound like Andar," she said mildly.

"I may not understand magic or Chaos, my Queen, but the High Sorcerer knows much about these matters. I am only sharing with you the wisdom he has shared with me."

"But how does his wisdom help me to sleep? Knowing the dream may not come true does not keep me from witnessing its horrors when I close my eyes."

From his belt Drake withdrew a small vial and presented it to her with an outstretched palm.

"Andar asked me to give you this, if I thought it necessary. He says it will shield you from the dreams. For this night, at least."

Rianna picked up the delicate vial and drained its contents in a single draught. Immediately the world began to list, slowly turning on its side. Drake caught her as she stumbled, his strong arms holding her up.

"Andar should have warned me it worked so quickly," he grunted as he half carried her over to the bed.

As she lay back into her pillow, Rianna felt the world become steady once more.

"I will be all right, Drake. Leave me. I'm certain Andar's tonic will help me sleep until morning."

With a final glance to assure himself of her safety and a curt bow Drake was gone, shutting the door behind him.

Alone in her bed the Queen closed her eyes. Sleep washed over her in a gentle wave, and the heavy veil of Andar's potion slipped down to cover her Sight in utter blackness.

The pains of labor woke her several hours later, blissful unconsciousness ripped away by the agony of impending childbirth. She cried out, and suddenly Drake was bursting into the room. Through the haze of her suffering she realized he must have stationed himself outside her door, determined to keep watch over her all night if need be.

"Summon the doctor!" he ordered one of the guards as he knelt down beside the bed and grasped her hand, placing his other palm on her forehead.

"She's burning up! Open the windows!"

Rianna clenched her eyes shut and moaned as another contraction tore through her, clutching desperately onto Drake's hand until it passed. When she opened her eyes again she saw the drapes had been pulled aside and the shutters thrown wide to reveal the Burning Moon, now hanging low in the gray sky of the predawn.

Against her will, her mind's eye conjured up the final gruesome image that haunted her dreams: the King's broken body at the manticore's feet beneath that same blood-red moon. The vision was shredded by the next wave of contractions, the pain driving everything else to the fringes of her awareness.

Yet even as she fought to bring her son into the world, Rianna knew she would never see her husband again.

Chapter 5

NAZIR THE RIGHTEOUS, forty-third Pontiff of the Order of the Crown, didn't move when the visitor entered his chamber. He remained kneeling on his prayer mat, a worn cloth garment so thin it did nothing to ward off the chill seeping up into the Pontiff's body from the stone floor. His hands rested palms down upon his thighs, the customary position when meditating. Apart from the mat there were no other furnishings or ornamentations in the room; as befitted a man of true religious conviction the Pontiff's chamber was a small, undecorated cell within the Monastery where he slept, ate, and prayed.

There was no need to look up with his blind eyes to recognize the woman who had come to interrupt his meditations; as with all members of the Order, Nazir's mystical second sight gave him a complete awareness of the physical world around him.

"The prisoner has spoken?" he asked in a calm voice.

"I always make them speak," Yasmin replied.

Nazir nodded in acknowledgment of what was a mere statement of fact.

Yasmin was a tall woman; taller, even, than most of the men in the Monastery. She was a far cry from the little girl who had been taken away from her parents nearly twenty years ago during the early days of the Purge.

"The heretic has confessed her sins," she continued.

She spoke with cold disinterest, her words a stark contrast with the burning passion of her holy devotion. All who served the will of the True Gods were fervent in their belief, but Yasmin's piety bordered on the fanatical. She had submitted to the initiation ritual within a year of her arrival at the Monastery, willingly giving up her natural sight for the sake of her convictions. A few years later, at the age of only twelve, she had joined the Inquisitors—the youngest to ever be granted the honor.

Even then, the Pontiff remembered, she had been fierce in her zealotry. It was customary for Inquisitors to shave their heads. Yasmin, however, was not content merely to shear off her long, dark locks. Once her scalp was bare she had doused it with boiling water, permanently scarring and discoloring the flesh so that her hair would never grow again.

The disfigurement, combined with her height and her sharp, angular features, gave her a terrifying appearance . . . all the better to serve the will of the True Gods in her chosen role. She had risen quickly through the ranks of her sect. Not yet thirty years of age, she was already the Prime Inquisitor's right hand, and the inevitable successor to the position when the old man passed away.

One day, Nazir thought, *she may even become Pontiff.*

"During her confession, she revealed the name of her leader," Yasmin continued, unaware of his train of thought.

The old man felt a surge of triumphant exultation at her words, though when he spoke his voice was calm. "Who does she name as the false prophet?"

"Ezra," the Inquisitor proclaimed, the single name causing the kneeling man's head to involuntarily tilt up toward her voice.

A scowl crossed Nazir's face. Ezra was one of the Order's oldest and most respected members, as well as one of the Pontiff's most trusted advisers.

"Is it possible the heretic is lying?" he asked.

"The Gods have given me the power to see through lies," Yasmin responded, making no effort to conceal the haughty pride in her voice.

Her arrogance was unbecoming in one sworn to act only as an instrument of divine will, but the Pontiff knew her words were true.

"Ezra's dedication to the cause has always been suspect," Yasmin added. "Was he not the one who urged you to abandon our crusade to eradicate Chaos from the Southlands?"

Ezra's voice had been among the loudest of those who counseled a course of appeasement rather than continued bloodshed in the final days of the Purge. Yet there had been wisdom behind his words—the Order would have risked losing everything had they entered into a war with the Free Cities. The Pontiff understood the need for moderates like Ezra to temper the fiery zeal of fanatics like Yasmin; something the Inquisitor had yet to grasp.

"Reluctance to push the Southlands into war is one thing," Nazir pointed out, hoping to educate the younger woman. "Spreading blasphemy and consorting with wizards is quite another."

Yasmin made no reply. For all her passion, she knew when to keep her words in check; she was not one to hurl speeches like storm-tossed waves against the immovable cliffs. Nazir was well aware she preferred action to discussion.

With a weary sigh, the Pontiff rose to his feet. "Summon Ezra," he said. "We will question him together."

"Ezra has fled," Yasmin replied. "I discovered his absence when I went to confront him with these accusations."

Nazir fought to keep the scowl from his face. By the ancient rites of the Order Yasmin was entitled to act on the information gained during her interrogation, but it was customary to inform the Pontiff first.

Yet this was not the time to take her to task for such a minor transgression. Ezra's flight had confirmed his guilt as readily as a confession drawn from the rack or scalding irons.

"No one can remember seeing him since the heretic's arrival," Yasmin added.

It had taken the Inquisitor two days to wring a confession from her prisoner. With that much of a head start, Ezra would soon be beyond the Pontiff's reach.

There was only one way to stop him.

"Leave this to me," Nazir said, dismissing his underling with a curt nod.

Ezra walked with a stoop to his shoulders; he was past eighty and he had already covered many score miles. Despite this he moved with a steady gait, surprisingly quick for a man of his age. He headed due north, never turning his head from his bearing, though this did not prevent his mystical awareness from watching for signs of pursuit from the south.

The burning sun beat down on his shaved scalp, a relentless heat that had transformed the farthest reaches of the Southern Desert into a barren waste devoid of all life.

To the north the monotony of the dunes was broken by the occasional oasis; thorny brushes and small, twisted cacti pushed up through crystal sands, struggling to survive. In the north, insects fed on the pulp and moisture of these stunted plants. Small lizards emerged at night to feed on the insects, then burrowed beneath the parched earth to escape the savage heat of the days. The northern reaches teemed with life.

But here in the south no creature could endure. So the old man walked utterly alone, his footsteps in the sand trailing far behind him to mark his progress. His destination was two more full days' march away. And still the sun beat mercilessly down.

The old monk barely noticed, for he was one of the Order. Six centuries ago his brethren had built their holy Monastery in the Southern Desert as a symbol of their detachment from the political strife and the mundane events of the Southlands and its people; they served a higher purpose. But the location had also been chosen as a sign of the Order's strength. The same power that gave them the ability to prophesize the future and to see without eyes allowed them to survive where no other creature could.

The Monastery represented the triumph of mental discipline imposed upon the physical realities of the world, and the monks of the Order were the manifestations of that triumph. Like all who served the will of the True Gods, Ezra was able to channel the power within himself to shield his physical body from the deadly effects of the blazing sun. He could sustain himself for weeks without food or water, and he had needed only the briefest of rests during his long trek.

Even so, a mount would have been quicker. But a mount required sustenance. Gathering supplies for the journey would have attracted attention; it might have aroused suspicions. It wasn't uncommon for Pilgrims to leave the Monastery in the service of the True Gods, but Ezra himself hadn't left the black walls in many years. His preparations would have been noticed. And so he had slipped away quietly into the vastness of the dunes, hoping to lose himself in the desert before the Pontiff realized he was gone.

It was inevitable the young woman Yasmin had captured would expose him. Her belief in Ezra's cause was strong and pure, but no amount of faith could withstand the tortures of the Inquisitors for more than a few days. Which was why she—like all of Ezra's followers save a precious few—knew only his name and no other. She could point the finger at him, not at any other of her fellow conspirators.

He pitied her: After her confession she would be burned alive at the stake. Nazir was not known for mercy or forgiveness. But there was nothing the venerable monk could do to help her now; she was beyond his reach. The movement she served, however, must continue. The cause of Ezra and his followers was of far greater import than any one life.

And so the old monk pressed ever onward, leaving the Monastery and the Order farther and farther behind.

Nazir moved quickly down the narrow staircase at the back of the Great Library. The folds of his loose-fitting robe swished softly as his bare feet pattered down the steps, descending into the deepest bowels of the Monastery. The Pontiff moved with a haste brought about not by desperation, but rather by surety of purpose, pausing only when he reached the heavy iron door at the bottom of the stairs.

There was great risk in what he was about to do, but Ezra's flight left him little recourse. For the crime of heresy the old monk's life was forfeit, along with the lives of all those who followed him in his blasphemy. And there was only one way the Pontiff could discover who else was working with him.

The archway of the door at the bottom of the stairs was etched with runes of warding, the door itself inscribed with powerful symbols barring entrance. Nazir barely noticed the magical safeguards. The glyphs were meant to keep others out; their magic was not meant to be unleashed against him. From within his robes he pulled out a large iron key, then used it to turn the lock.

The portal opened slowly, its hinges groaning beneath the ponderous weight. The small room beyond was shrouded in total darkness, though the lack of light mattered little to his blind but all-seeing eyes. The chamber was bare except for a small pedestal set against the far wall, atop which sat a simple iron crown. A thick layer of dust covered the floor; none but the Pontiff was permitted access to this sealed chamber, and Nazir hadn't been here for many years. Not since the days of the Purge.

But a time of crisis was upon them. For the past month the Oracles here in the isolation of the Monastery—separated from their brethren stationed in the Southland courts by fifty leagues of harsh, unforgiving desert—had shared a terrifying vision. A dark and dangerous power had been unleashed upon the mortal world: a child born under the Blood Moon; a child spawned in the fires of Chaos, its identity shrouded by smoke and flame. Some saw the child as male, others female. Some claimed it bore the features and complexion of an Islander; some claimed it was the spawn of the Danaan in the North Forest; others said the child was descended from Southland stock.

Such uncertainty was to be expected. The visions of the Oracles were themselves manifestations of Chaos; the details were meant to breed confusion among the faithful. But the true meaning of the augury was undeniable. It foretold the weakening of the Legacy; a warning that the Destroyer was about to return to the mortal world, reborn in human form. A prophecy confirmed by the manifestation of the Blood Moon earlier this month.

Nazir had summoned his wisest and most trusted advisers to discuss the visions, and decide on a course of action. They had debated what must be done long into the night, how they could find and stop this child, how best they could preserve and protect the Legacy. And throughout their debates, the Pontiff never suspected a traitor sat at his right hand.

The Purge had not completely snuffed out the Heresy of the Burning Savior. The Pontiff was well aware that some among the Order, particularly the young and headstrong, believed that the Legacy would one day fail. Misled by false prophecies, they imagined the salvation of the mortal world rested in the hands of a child schooled in the arts of Chaos magic, rather than in the endurance of the ancient spell of the True Gods.

Their belief defied the most fundamental tenets of the Order's teachings; it was an abomination to those who followed the will of the True Gods. Chaos can never be controlled; it can only be contained.

Nazir had thought that those at the heart of the movement had perished in the flames of the Purge. But if Ezra was one of the heretics—if he was, in fact, their leader—then how many others among the Order had been befouled by these profane teachings?

Not willing to dwell on such a question now, the Pontiff stepped through the rune-covered door and locked it behind him, sealing himself inside the room. Small clouds of dust stirred up as he crossed the floor to kneel reverently before the pedestal. He began a series of rhythmic breathing exercises to cleanse his mind. He had to set aside the urgency of his mission. He had to free himself from the anger of betrayal so his thoughts could be at peace. Unless his will was pure and focused he dared not use the Crown.

The holy Talisman had been bestowed upon the Order by the True Gods, a weapon to aid them in their never-ending battle to defend the Legacy. But it was a weapon of great and terrible power. If the Pontiff's will faltered—if the carefully constructed defenses that held the Crown's power in check failed—the weapon would be turned against them and Chaos would be unleashed to wreak havoc upon the mortal world.

Nazir knelt for several minutes, still as the black stone walls of the Monastery while he gathered his strength and courage for the coming ordeal. When he was finally ready he rose to his feet, steeling himself. Moving as if in a trance he reached out, a mortal about to touch the divine. Slowly, carefully, he lifted the Crown from its pedestal and placed it atop his own head.

His mind exploded with a rush of sight and sound. Night, day, darkness, light, heat, cold, fear, anger, joy: The thoughts, sensations, and emotions of every living creature in the mortal world bombarded him, overwhelming him, devouring him. His own consciousness was swallowed whole, drowned beneath an ocean of omnipresence.

Nazir collapsed, his hands reflexively clutching at his skull to hold the Crown in place as his body shook and trembled, thrust into convulsions by the awesome power coursing through him. But though his physical state was beyond his control, within his mind the Pontiff fought to restore a semblance of order. His identity broke free of the collective consciousness of all mortality, bursting forth from the surface of the churning sea of thought and sensation within his mind. Bit by bit, piece by piece, he began to impose his will on the Crown. One by one he blocked out each consciousness shrieking at him from across the world, building a wall to shield him from the cacophony of a million minds brick by brick.

He drew on the power of the Crown—the power of Chaos—slowly and deliberately. Using techniques learned through decades of study, he directed and focused the Talisman until a single image became clear: an old man walking alone across the desert.

Across the chasm of space and time, far beyond the shores of the mortal world, an enemy long exiled felt the call of Old Magic: pure Chaos, burning like a beacon. Still recovering from the recent spell cast over the bloodstained fountain, Daemron smiled, remembering the shards of stone he had cast into the boiling waters. The ripples of his spell had touched the shores of the mortal world.

For centuries, the Legacy had kept him at bay. Through it he had sensed the Talismans only as an echo, their power dull and faint. But his spell had punctured the Legacy, and through that still-open wound the sensation was now as sharp and keen as the blast of war trumpets in the bleak dawn before a battle.

He cast out with his own mind, seeking to make contact. Across the Sea of Fire, he chased the undeniable call to its source.

Ezra sensed it right away: a presence in his thoughts. He felt it probing, pressing, looking to uncover the secrets he had carefully hidden away. The Pontiff had found him. Nazir was looking to strip everything from him: what he knew, what he planned, who his allies were. A relentless assault on the fortress of his mind.

There was nothing he could do but press on and try to get far enough away that Nazir could not tear down the mental walls he had built up. But even as he fled, Ezra knew it was too late. The invasion had begun, and he lacked the strength to drive it back.

Then Ezra felt something else; something unexpected: the pulsing fury of untamed Chaos. Even muted by the Legacy, the Sea of Fire was still awesome in its angry power. He felt it rumbling far below the firmament of the earth; he sensed it churning above the arch of the sky itself. He could feel it coming for him, as surely as he could feel Nazir's presence in his mind.

Thick, black clouds appeared above him where an instant before there had only been clear blue sky. Ominous peals of thunder began to roll across the dunes—an event strange enough to momentarily divert the old monk's attention from his desperate inner struggle. Storms never formed in the Southern Desert. Never.

And then he felt another presence: an alien consciousness so vile and twisted that Ezra's mind recoiled from its mere touch. The old monk let forth a cry of pain and horror, and collapsed face-first onto the sand. Screaming against the twin rape of his mind, his body curled in upon itself as the first drops of hard rain began to pelt down from above.

Nazir felt the alien presence, too, and recognized it immediately: the immortal enemy of the True Gods. He felt the power of Chaos breaching the Legacy—a dark storm exploding into the mortal world. The coming of the one called the Slayer.

The Pontiff broke off his mental assault on the old monk, his consciousness fleeing back into his own body lying huddled on the floor of the Monastery cellar. He tore the Crown from his head and tossed it across the room, snuffing out his spell.

Daemron shrieked in agony as the link with the mortal world was severed. He flailed about with his mind, scrambling to reestablish the connection. But it was gone. Howling in frustration and beating his wings in furious rage, he was forced to pull back, before his own identity was drowned in the eternal flames of the Chaos Sea.

For a brief moment he had touched the mortal world, but now it had vanished once more. Weakened by the ritual of the fountain, he had been caught unawares. Yet even so he knew how close he had come to breaking free of his prison.

The Old Gods were dead, and his children had been born into the mortal world. Chaos had been unleashed; the Legacy had been momentarily breached. It was only a matter of time until it was breached again. And next time such an opportunity presented itself, he would be ready.

Nazir and the other had vanished, leaving Ezra alone. He lay where he had fallen to the ground, as the dark clouds of the unnatural storm boiled and churned above him. The breach in the Legacy had snapped shut, but the fires of Chaos had spilled through to wreak havoc on the mortal realm.

Torrents of cold rain lashed at his face, drenching his clothes and turning the ground to mud. Somehow Ezra summoned the will to gain his feet. But the ground had become a deadly quagmire, and the monk sunk in up to his knees when he tried to stand.

Fierce winds swirled around him, carrying small particles of sharp sand to tear at his exposed skin. Lightning forked the sky, shattering the blackness, and he felt the eruption of thunder in the back of his teeth. And then, above the fury of the storm, Ezra sensed a distant roar.

A flash flood spawned by the magical deluge was sweeping through the dunes; a great wall of water crashing in to obliterate him. Instinctively the old monk cast up a shield around his body, deflecting the Chaos-driven waves and temporarily holding them at bay.

Cocooned in a shell of protective magic as the wind and waves surged around him, Ezra had a brief hope he might survive the deadly storm of magic. Then a sizzling bolt of blue lightning arced down, sundering the protective shell and engulfing the old man. In a single, brilliant flash his body was reduced to a pile of ashes that were swept away by the raging floodwaters.

The Pontiff crawled across the cellar floor to the far corner of the room, his body drained by his ordeal. The Crown lay on its side in the corner where he had cast it away, undamaged. He reached out and clasped the Talisman with a weary hand, only then recognizing the true toll that had been extracted from him. His knuckles were gnarled and swollen, his fingers twisted and bent. His skin was creased with wrinkles and covered with dark brown spots.

Still prone, he reached up with one hand to feel his face, the other clenched tightly around the Crown. His cheeks were sunken and leathered, as if he had aged twenty years during the course of the spell—the cost of magic.

With a heavy sigh and a great effort he rose to his feet, the Crown clutched feebly at his side. *The body is only a shell,* he told himself, moving with deliberate, plodding steps as he made his way back to the pedestal. He placed the Crown on top, knowing the Talisman could never safely be used again—not with the Legacy so frail and the Slayer lurking on the other side.

He had failed in his mission; he had not had time to pierce the walls within Ezra's mind before he had been forced to break off the spell. But all was not lost. Ezra was dead; Nazir had felt the power of the storm that had formed when the Slayer had tried to force his way into the mortal world. He knew the old monk lacked the might to stand against such power. And without their leader, his heretical followers would be in disarray and confusion. Easy prey for Yasmin and the rest of the Inquisitors. With luck, the followers of the Burning Savior would be no more by the end of the year.

The Pontiff repressed an involuntary shudder, knowing his efforts to discover the identity of Ezra's followers had nearly opened the door for their ancient enemy to return. The Legacy was weaker and more fragile than he had feared. But he had sensed something else before aborting the spell, something that gave him hope. There was desperation in the alien mind that had brushed up against his.

The Slayer, their supposedly immortal enemy, was dying. All they had to do was protect the Legacy and wait, and victory was theirs.

The Pontiff used his key to unlock the door and exit the inner sanctum. Once outside he locked the steel door behind him, his hands trembling with a slight palsy he had not possessed only minutes ago.

He clenched his suddenly aged and arthritic fist around the key. *The body is only a shell,* he repeated. *True strength comes from the mind and spirit.*

Channeling all the power and energy of his will into his clenched fist he crushed the iron key into a twisted lump of useless metal, forever sealing the Crown behind the iron door and its impassable warding runes.

Chapter 6

IT HAD BEEN nearly a full day since Jerrod had passed any sign of civilization. Though traveling by foot, he moved with surprising speed, his long, steady strides drawing him ever closer to his ultimate destination. Those passing him on his journey—had there been any on the road to see him—would have found him unremarkable at first glance: a man in his early twenties of average height and fit build. His short, dark hair and pale skin were predominant features among many in the Southlands. His clothes were plain and simple: a light brown cloak, dark brown breeches, a sandy tunic, and a pair of calf-high leather boots. It was only his eyes that revealed he was anything more than a common villager upon the road: twin orbs of milky gray, completely dead to the world.

As a Pilgrim of the Order he was capable of far greater exertions than ordinary travelers, but he had pushed himself to his limits on this journey, driven by the news of Ezra's death. Four days at such a grueling pace had left him weary in both body and spirit. Now, however, his trip was nearing an end. The sun had reached its zenith in the sky and he was finally rewarded with his first sight of the wizard's manse—or rather, his first *awareness* of it, for sight was no true description of how his altered senses perceived the world.

The manse was a large, sprawling building of white stone, the spire of its central tower peeking up from behind the barren, rocky hills common to the region. There were no other buildings around; the nearest village was a full day's ride to the north. Like most Chaos wielders, Rexol—the owner of the manse—lived in isolation. Unlike others of his kind, however, his exile was self-imposed, a conscious effort to distance himself from the noble Houses that had turned their back on him twenty years ago during the Purge.

Yet as he had come to know Rexol, Jerrod began to understand that there was another reason he chose to live here. The deep Southlands were the frontier, the most remote edge of the kingdoms that had united over four hundred years ago under the rule of the Seven Capitals. The great cities that made up the Capitals themselves lay far to the north and west, in the lush fields of the midlands or along the coast of the Endless Sea. Other settlements had sprung up along the fertile banks of the many rivers that crossed the land, snaking from the mountains of the east to drain into the ocean to the west. But none of them ran this far south.

Here the land still echoed the uninhabitable realm of the desert. Water was scarce, the soil made up of scrabbling stone ill suited to farming. The few trees that pushed up from the raw earth were stunted and deformed. With plenty of good farmland only a few days' ride to the north, nobody was foolish enough to try to survive here. Nobody but one touched by the arrogant madness of Chaos.

By choosing to live here on the edges of the Southern Desert the mage was making a statement, one simultaneously echoing the Order's power while defying the Pontiff's authority. Rexol's dwelling dominated the horizon, looming above the barren hills in the same way the great Monastery loomed over the desert landscape a hundred leagues to the south. However, the stark white walls of the tower rising up from the center of the wizard's manse stood in sharp contrast with the black walls of the Order's ancient fortress.

Jerrod was drawing close now. He could see the high wrought-iron fence encircling the property grounds, constructed in the fashion of the wealthy noble estates far to the north.

To the naked eye, Rexol's manse was surrounded by a beautiful, self-sustaining garden. The estate was a flourishing paradise any lord within the Seven Capitals would be proud to have cultivated in his manor yard. The three-story marble tower was encircled by a verdant garden extending out twenty yards to the very edges of the iron fence. Lush grass covered the earth like a fertile carpet. Twenty-foot oaks lined the perimeter, their heavy, leaf-laden branches extending out over the railing to cast cool shade over the brown and barren dirt on the other side.

A dozen small ponds dotted the landscape, the three largest remarkable for the cascading fountains of crystal water arcing up from their centers. Lacing out from the ponds a web of small, babbling irrigation streams wove its way throughout the numerous groves of fruit trees and the abundant vegetable gardens scattered about the grounds.

But Jerrod was one of the Order, and his vision allowed him to recognize the oasis for what it truly was. The illusion of fertility amid the lifeless plains was shattered by the eerie emptiness of the garden, a smothering silence broken only by the soft whisper of the ever-running brooks. Absent was the buzz of insects, the chatter of birds, or any other sign of life. For all its beauty the garden was unnatural: an artifice of magic; a perversion of nature and true creation.

The monk shook his head. These were the thoughts of the Pontiff and his followers. They feared magic in all its forms, feared the destruction it could bring. The Order took individuals who were touched by the Gift or the Sight and taught them to internalize their power, shielding the mortal world from the potentially devastating effects of untamed Chaos.

In contrast, practitioners of the arcane arts sought to amplify their natural abilities through rituals and talismans. Their spells pierced the Legacy, opening a portal to the Chaos Sea. Wizards and witches served as conduits, channeling the flames of magic through their own bodies to unleash the fires of destruction upon the mortal world with no regard to the consequences. Or so the Order claimed.

Jerrod's mentor, Ezra, had taken a different view, however. The rituals of wizards and witches paralleled the meditations and teachings of the Order—two sides of the same coin. Chaos was not something to be feared, and magic was not an unholy abomination to be stamped out of existence. It was a tool, a weapon they could use against their ancient enemy when the Legacy inevitably crumbled.

Such beliefs were heresy, of course. A betrayal of everything the Order stood for, as was Jerrod's presence at the manse. This visit was an act of treason against the Pontiff; were he discovered he would be burned at the stake for his sins. Yet he had accepted this risk when he had chosen to follow Ezra, just as he accepted Ezra's command to recruit a powerful mage like Rexol to their cause.

They needed the wizard and his arcane knowledge of sorcery and magic. But even though Jerrod understood this as fact, the indoctrinations of the Order were not easily undone. The monk still felt an instinctive revulsion as he reached out and pushed on the iron gates.

He expected them to swing open at his touch as they had on previous visits. To his surprise they remained closed, though a soft chime could be heard ringing from within the tower. A few minutes later a young and rather portly man he didn't recognize emerged from the building, his silken robes stained with sweat. Despite his bulk, he carried himself with the light and haughty air of the upper nobility.

"A monk?" the young man exclaimed in a thin, reedy voice, seeing Jerrod's garb and the unmistakable silver-gray eyes. "What business do you have coming here?"

"My business is with Rexol."

The man's pink cheeks suddenly grew very pale, but he didn't reply. He merely stood there on the far side of the gate, his lip twitching in agitation or perhaps fear.

"I must speak with your master," Jerrod said at last. "Open the gate."

"The Pontiff has no authority here!" the young man blurted

out, his shrill voice rising to a sharp falsetto. "This is not the Monastery! You have no power over me! Go back to where—"

"Khamin!"

The strident babbling of the young man was mercifully cut off by the timely arrival of his master. The apprentice's head snapped around, drawn by the undeniable command in the voice of the wizard he served. Jerrod, of course, had no need to turn his blind gaze to take in the appearance of the man who spoke.

Even wearing a simple red robe, the wizard cut an imposing figure as he stood in the archway to his tower. He was thin and lean, and stood several inches taller than either Jerrod or the silken-clothed apprentice. His skin was a deep ebony common to the nomad tribes living along the Western Seas' southernmost shores.

The hood of his robe was thrown back, and his long, black hair was twisted in an elaborate braid that crawled down the front of his left shoulder. His face was covered by a short, scraggly beard that traced the line of his jaw, and Jerrod could make out the lingering traces of strange red markings scrawled on the skin of his cheeks and forehead—likely the fading tattoos from a recent spell.

Rexol looked to be in his forties, but the monk knew the wizard was much older than he appeared; at least sixty by Ezra's calculations. As it always did, the youthful visage unnerved him, a subtle reminder of the mage's willingness to use Chaos to disrupt the natural order. Yet it also reinforced Ezra's decision to recruit Rexol to their cause long ago.

Jerrod had heard the rumors of how the Pontiff had aged two decades in a single night, the terrifying cost of using the power of the Order's secret Talisman to kill Ezra. In contrast Rexol—a mage who had studied the ways of Chaos—had learned to harness the power of magic to keep himself young.

"There is a manuscript on the desk in my study," the wizard said to his trembling apprentice, dismissing him from the conversation. "Go transcribe a copy so I can study it without damaging the original. I will deal with this visitor."

The heavyset young man looked quickly back and forth, his

head turning several times from the wizard marching quickly forward from the tower to the monk standing calmly outside the gates. Rexol's approach seemed to help him regain his composure.

He gave a quick nod and muttered, "Of course, master," before scurrying away, obviously glad to have an excuse to leave.

"Khamin Ankha, my latest apprentice," Rexol explained once the man had disappeared back into the tower. "Not particularly gifted, but his family is quite influential among the Free Cities of the North. They gave me sanctuary during the Purge."

"Can he be trusted?"

Rexol laughed harshly, an unkind sound. "Khamin is too stupid to try and figure out why you are here, and too cowardly to do anything about it in any case."

"If anyone finds out we are speaking—" Jerrod began.

The wizard cut him off. "They won't. Forget about Khamin. It will take that slack-minded fool the better part of the day to finish transcribing the passage I left for him. I regret that you had to meet him at all."

Jerrod decided to let the matter drop. With Ezra gone the mantle of leadership passed to him. He had more pressing matters to discuss with the wizard, and little enough time to do it.

"I have troubling news. Something we should not be discussing out here on your doorstep."

"Then we will speak inside," Rexol replied briskly. He gave a simple wave of his hand and the sealed iron gates opened, swinging inward.

The monk scowled and shook his head before stepping through. "Chaos is not a toy to be played with."

"I doubt the Cataclysm was caused by all the wizards of the world opening their gates at the same time," Rexol answered with a mocking grin.

The sharpened tips of his gleaming white teeth stood out in stark relief against his red gums and black skin, giving his smile a savage—almost feral—appearance.

A retort sprang to Jerrod's lips, but he bit the words back. Arguing with Rexol would accomplish nothing. Instead he simply nodded and followed his host inside, leaving behind the unsettling stillness of the magic garden.

The wizard led him into a small dining area in the back of the manse. As had happened with his previous visits, Jerrod felt more at ease once they were inside. The purpose of each room they passed through was readily apparent from the sparse yet functional furniture within: a study, a research laboratory, a library, a meditation room.

Decorations and similar frivolity were nonexistent. This was the domicile of a man focused on a purpose, a man not given to material goods and worldly concerns lest they interfere with his pursuit of high knowledge. A man devoted to a cause . . . though Jerrod was smart enough to understand that this cause wasn't necessarily the same as his own.

When they reached their destination Rexol sat down at a small table, then motioned for his guest to do the same.

"Tell me why you are here," he demanded, forgoing preamble or courtesy.

Jerrod could sense the animosity in his voice. Despite Ezra's efforts to bring Rexol into the fold, the mage was still suspicious and mistrustful of anyone bearing the empty gray eyes of the Order. Understandable, given the years he had spent as a fugitive during the Purge.

"Ezra is dead," Jerrod said simply, cutting to the heart of the matter. "A week ago."

"He was old," Rexol replied, showing no real remorse over the news.

"It wasn't age. One of our people was captured by the Inquisitors. She exposed Ezra as the leader of our cause."

"Are they coming for me next?" The question was sharp and accusing.

"Of course not!" Jerrod shot back, his own temper rising. "Only Ezra and I know of your involvement with our cause, and Ezra fled the Monastery before they could question him. He died out in the desert. The Pontiff doesn't suspect either one of us."

The wizard chewed his lower lip with his pointed teeth, weighing the implications. "So why are you here?"

"I thought you deserved to know. Ezra spoke highly of you. I think he considered you a friend."

Rexol flashed a grin and gave a dismissive laugh. "It's easy to be a friend when someone has something you need." His voice was sarcastic and bitter. "Ezra was only interested in how I could help your great and worthy cause. He saw me as nothing but a means to an end."

"Then why did you agree to help us?" Jerrod demanded, slamming his fist on the table. He knew his pent-up grief over the loss of his mentor was coming out as anger against Rexol, but he didn't care.

The wizard shrugged, his tone suddenly mellow. "The same reason, I suppose. I want something from you. Having allies among the Order might someday be of great value to me."

It might even save your life, Jerrod wanted to say. But he knew threatening the wizard would get him nowhere.

"Besides," Rexol continued. "It's not as if Ezra actually ever asked me to do anything."

"That day will come soon," Jerrod warned him. "The Burning Savior has already been born into the mortal world. The Oracles have seen it."

"Really?" Rexol seemed amused by the monk's pronouncement. "Is our savior a boy or a girl?"

"I don't know," Jerrod admitted. "The details of the vision are unclear. The identity of the savior is shrouded in mystery."

Rexol barked out another short laugh. "What good are prophecy and vision if you can't act on them?"

"Ezra gave his life for this cause," Jerrod reminded him.

"That doesn't mean he wasn't a fool," Rexol answered more quietly. "What other signs do you have that this so-called savior is coming?"

"The Blood Moon heralds a time of momentous events," the monk solemnly declared.

"The Purge was marked by a Blood Moon," Rexol muttered grimly. "Maybe your brethren are about to unleash another massacre on the Southlands."

Jerrod chose to ignore the wizard's comment. "The coming of our savior is inevitable," he insisted. "Each season more children are born with Chaos in their veins. Wandering magicians have become a common sight in all the Seven Capitals. Outside the cities any villager can turn to the local witch or druid in search of magic. Only two decades after the Purge, all but the lowliest of lords has a court mage at his beck and call."

"Court mages, traveling magicians, briar witches: These people are nothing!" Rexol spat, replying with the haughty arrogance reserved for true wizards. "What power they have is weak and unfocused. Most are barely more than charlatans, relying on tricks to fool the ignorant and cheat them of their coin."

He stood with a sigh, turning away from Jerrod as if weary of looking at him. "I have apprenticed many of these so-called Chaos wielders, only to discover their power is a mere shadow of true talent. Khamin Ankha is not the first apprentice to disappoint me, only the most recent."

"Most of those born with true power are identified by the Order long before they come to your attention," Jerrod reminded him, rising from his seat and walking over to place a comforting hand on the wizard's shoulder. Rexol turned back to face him, shrugging the hand away.

"Nazir is reluctant to move openly against your kind," Jerrod continued. "The horrors of the Purge are still fresh in the memories of the people; he is afraid of uniting the common folk in sympathy toward you. But he still seeks to cleanse the Southlands of Chaos; my fellow monks wage a constant war against magic. The Pilgrims seek out children who show any sign of the Sight or the Gift. They are taken to the Monastery, conscripted into the Order so that they can be taught to control their power."

"Conscripted? Is that what the Order calls it when they tear a child away from its parents?"

"The Pontiff believes the power of magic can be tamed one child at a time," Jerrod replied calmly, refusing to be baited by the blatant hostility in the wizard's comment. "He thinks the Legacy can be preserved if they find and control all those children born with the Gift. But his people are not the only ones searching for children touched by Chaos.

"Ezra was willing to face the truth the Pontiff refuses to acknowledge: The Legacy will not last forever. And when it is gone we will need a champion to defend us against the invading hordes from the Burning Sea. We need a savior with the strength to use the weapon of our enemies against them—a child of power trained in the arts of magic and sorcery."

Jerrod chose his words carefully. The mage was an ally to their cause, but there were secrets the monk was not willing to share with him. He made no mention of the Talismans left behind by the True Gods, or the power they possessed. He told the wizard only what was necessary, taking to heart the words of warning his mentor had shared with him many years ago.

Rexol serves no cause but his own. He answers to no authority but his own. And he works with us for reasons that are solely his own. He hungers for the power of Old Magic, and he would betray us all to claim it as his own.

"I have the Sight," Jerrod continued, hoping to bolster Rexol's fading confidence in their cause. "I share the visions of the Oracles. The child we seek is out there, somewhere. The time of the Burning Savior draws near. I have seen it in my dreams."

"I don't have much faith in your dreams," the wizard muttered. His voice became louder as he added, "But I'm sick of watching the Southlands stagnate beneath the yoke of the Order. Ezra may be gone, but I will honor our arrangement: I will train your savior . . . if you ever find one."

Jerrod heard the mockery in his tone, but refused to back down. "I will find what I seek," he vowed. "I will not rest or waver until we have our champion. The child of destiny is out there somewhere, waiting for us."

"The child is not the only one waiting," the wizard noted.

"You must be patient, Rexol. It will take time. The one we seek may not be revealed for several years. But if you stay true to our cause I will bring you a worthy apprentice. I will find a child touched by true Chaos, a child with the power to save us all."

"Do so, and I will gladly train this wondrous child," Rexol answered, flashing his pointed teeth in another grin.

The smile was meant to further mock Jerrod's steadfast religious conviction, yet the monk sensed a hunger behind the wizard's taunting. Rexol was desperate for a worthy apprentice—as desperate as Jerrod was to find the Burning Savior.

Shared desperation was a poor foundation on which to build an alliance. But Jerrod could take solace in one undeniable truth: The wizard would never betray him to the Order.

Chapter 7

IT WAS WELL past dusk by the time Gerrit reached his front door, a regular enough occurrence during the harvest season. He was hot and tired and filthy from working the fields with his men, but he wasn't one to sit about while others labored, even if he was paying them. He was well off by most standards, and even wealthy according to some, yet he still felt an obligation to join in the harvest of his own crop.

His only regret about the long hours spent in the fields was the knowledge that Keegan—the son Nyra had given him before she died, the single most important person in Gerrit's whole world—would already be fast asleep in his crib by the time he returned home.

Gerrit opened the door carefully so as not to wake the sleeping child and made his way into the small kitchen. Alia, the serving girl hired to care for Keegan while Gerrit was out in the fields, had laid out a small meal of bread and cheese for his return. The young woman herself was sitting at the table, staring down at a plate of food in front of her.

"I hope you haven't been waiting for me since supper," Gerrit jokingly said as he removed his jacket and seated himself across from her at the table. "Your father won't be happy with me if he finds out you're starving yourself until I get home."

Alia looked up, startled out of thought by his arrival. "I'm sorry, Mister Gerrit," she said quickly. "I never heard you come in."

"You *didn't* hear me come in," he corrected her, though not unkindly. "I didn't want to wake the baby," he added, tearing eagerly into one of the rolls.

It wasn't unusual for Alia to have dinner with him, though usually on the nights he was late she would eat before. That way she could head back to her own home as soon as he returned from the fields.

"I expected you to be ready to leave as soon as I came through the door," he commented between mouthfuls.

"I got to tell you something."

"You *have* to tell me something," he said automatically.

It wasn't hard to pick up the concern in her tone. Gerrit noticed she hadn't even touched the food on her plate. He wondered how long she had been sitting there, waiting for him. And suddenly he knew something was very, very wrong.

"Is Keegan having the nightmares again?"

Alia nodded slightly. "He got another one tonight. He woke all screaming and crying. And I heard him say 'Mama.'"

Gerrit frowned. He had never spoken to Keegan about Nyra. There was no point; not yet. The boy was only two; he was just beginning to speak. He couldn't possibly have understood what had happened to his mother.

"Mama? Are you sure? Sometimes children can be hard to understand, especially when they're upset."

"I . . . I'm pretty sure, Mister Gerrit. He said 'Mama.' Like his nightmare was about Nyra."

"Impossible," he declared with a shake of his head. "She died when Kee was born. He never knew her. He probably meant the words for you, Alia. You take care of him. He probably thinks you're his mother."

Alia's eyes grew wide with horror. "Oh, Mister Gerrit! I wouldn't never make him think that! Not never!"

He held up a hand to placate her. "It's okay, Alia. I know you'd never do anything to dishonor Nyra's memory. I only meant that Keegan probably *thinks* you're his mother. He's a smart boy, he knows I'm 'Papa.' Maybe he somehow made the connection that you should be 'Mama.'"

The young woman cast her gaze down, as if she couldn't look him in the eye.

"He didn't mean me," she insisted, though her voice was soft and low. "He was just crying and crying. Took an hour till he fell back asleep." After a moment she added, "A baby ain't supposed to have nightmares."

"Maybe the hours I'm working are upsetting him," Gerrit said by way of explanation. "I'll bet he just misses me. I'll make more of an effort to get home early enough to see him before he goes to sleep. I'm sure that's all it is."

His answer didn't seem to ease Alia's concerns. "There's something else, Mister Gerrit. You had a visitor today. A woman. An *old* woman. Said she needed to talk to you about Kee."

An unexpected shiver ran down Gerrit's spine. "An old woman was asking after my son?"

"She didn't use his name. Just kept calling him 'the boy.' I didn't like her, Mister Gerrit. There was something wrong about her. Something nasty. She scared me. I told her to go away, but she wouldn't leave. She said she knew Nyra, so I . . . I told her to come back later. I just wanted her to go away. I didn't know what else to do. I'm sorry, Mister Gerrit."

He hesitated a moment before shrugging, trying to appear nonchalant for the young girl's sake. "There's nothing to be sorry about," he assured her. "If it's important I'm sure she'll show up later tonight. Don't worry, Alia. I'll find out what this woman wants."

"I stayed to tell you about her," the young woman said defensively, as if trying to atone for some crime Gerrit hadn't accused her of. "So you'd be ready in case she comes back."

"You did the right thing."

Satisfied with his answer, Alia pushed herself away from the table.

"You're leaving?" Gerrit asked in surprise. "You haven't even touched your food."

"I'm . . . I'm not hungry, Mister Gerrit."

He could see the nervousness in her; he could tell she was anxious to leave before this strange visitor returned. He found her behavior odd, but she was barely more than a girl and he wasn't about to chastise her for being easily spooked.

"That's fine, Alia. You go on home, now. Say hi to your father for me, and I'll see you tomorrow morning."

"I will, Mister Gerrit. Thank you. Good-bye."

And with that she was gone. Gerrit chewed his food slowly, trying to imagine what kind of woman could have made such an impression on Alia. And how that kind of woman would have known his wife.

It was well past midnight and the fire in the hearth had burned down to a few embers when the expected knock finally came at his door. For a brief second Gerrit considered simply ignoring it. The door was locked; whoever was outside would just have to come back another time. Then he laughed softly at himself for his foolishness and got up to greet his late-night visitor, his body casting eerie shadows on the walls as he crossed the floor of his front room to the door.

"Come in," he had been about to say as he opened the door, but the invitation died on his lips when he saw the figure who had come to meet him.

The woman was hunched over nearly double. Her scraggly gray hair fell uncombed from beneath the hood of her black cloak, partially covering her sunken, withered features. Though he had never seen Gretchen in person, he recognized the local witch-woman at his door.

She didn't try to invite herself in or make any move forward, as if she knew she wouldn't be welcomed.

"I've come about the boy," the hag said.

"You mean Keegan," was all Gerrit could manage by way of a reply.

"He's very special, that boy."

"Of course he's special. He's my son."

She pulled back her lips and bared her rotting teeth at him. "Don't speak to me like a fool! Your boy is different from other children. He is marked."

Gerrit resisted a sudden impulse to slam the door in the old crone's face.

Instead, he asked, "Marked? What does that mean?"

The witch ignored his question, responding with one of her own. "The boy, does he have nightmares?"

Somehow he knew there was no point in lying. "Yes."

"Nightmares about his mother?"

Gerrit didn't know much about witchcraft, but he was an intelligent man who wasn't easily fooled. Suddenly his earlier conversation with Alia made perfect sense.

"You spoke to Kee's nanny about this, didn't you? You're the one who filled her head with that nonsense about his mother!"

"Your son sees things in his dreams. He sees his mother dying. He's not old enough to comprehend what happened. But he sees it in his dreams and he *knows*."

"This kind of talk might have tricked a frightened young girl, but your games won't work on me."

The hag laughed, her shrill cackle sending shivers down Gerrit's back.

"This is no game. Your wife knew my power. She believed. She came to see me while the boy was inside her, to ask for my help. Did you know that?"

"You're lying!"

"Am I? She gave me something. Payment for services rendered." Gretchen reached beneath her robes and brought out a ring, holding it up high for him to see. It took Gerrit a moment before he realized it was an exact match of the one on his own finger.

"Nyra's betrothal ring! But she said . . . she told me she lost it."

"She traded it to me. Traded it for the life of her child."

"What . . . what are you saying?"

"The boy was dead inside her. Only my magic could give him life again. That's why your wife came to me. To beg my help. I warned her there would be a cost beyond the ring. A cost she was willing to pay."

A dawning horror crept across Gerrit's face as he began to understand. "You. It was your fault she died. You killed my wife!"

He balled his hands into fists and raised them up high, but he couldn't bring himself to strike a woman. Not even one as contemptible as this witch.

The hag never even flinched before his impotent rage.

"Your wife made a choice: her life for the boy's. There was no other way."

He lowered his fists, slowly unclenching them. Instead he held out his right hand, palm up.

"Give me back her ring."

He spoke with all the authority he could muster, but he doubted it would have any effect. He was certain she would simply snatch it away from him, but instead she set it into his waiting grasp. The skin of her fingers was dry and rough, and he instinctively pulled back at the contact, nearly dropping the ring.

"Yes," Gretchen whispered. "Take the ring back. It rightfully belongs to you: I have no use for it now."

"You had a bargain with my wife," Gerrit insisted. He had no wish to be in debt to this foul woman. "I will give you double what the ring is worth in coin. Come back tomorrow and I'll see you are paid."

"I don't want your coins. There is . . . something else."

"What, then? Out with it, witch! Or I'll raise my fists again, and this time they won't go unused!"

Though Gerrit was a large man threats and violence were not

normally in his nature. But this woman disturbed him. The longer he spoke with her the more agitated he became. He was anxious to end this meeting as quickly as possible.

"I want the boy. Give me your son."

"You're mad, woman!"

Gerrit tried to slam the door in her face, but the hag reached out with a single crooked finger and stopped it cold. She reached out with the same finger and touched Gerrit lightly on the arm. The chill of the grave swallowed Gerrit's entire body, freezing him in place. Paralyzed, he could do nothing but stand helpless before the monster who had come to take his son.

"The boy sees visions in his dreams—visions of things past and things yet to come. He is marked. I can smell him, I can taste him. Chaos burns in his veins."

The witch snapped her fingers, and the spell was broken. Gerrit stumbled back, his limbs suddenly his own once more. But his legs and arms were numb, and he collapsed to the ground by the fire-place on the far side of the room.

"But the boy must be given to me freely," the witch continued. "If not, his power will be of no use to me."

Gerrit rose slowly to his feet, leaning on the hearth for support, his legs functional but unsteady. He wanted to run, he wanted with every fiber of his being to turn and flee from the horrible creature that had invaded his home. But instead he held his ground, for Keegan's sake.

"I will never give my son over to you," he said, his voice defiant despite his fear.

"Right now the boy only sees things," she rasped. "But as he ages his power will grow. One day he will discover he can *do* things. Terrible, awful things. He must learn to control this power. If he doesn't, it could destroy him."

Summoning up his courage, Gerrit spat a reply filled with hate and venom across the room at the figure still hunched on the threshold of his door.

"So you will teach him to be a witch, like you? To cast spells and hexes on innocent villagers? To feed on their fear and weakness? I will die before I let that happen!"

"My power is weak," the crone whispered. "It comes from talismans and rituals. I know the spells to draw the magic out of a dragon's tooth, to shape it to my bidding. But the power is in the talisman. The boy is different. His power comes from within. Chaos is a part of him, and in time he will unleash it on the world. It is inevitable."

Gerrit's limbs were still tingling from the aftereffects of the witch's spell, but he could feel the sensation flowing back into them as the heat of the fire warmed him. He grabbed a poker from the fireplace and stirred up the dying embers, keeping an eye on the witch as he did so.

"You are not welcome here," he said as he jabbed at the fire, letting the tip of the poker grow ever hotter. "I want you to leave, now."

"I am not the only one who can see your son's power," Gretchen warned him. "Others will sense the Chaos in him. And some, like the Pilgrims of the Order, will not come to you as I have. They will simply take him away."

Gerrit turned from the fire to face the intruder, brandishing the poker like a weapon, its glowing tip extended far out in front. To his satisfaction, the startled witch took a quick step backward.

"Your wife made a choice when the boy was born," she hissed. "A difficult choice. Now you must make one yourself.

"Give the boy to me, let him be mine to raise and teach. In time, I will bring him back to see you, so that you can know him. Or refuse me, and lose your son forever when the Order comes and takes him away to the Monastery."

Gerrit didn't reply but took half a step forward, keeping the heated end of the poker pointed directly at the hag. In response she turned and fled out the still-open door, her shriveled form moving more quickly than he would have thought possible.

"I will be back tomorrow night for your decision," she called over her shoulder before being swallowed by the shadows of the night.

Heart pounding, Gerrit quickly closed and locked the door. He returned the poker to its place by the hearth, his hands shaking, his mind racing. He knew that much of what the hag had said was the truth. He had no doubt there was something different about Keegan; why else would the witch have come for him? And if she had sensed his power, others would as well.

But he would never give up his son. Not to the witch. Not to the Order. Not to anyone.

The next morning when Alia arrived at the house she found it deserted. Gerrit had taken his son and whatever valuables he could carry and vanished in the night.

Chapter 8

"YOU CALL THIS clean?" Madam Wyndham demanded of the maid, holding up the dinner napkin with a fingernail-sized stain on the corner. "Are you trying to embarrass me before Lord and Lady Hollander? Do you want them to think me so lowborn that I throw a dinner party with befouled linens?"

"No, mistress," the maid replied, setting down the knives she had been placing on the table and scurrying over to take the dirty napkin from her mistress's grasp.

"Take this to the laundry and fetch a clean one. I've worked too hard preparing for this dinner to let it be ruined by your shoddy napkin!"

The maid disappeared, but Celia Wyndham took no notice. She had set about examining each of the fourteen settings in turn, searching for some imperfection. Technically it should have been the Steward of the Manse who oversaw the final preparations for the coming dinner. But Celia Wyndham did not share her husband's high opinion of Roland; the ex-soldier's standards were sorrowfully lacking when it came to matters of culture and refinement.

She clucked her tongue in disgust at finding a tiny crusted particle of food on the tines of one of the forks, then set it aside so she would remember to tell the maid to bring a clean one. She made a mental note to deliver a savage tongue-lashing to the scullery girl for her lackadaisical efforts . . . she'd just have to be careful not to let Roland find out. The Steward could be irrationally overprotective when it came to the household staff under his charge.

He's too soft on them. Is it any wonder I have soiled napkins and dirty forks on my table?

Fortunately, everything else seemed to be in order. She wished her husband, Conrad, were here, but he had insisted his manorial duties required him to be away at least until the late afternoon. There was little argument she could make against such a claim—after all, it had been her idea for Conrad to apply to the Provincial Council for the rank of Manor Lord two years ago.

Conrad had been reluctant at first. He was a successful businessman; his ventures gave him great economic and political clout in the village, despite his lack of official standing. He saw the position of Manor Lord as a demotion: a glorified innkeeper whose sole task was to maintain suitable lodgings for the use of any nobility passing through the region.

But Celia knew better. The Manor Lord was the closest a low-born man like her husband could ever come to gaining a noble title, short of heroic acts in time of war. And her husband was no soldier. A noble would treat a Manor Lord as a virtual equal, at least within the confines of the manor. And it was not uncommon for the daughter of a Manor Lord to marry into true nobility.

Her husband made fun of her when she spoke of such things.

"Your social climbing is an amusing diversion, Celia," he had said when she first suggested applying for the Manor Lord's position, "but I am nothing more than a merchant to these barons and earls. I pay my taxes and they are happy. They don't want to speak with me unless they need gold to raise an army."

Celia knew better. Fortunes rose and fell quickly in the Southlands, and when those on top fell, those beneath rose. A dozen different cities had, at one time or another, been recognized among the Seven Capitals in the four centuries since the Southlands had been joined under the Treaty of Union. If cities could shift so easily in their station, surely so could families.

"You sell yourself short, Conrad," she'd replied. "The nobility respects the talent of those who can amass great wealth, as you have.

"And what of our daughter?" she'd added. "Would you not like Cassandra to have the chance to marry into the nobility?"

The last argument had finally swayed him, as she'd known it would.

Conrad loved Cassandra. Loved her too much, Celia sometimes fretted. When the time came to choose a husband for her he might object to seeing his daughter betrothed to an old baron desperate for an heir, or to a philandering viscount seeking the appearance of respectability by taking a lawful wife.

Though she loved her daughter, Celia knew she would have no hesitation. Her own family had climbed the social strata of the Southlands quickly through such marriages, and now she had achieved the penultimate step by getting her husband appointed the Manor Lord.

Besides, marrying for status could often lead to love, as it had between her and Conrad. But Cassandra was only four, and such thoughts were best left for later. Tonight there was too much to do.

Celia circled the table again, searching for anything that might jeopardize this evening's dinner. When she had heard the news of Lord Hollander's visit, her heart had leapt. When she learned his retinue would include Lady Hollander and ten other guests of rank she had nearly wept with joy. This was the opportunity she had prayed to the Gods, both Old and New, to grant her. Everything had to be perfect.

"The venison is exquisite," Lord Hollander proclaimed, and the other guests quickly added their agreement.

Celia blushed at the compliment. "Thank you, my lord."

"It is a shame your husband could not be here to enjoy it," Lady Hollander added. Celia wasn't sure if she detected sympathy or gloating in the lady's voice.

Before she could come up with a suitable response, Lord Hollander interjected on her behalf.

"Conrad is a busy man, as we all know. The revenues of the manor have nearly doubled since his appointment." The gracious lord raised his glass. "To Conrad, in appreciation for the fortune he has brought to this manor."

The others followed suit, raising their glasses and drinking to her husband. Celia beamed with pride, though inside she was silently cursing Conrad for being so late. He knew how important this evening was! Tradition held that the Steward of the Manse should fill in when the Manor Lord was absent, but Celia was damned if she was going to seat someone as uncouth as Roland at the table with Lord and Lady Hollander.

Yet she couldn't leave the seat empty; Conrad's absence had left thirteen at the table—an unlucky number. Celia had averted that catastrophe by bringing Cassandra down to dine with them. The girl sat picking at her food, obviously not impressed with the proceedings. Still, she had been quiet and well behaved under the watchful eye of the nanny who lurked unobtrusively in the shadows.

Celia made a mental note to congratulate the young woman on preparing her daughter so well for the dinner on such short notice—she had expected far less from someone raised as a simple farm girl.

And perhaps Cassandra's presence had not been a bad thing. Lady Hollander was well known for her love of children, and Celia's daughter looked absolutely precious tonight. The girl's perfect, cream-colored skin and curly blond hair were not unheard of in the middle provinces, but they certainly weren't common—oddly, neither Celia nor her husband was fair-haired. Her daughter's rare looks, combined with the emerald dress Celia had chosen to perfectly complement Cassandra's gorgeous green eyes, turned the little girl into an adorable living doll.

"Cassandra, darling, you haven't eaten a thing." Lady Hollander's words came unexpectedly, as if Celia's own thoughts had suddenly drawn attention to her daughter.

Celia tensed slightly in anticipation of the young girl's reply.

"I'm sorry, Lady Hollander," she mumbled, and Celia felt the tension slipping from her shoulders. "I'm not hungry."

"Cassandra has not been sleeping well," Celia said by way of apology. "Isn't that right, Nan?"

The nanny took half a step forward from the shadows. "Yes, madam. The young mistress has nightmares."

Celia frowned slightly. She hadn't wanted the dreams to come up, not tonight. She had foolishly opened the door herself, but the nanny should have known better than to mention Cassandra's vivid nightmares.

Lady Hollander, however, was suddenly filled with motherly compassion. "You poor child," she cooed. "What is it you dream about? Monsters?"

The nanny answered again, and Celia had to bite her lip to keep from shushing the stupid woman and causing a spectacle in front of everybody.

"Yes, my lady. She often dreams of ogres who walk the land and eat whole villages, and sometimes she speaks of great winged beasts breathing fire down from the sky."

There was a surprised chuckle from Lord Hollander. "Dragons, is it, my pretty child? I often dream of them myself, when I have too much wine at supper and heartburn plagues my sleep."

A round of polite laughter from the table was cut off by Cassandra's sudden shout.

"No! Not monsters. Not now. Now it's the horse dream!"

Cassandra suddenly broke down in tears.

Celia froze, mortified by the turn of events. The nanny hesitated, uncertain if she should invade the space of the other diners to try to placate the sobbing child. It was Lady Hollander who made the first move, pushing back her chair and coming around the length of the table to wrap a pair of comforting arms around Cassandra.

"Hush, child. Hush. Dreams cannot hurt you. They are only dreams, just like pictures in a book."

Cassandra's sobbing stopped, to Celia's relief. She was both grateful to Lady Hollander for easing her daughter's cries, and jealous that the noblewoman had usurped the mother's rightful role here at her own table.

"My dreams are different," Cassandra said softly, defiantly. "They're not like pictures in books."

"Tell me about your dreams," Lady Hollander urged. "Sometimes talking about them makes them seem not so bad."

"It's Gerald, the smith. He's got a horse. A gray one. He's doing something to its foot."

"Shoeing it, perhaps?" Lord Hollander offered from the other end of the table.

Cassandra shrugged, not understanding. Celia had never allowed her daughter into the stables, or even the smithy for that matter. How she even knew the smith's name, she couldn't begin to guess.

"Then the horse gets mad. It jumps and kicks. It kicks Gerald in the head." Cassandra traced a small circle on her own forehead. "Here. This part is all squished. Then Gerald is on the ground. There's blood on his head. Lots of blood."

For a second nobody spoke, but then Lady Hollander broke the awkward silence with a light laugh. "That is a scary dream for a little girl," she admitted, "but the horse can't hurt you. It isn't real."

"It's real!" Cassandra insisted with the absolute urgency only young children can muster. "It's gray and it hurts Gerald!"

"Nan," Celia said softly, "it's getting late. Perhaps Cassandra should go to bed now."

"Of course, mistress," the nanny replied.

Lady Hollander returned to her seat, and the nanny scooped Cassandra up in her arms and headed for the dining room's door.

She was almost knocked over by Conrad rushing in, still fumbling with the buttons on the clothes Celia had laid out for him. The nanny stumbled but regained her balance and glared at Conrad in cross surprise.

"My apologies, Nan. And to you, Lord Hollander," he added, suddenly aware all eyes had turned to him. "I went into the city yesterday to purchase some horses for breeding. I fully intended to be back in time to welcome you to our manor, Lord Hollander."

The lord waved his hand to show he felt no slight. "Your wife has more than amply filled in during your absence, Conrad. I trust all went well in the city?"

"No, my lord," Conrad replied, finally popping the final button of his collar into place. He still stood just inside the doorway, uncertain if it was polite to sit while being questioned by a nobleman. "We had some trouble with a skittish gray. I had taken our smith with me to examine the animals. I am sorry to say his skull was caved in by one of the animal's hooves. I had to see to his funeral arrangements. That is why I was late."

There was silence in the room as all eyes shifted from Conrad to Cassandra, still held in the arms of the nanny standing just inside the door.

"The Sight," Lady Hollander whispered.

At her words the nanny quickly set Cassandra on the floor and took a step back.

"The Order must know of this," Lord Hollander said at last.

Conrad only looked in confusion at the guests. "What's going on?" he demanded. "What are you talking about?" At last his gaze fell on his wife. "Celia, what's going on?"

But Celia couldn't answer him. She could only stare at Cassandra in horror, thinking over and over to herself, *Not her eyes! They can't take her beautiful eyes.*

At the sound of the horn Roland was instantly awake: a single, short blast that ended as if it was cut off prematurely. Not good. He grabbed his sword and rushed from the tent, not having time to don his armor as he raced toward the outskirts of their makeshift camp. The whole while he kept hoping to hear another signal—two blasts meant the odds were fairly even, three meant they were overmatched, four meant it was a false alarm. But there was nothing further, just the one blast. Which meant the sentries had been discovered and most likely killed.

The Rearing Lion mercenaries Roland had hired to protect Conrad Wyndham's only daughter during her flight were already gathering in battle formation, twelve soldiers armed with heavy broadswords. Those who had been on night-watch wore ringmail shirts. The rest, like Roland, were still in their sleeping clothes. But they were all here, except the two sentries on the perimeter and the two stationed outside Cassandra's tent.

Roland frowned. A dozen soldiers plus himself made thirteen—an unlucky number. But of course he hadn't yet counted Dalia and the five bowmen under her command. The archers added another six to their group, making a total of nineteen gathered in the clearing ready to face their enemy. Plus Bella.

Normally the Rearing Lions worked alone. They were elite soldiers for hire, specializing in protection for merchant caravans or important persons traveling along routes that were known for bandit activity. Ransoms and kidnappings were rare in the Southlands but occasionally a noble or wealthy merchant, or members of the family, would disappear before reaching their destination.

Roland knew these men were a strong deterrent to such an occurrence. Nearly a score of armed guards was usually enough to make would-be attackers rethink their intentions.

This job, however, was different. Following Conrad's instructions, Roland had recruited the hired blades on the condition that they be discreet. A mounted patrol would only draw attention to their carriage, and would do little to scare off their real enemies. Secrecy and stealth were their allies if they wanted to smuggle Cassandra out of the Southlands before the Order found her.

The other soldiers had to suspect something strange was going on. Roland had told them they were taking the girl from the Southlands to the islands of the West, where pirates and rogues ruled. There would be a ship waiting at the coast, a merchant Conrad knew. The mercenaries had to deliver the girl to him and then their job was done. The ship would sail away, and the girl and Roland would go with it.

No doubt the soldiers were curious about a wealthy father who would send his only daughter away to live in the Western Isles. There, if the girl was lucky and talented, she might become one of the infamous Women of the Waves, a band of fierce female brigands who sailed the Endless Sea. But most girls who crossed the waters ended up as thieves, prostitutes, or pleasure slaves to wealthy pirate lords . . . though Roland would give his life before he let such a fate befall Cassandra.

But in the end the fee Conrad had paid them, and the bonus they were told they'd receive should his daughter make it to the ship unharmed, was enough to make them set aside all their doubts. They'd even agreed to work with Dalia without complaint, despite the fact that her up-and-coming mercenary band of archers had underbid them on several recent jobs.

Yet the company had almost backed out when they learned Bella would accompany them. Roland could just make out the white witch's robed form huddled on the edge of the campfires, preparing some arcane recipe that would hopefully aid them in the attack.

Traveling with the silver-haired woman hadn't been pleasant. Each night she brewed up foul concoctions that polluted the entire camp with their stench. When she spoke her words were cryptic and mysterious, and her gaze made it feel as if she were looking deep inside you, judging you, and finding you wanting. It was easy for Roland to understand why the mercenaries balked at having her along, but Conrad had insisted the sorceress accompany them. In the end the mercenaries' love of gold had overwhelmed their distaste.

Cassandra had cried when they set out from the manor. She

cried the first night when they stopped to make camp. And she cried every night since until she fell asleep. It had been a full week now, and Roland could still hear her high-pitched, little-girl sobs in the darkness coming from her private tent whenever they stopped.

He had done his best to try to comfort her, but what could you say to a four-year-old who had been cast out by her own father? He knew it was more than this, as well: The strange nightmares that had driven them into exile hadn't been left behind. Sometimes Cassandra would wake screaming, but she wouldn't talk about her dreams to anyone. She'd just cry herself back to sleep.

Bella had taken an intense interest in the girl when she learned about the nightmares; she'd asked Roland for permission to speak to her in private. But Roland kept a pair of guards with Cassandra at all times, and they had strict orders to keep the witch away from her. This seemed to suit the girl just fine.

Apart from Cassandra's nightmares the trip had been uneventful until tonight, when the horn had awakened them all with its shrill note of alarm. Roland's fist tightened on the pommel of his drawn sword in anticipation. The sentries were dead, he was sure of that now. They would have signaled if they still lived. And whoever had killed them couldn't be far away.

At least they didn't have to worry about being flanked. The back of the camp was bordered by the rushing waters of the Marn River: No man could cross the rapids here, and the nearest ford was over a day's march away. The clearing they were in was large enough that they didn't need to fear an ambush from the trees, so they just had to wait for the enemy to reveal themselves. When they did, Roland's worst fears were realized.

Half a dozen figures in loose robes stepped into the light of the fire, slipping silently from the shadows as if materializing from the darkness of the night itself. They stood in two rows, a woman and two men in front, another three men standing close behind. Each was armed with only a simple wooden staff. Their hoods had been thrown back to reveal shaved heads and gray, empty eyes. It was obvious to all how the sentries had been found; their camouflaged hiding spots would have been useless against the Sight of the Inquisitors.

"The Order has no quarrel with you," the woman in the front declared in a strong, even voice, seemingly oblivious to the arrows Dalia and her archers aimed at her little group. "We have only come for the girl."

She was a tall woman, taller than any of the men accompanying her. Her scalp wasn't just shaved; it was scarred and disfigured. Roland could make out dark stains on her robes and a splatter of blood across her cheek. The blood was obviously not her own.

"We have orders to take this girl to the Western Isles," Roland replied quickly, hoping to bolster the courage of those hired to protect Sir Wyndham's daughter. "And we intend to do just that."

"She belongs to the Order," the woman insisted. "She has the Sight. It is heresy to refuse our request, punishable by death."

Despite himself, Roland hesitated before replying. All his life he had lived in the Southlands. He had seen the political power of the Order. Even the most powerful lords bowed down to their will. Who was he to defy them? What weight did his vow to protect Cassandra with his life have against the will of the Gods?

In the silence of his self-doubt, Dalia answered for him.

"How will you report us to the Pontiff with your throat torn open by my arrow?"

In unison all six archers fired at the three figures in the front rank. At this close range there was barely time to hear the twang of their bows or the hiss of the arrows through the air before the missiles reached their targets.

The Inquisitors reacted with superhuman speed, seeming to move even before the arrows were fired, twirling their staves to deflect them harmlessly away . . . all except the woman in front. Instead, she caught Dalia's arrow with her free hand, casually reaching up to pluck it from the air mere inches from her throat. Behind them, the other monks fanned out and moved forward until they stood beside their comrades.

Roland raised a clenched fist and the first wave of soldiers rushed forward to attack, eight trained and armored men with swords against six members of the Order wearing robes and carrying only wooden staves. The slaughter was over in seconds.

Three of the Rearing Lions went down before they could even swing their blades, dropped by the lightning-swift strikes to the sides of their heads, the hard wood of the Inquisitor's staves caving in their soft temples. Another had his leg broken, the bone snapped by a sharp kick from one of the monks striking just below his knee. A fifth had his ribs shattered by a flurry of punches to his midsection, the force of the blows penetrating his mail shirt.

The remaining three soldiers managed nothing more than a few wild blows that were either parried or easily sidestepped by the spinning, whirling robed figures. A sharp fist to the throat, a knee to the groin, an elbow to the face and the soldiers still standing were standing no longer.

Roland had always dismissed the rumors he had heard about the martial prowess of the Order, believing them to be nothing but another political tool to ensure the obedience of the masses. He had scoffed at claims the Inquisitors could see into the minds of their enemies to anticipate and counter attacks even before they came. But there was no way to deny the ruthless efficiency of the massacre he had just witnessed. For the first time in his career as a soldier, Roland felt the urge to flee from a battle. Only his loyalty to Cassandra—and the knowledge that there was no real hope of escape—enabled him to hold his ground.

A second volley of arrows launched by Dalia and her now desperate archers into the melee was as ineffective as the first. The Inquisitors simply ducked and twisted out of the way, or calmly knocked the deadly projectiles aside.

"Taste my Chaos, you sightless bastards!" Bella screamed, rushing up from her spot at the back and hurling what appeared to be a small silver egg at the nearest of the enemy.

The sorceress was spewing forth a mountain of foul-sounding but senseless words, an arcane language to shape her spell. The egg struck the ground just in front of its targets and erupted in a ball of blazing white fire, engulfing all six of the robed assassins. Roland and what remained of his troop staggered back, knocked off balance by the concussive force of the explosion and recoiling from the heat.

For the first time since setting out, Roland was glad Conrad had insisted they bring Bella with them.

Inside the conflagration one of the male Inquisitors screamed, his body barely visible through the smoke and flames as it collapsed writhing to the ground. One of the figures beside him also fell, but a second later the woman and her three remaining companions stepped calmly from the wall of fire, completely unharmed. Their clothes weren't even singed.

"Uriah and Saergul were weak," the tall woman explained coolly, sparing a brief glance at the now still corpses in the rapidly sputtering flames behind her. "But the divine will we serve is stronger than your profane magic."

Her hand fluttered at her side, a quick flick of the wrist so subtle it may have been imagined. And suddenly a long, sharp throwing dart was lodged in Bella's neck.

The witch clutched at the metal impaled in her windpipe, choking as her hands flailed helplessly at the shaft protruding from her flesh. A thin rivulet of blood crawled down from the wound. The witch managed to wrap her fingers around the invading object and yank it free, and the blood gushed forth from her throat like a crimson geyser, staining her white robe. A look of dumbfounded shock passed across her face and she collapsed to the ground.

Roland tore his eyes away from the grisly scene to discover that Dalia and her archers were also dead, slain in the few brief seconds he had been entranced by the witch's futile struggle to survive. The two guards from Cassandra's tent had joined them now, drawn by the explosion. That made the odds seven against four, thanks to the witch's spell. But Roland had seen enough of their foe to know that none of them would survive this fight.

Grim determination set their jaws as they stood to meet their end and the Inquisitors slowly advanced.

- - - -

Cassandra heard an explosion outside and the crackle of fire, followed by the sound of screams. The two men sitting with her in the tent grabbed their swords and ran out to see what was happening. They could have just asked her. She had seen it all in her nightmares. She knew the men wouldn't be coming back.

A second later the tent flap opened and another man walked in, soaking wet from head to toe. She didn't recognize him. He wasn't one of the soldiers and he wasn't one of the strangers from her nightmares. They were all bald; this man had short, dark hair. Then she noticed he had no eyes.

"You're like the others," she whispered, a little afraid and a little excited.

"No, Cassandra," he said softly, crouching down to scoop her up in his arms, "I'm not like them at all."

He knew her name. Nobody called her by her name anymore. They all called her "the girl" now.

"My name is Jerrod. I'm going to take you somewhere the Order will never find you."

His wet clothes were cold against her skin as he lifted her in his arms, but she found his embrace safe and comforting.

"Can you piggyback, Cassandra?"

The little girl nodded. Her daddy used to piggyback her all the time.

The man swung her around onto his back. She wrapped her arms tight around his neck, and he reached back to hook her legs in the crooks of his elbows.

"Good girl," he said as they slipped from the tent, leaving the sounds of the still-raging battle behind them as the man jogged toward the river.

"Where are you taking me?" she whispered into her rescuer's ear.

"To a man who will keep you safe."

"Does he have no eyes, like you?"

"No, he's not like me at all. He's a wizard. His name is Rexol."

Cassandra smiled. This seemed like the stories her nanny used to tell her, about faeries and trolls and princesses whisked away in the depths of the night.

"Hold on tight," the man warned as he reached the edge of the raging river. "We're going for a swim."

Chapter 9

"HOLD OUT YOUR arm, Cassandra," Rexol ordered.

The girl hesitated, glancing quickly from the small ink pot to the glowing metal tip of the quill in his hand. She turned her emerald-green eyes up to meet the wizard's own.

"What are you going to do?"

The mage rubbed his free hand along the side of his dark-skinned cheek, showing her the tattoos inscribed on his own face.

"I'm going to paint a design on your arm. Like these."

If she were older he would have explained to Cassandra what the symbols were for, and how they helped to channel Chaos. But Cassandra was only eight. Though she had been under his care for nearly four years, she was still his ward, not his apprentice—she was too young to comprehend the intricacies of magic. Chaos was strong in her, but it was latent and unharnessed. Her power only manifested itself subconsciously, through her strange and sometimes prophetic dreams. She wasn't ready to begin her training in the arcane arts.

He had planned to teach her true magic once she was more mature. She would learn the words to call the Chaos out, and the rituals to shape and control it once its power was unleashed into the mortal world. Given time, he could transform the girl into one of the greatest sorceresses since the Cataclysm.

But now it seemed he would never be given that time. The Pontiff had issued an official summons for both him and his young charge to present themselves at the Monastery. Rexol could think of only one reason for such a summons: The Pontiff knew who Cassandra was, and how she had been snatched away from the grasp of the Inquisitors four years ago.

He had tried to keep her identity secret, shrouding her from head to toe in the manner of the Western nomads whenever he went into town to purchase supplies. Few of the townsfolk dared to ask him about his mysterious shrouded companion. Those who did were told she was a relative from one of the tribes in Rexol's ancestral homeland.

But careful though he was, Cassandra was only a little girl. She was incapable of understanding the urgency of maintaining the ruse. There were times she pulled the shawl from her face to catch a cool breeze, or lifted her veil to get a better glimpse of some item of interest. Anyone who caught sight of her complexion or shocking green eyes would know she was not Rexol's kin.

He should have seen this coming. It was inevitable that rumors would spread of the pale-skinned girl with the emerald gaze. These rumors would eventually make their way to those who served the Order; it wouldn't be hard for them to piece together the truth.

In the end, though, he'd accepted the risk out of desperation: Unlike all the apprentices who had come before, she had real potential. Potential that might never be fully realized. The Pontiff had summoned them to the Order's stronghold, and Rexol knew there was a chance neither one of them would ever leave the Monastery again.

Yet refusing to obey the summons was in itself a crime punishable by death. If he tried to run he'd become a fugitive, hunted by the assassins of the Order. Better to capitulate, at least in appearance. If he went to the Monastery of his own free will they had no legal right to hold him.

In the royal courts of the Southlands there was a growing undercurrent of resentment against the power the Order exerted. Rexol was betting that Nazir wouldn't risk evoking memories of the Purge by holding a wizard of his reputation without cause. Not if it meant alienating his allies among the noble Houses. It was a dangerous political gamble, but one the mage was willing to take.

Even if the Pontiff did arrest him for heresy, he still had his secret allies within the Order. He believed Jerrod and his followers would find a way for him to escape; they needed him. And he had one final card he could play, if necessary: Cassandra's recent dream.

He wasn't going in unprepared, of course. He was no helpless lamb to be led to slaughter. The monks of the Order had power, but so did he.

Dipping the glowing quill into the ink pot with his left hand, he reached out and grasped the young girl's wrist with his right: firm, but not cruel. She didn't resist as he held her bare arm straight out, the palm of her tiny hand facing the ceiling.

"Will it hurt?" she asked, only the faintest hint of a tremor in her voice.

"Only for a few seconds."

He had never lied to her. Whatever else his young charge might feel toward him—and Rexol knew he was not an easy man for a child to love—at least she trusted him.

She gasped once when the searing metal first touched her skin, then bit her lip against the pain as the wizard burned an arcane symbol of binding into her flesh. The glyph sizzled and smoked before slowly melting away beneath the skin, leaving no trace it had ever existed.

Rexol pushed his way through the small crowd of supplicants camped before the Monastery's gate. His long fingers clenched even more tightly around Cassandra's tiny hand as he dragged her through the ceaselessly praying throng.

The walls of the Monastery towered over them, thirty feet above the surrounding desert sands. They were made of an otherwise unknown stone, perfectly smooth and without visible defect. The black rock gleamed like polished marble, and if one stared at it long enough it was possible to see dark shadows moving beneath the surface. Legend held that the souls of the monks who died within the Monastery walls still dwelled within the stone, giving power and strength to their brothers and sisters inside.

The only entrance was the massive gate on the eastern face: two enormous slabs fashioned from the same black stone that made up the rest of the fortress. If not for the barely visible seam where the hinges swung open and the faint line between the two slabs, this section of wall would have been indistinguishable from the rest of the structure. If permission to enter was granted the gates would open and the stone would part, soundlessly opening inward to grant entrance, then sealing behind once more to preserve the inner mysteries of the structure.

In the first century following the Cataclysm, the supplicants camped outside the gates would have numbered in the thousands. Today there were fewer than fifty ardent believers. The Old Gods rarely answered prayers, and many of the common folk had turned to the New Gods to make their pleas. Not that they answered any more prayers than the Old, but at least they were *New*.

Despite this, the Order still held significant influence across the Southlands. Though many Southerners had fallen from the path of true worship, the common folk still generally heeded the wishes and demands of those who served the Pontiff. Some obeyed out of fear, some respect, and others simply because of the political influence the Order wielded.

Oracles were common in most noble courts, using their visions to give guidance and counsel to the various ruling houses . . . along with frequent donations to their liege lords from the Monastery's substantial coffers. In return, Pilgrims were given free rein to spread the faith of the so-called True Gods from the impregnable stronghold to each of the Seven Capitals and every city, town, and village in between.

And the ancient law that permitted those with the Sight or the Gift to be recruited into the Order against the wishes of parents or guardians had never been repealed . . . though rarely was a child of noble birth ever taken from his or her family.

Had Cassandra's parents been true nobility, instead of members of the merchant class, she would never have ended up under Rexol's care. Some would attribute her fate to the whims of fortune and chance, but Rexol knew better. Chaos turned the wheels of destiny in ways even the prophets could not see.

What the supplicants outside the Monastery walls lacked in numbers they more than made up for in religious fervor. The faithful pushed and shoved one another without regard, bowing and prostrating themselves, their voices rising up in a discordant cacophony of chants and prayers.

The nearer Rexol and Cassandra came to the gates the more insufferable the crowd became. Eager worshippers pressed forward, desperate to bring themselves ever closer to the smooth black stone of the Monastery, never quite daring to touch the holy yet forbidding walls.

Rexol and his charge passed through the throng with relative ease, the people scrambling in their haste to clear a path before him. A Chaos mage in full wizard's regalia cut a fearsome figure.

The dark skin of Rexol's face and bare torso were painted in fierce glyphs, both symbolic and functional in the unleashing of Chaos. His long black hair was knotted in dozens of wild, uneven braids interwoven with the feathers of a young roc.

His body was adorned with all manner of magical talismans: Smooth white hoops fashioned from the bones of long-extinct beasts pierced his lips, nostrils, ears, tongue, and even the nipples of his chest. Frozen giant's tears glimmered in the rings on his fingers, and he wore a necklace strung from ogres' teeth. His left arm jangled with a dozen bracelets wrought from a young dragon's scales; they completely covered his tattooed skin from his wrist to his elbow. In his right hand he clutched a six-foot ebony staff topped by a gorgon's horned skull.

Rexol had drunk deep of the witchroot this morning in anticipation of this meeting. His body quivered with barely contained energy; it shimmered with the aura of a terrible latent power. The worshippers at the gate recoiled from his presence, withering before the harsh glare of Chaos bubbling just beneath the surface of his wild yellow eyes. The wizard had come ready for battle.

He reached the gate, the young girl who had been his pupil for the past four years still in tow. He rapped his staff hard upon the flawless stone surface, the gorgon's skull bringing up tiny sparks with each blow.

"I have been summoned by the Pontiff," he growled at the featureless stone before him.

A somber, low-pitched bell rang out from within, and the supplicants obediently backed away. The massive gates opened inward slightly, leaving barely enough space for one man to step through, even though Rexol knew it was possible for the gates to spread wide enough for an entire caravan of wagons traveling side by side to pass within.

Aware of the slight he had been given, he stepped through angrily, yanking Cassandra after him. The gates closed silently behind them. Despite the euphoria brought on by the witchroot flowing through his body, he felt a twinge of fear as he took stock of his surroundings.

Immediately inside the Monastery gate was a large courtyard; beyond it were the buildings that served as the living quarters and bureaucratic offices of the Order. Catwalks had been built four feet below the top of the stone walls along the inner entire perimeter, forming battlements so the monks could patrol them during the unthinkable event of an enemy siege.

The courtyard contained a few monks wandering through as they performed their various religious and secular duties, seemingly oblivious to his presence. They were clad in simple garb, functional and unremarkable. Muted colors were their only distinguishing feature; beyond the walls Rexol would not even have recognized them as members of the Order. Not until he was close enough to see their gray and lifeless eyes.

From the buildings on the other side of the courtyard a figure was approaching, dressed as the others save for a rather unremarkable chain of office around his neck. Flanking him on either side, following a single step behind, were six more monks: Inquisitors; guards to protect the leader of the Order as he met with one of their sworn enemy.

Rexol had never met the Pontiff before; he was momentarily taken aback by the physical frailty of his rival. Nazir seemed an old, old man. He walked with slow, measured steps, stooped forward and leaning heavily on a simple walking stick. His face was lined and weathered; his wrinkled scalp was speckled with dark brown age spots that could not be hidden by his few wispy strands of white hair. Like all the monks his eyes were sightless orbs of solid gray. Yet despite the obvious diminishments of age he carried himself with an air of authority.

"I am here," the mage declared once the Pontiff had crossed the distance between them. "I have answered your summons."

No more words were needed; Rexol's appearance spoke for itself. He had come girded for battle, weighed down with so many talismans and ornaments of power that he was barely able to contain the Chaos within himself. If this was to be his last stand, he wanted his foe to realize that victory would come with a terrible cost.

The old man did not reply immediately, and Rexol knew his none-too-subtle point had been made.

Nazir studied the spectacle before him, evaluating his enemy. Though not a sorcerer, he understood the violent purpose of the fearsome glyphs etched on the bare-chested man's dark skin. He felt the awesome potential of the Chaos bound within the rings and necklaces adorning the wizard; the Sight allowed him to see the shimmering nimbus of crackling power enveloping his foe.

Typical of his kind, the mage had pushed himself to his very limits with no regard for the possible consequences. His yellow eyes gave undeniable proof that his mind was addled by the narcotic effects of witchroot, further impairing his judgment.

The Pontiff realized he would have to be aware of the potential consequences for both their sakes. A single lapse in the wizard's mental control could unleash the devastating fury of the Chaos trapped within the talismans, resulting in a storm that would consume them all.

"I see you have brought the child," the Pontiff said, turning toward the young girl.

She recoiled slightly, half hiding behind Rexol's leg. A common enough reaction in the children brought here. In time she would get over her fear of his gray, sightless eyes.

"Cassandra is in my charge. I have taken her as my apprentice." The wizard made no effort to veil the implied threat in his tone.

"She belongs in the Order," the Pontiff replied, his voice even but firm. "Her parents should have brought her to us when she first manifested her power."

"They didn't. They brought her to me. She is my responsibility, not yours."

"Her parents did not bring her to you. She was stolen away even as our emissaries came to escort her to the Monastery."

He paused as if expecting the wizard to protest his innocence, but Rexol said nothing.

The Pontiff continued in the same passionless voice with which he had leveled the initial accusations. "By hiding her from us you have violated the doctrines of the Order. I could try you for heresy."

"The cost would be high," came the wizard's brazen reply, confirming the Pontiff's fears: The heady rush of witchroot had made him bold and reckless. "The Seven Capitals will only follow you down the path of moderation. Return to the fanatical ways of the Purge and they will abandon you!"

"We are not concerned with the politics of the Seven Capitals," the Pontiff declared. "The Order serves a higher purpose, and we are all united in our cause."

"United?" Rexol sneered. "We both know the Heresy of the Burning Savior did not die with Ezra! How many of your own people have turned against you? How many heretics do you have here in your walls right now?"

These were questions Nazir could not answer; questions that haunted his days and brought the demons of self-doubt during the night. He had suspected Rexol was in league with the heretics. He was all but certain one of them had delivered the girl into the mage's possession. And now the Pontiff was determined to take her away no matter what the cost.

"The loyalty of my Inquisitors is not in question," the old man replied with confidence, tilting his head to indicate the six monks flanking him. "Do not believe you have allies within these walls," he added. "The heretics will not expose themselves simply to come to your aid."

A sly smile twisted the mage's lips, as if he knew something the Pontiff didn't.

"Are you so sure?" the wizard mocked. "Cassandra has the Gift of prophecy. Her dreams have revealed a vision of what will happen if you dare to attack me."

"Our Oracles also dream," came the Pontiff's calm reply. "I have seen what will happen if blood is spilled within the Monastery walls. I know it will herald my own impending death.

"But if I fall, a successor will rise to replace me," Nazir continued, his voice unwavering in his conviction. "And you would still burn at the stake for your crimes. That is a price I am willing to pay if necessary."

A flicker of doubt flashed across the wizard's face, giving further strength to Nazir's resolve.

"The followers of Ezra do not have the will to stand against us. They are cowards; they live in hiding, surrounded by fear. We are the hunters and they are the meekest of prey!" His voice rose up in a righteous shout. "One by one we will find them—and those who serve them—and crush them in the name of the True Gods!"

"Your Gods are dead!" the wizard spat out.

Nazir showed no reaction to his words; he gave no sign that might betray his emotions or intent. The Inquisitors behind him, however, stiffened at the blasphemy spewing from the wizard's mouth.

Sensing their anger, the mage thrust his staff toward the sky. The aura surrounding him sparked and flared, the air crackling with the brute force of barely contained power.

Chaos surged through Rexol's body, a wave of heat coursing through his veins. It rose up like smoke from the charms dangling off his necklaces and jewelry, coalescing and enveloping his tattooed form. He breathed the sweet mist in through his nostrils until it filled him to near bursting. His ears buzzed with the growing power, his bare skin tingled, and he could feel his hair standing on end as the energy flowed through him.

With a single word or gesture he could unleash the magic of his talismans on the Pontiff; blast him from existence; sweep away those who dared oppose him in an ecstasy of unbridled violence. Yet at the last instant, he stayed his hand.

A small crowd of monks had gathered in the courtyard, joining the Pontiff and his Inquisitors. Several more had moved silently behind Rexol, surrounding him and Cassandra. They stood motionless, arms at their sides. Their unseeing eyes were focused intently on the mage and his apprentice.

With great difficulty Rexol managed to hold the gathering Chaos in check as he quickly weighed the odds. Physically, he doubted he was a match for any of them. Even the frail old Pontiff was likely a master of the martial arts. If his magic couldn't destroy them—all of them—Rexol knew he wouldn't survive.

The Order collected those who were strong in the Sight and nourished their talent, but it also trained them to resist other manifestations of Chaos. Individually they were no match for Rexol's magic, but collectively they might withstand his sorcery through sheer force of will.

And there was one final consideration: the imposing black walls of the Monastery that surrounded them. It was said that the dark stone devoured and imprisoned Chaos, giving strength to the monks' ability to resist the arcane within the fortress.

Despite his formidable battle raiment, Rexol doubted he would ever make it out past those black stone walls again should he attack. And while the Pontiff was willing to sacrifice his life for a greater cause, the wizard was not.

He lowered his staff and released the Chaos in a long, slow sigh of gentle wind. The breeze ruffled the thin wisps of hair on the Pontiff's head, but otherwise there was no indication of how close Rexol had come to loosing a spell of massive destruction within the Monastery walls.

"You will not leave the walls of the Monastery with Cassandra," Nazir declared, his voice hard and cold as tempered steel.

The battle was lost; Rexol was smart enough to see that. His strategy now turned to one of retreat . . . and survival.

"If I give you Cassandra, then I am free to go?"

The Pontiff shook his head. "Renouncing your claim on the girl is not enough. You will not leave as long as you are an agent of those who follow the teachings of Ezra. You are in league with those who preach heresy. You must stand trial for your crimes . . . or atone."

It was clear what the Pontiff was demanding. He wanted Rexol to reveal his allies within the Order; he wanted a name.

The wizard hesitated, but only for an instant. He had sided with Ezra's followers only because it had cost him nothing. In exchange they had given him Cassandra, but she was about to be taken away—there was nothing left to bind him to them now. He no more believed in their quest to find the Burning Savior than he believed in the Order's crusade to stamp out all manifestations of Chaos to try to preserve the Legacy of the Old Gods. And Rexol had no intention of becoming a martyr for a cause he did not believe in.

"Jerrod," he said flatly. There was no point in lying; the Pontiff would know. "He's the one you want. Jerrod."

The Pontiff gave a short nod of acknowledgment. "You are free to go," he said. "But be warned—the Southlands are the domain of the Order. Seek another apprentice from among those who swear fealty to the Seven Capitals again, and you will burn."

One of the Inquisitors stepped up and took Cassandra's free hand. Rexol released his grip on her other one, taking a last look down into her emerald eyes as they filled with tears of fear and confusion. There were no words he could say to her, nothing more he could do. So he simply turned and walked out the way he had come.

The massive gates of the Monastery opened once more, just wide enough to accommodate a single person. Rexol stepped through the portal and trudged slowly down the stairs, the crowd parting for him as it had on his arrival. At the bottom he crossed the empty plain until he reached the two horses that had served as their mounts for the five-day ride from his manse across the Southern Desert to the Monastery's gates. He tied the lead of Cassandra's horse to his own mount's bridle, then swung himself up into the saddle and set off for home. He never once looked back.

He briefly thought about the man he had exposed, wondering how long it would be before the Inquisitors hauled him in to be tried. Jerrod was smart and careful; he had no doubt planned for this day. Most likely he had agents inside the Monastery who would warn him they were coming. Rexol was confident his former ally would have ample time to flee to the safety of the Free Cities, though he wasn't certain Jerrod would chose to do so.

Eventually his thoughts turned back to Cassandra. She still bore the mark of his final spell, a powerful incantation binding her to him with the symbol he had branded into her flesh, invisible to all eyes but his own. But the magic meant nothing now that she had been seized by the Inquisitors. She was lost to him forever, just one more child claimed by the Order.

He needed to find another worthy of learning at his feet. He couldn't expect help from Jerrod or his followers—not after he had exposed them. And the Pontiff had forbidden him to take another apprentice from among the children of the Southlands. But there were other places he could seek out those with power: the Free Cities; the Frozen East; even in the forests of the Danaan.

He suspected there might even be a precious few who could match the potential of the girl he had just sacrificed to save himself. Jerrod had found Cassandra for him; her power had dwarfed any he had seen before. Based on this, Rexol was willing to admit the so-called Burning Savior that Jerrod had seen in his dreams might even be real.

There were other children out there who were touched by Chaos, just as Cassandra had been. They might live seemingly normal lives for a time, but power flowed through their veins. Born under a shadow of death, their lives would be marked by turmoil and danger. Their untapped potential would twist the world around them, shaping events, driving them toward their destinies until their true natures were exposed.

Those of the Order would continue their relentless hunt to identify these children and spirit them away to the Monastery. But Rexol knew their attempts to snuff out the sparks of Chaos would ultimately prove futile. If he was patient he would eventually find one of these extraordinary pupils before his enemies could lay claim. They would be drawn to him by the burning power coursing through their veins; like calling to like. It was inevitable.

However, contemplating the victory of a distant future couldn't help him push away the defeat of his immediate past. As he rode off into the dunes, he couldn't shake the image of Cassandra staring after him as he abandoned her, her brilliant green eyes wide with fear and betrayal.

Chapter 10

"Leave me alone!"

Scythe recognized the blubbering voice crying out from down the alley. Eiger was ten—two years older than Scythe herself—but he still sounded like a baby when he was scared.

She couldn't hear what insult was said in reply to Eiger's plea but she recognized Petir's mocking laughter. And wherever Petir went Bander and Corbin were sure to follow. Methodis didn't like it when she got into fights; he always said it was better to walk away. But three against one wasn't fair, even if the one was a full year older than any of his tormenters.

Methodis had told her to hurry back. He needed several of the items on the crumpled ingredient list clutched in Scythe's grimy fist for a patient who was coming back this afternoon. And she didn't even like Eiger. Not really. He was too fat to climb or play tag or duck-and-cover. He was too clumsy to play toss-rocks. And he cried if he fell down or stubbed his toe or scraped his knees.

But it was three against one. And Scythe hated Petir.

"Please, don't make me!" came Eiger's pitiful cry from the alley just ahead.

"You better eat up, Butter-boy!" Petir snapped back. "Your Islander girlfriend isn't here to save you this time!"

Scythe flew down the alley like the harsh wind of vengeance, the list of ingredients fluttering forgotten to the dirty street in her furious wake.

"I'm not his girlfriend!" she screamed as she came hurtling around the corner.

Eiger lay flat on his back in the dust of the empty street. Petir was sitting astride the other boy's ample belly, pinning him down. Dozens of inch-long maggots snatched from one of the bait shops by the dock crawled blindly over one another in a small pile on the ground beside them. Petir held one of the wriggling worms pinched between his thumb and forefinger, dangling it over Eiger's plump, tear-streaked face.

Bander and Corbin were standing safely off to the side, watching as their ringleader tortured his latest victim. At least, they were until they caught sight of Scythe barreling onto the scene. With a startled cry both boys turned and fled before her charge; they'd learned long ago not to tangle with the slight but savage waif being raised by the local healer.

Petir tried to rise to his feet, too—perhaps to join his companions in flight, perhaps to do battle with Scythe once again. However, his intentions were never given a chance to crystallize as Scythe launched herself feetfirst into his back. The impact knocked him sprawling off Eiger and onto the hard-packed earth of the street, where he landed facedown.

Before he could get up Scythe jumped on her prone opponent again, her knees connecting between his shoulders. The painful grunt of air escaping Petir's lungs was drowned out as Scythe punctuated her landing with another cry of, "I'm not his girlfriend!"

She threw herself down across Petir's back and wrapped a wiry arm under the older boy's chin in a fierce choke hold. With her other hand she reached around and hooked her index finger into one of his nostrils, bending his head back and up.

Eiger still lay on his back, gasping for breath and sobbing in fear, though his cries were now drowned out by Petir's shrieks of pain. He bucked and thrashed beneath her, but Scythe wasn't about to let him break free so easily.

In past fights the pair had exchanged fat lips, black eyes, and bloody noses. She'd bitten him hard enough to break the skin on more than one occasion. One time she'd actually cracked his knuckle when she had him in a finger lock. And another time she'd cut open a four-inch gash on his forehead with a rock thrown from a dozen feet away. But this time she was really going to teach Petir a lesson.

Without releasing her choke hold or her grip on his nostril, she cast her head about from side to side. The maggots were still squirming in the dust a few feet away. All the better. Petir would have to eat them from the dirt.

But before Scythe could maneuver her victim into position to begin his forced feast she felt a pair of large, rough hands wrap themselves around her waist and yank her off. She screamed and tried to kick whoever was holding her but the man was too strong and too careful to let her land a solid blow, and she couldn't break free.

Eiger and Petir were both still on the ground, staring up in terror at whoever had grabbed her.

"Get out of here ye little bastards!" the stranger spat in a rasping voice.

His breath smelled like the stuff Methodis used to burn infection from a raw wound. And there was another smell on him: not the fishy stench of a dockworker, but the sour stink of a man who lived in the cramped streets of the city core.

The two boys scampered away, fleeing down the alley. Scythe struggled to join them but was powerless against the man holding her.

"Yer quite the little hellion," the man said, setting her down. "Go on. Get out of here if yer scared."

Released from his hold, Scythe took several quick steps away from the man then turned to face her attacker. The man's clothes were dirty and stained, but they weren't the rags of the beggars who wandered over near the churches of the New Gods. He was tall—much taller than Methodis. Bigger, too. He had long, stringy hair and a dark, scraggly beard. An ugly scar ran down the left side of his face, ending in an empty socket where an eye had once been.

"I'm not scared of you!" Scythe declared, though it wasn't entirely true.

The man laughed. It wasn't a pretty sound. "You dropped this, girlie." He held up a crumpled piece of paper.

"That's mine!" Scythe snapped, suddenly remembering why she had been out in the street this morning in the first place.

The man smiled at her as his eye glanced over Methodis's shopping list. "You work for the doctor, eh." It wasn't a question. "My name's Luger, girlie. What's yer name?"

Scythe was suddenly very sure this man already knew her name.

"Give me back my list," she demanded, her voice trembling ever so slightly.

He extended the paper to her only to snatch it back as she reached for it. "Yer the one they call Scythe, ain't that right? You know what a scythe is, girlie?"

"It's an Old Tongue word," she replied instinctively. Questions about her name were familiar enough by now that she could answer while trying to figure out a way to get her list back from this smelly man. "It means 'spirit.'"

"Methodis tell you that, did he?" the man asked with a sneer. "Out in the fields a scythe is something they use to harvest the crops. Slice them crops real good with a scythe, you know. Just like you sliced your mama's belly open when you were born."

Scythe didn't say anything, only shook her head in confusion. She didn't know anything about her mother. Methodis never talked about her. But she couldn't believe this foul, ugly man had actually known her.

"What's the matter, girlie?" Luger whispered. "Methodis never told you that? He never told you that when you were born you ripped your mama right apart? Tore her insides wide open, you did. Killed her."

"You're a liar!" Scythe screamed, tears welling up in her eyes. "Give me back my list!"

Luger laughed again. "You want it, girlie? Come get it." He held it out again, taunting her.

She leapt forward as if to grab it, knowing the whole while that he would just snatch it away again. She didn't care; the paper wasn't her real target. Methodis didn't know much about fighting. He always said it was better to learn ways to stay out of fights than to learn ways to win them. But he knew lots about the body. About where it was weak. And he'd taught her what to do in an emergency if a man ever attacked her.

As Luger yanked the paper up above her reach, Scythe simply followed through with her lunge, crouching down to drive a tiny, balled-up fist into the spot between Luger's long legs just like Methodis had taught her.

The one-eyed man staggered back and doubled over clutching at his groin with a long, loud groan. The list slipped from his fingers and Scythe snatched it from the air before it hit the ground, then fled down the alley. A second later the man's voice chased after her, spewing profanities. But his words couldn't hurt her and they quickly faded away into the background noise of the city as Scythe emerged from the alley onto one of the busy streets of Callastan's market square.

She glanced back to see if Luger was following her. Once assured the coast was clear, she took stock of her surroundings. To her surprise, she was only half a block away from the first of the shops she'd need to visit to acquire all the items on Methodis's list.

"What took you so long, Scythe?" Methodis asked as he took the small bag of medicinal components from his adopted daughter's hand.

Even the learned doctor had fallen into the habit of calling her by the more familiar name and not the one with which he himself had christened her.

"Marigus was out of goldenbreath. I went to Wilmer's shop, but he was all out, too. I had to get you sunstar petals instead."

She spoke with a smooth confidence that belied her age. His young charge was only eight, yet she already knew her letters well enough to read an ingredient list.

And she's smart enough to know which substitutes to get when the primary agents are unavailable, he silently noted with a twinge of fatherly pride.

Her explanation seemed completely reasonable, and it was delivered without a hint of guilt or hesitation. But Methodis was a man of medicine, a man used to observing minute physical details to aid him in his diagnoses. The fresh dust and stains on Scythe's clothes and the faintly discolored contusions just above the wrists had not escaped his notice. And he knew Scythe's character as well as any doting father might know his own flesh-and-blood daughter.

"Were you fighting again, Scythe?" he asked, without any real anger. "Did Petir give you those marks on your arms?"

The young girl hesitated, her brow momentarily furrowing in concentration. Methodis realized she was assessing the situation, calculating her odds of escaping punishment even as she tried to devise a convincing cover story to explain the telltale bruises. As always, he found her stubborn refusal to admit defeat amusing.

Scythe's shoulders slumped ever so slightly and she sighed in resignation. "I was fighting with Petir," she said contritely. "I'm sorry I lied to you."

"I notice you're sorry for lying, but not for fighting," the doctor remarked even as he reached out to ruffle her short, silky black hair. She hopped back quickly and gave him a petulant frown as she smoothed down her locks.

"Don't muss my hair! It feels all icky when you do that. And Petir asked for it. He was picking on Eiger."

"I should have guessed," Methodis replied. "Even so, you'll have to copy out a page from one of my medical texts tonight." He held up a stern finger to quell Scythe's forthcoming protest. "As a punishment for lying," he added, "not for helping Eiger."

Scythe rolled her eyes in exasperation but didn't offer further opposition. In all truth the punishment wasn't that severe. No more than an hour of her time this evening would be occupied with the task, and on some occasions she actually seemed to enjoy transcribing his texts. Methodis made a mental note to give her a passage detailing the Creeping Rot, an obscure and particularly gruesome affliction. Scythe seemed to enjoy such graphically macabre subject matter the most.

He turned his back on her and began to stock the recently purchased supplies, placing them carefully onto their respective shelves. Proper organization was essential to any respectable medical practice. He expected Scythe would disappear into the street as she typically did, searching out Eiger or some of the other local urchins to try to goad them into stirring up minor mischief until it was time for her to come in for dinner. When she spoke, her presence startled him enough that he almost dropped his powdered blackroot into a mustard salve he had prepared that morning.

"Methodis, how did my mother die?"

He paused before turning back to face her. He had known this question would come, but even after eight years he didn't know how he should answer it.

"She was injured when you were born, Scythe. Someone had hurt her very badly."

He could tell by the look on her face the answer wasn't satisfying, but he didn't know what else he could say to fill the heavy silence that had fallen over the room.

"Was it 'cause of me?" she blurted out suddenly. "Did my mama die because I was born?"

"No, Scythe," he said. "It wasn't your fault. You didn't kill your mother. It was the man who hurt her. Who told you this nonsense?"

"A man in the street said my mama died because I split her open."

"A man? What man? Where?" A fierce protectiveness flared up inside Methodis, making his words come out sharper than he had intended.

"I . . . I can't remember his name. He was in one of the alleys.

He smelled funny. He only had one eye. And a scar. Like this." She traced her finger along her face.

"Luger," Methodis muttered, all the pieces suddenly becoming clear. He should have known a boy Petir's age wasn't strong enough to leave those kinds of bruises on Scythe's arms. "The man with one eye is named Luger."

Scythe nodded. "Is it true, Methodis? What he said? Did I . . . did I kill my . . ." Her voice caught in her throat with a hitch.

The doctor set the ingredients on the floor and knelt down facing Scythe, arms held out. She stepped forward and he clasped them in a tight hug around her. He felt her chest heaving as she fought back sobs.

"It's not true, my little spirit. Never, never let anyone tell you that it was your fault."

He held her in his arms as the tears came. They didn't last long; with Scythe they never did. She sniffled and wiped her running nose on the shoulder of his tunic.

Methodis loosened his hug and placed his hands firmly but gently on the little girl's shoulders so he could look directly into her eyes. "Listen to me, Scythe. Luger is a very bad man. He tells nasty lies because he just wants to hurt people. If you see him again, you run away as fast as you can. Okay?"

"Okay," she mumbled in reply, her voice still thick.

He could tell from the expression on her face he didn't need to emphasize the warning again. He stood up and ruffled her hair a second time, eliciting a small laugh as she playfully slapped his hand away.

"Can I stay inside with you today, Methodis? I'll go in the back whenever a patient comes. I'll be real quiet and I won't make any trouble."

"Of course," the doctor said with a warm smile. "You can stay with me as long as you want."

— — — —

"Are you sure about this, Methodis?" Captain Trascar asked once he had heard the doctor's offer. "Have you really thought this through?"

Methodis had thought it through. He'd thought it through dozens upon dozens of times. In the three days since Scythe had mentioned her meeting with Luger he'd thought of little else.

Luger had fallen on hard times. Last winter he had caught one of his customers cheating at dice in the gambling rooms at the back of his inn. Caught him red-handed. Everybody saw it—the man was marked for a cheat in a part of town where cheaters turned up dead the next morning. But Luger was never a patient man and he had stabbed the customer in the throat, right in front of everybody. At the time nobody cared.

And that would have been the end of it. Except that the man turned out to be a member of Callastan's city patrol. Methodis had heard all this from a reliable source after the fact, and the story was even more plausible given what happened next.

Nobody ever came forward to charge Luger with the murder. The constables in charge of the city patrols wouldn't allow that. How would it look if one of their own was known to have been lurking in the docks while off duty, gambling at one of the worst taverns in the district . . . and cheating, to boot? No, they weren't about to let that story be entered into the public records with a trial.

Instead they brought a very different kind of justice crashing down on Luger's world. They raided his establishment. They seized the illegal alcohol brewing in his cellar, and confiscated from his storerooms the banned roots and leaves people would smoke or chew to alter their conscious states. They arrested the girls in his back rooms and, more shockingly, arrested their customers, too.

A week later they raided the place again. And again. And again. Luger tried to pay them off; bribing the patrols was a necessary cost of the business he had chosen. But no amount of coin could keep the raids from happening.

They never arrested Luger himself. They didn't have to. He went out of business within two months, after running up huge debts with other whorehouse and tavern owners in the district. Debts he couldn't pay back. The patrols didn't have to execute Luger for murdering their comrade; the men Luger owed money to would do it for them in due time.

Word on the street was that the time was drawing very, very near. That was what scared Methodis the most. Luger knew he was finished. He was desperate and drunk and looking to settle old scores before he turned up gutted, swollen, and floating in the harbor.

"I've thought this through," Methodis said in answer to the captain's question still hanging in the air. "Your ship is setting sail tomorrow morning. Scythe and I want to be on board. Most captains would jump at the chance to have a healer join their crew."

Trascar shook his head. "I'm not going to lie; the crew would string me up if they knew I was trying to talk you out of signing on. We've been without a healer ever since Obler contracted the spotted plague and died last summer.

"But I'm also your friend, Methodis. And I don't want you to do something you'll regret. If this is about Luger why don't you just leave town for a while? A few weeks and he won't be a problem anymore, or so I hear."

Methodis had already considered that option. He had considered many options. He was an observant and analytical man, after all.

"Luger is a vengeful whelp spawned from a diseased bitch," he said with uncharacteristic hatred. "He's just mean and petty enough to use his last few coins to pay someone to settle his scores for him after he's gone. I don't want to take that chance."

Still, the captain resisted. "This is no kind of life for a girl! Weeks, even months at sea broken up by a day or two docked in some stinking port teeming with unwashed Islanders."

"Scythe is an Islander herself," Methodis noted. "And the ports aren't as bad as you claim. I traveled often in my younger days, Trascar. Or have you forgotten our voyages together?"

"I haven't forgotten. But we were both young men then, looking for adventure. You gave the life up for a reason: You wanted to study and learn your craft.

"Besides, things are different now, Methodis. Every season spawns a dozen storms the like of which you've never seen! The seas seem to grow rougher and wilder with each passage, as if some great power was stirring the waters up against us. Shipwrecks aren't unheard of these days.

"And what about my crew?" Trascar continued, furthering his point. "Long trips at sea can do things to a man. Urges can make him try to . . . take liberties . . . with a woman. Things he wouldn't do on land."

"You're too good a sailor for me to worry about storms and shipwrecks," Methodis countered. "And you're too honest a man to hire on a crew that would do those kinds of things to Scythe."

"What about pirates?" Trascar added, though from his voice it was obvious he was reaching for arguments now. "If they capture a young girl you know what they'll turn her into."

"No worse than what Luger would do. No worse than the other brothel owners that will come prowling around her as soon as she comes of age. Say what you want about the life at sea, it can't be any worse than the cesspool here in the slums of Callastan.

"I've thought this through, Captain. If anything happens to me Scythe will be just another young girl alone on the street, meat for the wolves. Even if nothing happens to me a smooth-talking flesh trader could lure her away to someone's hidden back rooms with promises of easy wealth and I'd never find her. Or she could fall in with the gamblers and the drunks and degenerates that crawl out of every alley in this festering hole."

Trascar tilted his head, trying to come up with some other argument to oppose Methodis. When the seaman stayed silent the doctor knew he had won.

"Say whatever you want about the hard life at sea," Methodis added to sew up his case, "but things are far worse here on land."

A wide grin spread across the captain's face. "That's why I'm hardly ever in port. Okay, old friend, you've got a deal. Glad to have you on board, truth be told. The men were anxious for me to pick up someone who knows the difference between heat rash and leprosy.

"I'll give you the largest quarters I can spare, but our cabins aren't designed for a man of your profession. Don't try to bring your whole shop with you. Just the stuff you think we'll be most likely to need before we reach Staeros and the other islands. We leave at daybreak. I can't afford to miss the tides, so if you're late the whole deal's off."

They weren't late. The *Shimmering Dolphin* set sail from the Callastan ports on the morning tides as scheduled. Belowdecks, one of the most respected and knowledgeable healers in the city unpacked his belongings in what had formerly been the first mate's cabin. On the deck above his traveling companion—a young girl with dark hair, olive skin, and fierce, almond-shaped eyes—stood beside the captain at the bow, laughing and squealing with delight each time the windswept spray flew over the *Dolphin*'s prow to sting her smiling face.

Chapter 11

"KEE?" GERRIT CALLED out, hearing the sound of the cottage door open. "Keegan, what are you doing home? I thought you were out playing with the others."

When there was no reply he rose up from the table where he had been finishing his lunch and went out into the entryway. Keegan was standing there: a slight, dark-haired boy of eight, though there was a seriousness about him that made him seem older despite his small size. One of his eyes was purple and swollen shut.

Gerrit sighed and came over to look at his son's injury. They had only been in the town a year, yet this was an all-too-familiar sight. Ever since their arrival Keegan had been picked on by the other children. Partly because he was new, partly because he was small, but mostly because he was different in a way others could sense but not explain.

Other children, and even some adults, found Keegan's mere presence to be discomforting. He was too quiet, too somber. Too smart and insightful for his age. Children should laugh and play, but Keegan tended to just sit and watch with dark, intense eyes that rarely blinked. Even Gerrit himself found it unsettling at times.

"What happened?" he asked, tenderly inspecting the eye. The

damage wasn't serious; the swelling would go down in a day or two.

"Fenthar hit me," was the simple reply.

"I should have known."

Fenthar was the son of Alferon, the local blacksmith. Though roughly the same age as Keegan he was nearly twice his size. It wouldn't be the first time the bully had fought with Keegan, though Gerrit understood such altercations were rarely unprovoked.

"And did he just hit you for no reason, Keegan? Or did you say something to upset him?"

Keegan didn't speak often, but when he did it could sting. Most children his age would use their fists to hurt, but his son knew how to use his words as a weapon. Perhaps it was because he was so small compared with the other boys. A sharp tongue was his only defense when the others picked on him—a defense that often led to black eyes and bloody noses.

"We had a race. I lost and Fenthar was teasing me because I can't run like the others. He was calling me names. He wouldn't stop. So I told him about his mother."

It was common knowledge that Fenthar's mother had left several weeks ago to help her sister with a new baby in a nearby village. But Gerrit couldn't see how this information could earn his son a punch from the other boy.

"I don't understand, Kee. What did you say about his mother?"

"Everyone thinks she just went away for a bit, but she's not coming back. Not ever. I told him that."

"Keegan! That's a horrible thing to say! No wonder he hit you. Why would you say something like that?"

The boy shrugged. "It's true. She's dead."

A shiver ran down Gerrit's spine. It wasn't what his son said, it was the way he said it. This wasn't the hurtful wish of an injured child; there was no petulance or sullenness in the declaration. He said it as if it was simple fact. Gerrit didn't know what to make of such a statement, so he pretended not to have noticed.

"You have to go apologize to Fenthar, Kee. We have to go right now."

"I didn't do anything! Fenthar hit me! This isn't fair!"

The boy crossed his arms over his chest and thrust out his lower lip, pouting. Gerrit found the outburst comforting: This was the type of reaction he expected from an eight-year-old.

Keegan continued to sulk as Gerrit dragged him through town to apologize to the boy who had hit him. He didn't release his son's hand until he reached out to knock on the blacksmith's door.

"Gerrit?" Alferon said upon opening the door and seeing who was there.

The smith was a giant of a man, his neck and shoulders a mass of knotted muscle clearly visible even beneath his coarse, heavy work shirt. He had a reputation as a brawler and had been known to blacken a few eyes of his own, though usually only after he had been drinking. He seemed sober enough now, though he looked haggard and tired.

"What do you want?" The smith's voice was short and curt; he was a man who didn't want company.

"There's trouble between our lads, Alferon," Gerrit said, getting right to the point. "They're fighting again."

"I should've known," the smith grunted, his voice getting louder. "What happened? Your boy use a stick to beat on Fenthar's head?"

"What are you talking about?" Gerrit asked, confused. "Keegan's half Fenthar's size! Look at my boy's eye, Alferon. Your son did that. And it's not the first time he's beaten Keegan up!"

The smith snorted. "Well, your lad must've gave as good as he got. Fenthar came home and ran right to his room, howling and crying like he was a little baby. He still ain't stopped yet!"

Your son came home in tears and you didn't even bother to find out what's wrong? Gerrit wanted to shout, *What kind of father are you?*

Instead he took a deep breath, trying to remain calm. They were here to apologize. He had to keep that in mind.

"Yes, well . . . I'm sorry about that. Keegan said something to him. Something awful. Something he never should have said. And now we're here to apologize."

"He *said* something to him? That's it?" The smith squinted one eye and gave them a dubious stare. "What in all the fires of Chaos did your little bugger say?"

"That's not import—"

Keegan cut him off. "I told him his mama wasn't coming back because she's dead."

"My son was upset," Gerrit quickly offered by way of explanation. "Your boy was teasing him. Not that there's any excuse for this, of course. I'm sorry for—"

His apology died when he saw the expression on Alferon's face. It wasn't anger or outrage or shock; it was fear. Pure, abject fear. He stood as if paralyzed with it, his eyes empty, his mouth hanging slightly agape. And suddenly Gerrit knew.

"It's true, isn't it?" he whispered.

Alferon shook his head, dispelling the strange stupor that had momentarily gripped him. "No! Ridiculous. She's away with her sister, is all. Helping with the baby."

"No," Keegan said quietly. "She's dead. She got sick, and you took her to her sister so Fenthar wouldn't get sick, too. But she got more sick after you left and her face got all these spots and then she died last night in her sister's bed. And now you're sick, too."

The big man took a slow step back, holding his palms up in front of him as if trying to ward off the visitors at his door but afraid to touch them.

"What kind of a monster have you raised, man?" he asked in a terrified whisper.

There was a faint rash on his trembling hands, and a telltale discoloration in the fingertips.

"The pox," Gerrit muttered, all the pieces suddenly falling into place. "Your wife got the pox so you sent her away!"

For a second it seemed the smith would deny it. Then the big man noticed the markings on his own hands and his shoulders slumped.

"They would have quarantined us all," he said, his voice pleading. "Locked us all together in this house until the pox had run its course. Abandoned us here to watch and wait and see if we'd all die."

"You could spread it to the whole village!" Gerrit snapped back, horrified at Alferon's selfishness.

"No!" he protested. "We saw it in time. That's why we sent Penelope away. Her sister had the pox once, but she lived. You only get it once, she can't catch it again. Penelope's just going to stay there until she's better. Her sister will look after her. Until she's . . ."

He trailed off and looked down at Keegan, remembering the boy's pronouncement that his wife was already dead. When he turned back to Gerrit there were tears in the smith's eyes, and his words came out in a desperate rush of half-choked sobs. "We couldn't tell anyone. They would have locked us all up together in this house. Me and my son would have caught the pox for sure! This was the only way!"

"By the Gods, man, look at yourself! You've got it anyway!"

"No! It's the forge, is all. The heat makes my skin raw and red. And . . . and the iron rubs off on my fingers, giving 'em a funny color. That's all!"

Gerrit placed a protective hand around his son's shoulder and pulled him back a step. "I'm sorry, Alferon. I have to tell the authorities. If the pox isn't contained it could kill us all."

The smith's expression suddenly changed from desperation to anger. His pleading hands became fists and he took a step forward. Gerrit was certain he would keep coming, but he stopped short when Keegan spoke up again.

"Fenthar's going to get sick, too. Like you. Like his mom. But you two won't die."

Alferon's head snapped down to glare at the small boy standing on his doorstep, then slowly turned back to face Gerrit.

"Sorcery. That's what this is. Your boy did this!"

"Don't be a fool!" Gerrit spat. "The days of the Purge are over. The Order doesn't look kindly on false accusations of witchcraft anymore."

A look of evil cunning crossed the smith's face.

"No, they don't. You're right about that. And maybe I can't prove your boy caused this. But he knew about it, sure enough. Nobody else did. The Order might be interested in that, now, wouldn't they?"

When Gerrit made no immediate reply the smith continued, his voice low and dangerous, like the growl of a trapped animal.

"Think carefully now. You tell anyone about my wife being sick, and I'll make sure the whole town knows about your son. You may get them to lock me and Fenthar up for a month, but if you do the Order will take your boy away from you."

"Now who's the monster, Alferon?" Gerrit asked, his voice filled with contempt and disgust.

"A man does what it takes to protect his family."

The smith stepped back, his glance moving from father to son, though he was unable to look either of them in the eye before he closed the door.

His words resonated with Gerrit, for he knew them to be true. He had thrown away everything he had worked his whole life to build for the sake of his son. Since the night of the old hag's visit six years ago he had moved several times, hastily packing up everything whenever he heard a rumor that a Pilgrim or Inquisitor was in the area. Half a dozen times he had fled like a thief in the night, forced to build a new life in a new place, afraid a passing member of the Order might sense something in Keegan the same way the old hag had.

There was no doubt in his mind that the smith would make good on his threat to expose Keegan if reported. The Order would arrive soon after to investigate these rumors. But something was different this time. Gerrit now realized that he had been living in denial, just like Alferon. Deep down he had always refused to believe what the witch-woman had said about his son. He could ignore the truth no longer: Keegan had the Sight. By the ancient laws, he belonged to the Order.

Hand in hand, father and son made their way back through the town. But they didn't head home. Instead, Gerrit took them to the mayor's house to tell them what he had seen. He made no mention of Keegan's dream, but instead noted the unexpected departure and prolonged absence of Alferon's wife. He commented on the discoloration and rash he had seen on the smith's hands. And he left it at that.

As he returned home, he knew the mayor would send someone to investigate. An outbreak of the pox was too dangerous to ignore. By the morning Alferon's house would be quarantined, the smith and his son kept inside until the pox had passed.

The village council would work quickly to institute the plague laws. All residents would be required to undergo an inspection every third day throughout the next month until it was certain nobody else had contracted the potentially deadly disease. Guards would be set up on both roads to warn potential visitors away and to keep potential pox carriers from leaving. A call would be sent out for healers to treat the ill, and another for soldiers to help enforce the restriction. By midday tomorrow nobody would be allowed in or out of the village for the next several weeks. And by then Gerrit and Keegan would be long gone, vanishing into the night as they had done so many times before.

Keegan had the Sight. He had Chaos in his veins. But he was still his son, and Gerrit wasn't about to let anyone—not even the Order—take him away.

Chapter 12

VAALER LAY ON his back staring at the ceiling, eyes wide despite the lateness of the hour.

He reached over and gently rubbed the moonstone on the night table beside his bed. The gem began to glow, its soft blue light casting strange and unsettling shadows on the walls. He knew the shadows were only his bedroom furniture, but sometimes they looked more like monsters, watching and waiting for him to fall back asleep so they could pounce.

He thought of calling for the servants—they were there, just outside the door awaiting his every command. He was, after all, a prince. The crown prince, in fact, direct descendant of Tremin Avareen, the first Danaan King. Though he was only nine, Vaaler already understood what that meant. Someday, when he was older, he himself would become King of the North Forest.

The young Monarch-to-be shifted in his bed but didn't call for the guards. The shadows didn't really bother him. Not much. It was the dreams. Not his dreams. His mother's. He wasn't supposed to know about them, but he did.

Vaaler couldn't tell anyone that he knew about the dreams. If he did, they would ask him how he knew. And he would have to show them how the tapestry on his wall was actually hiding a secret door to a warm, dark tunnel. He didn't want to show them the tunnel. The tunnels were his own special place.

He only went in them at night, when his attendants thought he was sleeping in his bed, his way lit by the glow of his moonstone night-light. He'd found them by accident a few months ago, and since that day he'd spent many hours exploring them.

Sometimes the secret hallways inside the walls took him past the council room, and he would hear his mother and her advisers talking about her dreams. Scary dreams, mostly. About fire and monsters. And then in the night his own mind would dance with dark visions and the terrified imaginings of a child.

But he couldn't tell anyone. He had to pretend he didn't know about his mother's nightmares, or they'd find his special hiding place. He had to pretend he didn't know about the Sight.

He heard one of her advisers say it, once, just like that—"the Sight." The Queen had the Sight. Vaaler didn't understand what that meant, exactly, except that his mother saw things in her dreams. Things that sometimes made her wake screaming in the night.

Yet it wasn't the manifestation of his mother's fears that had woken the young boy on this evening. Tonight Vaaler—the only child of Queen Rianna Avareen, the crown prince of the North Forest and the future leader of an entire nation—wanted a drink of water.

He sat up in his bed, a slightly undersized nine-year-old Danaan boy. He had the brownish green skin common to all the Danaan, and he'd inherited the sharp features of his father's royal bloodline . . . though his father had died before Vaaler was even born. For all intents and purpose, he was a typical child; unremarkable in every aspect, save for the fact he was destined to one day rule a kingdom.

Turning and casting his covers aside, Vaaler dangled his feet over the edge of the mattress, suddenly reluctant to let them touch the floor. He didn't believe in monsters anymore. Not really. He was too old to think an ogre or dragon lurked beneath the bed. Not during the day, anyway. At night, however, he wasn't so sure.

In a sudden spurt he leapt to the floor and darted across the room, yanking open the door and letting the light from the torches burning in the hallway beyond spill into the chamber, overpowering the soft glow of the moonstone. The attendants outside were caught off guard by his sudden appearance; they had been sitting on the floor with their backs against the wall.

Vaaler giggled as they scrambled to their feet, brushing themselves off and bowing toward the royal heir. The boy gave a slight wave of his hand as he'd been taught; the monarchal equivalent to returning their gestures of supplication.

"Does His Highness require anything?" one of the attendants asked.

"Water, please," Vaaler replied.

His mother had taught him to always be polite, especially to the personal attendants assigned to serve and protect him. *They will serve out of duty to House Avareen,* she had once explained, *but it would be better if they served with pride.* And his mother was the Queen, so Vaaler had to do what she said.

"Shall I fetch you a glass from the kitchen, Your Highness?"

"I want to get it myself. Please."

"As you wish, Your Highness."

The two attendants fell into step behind the young prince as he padded down the halls of the vast castle complex. Vaaler barely noticed them. After a lifetime of having attendants always following in his wake, even a lifetime of a mere nine years, he had grown accustomed to their presence.

"The dream is the same, always the same. Fire, flames, the Destroyer of Worlds. Always the same."

Vaaler halted on recognizing his mother's voice. The halls in the castle often played tricks with sounds, making noises seem much closer or father away than they truly were. But Vaaler could guess the room that was the origin of his mother's words.

"Perhaps the dream has some symbolic meaning, my Queen."

He knew it was High Sorcerer Andar speaking this time, confirming what he had guessed—his mother was in the council chamber. Vaaler turned down an intersecting hallway, suddenly eager to see his mother's face. His attendants followed wordlessly behind.

"If this vision is symbolic, we should consult the ancient texts for possible interpretations."

This voice belonged to Drake. He liked Drake. Drake knew how to ride and fight and wrestle. He knew fantastical stories about Tremin and Exter and all the ancient kings; he knew about the Gods' War and the Cataclysm and the Chaos Spawn. Sometimes he'd talk about the years he spent beyond the boundaries of the North Forest, exploring and adventuring with the humans in the Southlands. And sometimes Drake even let Vaaler practice archery with his bow, as long as the prince promised not to tell his mother.

Vaaler heard people say Drake was his mother's consort, but he didn't know what that meant. He had asked once while Drake was teaching him how to fletch an arrow, but the man had stammered and turned red and hastily excused himself. Vaaler liked it better when Drake was around, so he hadn't asked again.

At the door to the council chamber a pair of armed guards stood watch. They stepped aside at the crown prince's approach, each man giving a slight bow in Vaaler's direction. Almost subconsciously, Vaaler raised his hand in royal acknowledgment of the gesture.

"It's not symbolic. The dream is too consistent to be . . ."

His mother trailed off upon catching sight of her son, her right hand unclenching and releasing its grip on the plain gold ring that hung from the chain on her neck. The ring was the symbol of the Avareen House, she had once told Vaaler. She had to wear it because she was the Queen, and one day when he was King he would have to wear it.

Vaaler wasn't much looking forward to that. He thought the ring must be very uncomfortable. His mother was always tugging and grabbing at it or wrapping her long, thin fingers around it, hiding it from view with her tight fist pressed up against her chest.

The Queen crouched down, arms held out to embrace him.

Vaaler trotted obediently up and into her loving embrace. Her thin but surprisingly strong arms wrapped around his body, clutching him to her breast. He felt the metal of the ring on her neck pressing through his thin nightshirt, cold against his chest. She held him for a second then pushed him back just far enough to plant a brief kiss on his forehead.

"What's the matter, Vaaler dear?"

"I couldn't sleep, Mummy." The words were out before Vaaler even realized his mistake. He wasn't a little boy anymore; he was supposed to use the proper forms of address now. "I mean, I couldn't sleep, my Queen."

Neither his mother nor the other half a dozen men and women in the room seemed bothered by his breach of royal etiquette.

"Has the young prince had a nightmare, perhaps?" It was Drake who asked the question.

"No, Drake. I was just thirsty. It's hot in my room."

"The summer heat makes sleep difficult for us all," Andar agreed. Though his tone was kindly, Vaaler sensed something odd about his voice. Almost as if he was disappointed to learn Vaaler hadn't been awakened by a nightmare.

"Why didn't you have one of your attendants bring you a drink?" his mother asked, stroking back the lock of hair that always seemed to fall down over his forehead.

Vaaler shrugged. "I can do it myself."

The prince sensed they had important business to attend to. Business that did not involve him. But for some reason he was reluctant to leave.

The Queen kissed him once more on his forehead then rose to her feet.

"Hurry off and get your drink, my love. Then back to bed. You need your sleep, and the Queen must continue to receive the council of her advisers."

Normally he would have gone without question. His mother was the Queen; everyone had to do what she said. But Vaaler didn't want to leave, not yet. His room was hot and stuffy, and the shadows would still be there waiting for him to make his mad dash from the door to the safety of his bed.

And this was his chance to finally ask the question he could never ask. They had been talking about the dreams when he had come in. He could ask about them now and nobody would wonder how he knew. Nobody would go looking for his secret tunnels in the castle walls.

"What kind of dreams were you talking about, Mummy? I mean, my Queen?"

The Queen exchanged concerned glances with her council then turned back to her son. "They are nothing for you to worry about. Mummy has many dreams."

"Why don't I have any dreams?"

The question hung in the air for a long, long time. Drake shifted uncomfortably from foot to foot; Andar stared down at the floor. One of the other advisers coughed softly into her fist.

"Now is not the time for this discussion, Vaaler."

The Queen's voice was firm and insistent, but not angry. She never got angry. Not at him. But Vaaler had learned there was no use arguing with her when she used this particular tone of voice. He called it her queen voice.

"Yes, Mother." He turned to go.

"Vaaler, remember your manners." His mother's voice was soft and warm once more.

"Please excuse me for interrupting," the young prince dutifully recited.

"'Twas no trouble, Your Highness," Drake responded.

The others murmured similar sentiments as Vaaler left to resume his quest for a drink of water. At a word from the Queen the guards closed the doors to the council chamber as soon as Vaaler had stepped out of the room.

- - - -

A silence fell upon the council chamber in the wake of Vaaler's exit. The Queen seemed lost in thought, and none of the others were inclined to break her concentration.

"When the prince came in I had hoped . . . ," Andar began at last, but when the Queen glanced up to meet his gaze he trailed off.

Typically, it was Drake who had the courage to say what had to be said.

"He should have had a dream by now, my Queen. A vision. Something. You yourself had manifested the Sight by the time you were four."

The Queen sighed and gazed down at the floor. "Llewellyn also had the Sight. He understood the vision in ways not known since the days of the Cataclysm. Perhaps if Vaaler's father yet lived . . ."

"My Queen," Andar reassured her, "your husband was a great Seer and prophet, but you are easily his equal. If anyone . . . that is, you cannot blame . . ."

Realizing Andar had trailed off the Queen looked up. "Speak freely," she said to her advisers. "What is said shall not pass beyond the walls of this council room, but I command you to speak freely."

After a deep breath, Andar continued. "Your son will one day sit upon the throne, my Queen. He is the sole heir to the crown. But will he be fit to lead our people?"

"My son is a bright and capable boy with a good and noble spirit!" Despite her intentions, the Queen's voice was tinged with the anger of a mother defending her child.

"Chaos is thin in his veins. There is no blame in this, it happens sometimes. There have been Monarchs in the past who have been weak in the Sight," Andar said softly, trying to cushion the blow.

The Queen made no reply. His words were meant to be kind, but the true meaning lay just below the surface. Other Monarchs had been weak in the Sight, but her son was not weak. He was blind. Such a thing was unprecedented in the unbroken line of the Avareen House, descending from Tremin himself through thirty generations.

Her husband had been a prophet of rare talent, surpassed only by her own remarkable abilities. They were the preeminent Seers among all the nobility of the Danaan Houses. Chaos burned strong and pure within both male and female, and their union was expected to produce an heir whose blood would also be thick with Chaos.

But somehow the mingling of their rich bloodlines produced a child without the Sight. A beautiful, intelligent, kind, and perfect child save for this one inexcusable flaw. In all their history, the Danaan people had never rebelled against or refused to accept the rightful successor to the throne. But the Danaan people had never been asked to bow down to one such as her son.

It was Drake who jumped to her defense, as always. He had been there for her when they brought news of her husband's death in the battle with the manticore. He had led the army out to destroy the creature that had widowed the Queen. He had been there to provide her comfort and support and even love once her mourning time had ended. And he had been there to help her raise Vaaler and teach him all the things only a father can teach a son.

"We all know Vaaler does not possess the Sight. But his bloodline is pure and Chaos runs deep in the wells of his family. Perhaps he possesses the Gift."

There was a murmur of surprise and even disbelief from the advisers at Drake's bold statement.

"Surely if he had the Gift we would know by now," Andar objected. "It's not something that can be hidden. Other wizards can sense the power dwelling in the child.

"I was barely three when my own talents were recognized," the High Sorcerer continued. "It is the same with all the mages who serve in the court: Their Gift was noticed well before they reached the prince's age."

"Perhaps we do not know what to look for," Drake countered. "Among our people Chaos is strong, and those with the Gift perform magic naturally and at a very early age. But in my travels among the Southlands I encountered many human mages who had not learned to shape Chaos until well into their teens. Maybe Vaaler's Gift is hidden, locked away like the power of the humans."

"Even if it was," Andar said, "we would not know how to unlock his talents. The rituals we use are very different from the strange arts the humans use to unleash and control their power."

"The humans study Chaos and magic in ways foreign to us," Drake agreed. "The Gift does not come naturally to them. But through years of patience and practice they can unlock power that rivals that of any Danaan sorcerer."

Drake hesitated before continuing, as if he was afraid of what he was about to suggest. "In my travels among the humans I encountered many individuals who possessed great knowledge of Chaos and magic. Perhaps if Vaaler were to be given to one of them—"

"No!" The Queen's voice was filled with the anger of betrayal. "I will not send my son out among the savages! I will not give him over to the Order to have his eyes plucked from his head!"

"Please, my Queen," Drake implored, "hear me out. I would never allow your son to fall into the hands of the Monastery's butchers. They seek to destroy the Gift, not nurture it. But there are others who wield Chaos among the humans: witches, alchemists, and mages. Near every village lurks a man or woman who uses strange rituals to shape spells. They bring rain or heal the sick; some have the power to forever change the fortunes of those who seek them out. All for a price.

"The Order tried to wipe these people out during the Purge, but despite their efforts nearly every noble House in the Free Cities employs a wizard or court mage. Often these mages will take apprentices, to nurture their untapped talent and teach them the art of shaping Chaos."

"Are you suggesting we offer my son as an apprentice to one of the Houses in the Free Cities?"

"I would strongly advise the Queen against such a course." Andar's interruption was sudden and urgent, but he still maintained the formal speech expected of the High Sorcerer. "The Houses of the Free Cities are in a perpetual state of unrest. Their fortunes rise and fall and rise again on the whims of politics and chance, and they are not above exploiting a situation for their own gain. To

deliver the heir to the Danaan throne into the hands of one of
these noble Houses would present them with an opportunity to
leverage the young prince for promises of alliance and political
support from our nation."

The Queen was aghast at Andar's words. "Are you saying the
humans would use my son as a hostage against our kingdom?"

"I have studied the political history of the Free Cities in great
detail, my Queen," Andar reminded her. "Vaaler would be little
more than a political commodity for whichever House possessed
him. Needless to say, rival Houses would be anxious to acquire
such a valuable bargaining chip for their own purposes—or at the
very least, to eliminate its presence from the political table. Your
son's life would be in constant danger from both enemies and supposed allies in such a situation."

"I am not suggesting we send him to the Free Cities," Drake
countered. "My agents in the Southlands have brought me news of
one particular man who could be the answer to our problems. A
Chaos mage of immense power who has studied and researched his
craft over many decades."

"It sounds as if you have been preparing for this for some time,"
Andar interjected.

"Forgive me, my Queen," Drake said, ignoring the High Sorcerer to address Rianna directly. "I had hoped this day would never
come, but I thought it best to be prepared. For Vaaler's sake."

The Queen nodded for him to continue. Drake had clearly
overstepped his authority, but he had done it out of affection. She
wasn't about to chastise him for helping her son.

"What else do you know about this human?" she asked.

"His name is Rexol. Several of the more prominent families in
the Free Cities employ mages who once studied under him, though
he himself has no political affiliations. He is rumored to be looking
for a new apprentice. And it is well known that he is no friend of
the Order."

"How can we trust this man?" Andar demanded.

"His reputation for neutrality is well known," Drake assured them. "He dwells alone on his grounds near the borders of the Southern Desert, so as to remove himself from the earthly concerns of the various political factions. According to my agents, he quests for what the humans call Old Magic, and he is obsessed with ancient documents that predate the Cataclysm. Such documents are rare among the human kingdoms.

"We could offer Rexol historical tomes from our libraries should he agree to accept Vaaler as his disciple. Each year Vaaler studies under him we will bequeath a new batch of volumes to Rexol for his use. Should anything happen to the prince, he will see no more of the ancient knowledge we have preserved."

"You would protect the safety of my son with the promises of mere books?" The Queen was incredulous, shocked at the cavalier attitude of Drake toward her own flesh and blood.

"You forget, my Queen: The humans are a young people. They have no history, no ancient learning. From our dealings with the Free Cities we know they hunger for this knowledge; they lust for it. To a man such as Rexol our ancient arcane texts are more valuable than any material wealth."

The Queen considered Drake's words carefully. He was not a man to speak lightly of such things, or to make such declarations without strong evidence to support them. She had learned to trust his judgment. And she knew he cared about Vaaler. Still, the Queen had her reservations.

"What say the rest of you?" she asked the room.

"I do not like to send the only heir to the throne out beyond the safety of our kingdom's borders, but this wizard may be our only hope to discover if your son has the Gift," Andar conceded. The others murmured their assent.

The Queen closed her eyes, hoping for a vision to guide her in this decision. She prayed for some sign that her son would be safe in the hands of a human she had never met, a man whose only allegiance was to himself and his lifelong pursuit to master Chaos. She saw nothing but the flames that haunted her dreams, a warning of the destruction of her kingdom. Would it happen in her lifetime? Perhaps in her son's? Without either the Sight or the Gift, would Vaaler be able to withstand the coming of the Destroyer of Worlds?

It was a terrible risk, but one she had to take. Vaaler would rule the kingdom one day. Despite her reservations about sending him into these strange lands she had a responsibility to the Danaan people to try to discover if her son had the Gift.

"So be it," she said, not even aware her right hand had risen up to clutch the ring dangling from the chain at her throat in a tight fist. "Send a messenger to this Rexol with our offer and terms."

Chapter 13

BEYOND THE BLACK Monastery walls, the night sky is obscured by thick clouds and sheets of driving rain. In the darkness she can't see them, but she can sense them. Monsters at the gate.

The pealing bells that heralded the first light of dawn rang out through the Monastery, waking Cassandra and cutting the all-too-familiar vision short before it could reach its gruesome climax.

The dream had plagued her for the past several days. She knew by the rules of the Monastery that the Pontiff was supposed to be told whenever someone kept having the same dream. But Cassandra had no intention of telling anyone about what she had seen. Her dreams scared people. That's why her parents had given her to Rexol; and that's why he had given her to the Order. Because of her dreams.

The morning bells ended, and Cassandra scrambled up from her sleeping mat and pulled off her nightclothes. She slipped into her undergarments, then into her warm, gray robe—a robe just like the one the monks wore.

When Rexol had first left her with the Pontiff she had been terrified of the monks. They rarely spoke, and with their strange, all-white eyes they seemed more like ghosts or spirits than real men and women. But they treated her with kindness, and within a few weeks her fear had given way to curiosity. She wanted to know more about the Order, and the Pontiff and the others had been eager to teach her.

Now, four years later, she considered the Monastery her home. She couldn't recall much about her parents or her life before Rexol: Vague memories of her father's kind eyes and her mother's tight, pinched face were all that remained. And even her years with Rexol were starting to fade, though she remembered enough to know she preferred living in the Monastery.

There were other children here, for one thing. A few were younger than her, several were older; more boys than girls. And even though Cassandra didn't speak to them often—like her, the other children were focused on their individual studies—it was nice just to see them around. But it was more than that. Living with the Order meant she was serving the will of the True Gods.

The young girl opened the door to her tiny room then moved quickly down the dimly lit hall, eager to get some breakfast before beginning her daily lessons.

Before coming to the Monastery, Cassandra had never heard of the True Gods. Now, thanks to her lessons, she knew all about them. How they were born from the fires of the Chaos Sea. How they created the world and all the animals and people. And how they used their power to form the Legacy to protect the world from the Slayer.

Cassandra enjoyed her lessons. She liked the stories of the True Gods. She liked that the Order was working to preserve the Legacy and keep the world safe. She wanted to help them, maybe even one day join them.

Which was why she couldn't mention her vision. If she told anyone about what she had seen, they would send her away. Like Rexol. Like her parents.

"The girl is hiding something," Yasmin declared.

The Pontiff set down his spoon with a weary sigh. He didn't need to ask who Yasmin was referring to; there was only one of the Order's wards she bothered to keep an eye on. The Inquisitor had been suspicious of Cassandra ever since the girl's arrival, as if the child had somehow been corrupted by Rexol's foul magic.

"This couldn't wait until after breakfast?" the Pontiff asked, keeping his voice low so the monks at the other nearby tables in the dining hall wouldn't overhear. "You couldn't even let me finish my porridge?"

Yasmin shrugged indifferently. The tall, thin woman rarely ate with the others. She slept only a few hours each night, and by the time the morning bells called the rest of her brethren to the tables she had already finished her only meal of the day.

"It is my duty to report what I see," she insisted. "When you decide to take action is up to you."

"Action for what, exactly?"

"The girl is hiding something," she repeated. "She is carrying a secret."

The Pontiff didn't bother to ask Yasmin how she knew this. Inquisitors were trained to sense deception and concealment; it was integral to their function. And Yasmin was very, very good at what she did.

"I will speak to her now," he said, rising from his seat. "Will that satisfy you?"

"I will come with you," Yasmin offered.

"No," the Pontiff corrected. "You will not."

If he was going to speak with Cassandra, the last thing he needed was Yasmin looming over them. Even full-fledged members of the Order found the burned scalp and intense presence of the Inquisitor intimidating.

"The girl is dangerous," Yasmin warned. "We all sense her power. We all know the wizard was teaching her."

"Cassandra is not our enemy," the Pontiff told her, his voice calm but his tone hard as steel. "She is one of us now. She has power, but we must not fear it. We must teach her to control it."

Sensing the matter was resolved, Yasmin bowed and retreated to a far corner of the room without further argument.

The Pontiff picked up his bowl and spoon and made his way

through the dining hall to where Cassandra was sitting alone at one of the smaller tables. He had noticed she often ate alone, but that wasn't uncommon. Many of the monks, and even several of the other children, preferred solitude.

"Cassandra," he asked in a soft voice, "may I share your table?"

The blond girl looked up at him, her emerald eyes wide, her spoon frozen halfway between her bowl and her mouth. She gave a nearly imperceptible nod, and Nazir set down his own bowl and took a seat across from her.

Instead of saying anything, he silently turned his attention to the task of finishing his porridge. After a few seconds the girl seemed to relax and did the same. Only once they were both finished did he speak.

The Pontiff had an idea of what Cassandra might be hiding. Given her talents, and her history, there was only one logical conclusion. But he had to approach the matter carefully if he wanted to bring her into the fold.

"Cassandra, are you happy here?"

Her head snapped up and her shoulders suddenly tensed; it wasn't necessary to have an Inquisitor's training to see her obvious anxiety at the question.

"Yes, Pontiff," she said softly. "I like it here. Very much."

"That's good, Cassandra. Because I want you to be here. We all want you to be here."

"All of you?" the girl asked, her eyes darting for an instant to Yasmin standing watch from the far corner.

"Yasmin can be scary," the Pontiff admitted, "but she serves the will of the True Gods."

"I want to serve their will, too," Cassandra said urgently. "I do!"

"I know," the Pontiff assured her. "You've worked hard at your studies. You've learned the history of the True Gods. But if you really want to serve the True Gods, that is not enough."

"Yes, Pontiff," she said, casting her eyes down to her empty bowl.

"You know that many of the monks here at the Monastery are Seers, right?"

"Yes, Pontiff."

"The Seers are very important, Cassandra. Their visions guide us. They show us the righteous path we must walk."

"Yes, Pontiff."

"But the Seers must be properly trained before they can do this. They must learn to focus their talents.

"Without this training, their dreams are nothing but the echoes of Chaos. Without the training, they have violent nightmares showing only death and suffering."

He paused, waiting for the girl to say something. She shifted in her seat, but only continued to stare down at her bowl.

"Cassandra, would you like to become a Seer?"

The girl shook her head. "I don't have any dreams," she mumbled.

The Pontiff reached across the table to rest his wrinkled hand on the young girl's wrist, his touch gentle and reassuring.

"It's okay, Cassandra. Whatever you saw, you can tell me."

The young girl shook her head, and he saw she was struggling to hold back tears.

"Don't be afraid, Cassandra. It was only a vision. It can't hurt you."

"If I tell you," she whispered. "You'll send me away."

"No," the Pontiff promised. "You are one of us. The Order will never turn its back on you. We will never send you away."

"My parents did. Rexol did."

"We are not like Rexol," the Pontiff said softly. "And your parents didn't want to send you away."

"They didn't?"

Her confusion was to be expected; she had been only four at the time.

"Do you remember how you came to be with Rexol?"

Cassandra shook her head uncertainly.

"You were very young," the Pontiff said, patting her wrist. "Too young to remember, I guess.

"Rexol stole you from your parents. They wanted you to come

live with us; they wanted you to join the Order. And he stole you away from them. From us."

"And you stole me back?" Cassandra asked, her voice hesitant.

"The will of the True Gods brought you back to us," the Pontiff explained. "This is where you belong, Cassandra. With us. With the Order."

The Pontiff released his grip on the girl's wrist and leaned back. Cassandra nodded, took a long, deep breath, and wiped her eyes. She seemed more relaxed. Even calm.

"Do you trust me, Cassandra?" Nazir asked.

"Yes, Pontiff."

Her reply was short and simple, but he could sense the earnest sincerity of her words.

"Then you must tell me your dream."

She hesitated only for an instant before speaking.

"We are in the Monastery: you, me—everyone. It's night. It's raining. The storm is so dark it blocks out the moon. There are monsters at the gate."

"Monsters? What kind of monsters?"

"I don't know," Cassandra said, shaking her head. "They're just shadows in the night. And then the monsters are inside.

"They break open the gate. They climb over the walls. And then they kill us all. Everyone. They rip us apart and leave our bodies piled in the courtyard."

Though her voice never wavered, Cassandra's face had gone even more pale than usual as she recounted her nightmare. The Pontiff knew she was looking for reassurance—something to put her young mind at ease.

"Do you know what *symbolic* means, Cassandra?"

"No, Pontiff."

"It means sometimes a dream shows one thing but means something else. The monsters might not be real. They might represent some other threat—an enemy of the Order."

"Like Rexol?"

"Him, or others like him."

"What about the bodies? The killing?"

"Your visions are spawned in the fires of Chaos, Cassandra. Until you learn to control them, they will always end in violence and death. But that does not mean they will come true.

"Do you want to learn to control your visions?" Nazir continued. "Do you want to learn to use your power as Seer, in the service of the True Gods?"

"Yes, Pontiff. I do. I really do."

"The training is difficult. It will take many years. You must be certain you are ready."

"I'm ready, Pontiff," she insisted, and there was no mistaking the conviction in her voice. "I want to serve the True Gods!"

"We are all merely instruments of their will," the Pontiff agreed, giving her a warm smile. "I will send word to the Seers. We will begin your training at once."

With his mystical second sight he didn't need to turn his head to sense Yasmin storming angrily from the dining hall.

Chapter 14

AND TO DAEMRON were given the gifts of the Gods, the Talismans imbued with the power of the Immortals that their champion might battle and defeat the Chaos Spawn. And with these Talismans the Slayer, greatest of the mortal kings, became himself a God.

Rexol read the passage of the slender volume a second time: slowly, carefully, word by word, then letter by letter. He spoke the Danaan language fluently, but this text was written in an ancient tongue five hundred years removed from any of the dialects spoken in the North Forest during the present day. The vocabulary and syntax were strange and alien. Even the alphabet was different, with characters and symbols that had long ago fallen into disuse. He wanted to be sure he had made no mistake.

And to Daemron were given the gifts of the Gods, the Talismans imbued with the power of the Immortals that their champion might battle and defeat the Chaos Spawn. And with these Talismans the Slayer, greatest of the mortal kings, became himself a God.

Rexol rubbed his eyes, blinking rapidly as his vision blurred. A bolt of pain shot through his skull, causing him to wince. The glow from the witchroot in his system was fading, making it harder to pierce the veil between the mortal world and the realm of Chaos.

Spells of understanding were never easy. Unleashing Chaos to bring about death and destruction was elementary, but subtly manipulating its power to translate an ancient text was infinitely more complex. The safeguards necessary to contain the spell's backlash—the unforeseen consequences Chaos inevitably wrought upon the mortal world—were many, and maintaining them required great discipline and patience.

The strain was taking its toll, but Rexol had no intention of stopping. Ignoring another searing flash of pain between his eyes, he shook his head and forced himself to refocus. In response, his blurred vision became clear once more.

He read the passage a third time, taking particular care with the last line as he struggled to contain his growing excitement. *And with these Talismans the Slayer, greatest of the mortal kings, became himself a God.*

For the last six years Rexol had been entrusted with the education and training of the heir to the Danaan throne. In exchange the royal family had sent him a steady stream of books and manuscripts that predated the Cataclysm. But despite their promise to exchange ancient knowledge for Rexol's vow to train the crown prince, it was obvious the Tree Folk didn't trust him.

The works were written in a dozen different languages, none of which was spoken anywhere outside the Danaan kingdom. Most were so archaic that even the present-day Danaan scholars would be hard-pressed to translate them accurately. They never imagined a human would be able to comprehend the true subject matter of what they had delivered.

But the Danaan sorcerers had only a rudimentary understanding of magic. Chaos came naturally to them; it flowed through their veins and wove its way through the forests of their kingdom. It was easier to call upon—they relied more on natural ability, and less on the complicated spells, incantations, and rituals that were necessary to summon Chaos in the Southlands.

In contrast, Rexol had spent decades learning to control and manipulate Chaos. The manuscripts had been preserved with the power of Old Magic—without it most of the works would have crumbled into dust centuries ago. Rexol knew how to draw on the lingering remnants of the Old Magic's power. He knew how to bend and twist it to his own desires.

It had taken nearly five years of study and research, but eventually he was able to read the manuscripts the Danaan had sent him, and he quickly discovered how he'd been betrayed. He'd expected to receive the works of historians and philosophers—accounts that would detail the lives and deeds of the great wizards of legend who had drawn on the raw power of Chaos before the Legacy had cut the mortal world off from the source of all magic.

Instead, he received census reports, royal proclamations, storehouse inventories, diaries and logs recorded by insignificant bureaucrats working for the royal family—mundane works focusing on the minutiae of daily existence rather than the epic events that shaped history itself.

Outraged at their treachery, Rexol had briefly considered ending the arrangement. But there was no other source he could call upon in his quest to unlock the secrets of the past. In the Southlands, all surviving documents that predated the Cataclysm had been locked away by the Order in the depths of the Monastery. Trivial as the meager scraps the Danaan fed him were, they were all he would ever get.

Hoping to unearth something of value from the thousands of seemingly worthless texts, Rexol had devised powerful incantations that enabled him to read and comprehend the ancient writings. And as he read volume after volume, he was able to glean small kernels of the kind of information he hungered for, tiny threads of a much greater tapestry.

This particular volume was the diary of a steward who had served beneath one of the many Danaan kings named Lassander. Since the first Lassander ruled nearly three hundred years before the fourth and final Monarch of that name, it made pinpointing the exact year of the manuscript's compilation difficult. However, for Rexol's purposes exact dates usually weren't necessary.

And to Daemron were given the gifts of the Gods, the Talismans imbued with the power of the Immortals that their champion might battle and de-

feat the Chaos Spawn. And with these Talismans the Slayer, greatest of the
mortal kings, became himself a God.

The excerpt was hardly what one would have expected in the diary of a minor court functionary. It was buried between the inscribed guest list for an upcoming social event and the item-by-item description, including cost, of a new wardrobe the author had recently purchased.

A scribbled quote from a better-known text of his era, perhaps? An entry the steward made on that day to . . . what? Inspire himself? To give himself confidence about an upcoming event by reminding himself how anything was possible, even a mortal becoming a God?

Rexol mulled the words over once more. He had found mentions of Daemron before in the Danaan texts. According to the legends, he was a great champion who ruled the Danaan people before the Cataclysm—a wizard, warrior, prophet, and king. Over time, the legends explained, he earned the title of the Slayer for his many victories over the monstrous creatures that rose from the Sea of Fire to threaten those under his dominion.

The Order also had legends of a mortal hero called the Slayer. In their accounts, he was an arrogant wizard who dared to challenge the Old Gods. Rallying his followers, the Slayer made war against the Immortals. The Chaos unleashed in the battle caused the Cataclysm, and the world was nearly split in two. But in the end the Slayer was defeated and the Old Gods created the Legacy to keep the mortal world safe from the destructive power trapped in the Sea of Fire . . . or so the Order claimed.

It was dangerous to make unfounded assumptions, but evidence seemed to indicate the Danaan Slayer and the human Slayer were one and the same. The implications of a shared legend opened the door for interesting questions regarding the origins of the two races. Were the Danaan and humans once a single people?

However, speculations on ancestry and anthropology were not Rexol's primary focus. He was much more interested in the reference to the Talismans—the gifts the Immortals bestowed upon their champion. Rexol had seen brief mentions made of the Talismans in other Danaan texts, though never in connection with the Slayer or the Old Gods. He had assumed them to be items of great religious significance but no real power. Was it possible he had been wrong?

And with these Talismans the Slayer, greatest of the mortal kings, became himself a God.

Rexol didn't believe in Gods—not in the way the Order described them. But in the age before the Cataclysm, before the Legacy was formed, mages had reached freely into the Sea of Fire—the source of pure Chaos—to work their art. Such power would have made the ancient wizards truly seem like Gods. Were these Talismans artifacts forged with the power of the Old Magic? Was it possible the Talismans had survived the Cataclysm? Were they a link to the great magic of the past?

His musings were interrupted by a rap on the door as Vaaler poked his head in.

"Forgive my intrusion, master, but it's getting late. Should I start supper soon?"

"Prepare something for yourself," he said to his apprentice. "I won't be coming down for some time."

The prince nodded and slipped out without another word, closing the door behind him.

In the years since Vaaler had been under his care, the teacher had come to learn many things about his young charge. The boy was intelligent and quick, his mind was active and hungry for learning, he was driven to succeed at his studies, and he desperately wanted to satisfy the hopes of his people and his Queen. But even though he was born under the Blood Moon, he was as dead to Chaos as an Eastern savage.

The young heir was a lesson in the dangers of trying to control Chaos. The Danaan people had sought to breed a great prophet to rule and guide their kingdom through the union of two of their kingdom's most powerful Seers. But Chaos could not be controlled by heredity or bloodlines, and their offspring had been born stone-blind to the visions of his parents.

In desperation the Danaan had sent the boy here, hoping he possessed the Gift rather than the Sight. But after only a few months of working with him Rexol knew Vaaler would never be a wizard. Not even a minor enchanter or a traveling magician, unless he chose to become one of the charlatans who used sleight of hand and trickery to compensate for their inability to touch the true essence of Chaos. Yet Rexol had never admitted this to the Danaan, for fear they would recall the young prince and the stream of ancient texts—however mundane—would dry up. Even the small drops of knowledge he was gathering from the manuscripts were well worth the expense and effort of keeping Vaaler around.

Rexol stood from his chair, leaving the document he had been studying open on the table. He needed to take a break. One couldn't channel Chaos too long without risks, and he had been working with the manuscript for several hours already.

He stretched his hands up toward the high ceiling of his study as he turned to face the full-length mirror on the near wall. The markings painted on his arms and bare torso had begun to fade. This morning the ink had completely covered Rexol's lean frame like a second skin; the intricate red and white symbols traced over every inch of his exposed flesh. Now the ebony of his natural complexion could be clearly seen beneath the washed-out color of the ink.

The circles etched around his eyes and over his cheeks—glyphs to give him sight and understanding, and to protect his mind from the terrible power he sought to control—had vanished completely, devoured by the hungry fires of magic as the Chaos tried to wrench free of the constraints Rexol had enforced upon it.

His safeguards were gone, and there was a weariness deep within him, a mental and physical exhaustion. The complicated spell of understanding had sapped much of his strength; it was time to stop.

But there were many, many more passages still to be read in this diary alone, and hundreds of other manuscripts that he hadn't even started trying to decipher. It was likely most of them would contain nothing but useless dreck, but there might be more valuable nuggets buried inside—more references to the Talismans.

He had never heard mention of them before he started studying the ancient Danaan texts. But that wasn't enough to dismiss them as legend. If the Talismans actually were relics imbued with the power of Old Magic, the Order would have made sure to purge all knowledge of their existence from the Southlands.

Even if they were real, Rexol reluctantly admitted, it was possible they had been destroyed in the Cataclysm. If the Slayer, a great wizard, challenged the Old Gods—whom Rexol suspected were also nothing more than extremely powerful wizards themselves—the Chaos unleashed in their epic battle could easily have consumed the Talismans, just as Rexol's spell of understanding had eaten away the tattoos on his skin.

But it was also possible the Talismans were strong enough to survive. Maybe they hadn't been destroyed, but were only lost or hidden. Their power now would be muted by the Legacy, possibly even locked away so that they didn't appear to have any special properties at all. The Talismans could be anywhere, just waiting for someone with the rare combination of talent, will, and knowledge to find and awaken them.

Drawing on Chaos to decipher the pages was a slow and tedious affair. It would take him years—maybe decades—to go through all the manuscripts without help. He needed another apprentice. Not someone blind to Chaos like Vaaler, but one who could be taught the ways of magic. One who could learn to cast spells of his or her own; one Rexol could draw on to augment his own power.

Someone like Cassandra.

He shook his head, dispelling the unwelcome memory of the young girl's emerald eyes staring after him as he'd abandoned her to the Order. Cassandra was lost to him, but there were others like her: children touched by Chaos and born under a Blood Moon. Surely one or two had managed to stay hidden from the Order . . . and from him. But they couldn't stay hidden forever.

The power of Chaos was cyclical. Despite the Order's efforts, Chaos could never be kept at bay for long. Rexol could feel its influence in the mortal world slowly spreading once more, shaping events to alter the course of history. Perhaps that was why he had discovered this passage only now: The latent power of the Talismans was calling to him, urging him to find them.

In the same way, he would find another apprentice. Eventually the true nature of those touched by Chaos would be exposed— violently; tragically. Some called it destiny or fate. The Order branded it a curse. He knew it for what it really was: opportunity.

And while he waited for a worthy apprentice to be revealed, he would continue his studies. He would learn everything he could about the Talismans. When the time came, he needed to be ready and willing to claim their power.

Rexol glanced down at the book he had spent the better part of the day reading. It was late. The witchroot in his system was fading, and taking more now could cause an overdose that would send his body into convulsions, shock, and even death.

Better to resume the work tomorrow; continue his quest to find more hints and clues about the Talismans once his strength had returned. Whatever secrets he might uncover weren't going to vanish in the night. Pressing on in his exhausted state was foolish. Reckless. Dangerous.

For several minutes the wizard simply stood and stared at the volume, trying to force himself to turn away and leave the study until tomorrow. Instead, when he finally broke his gaze, he picked up the small bottle of ink and began to retrace the faded markings on his face.

Chapter 15

"PAY ATTENTION, SCYTHE," Methodis chided, glancing up from the medical ledger on the table in front of him. "You need to grind the root into fine powder, not the lumpy mess you've got there."

Scythe snapped out of her daze at the sound of his voice, glancing quickly around the small cabin that served as the *Shimmering Dolphin*'s infirmary. She was sitting cross-legged on the floor, a mortar and pestle in her lap. Against the wall behind her was the massive wooden footlocker Captain Trascar had given Methodis to store all the supplies of his trade when he had first signed on with the crew.

"Sorry, I was thinking about something else."

"You mean *someone* else, don't you?" the old man teased. "You were daydreaming about that new man Trascar signed on, weren't you? Rickard, isn't it?"

"I was not!" Scythe snapped back a little too quickly, and the healer knew he had hit his mark.

Methodis allowed himself a smile as he reviewed the list of medical supplies on hand, ticking off ingredients that had been used since he updated his records last week. From the corner of his eye he noticed Scythe attacking the mortar and pestle with renewed vigor to hide her embarrassment.

She's fifteen now, the doctor reminded himself as he flipped the page. *It's natural for her to notice some of the young men on the ship.*

More than a few of them were beginning to notice her, as well. Fortunately Trascar wouldn't sign anyone on with his crew unless he was sure of his moral character. Scythe could do a lot worse than the likes of Rickard.

At the top of the new page, Methodis jotted down the date, then made a short entry: *General health of crew seems excellent. Two cases of flux yesterday. Treated with vinegar wine mixed with silton powder. Both patients showing marked signs of improvement.*

He closed the ledger and turned in his seat toward the young woman still sitting on the floor. "If you like, I can invite Rickard to dine with us in the captain's cabin tonight."

Scythe shrugged without looking up. "If you want to. Why should I care?"

Methodis knew her well enough to realize her seeming indifference was purely for show. He was about to say something else, just to see if he could get a rise out of his young charge, when he was interrupted by a frantic rap at the door.

Before he could open his mouth to say *Enter,* the door flew open and Dugal, the first mate, popped his head in. Methodis could see right away something was wrong. Very wrong.

"There's a ship coming up hard on us. We're trying to outrun her, but she's fast."

"What colors are they flying?" Methodis asked, already knowing the answer.

"None."

Only pirates sailed without flying the flag of a home port.

"If we get some luck and some favorable winds they might not catch us," Dugal continued. "But the captain wants you to stay here in your cabin in case they try to board us." He cast a meaningful glance in Scythe's direction. "Both of you."

"Don't keep me locked up in here!" Scythe protested, jumping to her feet, the bowl of medicine she had been grinding forgotten on the floor. "I know how to use a blade as well as any man on this ship!"

The first mate didn't say anything, but instead looked over to

Methodis, who only sighed. Ever since she had come aboard seven years ago, Scythe had practiced fencing and fighting with anyone who would spare her the time. She had quick hands and excellent instincts, and her technique had been honed with thousands of hours of practice. But this was not the time to put those skills to their first real test.

The healer gave a slight nod and Dugal slipped out, shutting the door behind him. Scythe snorted in surprise, then turned to get the rapier she used during her drills from where it hung on a peg in the wall.

"No, Scythe. We have to stay in here."

The tone in the doctor's voice stopped her short. But she turned angrily to face him, refusing to give up so easily.

"I can help them! You know I can."

Methodis rose slowly from his seat and crossed the floor to put his hands on Scythe's shoulders. He looked her straight in the eye, making no attempt to hide the fear in his voice when he spoke.

"You know what will happen to you if you're caught. The pirates . . . they aren't like Trascar's crew. It isn't safe for a woman."

The girl's eyes went wide as understanding slowly dawned on her. Despite all she had learned in her time at sea, despite everything Methodis and the others had taught her, she was still innocent about many things. She was still barely more than a child.

Scythe wasn't easily daunted, however. "Things won't be much better for the others," she pointed out, her wide-eyed surprise now replaced by a look of grim determination. "Pirates don't take prisoners and I'd rather die fighting with the rest of the crew than let them . . ." She trailed off, unable to even say the words.

Methodis shook his head. "Just do as the captain says. Stay here in the cabin. If you go up there, all you can do is serve as a distraction. Please, Scythe. For me."

For a second she seemed about to protest further; then she simply nodded in acceptance. Methodis turned away, relieved. He took a step back toward the writing table, then suddenly felt too weak to even stand. He was forced to sit down on the top of the enormous footlocker, the gravity of their situation momentarily over-whelming him.

Scythe came over and sat beside him, taking his hand in her own. "Maybe they won't catch us," she whispered, though her voice didn't hold much hope.

Methodis knew she was smart enough to grasp the truth. Pirate ships ran light; they didn't carry much in the way of cargo or stores. The *Shimmering Dolphin,* on the other hand, was laden down with trade goods they planned to sell back in Callastan.

He gave her delicate hand a reassuring squeeze but didn't reply. He was desperately trying not to think of what the pirates would do to the young girl he had raised for the last fifteen years if they found her. And at the same time Methodis was scrambling to come up with a way to save her.

"Open the damn latch!" the voice barked from the other side of the infirmary's door. "Yer only makin' things worse!"

A second later the entire cabin echoed with the sound of a heavy body slamming itself against the locked door, and Methodis heard the sharp crack of splintering wood coming from the chair he had propped up against the entrance. One more hit and they'd be through.

The healer stood alone in the center of the room, facing the portal. Grasping the handle of Scythe's rapier with both hands, he held it straight out in front of him. Scythe may have been an expert with the blade, but Methodis had never bothered to learn the art of killing.

"One more time!" the voice outside shouted, and this time the wooden legs of the chair gave way. The door flew open, sending a large, bare-chested pirate tumbling into the room. Instead of lung-ing forward, the doctor took a step back as the man quickly scram-bled to his feet and pulled out his own weapon: a cruelly curved saber.

Before his enemy could strike, however, another figure stepped through what remained of the cabin's door. Like the first pirate he wore no shirt; a thin, sleeveless vest of tanned leather covered the scars and tattoos of his torso's bronze skin. His beard was bound in half a dozen braids by gold and silver ties, as was his long black hair.

He stepped forward, the gold hoops in his ears jangling against each other, and quickly surveyed the room. When his gaze focused on the slight man standing defiantly in the center, the thin rapier's blade held out straight before him, he raised his saber and grinned.

Methodis made an awkward lunge, which the pirate easily slapped aside, knocking the rapier from the healer's unsure hands. A heavy fist to the side of the jaw sent Methodis reeling. He stumbled backward until he bumped up against the footlocker on the far wall. He lost his balance and fell awkwardly, ending up sprawled on the floor.

Several other pirates standing just outside the door laughed at the spectacle, but the man who struck him wasn't laughing.

"What are you?" he snapped in a heavy accent. "You're too old to be the captain's cabin boy, and too ugly to be his bum-boy. You don't even know how to hold a sword. So why are you on this ship?"

Methodis looked up into the eyes of his conqueror from the floor, his gaze steady. "I'm a healer. I help Captain Trascar and his men when they are injured."

The pirate held the blood-smeared blade of his saber aloft. "You can't help them now."

The first pirate who had entered—the large man who had broken down the door—asked, "Should we kill him?"

"No," the other replied thoughtfully, not taking his eyes off the old man on the floor. "Not just yet. Tell me, healer, are you any good?"

"I am," he replied, with just a hint of cold defiance.

The pirate nodded. "Shoji, take him to the ship. We could use a good healer. The rest of you, search the room. Tear it apart if you have to, but I want everything of value found. Then we sink the ship."

"Wait," Methodis blurted out. "My footlocker. It has all my tools and medicines inside. Powders and potions I'll need if you want me to help you."

"Open it. Let me see."

Methodis shook his head, knowing he couldn't let them see the precious cargo inside. Not if he wanted Scythe to live.

"Many of the components I use are sensitive to light and air. The inside of the box is tightly sealed to protect them, but they will become worthless if they are exposed unnecessarily."

The pirate captain was silent for several seconds, balancing his inherent distrust of others against the potential value of the healer and the mysterious contents of the large footlocker. His impulse was to ignore the warning and smash the container open. But he was the leader for a reason. Unlike the rest of his crew he knew how to control his impulses when necessary.

"Two of you, grab this footlocker and go with Shoji. Take it and the healer down to the hold."

One of the pirates—Shoji, most likely—grabbed Methodis and yanked him up from the floor. Two others seized the massive foot-locker, each one grabbing the handle on either end. They groaned under its weight as they hoisted it up, but between the two of them they managed to keep it aloft.

"Chain him up," the captain ordered as they were leaving. "Then come back and help the others. I want this ship stripped and burned within the hour."

Alone in the darkness of the pirate ship's hold, Methodis fumbled to open the latch on the footlocker's lid. He didn't know how much longer Scythe could last inside the airtight container, and he was desperate to get her out. But the latch had a complex locking mechanism, and the only light was from a few slivers of sun shining in through splits in the hull. After what seemed like hours but was likely only a minute or two, the lock clicked and the lid flew open.

Scythe all but leapt out, gasping for air.

"Slow, deep breaths," he told her in a firm but quiet voice. "Try not to make any sound to draw attention."

Scythe nodded and did her best to follow his instructions, taking in air with a slow, steady rhythm rather than panicked gulps. Her pounding heart began to slow as her starving lungs were sated once more.

"We don't have much time," Methodis said in an urgent whisper. "They'll be back soon. You have to find somewhere better to hide."

Her eyes began to adjust to the disorienting shafts of daylight piercing the darkness of the hold, giving her a first look at her new surroundings. Boxes and barrels were piled haphazardly all about, seemingly without rhyme or reason. The most valuable cargo from several ships had been seized and thrown down here as quickly as possible, with no thought given to any kind of organization or order. Soon, she knew, the haul from the *Dolphin* would be added to the hoard.

"This ship has to go back to port soon; I'm guessing they're almost out of provisions. Their meat's gone bad."

Now that she was no longer gasping for air, Scythe noticed the stench in the hold. Methodis was right; it stank of rot and maggots.

"If they're smart, they'll salvage enough from the *Dolphin* to last them a week and get them back to Callastan. That's where they'll get the best price for most of what they've stolen. You have to stay out of sight until we get there."

Scythe nodded. It was dark here, and with the boxes and crates strewn about she should have no trouble staying hidden.

"Once we get into port, wait until nightfall. Most of the pirates will go ashore. That's when you sneak off the ship."

"What about you? Aren't you coming with me?"

"As soon as we get anywhere near port they're going to have guards watching me at all times, Scythe. I won't be able to get away. But you will."

She nodded again. "I understand. Don't worry—I'll tell someone what's happened. I'll tell them you're a prisoner here."

Methodis shook his head. "No, Scythe. It won't do any good. While docked, only the port authority has the right to board a ship without the captain's permission. The pirates know enough to bribe them to stay away."

"Then I'll find someone else," Scythe insisted. "There's got to be someone who can rescue you."

"No, Scythe! If they think there's any chance of someone finding me, they'll kill me. Then they can make up any story they want to explain my body. They could say I was a crew member they were bringing back for burial on land. Just leave me behind."

"I can't! I . . . I . . ." She broke down in tears as the truth of what Methodis was saying finally dawned on her.

"You can, Scythe. There's nothing you can do for me. You have to save yourself. You have to hide before they get back. And stay hidden. Don't try to talk to me. Don't try to free me from the guards. Just stay out of sight until we reach the port, then get off the ship."

She didn't answer him but stared down at the ground, crying softly. Methodis reached out and lifted her chin so she was looking him in the eye. "Please, Scythe," Methodis begged. "They won't hurt me. I'm too valuable. But you . . . you can't let them find you! Now go. Hurry. Go now!"

Scythe climbed out of the footlocker and gave Methodis a fierce hug. He wrapped his own arms tight around her, and for several seconds they just held each other in silence. Then he whispered in her ear, "Promise me you'll do this, Scythe. Promise me you'll do whatever it takes to save yourself."

"I promise," she whispered back, choking on a sob.

He held her for a few brief seconds more, then gently pushed her away. She sniffed once and wiped away a final tear. Then she gave her mentor a quick kiss on the cheek and disappeared into the clutter of the hold.

– – – –

Five days later they reached port at Callastan. Scythe knew they were docked in the city of her childhood because she had overheard two of the pirates talking about it earlier in the day.

She had gotten quite adept at hiding among the crates and boxes of the pirate ship's hold. At first she had cowered in the farthest corners, terrified she might be discovered, only emerging at night to steal scraps of food from the unguarded stores. But by the third day she had become bold enough to creep up silently whenever she heard anyone enter so she could listen in on their conversations. She had even gotten into the habit of spying on Methodis in the hope she could find a way to help him escape, too. Or at least get another chance to speak to him. So far she hadn't accomplished either of her goals.

He had tended to the wounds of at least ten men by her count. Some of the injuries were from the battle with Trascar's crew while others were from drunken skirmishes among the pirates themselves. None of the men had died, and from what she had overheard the captain was quite pleased with his new healer.

That made Methodis even more valuable, and it made it that much harder for Scythe to come up with a plan for him to escape. They only time he was ever allowed above deck was when he was treating a patient. The rest of the time he was in the darkness of the hold, shackled around his wrists and ankles with heavy iron chains bolted into the ship's hull. And he always had at least one guard watching him.

Despite all this, Scythe had no intention of leaving him behind.

It was night now, all but a handful of the crew had left the ship to go whoring, drinking, or gambling on the mainland. There was only one guard watching over Methodis, and he was two-thirds of the way through the bottle of rum he was using to drown his disappointment at being left behind. If she waited long enough he might pass out in a drunken stupor . . . but the longer she waited, the greater the chance that someone else might come down to relieve him. She had to act now.

The guard was half standing, half leaning against a pair of barrels, mumbling to himself about his bad luck. Moving without a sound she slid into position behind him. In her white-knuckled fist she grasped the thin knife she had salvaged from one of the many pilfered crates in the hold.

She had never killed a man before, but the crew of the *Dolphin* had taught her how to do it in half a dozen different ways. She stabbed the knife into the pirate's back at an upward angle, striking under the bottom edge of the shoulder blade. The sharp steel slid through his ribs and into his lung, and when he tried to scream all that came out was a soft sigh and a spray of sticky, bubbling blood.

The man stumbled forward, wrenching the blade from Scythe's grasp. He turned to face her, grasping and flailing behind him in a futile attempt to seize the handle of the knife lodged in his back. He took a step forward, then slumped to his knees. His chin and chest were soaked with the blood pouring out from his half-agape mouth. He reached out with his hands, though whether his feeble gesture was an attempt to grab her or a plea for help Scythe couldn't say. He gave one last gurgling gasp, then slumped forward onto the floor.

Scythe stepped over his body, only pausing long enough to yank the dagger free from his corpse, and rushed to Methodis's side.

"Scythe, what have you done?" he asked in a horrified whisper. "He's dead!"

"I'm getting you out of here," she replied. She found the heavy padlock of his chains and tried to pry it open with the slim blade of her knife. The tip broke off but the lock didn't budge.

"You have to go," Methodis pleaded, his voice urgent. "Get off the ship before they find you!"

She ignored him and instead turned her attention to the body of the guard. She rolled him over onto his back, grunting with the effort, then rummaged through his clothes, searching every pocket. Her hands were sticky with blood and gore, but she fought back the urge to retch. She had to find the key! She had to!

"Scythe!" Methodis hissed, his voice as loud as he dared. "The guard doesn't have the key! The captain keeps it on his belt. It's hopeless."

Giving up her desperate search, she raced back over to the chains. She wrapped one around her forearm twice and pulled with all her might, trying to wrench the bolt free from the wooden hull. It didn't even budge.

"This is pointless, Scythe. Just leave me here."

"I can't leave you here now," she grunted as she pulled on the chain again. "If they find you here with that guard's body, they'll kill you."

"I'll say he was drunk. I'll say he was mad at being forced to guard the prisoner. That he blamed me. I'll say he attacked me and I was just defending myself."

Sweat broke out on her forehead as she strained against the bonds keeping Methodis captive, but still the bolt held.

"You can't fool me, Methodis," she panted as she stopped to gather her strength again. "They won't care if it was self-defense. They'll kill you anyway."

"No, I'm too valuable. The captain knows this. He might flog me, but he won't let them kill me. Go, Scythe. There's nothing you can do for me."

Scythe cast her head from side to side, looking for some way to gain some leverage. Nothing.

"Maybe I can find something in one of these crates. Just give me a—" Her voice was cut off by the sound of heavy footsteps coming down the stairs.

"Yoskur?" a drunken voice called out. "Shift's done, you lucky bastard! The captain sent me to take over."

"Go, Scythe. This is your last chance."

Methodis's voice was firm yet calm. But when Scythe looked into the eyes of her mentor she saw a fear unlike any she had seen before. And she knew he was afraid for her.

"Yoskur? You down there? Hello?"

She dropped the chain and sprinted across the hull toward one of the portholes. Behind her she heard the footsteps coming down the stairs. She clambered up onto a stack of crates and slammed her shoulder into the porthole, forcing it open. It would be a tight fit, but she was slim. She heard a gasp and an angry shout, followed by the sound of a hard slap and a grunt of pain from Methodis.

She wriggled her shoulders through the narrow opening. Outside the moonlight made it easy for her to see; compared with the dingy shadows of the hold it was almost like daylight. She could see reflections of the pale light on the water twenty feet below her.

More pirates had come down into the hold; the sound of running footsteps and their angry shouts spurred her on. She twisted her body and pulled herself the rest of the way through, then fell like a stone into the cold ocean water.

With powerful strokes she made her way through the waves until she was safely away from the pirate ship. She listened for the sounds of pursuit, of someone diving into the water after her, but heard nothing.

Slowly she swam along the docks, parallel to the shore, passing pier after pier, trying to put as much distance as she could between herself and the ship she had left. After twenty minutes the ship-yards were behind her and she was swimming through the open water. She kept going until her limbs became heavy and she was struggling just to stay afloat. At last, she angled in toward land.

Ten minutes later she crawled up on shore on the very outskirts of the city. She rose to her feet and stood shivering in the chill night air: a fifteen-year-old girl, alone for the first time in her life.

Chapter 16

"I MUST SPEAK with you, Nazir."

The Pontiff remained kneeling on the prayer mat in the center of the room, not turning to acknowledge the speaker who had barged in unannounced.

"You have come to protest Cassandra's candidacy," he guessed.

"I fear what will happen to the Order if she is to join our ranks," Yasmin admitted.

Her reaction was not unexpected. Seven years had passed since Cassandra had been rescued from Rexol, yet there were many in the Order who felt she was forever tainted by her brief apprenticeship with the wizard.

"Cassandra has embraced our teachings and our faith," the Pontiff replied. "Is that not what we hoped for when she first came into our charge?"

"She served under a Chaos mage," Yasmin pressed. "One with a history of openly defying the Order in the past."

Like the Pontiff, her voice was calm. But the scarred flesh of her disfigured scalp had turned a darker shade of purple, giving hint to the true state of her emotions.

"That was not her choice," Nazir countered. "She was abducted and forced to serve the wizard. We cannot punish her for Jerrod's crimes."

At the mention of the heretic's name, Yasmin turned her head and spat on the dusty stone floor in the corner of the room. The Pontiff frowned in disapproval, but didn't bother with further comment. He understood that name was anathema to Yasmin.

In the years since Jerrod had been revealed as a traitor and a student of Ezra's heretical teachings, nearly two dozen of his followers within the ranks of the Order had been flushed out and executed by the Inquisitors. Jerrod himself, however, had avoided capture. Yasmin had spent two years pursuing him as a fugitive across the Southlands and through the Free Cities, but each time she thought she had him cornered he somehow managed to escape.

Her efforts had ended only after Beloq, the aging Prime Inquisitor, commanded her to return to the Monastery to serve at his side in the twilight of his days. Over the next three years the intensity of the hunt waned, as did Beloq's health. With his inevitable passing, Yasmin had assumed the mantle of Prime Inquisitor; she was only the fourth woman in the seven-hundred-year history of the Order to be granted the honor, and the youngest of either gender to hold the position.

Under her reign, the hunt for Jerrod had been renewed in earnest . . . only to yield two more years of frustrating, fruitless results. In Yasmin's own eyes, failing to make Jerrod answer for his crimes was the only blemish on her otherwise perfect record. Now Cassandra, whose name would be forever linked with that of the traitor, was about to undertake her final initiation and become one of the Order.

"You have questioned her," Nazir reminded the fiercely devoted woman who now served as his right hand. "If you sensed a lack of conviction in her—if you sensed any uncertainty in her, or a wavering in her loyalty to the Order or her belief in the True Gods—you have the right to deny her candidacy."

Yasmin was silent for a long time before answering. Yet the Pontiff knew that as much as she might despise Cassandra for her past relationships, the Prime Inquisitor could not bring herself to falsely accuse the girl.

"She is a true believer," Yasmin confessed. Then she quickly added, "But we cannot simply ignore the visions of the Seers! We must remain ever vigilant!"

"We must remain ever vigilant," the Pontiff echoed. "But the dreams of the Seers are often difficult to interpret."

Yasmin's fears were understandable. Jerrod's exposure had dealt a crippling blow to his cause. Those followers who weren't captured fled, or turned their back on the Heresy of the Burning Savior. Cleansing the ranks of the Order had snuffed out an imminent threat to the Legacy, and the visions of the Monastery's prophets confirmed that they had entered an era of nearly unprecedented calm and tranquility. The flaming figures—the so-called Children of Fire—that plagued their dreams faded away, leading many in the Order to believe the Legacy was safe and secure.

The Pontiff was not so easily fooled. He understood that though Chaos could be quelled, it could never be fully quenched. During the past decade of peace, the Sea of Fire continually lapped against the Legacy; weakening it, eroding it. And as the power of Chaos waxed like an incoming tide, the dreams of the Seers had once again been engulfed in smoke and flames.

"The return of these visions warns us that a time of great danger approaches," the Pontiff explained. "We need Cassandra to join our ranks.

"I have watched her closely ever since she came into our provenance. I know her heart and mind; I see her devotion. I see her strength. Under Rexol she may have been a threat to the Legacy, but once she is initiated into the Order she will be one of its most stalwart defenders."

"If the vision is not a warning against Cassandra," Yasmin suggested, "then maybe it is a warning against her old master. Rexol still embraces the ways of Chaos. Let me bring him in for questioning."

The Pontiff had considered and discarded her idea many moons ago.

"Rexol has taken the crown prince of the Danaan as an apprentice," Nazir reminded her. "Moving against him without clear and just cause would be seen as an attack on the Danaan people."

"Would that be so bad?" Yasmin wondered. "Their blood is befouled by Chaos. Perhaps now is the time to rally the Southlands and wipe the Tree Folk from the face of the earth."

"The Southlands is not ready for a crusade," the Pontiff warned. "And the Free Cities are building trade with the Danaan—they would stand with them, not us.

"War brings suffering and death; these are the seeds of Chaos," he cautioned the overeager young woman. "Seizing Rexol now might be the spark that sets the world ablaze. In trying to prevent the collapse of the Legacy, we might actually bring it about."

"I had not considered that," Yasmin admitted after a few moments of silent contemplation.

"Chaos can ensnare us in many ways," Nazir reminded her. "We must not fall prey to its tricks and traps. We must not be rash and foolish; we must be patient and careful.

"The strength of Chaos ebbs and flows. These visions warn us that its power is growing in the mortal world once more. We must stay vigilant. We must continue to seek out those touched by Chaos and contain them, as we have done with Cassandra. And we must do so without plunging the Southlands into a war that could destroy us all."

"I understand, Pontiff," Yasmin said, bowing her head in acceptance of his wisdom.

"Go and tell Cassandra to get ready," Nazir ordered, returning to their original purpose. "It is time for her to become one of us."

Cassandra trembled, but it wasn't from the cold. Though there was a chill in the desert night, she had grown accustomed to it after seven years at the Monastery.

"Are you afraid, child?" the Pontiff asked.

She shook her head. "I'm not afraid."

That wasn't entirely true. The Monastery was her home, the only home she really remembered. The devoted servants of the Order had taught her their ways and instilled in her an understanding of and a belief in the True Gods; they had shared their wisdom with her as she had grown up among them. They were her family now. The only family that mattered. She had been waiting for this moment for many years, eager to take the final step and truly become one of them. As this day had approached she had felt an ever-growing excitement and anticipation. Now that the moment was at hand, however, she couldn't help but feel a bit overwhelmed with the gravity of it all.

A dozen monks of the Order had gathered in a circle here in the courtyard to be part of her initiation. Their faces and forms were hidden by heavy cloaks, the hoods pulled up to conceal their identities. They were not individuals here—they were the Order.

Those surrounding her didn't speak, only stood in somber silence as she had made her way to the center of their ring. There, the Pontiff had been waiting for her. She hoped his question was one he asked all of the initiates; she hoped he didn't sense the fear she refused to openly acknowledge. She didn't want anything to get in the way of the ceremony.

The Pontiff placed a reassuring hand on her slim shoulder. "Prepare yourself. We are about to begin."

The monks around her began to chant softly. She glanced up at the night sky above her, gazing at the stars for what might be the last time. But the loss of her sight was a small price to pay for what she was about to gain.

"Close your eyes, Cassandra. Do not rely on them to guide you; look to the power within. Let the True Sight guide you now."

She did as instructed, shutting her eyes. At first there was only darkness. Cassandra began to breathe, channeling her energy, focusing her power as the monks had taught her, drawing upon all the lessons she had learned over her years of study.

When she had first arrived as a little girl her power had manifested itself only in her dreams. She would wake screaming in the night, the terrible visions overwhelming her. But with the guidance of the prophets she had slowly learned to control her visions. The nightmares became less frequent, finally stopping altogether—with one exception.

There were still nights when she would see the face of Rexol, the mage who had abducted her as a little girl. Sometimes she would awaken with the image of the man who had been her master until the Order had rescued her burned into her mind's eye, her left arm tingling with a terrible heat. Even after all these years, Rexol still haunted her, a dark and shadowy figure she could only half remember.

Apart from these episodes, however, she was no longer at the mercy of the power within her. She had learned to redirect it, to turn it to her advantage. Now she used her power to see the world around her. Eyes still shut, the world around her slowly came into view. Not the shadows and twilight she would see if she were to open her eyes, but a full and complete awareness of her surroundings that transcended the physical world.

Sensing her achievement the Pontiff removed his hand from her shoulder and placed his palms firmly but gently over the lids of her still-closed eyes.

"Cassandra, do you understand what you are about to do?" he asked in a deep voice, enacting the first line of the initiation ritual.

She gave the traditional response. "I must sacrifice my sight so that I can truly see."

"And do you do this of your own free will?"

"It is my honor and privilege to do this." She spoke slowly, carefully. She was about to undertake a sacred oath, and she was determined to recite it without flaw. "I believe in the True Gods. I give my life to their service, and to the service of the Order that was founded to protect their Legacy. I vow to defend this Legacy against any who would destroy it, be they man, woman, or child."

"No one life can be held before the greater good. Any in the

Order must be willing to sacrifice his or her life to protect that which we believe in. Do you understand this, Cassandra?"

"I do, Pontiff."

"Then cast aside the trappings of the mortal world, and see with the Vision of the True Gods!"

The Pontiff thrust his palms forward, throwing her head back. She fell to her knees and cried out as her vision dissolved in an agonizing blaze of blue fire, blinding her. She shrieked as the intense heat seared the lenses of her eyes. She screamed and clawed at her face as the soft tissue of her eyes melted away, molten tears crawling slowly down her cheeks. The fire burrowed deep into her skull as the Pontiff's power burned away the last vestiges of her mortal sight and she could do nothing but scream and writhe at the unbearable agony.

And then suddenly the pain was gone. The veil of blue fire obscuring her sight slipped away to reveal the world around her, blazing with a pure and glorious intensity she had never witnessed before.

"It is done, my child."

Responding to the Pontiff's words Cassandra opened her once emerald eyes to reveal two gray, lifeless orbs.

Chapter 17

THE SOUND OF Keegan's scream woke Gerrit immediately. Pulling on his robe, he slipped quickly from his bed and into the hall. The moonlight through the window cast just enough light for him to find his way without a lantern. He knocked once on the door of his son's room. "Kee, are you all right?"

Keegan had always had nightmares, ever since he was a little boy. Two or three times a month he would wake from a dream so terrifying it would leave him trembling and crying, afraid to go back to sleep. There were many explanations, of course: the anxiety of growing up without a mother, the stress of having to move every few years, the difficulty Keegan had making friends with others his age. Plausible explanations, all of them, though deep down Gerrit knew none of them was the real truth.

But things had seemed to get better when they had settled here in Tollhurst just over five years ago. Since then the terrible dreams had become less frequent. His son was fifteen now—a young man—and it had been over a year since his last nightmare. Gerrit had even allowed himself to believe the nightmares were gone for good.

"Keegan?" he called out again, not hearing an answer. He gently pushed the door open and came into his son's room. The young man was sitting on the edge of his bed, wearing only his breeches.

His naked body, pale and thin, was bathed in sweat despite the chill of the night.

He looked up at his father with his dark eyes—eyes that seemed to grab you and hold you in their gaze. "We have to leave," he said, his voice a choked whisper.

Moving slowly, Gerrit crossed the room and sat next to Keegan on the bed. He draped a strong, comforting arm across his son's bare shoulders. "Another dream, Kee?"

The only response was a slight nod.

"Tell me about it. Maybe it will help."

For several moments there was only silence as Keegan stared down at the ground. Gerrit said nothing, knowing it was better to let the lad tell things in his own time. At last, he began to speak.

"They're going to destroy the village. All of it. Burn it to the ground."

"Who? Who's going to destroy the village?"

"Raiders. Everybody dies. Nobody gets away."

Gerrit hesitated, not sure what to say. He knew his son's dreams were special; he knew they were more than just dreams. But he didn't know what to make of them.

The young man turned his head to face his father, his cheeks stained with desperate tears. "We have to leave, Father. If we don't, they'll kill us, too."

It wouldn't be the first time they had fled a town in the night, though each time Gerrit prayed to the Gods that it would be the last. But this time they wouldn't be running to keep their secret hidden, or to escape angry and frightened neighbors, or to keep the Order from finding them. This was different.

"We can't go, Keegan. We have to warn them."

"They'll never believe me," Keegan replied. "Nobody ever does."

"Maybe this time they will. Maybe this time it will be different."

"It won't be."

"These people are our friends, Keegan. We have to tell them what's going to happen so we can try and stop it."

"We can't stop it. No one can. My dreams always come true."

His son's words, delivered with such simple finality, sent a shiver down Gerrit's spine. It was a statement of inevitable fact, utterly devoid of all hope.

"Listen to me, son," he said with a sudden urgency, "I admit I don't understand this . . . this power you have. I'm a simple man, such things are beyond me.

"But I believe these dreams are more than just visions of the future. There has to be some purpose behind them. There has to be a reason you see the things you do."

"What reason? What purpose?"

He wanted to be able to give him an answer. More than anything, the father wanted to say something that would ease his son's suffering, give him some hope. But the truth was he didn't know what to say.

"I can't answer that, Keegan. All I know is that you have been shown something terrible. I don't know why you've seen it and I don't know if there's anything we can do to prevent it. But I know we have to try."

He gave his son a reassuring squeeze with the arm draped around his shoulders, and felt him shiver from the perspiration on his bare skin.

"Get under the covers," Gerrit said, rising to his feet. "Tomorrow I'll call the town council and we'll tell them what you've seen."

"So we're not going to leave?" Keegan asked as he tucked himself back in. Gerrit wasn't sure, but he thought he sensed relief in his son's voice.

"No, we're not leaving. There are times in a man's life when he has to take a stand."

"There haven't been Raiders this far into the Southlands since before the Purge! Long before that, even. Fifty years ago, at least. This is preposterous!"

Gerrit Wareman, general store owner and recently elected mayor of the town of Tollhurst, replied to the angry outburst in a calm and level voice. "Maybe so, Willan, but there have been Raiders here in the past."

As he spoke, Gerrit let his eyes drift over the ten men and women who made up the village council. They had come to the local inn that served as the town hall in time of need to hear him speak. They watched him with curious eyes from their seats around the tavern's tables, looking very much like a crowd of hungry customers. It wasn't unusual for a village council meeting to end with a good meal, strong drink, and boisterous song. But this meeting was different. There would be no singing tonight.

"Adrax fought the Raiders when he was a young man, Willan," Gerrit noted. "Perhaps he can make you understand the danger."

A stooped, gray-haired old man rose slowly to his feet. Adrax was nearly eighty now, the oldest council member, the oldest man in the village. He seldom spoke at the meetings, and his voice was thin and nervous on this night.

"Gerrit speaks the truth. If Raiders come to Tollhurst our houses will be burned and our livestock slaughtered. Everything of value will be seized, the men will be killed, and the women will be taken for purposes too vile to mention. Raiders are not men—they are inhuman monsters. They have no remorse, and no conscience. If Raiders are coming, we need to prepare for war."

Willan Coburd, owner of the Smiling Drake Tavern and long-serving mayor of Tollhurst before Gerrit had run against and defeated him last spring, renewed his protests.

"I do not doubt the savagery of the Raiders—I doubt their very existence! A full generation has passed since they were last seen in this province. Raiders are a threat to those who live in the borderlands, not us. If the barbarians of the Frozen East had entered the Southlands we would know!"

"Raiders do not necessarily have to be barbarians from the East," Gerrit pointed out, trying not to let his exasperation show. Ever since he'd become mayor, Willan Coburd had opposed every idea he had put forth on mere principle. "Outlaws—men of no conscience and no honor banding together to prey upon the weak: The Southlands breeds such animals as readily as the Frozen East."

"Save your scary tales for the children," Willan scoffed. "The patrols scour the province regularly for brigands and highwaymen. They keep the roads safe. Everyone knows Raiders no longer dare venture within three days' ride of any of the Seven Capitals. But you would have us disregard all this?

"You would have us believe that after fifty years Raiders are about to return, Gerrit? We are supposed to believe this because a *boy* has had a bad dream?"

"I told you they wouldn't believe us," Keegan muttered from his chair in the corner.

Normally only the council was permitted to attend town meetings. Given the circumstances, however, Gerrit had insisted his son be present. Despite Willan's strong objection.

"Nobody ever believes," he continued. "Not until it's too late."

Gerrit held up a hand to silence his son. He would make them understand. He had to, no matter what the cost.

"My son . . . ," he began uncertainly, staring at the floor, ". . . my son knows things. Things he shouldn't—couldn't—possibly know. Sometimes he has dreams. Dreams that come true. We have kept this secret, my son and I."

The mayor of Tollhurst raised his eyes to the other councilors. His neighbors and friends were staring intently at him, trying to weigh the merit of his words.

"Dunkirk," Gerrit said, addressing the village smith, "Keegan told me your daughter would marry a minstrel. He told me this two seasons ago. A week later Pellin first arrived in our town, a kind stranger with his lute slung across his back. And now in less than a fortnight you will celebrate his union with your daughter." Gerrit spoke softly, yet the silence in the room carried his words clearly to every ear.

"And Lassinda," he said, addressing the matronly woman who served as the village midwife. "Last High Season he told me Juliana would have twins. He knew she would have twins before anyone even knew she was with child, including you."

Turning his attention back to Willan, Gerrit continued to plead his son's case. "And he told me of Lord Selkirk's visit. Did I not suggest to you that we stock up on the most expensive wines? I told you we should always be prepared, just in case. Do you remember, Willan?

"What would have happened if such an important noblemen had graced your tavern's door and found nothing worthy to refresh his thirst? Do you think it was simple good fortune that prompted my suggestion?"

Uncertain what more he could say, Gerrit paused before concluding. "If my son tells me Raiders are coming to the village in two nights, I know it to be true."

There was silence from the council, until Elimee, oldest of the female councilors, spoke up. "Keegan has the Sight. He's a Seer!"

"I always made him hide it," Gerrit admitted softly. "I was afraid. Afraid of losing him. Afraid the Order would come to take him from me. My wife is dead and Keegan is all I have left of her. I could not bear to lose him."

Willan's voice cut through the awkward silence. "How do we know you speak the truth, Gerrit?"

Keegan looked up from his chair, his dark eyes burning with the fire of a fifteen-year-old youth called to a challenge. "Are you calling my father a liar, Willan?"

Willan ignored Keegan and addressed himself to the council instead. "Our mayor is a fine, upstanding man; he is an important part of our community. But the same cannot be said of his son."

"Watch what you say about my boy," Gerrit warned ominously.

"Forgive me, Mayor," Willan apologized without sincerity. "I'm sure Keegan's a good boy deep down, but the fact is he doesn't fit in. He's too quiet, too withdrawn. The other children never took to him."

"Willan!" Elimee shouted. "How can you say such a thing? The boy is right here!"

"I'm only saying what we all know to be true. I don't begrudge a father for wanting to believe his son is special, that he has some gift. But to the rest of us it should be obvious that this so-called dream is nothing but a frustrated boy's desire for attention."

"You go too far, Willan!" Gerrit snapped. "You have no idea what is at stake here."

"No? Then let the boy speak for himself, Mayor. Let him tell us of his horrible dream in his own words."

"I've seen fire and blood as our village burns and our men are slain," Keegan said in response. He spoke slowly and without emotion as he recounted the most vivid details of his dream. "I've heard the screams of the women as they are ravished while the corpses of their husbands and fathers lie beside them.

"I've even seen your death, Willan. Cut down like a dog in the street by a Raider's scimitar, the blade biting into your back as you run in terror, leaving your wife and daughter behind."

"Damn you, boy!" Willan shouted, his fists clenching as he leapt to his feet. "Nobody threatens me!"

"Enough!" Gerrit ordered in a loud voice. "Keegan, no more. Willan, sit down!" Reluctantly Willan did as he was told. "My son isn't threatening you, you fool! He's trying to warn you. He's trying to save your life!"

Face twisted into a contemptuous sneer, Willan shot back, "So you say. But we have no proof of his talent but your own claims. I hardly think that is enough to act on."

It was Elimee who brought reason back to the meeting. "In the years since Gerrit arrived I've never known him to lie to anyone about anything. He's a good man, we all know that. That's why we chose him as our mayor.

"I see that same character in Keegan," the old woman continued. "If what they say is true we cannot afford to ignore them. If they are wrong we will know in two nights and we can deal with them then. But if they are right we must begin our preparations tonight."

Murmurs of assent greeted the old woman's words.

"Very well," Willan conceded as he took his seat, "we will make preparations. But if your son is wrong . . ."

"I truly hope that he is," Gerrit somberly replied.

Keegan's voice was calm and cold. "I'm not."

Chapter 18

THE RUMBLE OF horses' hooves filled Herrod's ears, making his heart race and his blood boil. The village was just ahead; in the moonlight he could see the outlines of the buildings. He raised his hand, his wicked scimitar glinting in the moonlight. Behind him a score of torches were lit and raised in answer as his band of followers—violent and depraved men like himself—prepared to burn out the unsuspecting citizens as they slept.

They charged into the silent village, mounts swooping and dashing among the homes and buildings as they threw their burning brands onto the dry, thatched roofs. Smoke curled up and the flames began to catch. Soon the fire would devour the buildings and the shrieking townspeople would pour out of their blazing homes. Confused and panicked, they would be cut down in the streets by his men. Only the young women would be taken alive, for their later use. After the slaughter, they would loot the charred remnants of the buildings. It would be as it had been in half a dozen villages in the past month: They would take what they could, destroy the rest, and gallop off into the night, leaving the patrol dispatched from the Seven Capitals to stumble onto the grisly scene days later.

Herrod wheeled his horse around, his long black cape billowing behind him like an inky cloud, and galloped to the open square in the center of the village. Bloodlust filled his head, but he could sense something wasn't right. He could hear the shouts and cries of his own men—but where were the screams of the villagers?

He pulled his horse up short and surveyed the scene. The buildings smoldered but did not blaze up in flame. It was as if the roofs and walls had been drenched with water. And the town was empty; only his own men on their horses could be seen, rushing through the streets among the buildings.

Was the town deserted? Had something else driven the people away? Disease, maybe? Or famine? From his belt Herrod pulled a curled, twisted horn and blew three staccato blasts on it.

Within a minute his men had gathered with him in the central square, their horses standing impatiently, hooves stamping uneasily on the ground. Herrod quickly counted: sixteen riders. Four were unaccounted for.

"Who's missing?" he demanded gruffly, already made uneasy by the ghost town they had stumbled into. "Who's missing and where in the fires of Chaos have they gone?"

A single voice answered him from the far end of the square. "They are dead, killed by archers. As you will be if you do not throw down your weapons and dismount."

The Raiders all turned to face the speaker. A lone man stood at the far end of the square, unmounted, and unarmed.

Gerrit had insisted he face the bandits alone; the rest of the townspeople either had been evacuated or were strategically placed about the village. Some had wanted to kill the Raiders with no warning, no offer of surrender. Just kill them all. But the mayor had vetoed the idea. He would bring these men to justice alive if he could.

The Raiders had as yet made no reply. "You are surrounded," Gerrit told them. "Our archers will shoot you where you sit if you do not surrender immediately. This is your last warning."

He doubted they would accept, but if he could Gerrit wanted to capture them without more bloodshed. Resistance by the Raiders could lead to one of the villagers getting hurt.

There was no reply from the Raiders, though he could tell the leader was studying the surrounding buildings intently, trying to locate the ambush.

Herrod couldn't see the archers, but he didn't doubt they were there. Yet he refused to be captured by a bunch of common villagers. The night was dark, his armor strong, and he could see they had not thought to barricade the roads leading from the square out of the town.

The Raider made his choice. Without a word he spurred his horse forward. The sound of arrows filled the air; he heard the cries of his men as they were plucked from their seats behind him. An arrow ricocheted off his mailed shoulder, deflecting harmlessly away. He could hear the battle cries of the villagers as they poured out from their hiding places, lining the four edges of the town square.

A second later a dozen flaming arrows struck the ground around the horses. The earth, which had been soaked with oil, erupted into a wall of flame. Herrod's horse reared and he was thrown to the ground amid the flames.

Gerrit watched wordlessly as the Raiders were consumed by the inferno. A few were lucky enough to escape the burning trap, spurring their horses through the wall of flames. But as they emerged from the conflagration they were met by the men of the village wielding homemade pikes. Just as Adrax had shown them they braced their ten-foot spears into the ground while they met the charge of the panicked horses. The beasts were impaled on the pikes, the riders thrown from their mounts. Even as the Raiders struck the ground they were set upon by the villagers, now brandishing picks and scythes, shovels and axes. Kill or be killed—the men of the village knew it had come to that. They fought for themselves, for their homes, for their families, using their weapons with a grim determination on a merciless foe.

Gerrit turned his attention back to the flames. So far the trap had been perfect—not a single Raider had escaped. He could hear their screams, the shrieks of men and horses as they were consumed by the fire. The perfect trap, perfectly executed, but it brought him no pleasure.

Deep within the blaze Herrod rose to his feet. All around him his men were dying: choking on the smoke; cooking in the fires; being hacked down by the makeshift weapons of the townsmen. But the Raiders' leader was not so easily beaten.

As the strongest of the band, he had his choice of treasures. On one of their raids he had claimed a cape of magnificent properties: a cape woven from the hair of a giant; a cape that now protected him from the flames. The fire licked at the garment, but it did not catch. Yet he knew the protection was not absolute. Even now he could feel his armor searing his skin, could feel his breath being choked from his lungs.

Wrapping the saving cloth tightly around his body, Herrod marched directly through the blazing wall of flame and into the cool night beyond. He emerged singed but unharmed, and found himself facing two startled young men brandishing long spears.

The townsmen hesitated, unsure how to attack. They had been trained only to meet a charging horse, yet now they faced an armored opponent on foot. Herrod had no such hesitation. Two strides and he was too close for them to effectively use their spears. The first man was dead even before he could drop his now useless pike, his head nearly severed by a single chop of Herrod's deadly scimitar.

The second dropped his pike and fumbled for the axe at his belt, too surprised even to scream as his companion dropped lifeless beside him. He managed a single off-balance swipe at his foe, which Herrod easily parried. A forward slash across the chest and a back slash across the stomach and the melee was over. The man slumped beside his friend; his warning cries to his fellows a silent bubbling of blood in his throat.

The Raider moved quickly now, heading toward the shadows of a nearby building. No one else had noticed his escape; they were too concerned with finishing off his followers. He slipped into the darkness and crept along the edge of the building, heading for the outskirts of town. Now that he had left the battle scene undetected he could sneak into the surrounding farmlands, steal a horse, and ride off into the night. But even as he planned his escape Herrod vowed he would return to seek vengeance.

Gerrit had seen Herrod emerge from the fire, had watched in horror as the Raider had cut down the two young men—men with families, one with a newborn child not a year old. He had screamed a warning, but his voice could not be heard above the roaring flames and the screams of the dying bandits. He watched the butcher vanish into the shadows, and he knew what he had to do. None of the Raiders could escape alive, not if the town was to be safe again. Moving quickly but silently he followed his enemy into the darkness of the fields beyond the town, armed only with the half-sized ceremonial mace the town mayor always wore at his belt.

The nightmare woke Keegan with a scream; his scream woke many of the other sleepers in the evacuation camp. Elimee was at his side almost instantly, cradling him in her frail arms.

"Hush, my young Seer," she whispered in his ear.

Since the town meeting only Elimee had spoken to him. Everyone else at the evacuation camp—all the women and old men who had known him since he had arrived in the town, the girls and boys he had grown up with, all the young children he had looked after and played with during festivals and feasts—kept their distance, shunning him because of his dream.

Only Elimee, wise old woman of the village, still treated him the same. Only she could meet his gaze, only she looked at him without fear.

Keegan gently worked himself free of her protecting arms. "Something is wrong," he told her in hushed but urgent tones.

"Have you had another dream?" she asked.

Keegan nodded. "This one wasn't clear. I can't remember it. But I know something is wrong. I have to go back to the town."

He thought she would object, but instead Elimee was silent for several seconds, lost in her own thoughts. Then she gently stroked his cheek.

"My young prophet, you have done so much for these people, though they know it not. You have risked much by revealing your secret; you have sacrificed more for the people of this town than they can possibly know."

"I . . . I did what I had to. Father said it was the right thing to do. We had to warn you."

The old woman smiled at him. "You are a fine young man, Keegan. You truly are your father's son. But your dream has taxed your power. You are tired. I can see the weariness in your eyes.

"I do not know much about the Sight, but I know it comes from the power of Chaos that flows within your veins. Every vision, every dream saps your strength. You need time to rest before you will dream clearly again. Right now you are exhausted. Your talent is drained. I do not know if you can trust your dreams as you normally would."

"Something is wrong," Keegan repeated. "I know it. I have to go."

Elimee cast a quick glance around the makeshift camp. Everyone was either sleeping or pointedly ignoring her conversation with Keegan.

"I believe in your power, Keegan. I believe in you. Now you must believe in me."

She pulled him close, her gnarled hands clenching his shoulders as she stared deep into his eyes.

"You are not the only one is this town who dreams, Keegan," she whispered, "though my Sight was weak to begin, and has weakened further with age and neglect." The old woman smiled gently. "Like your father, my parents also feared the Order would come to take me away."

Keegan did not react to the confession. He had long suspected the old woman of having Chaos in her veins—sometimes he could feel it calling to him from within her, like calling to like. His father had forbidden him from ever mentioning it. Now she merely confirmed his suspicions.

The old woman released his shoulders and reached down inside her blouse to withdraw a small pendant of gleaming white. It was carved in the shape of an eye.

"Unicorn horn, a gift from my aunt. She was a witch-woman. I suppose the Chaos in my veins came from her."

Elimee took his hand in her own and wrapped his fingers around the charm.

"There is power in this," she whispered. "The Chaos Spawn are gone, but their magic lingers. Draw strength from it, feel its power fill your mind and heart. We will know the truth of your nightmare."

Keegan hesitated, uncertain how to proceed. Gently he reached out with his mind. Reached out with his spirit. Reached out to the charm carved from the horn of a beast that had been extinct for centuries, and to the frail old woman before him.

At first there was nothing. And then he felt it. A faint ember of flickering power. Instinctively, without even knowing how, Keegan began to fan the flame.

The ember he saw with his mind's eye flared to life, bursting into a blazing blue fire. Keegan drew the fire into himself, his starving talent devouring the power of the old woman's charm.

The dream exploded in his mind; the image dim and faint, but discernible. It lasted the briefest of moments, the images crystallizing in Keegan's mind almost instantaneously. His father in a field, leaping onto the back of a man in a black cape. They fall to the ground and wrestle briefly. The man breaks free, and draws his scimitar. Gerrit tries to protect himself with the pitiful little mace on his belt but the scimitar slashes down . . .

"No!" he screamed, tearing the charm from its cord around Elimee's neck.

The carved eye slipped from Keegan's fist and clattered on the floor as he leapt to his feet. The old woman stiffened, her fingers clenching Keegan's own. Then she slumped weakly onto the floor, her withered hand sliding from his grasp. Others nearby turned to look, their faces a mix of confusion and fear. None dared to interfere.

Keegan hesitated, torn between the vision of his father and the plight of Elimee on the ground at his feet. The old woman raised her head.

"Go, Keegan," she whispered, "I will be fine. Go to your father."

Keegan sprinted across the moonlit fields, stumbling over the furrows in the near darkness. Guided by the memory of his vision he raced to where he knew his father faced certain death.

He crested a hill on the outskirts of the town and saw his dream unfolding less than a hundred yards away. Two dark figures grappled on the ground, silhouettes wrestling in the silver moonlight.

Engrossed by the scene before him, Keegan tripped on the uneven ground and tumbled down the hill. He flipped and bounced down the steep mound, the fall knocking the wind from him. For several seconds he lay on his back at the bottom gasping for air, trying to regain his breath and clear his head.

When he rose unsteadily to his feet he saw only one figure standing; the other lay writhing on the ground at its feet. Keegan staggered toward the pair, his warning cries lost in his still-gasping lungs.

The standing figure raised his arm; the sickle curve of a scimitar blade sliced through the darkness, slashing at the figure on the ground. Once, twice, a third time as Keegan could only sob and cry, stumbling toward the massacre.

Herrod brought his sword down for a fourth time, certain his enemy was dead yet wanting to disfigure and mutilate the corpse out of pure malice. Above the grisly sounds of his butchering his ears picked up another familiar noise: grief-stricken sobs.

He turned from his bloody work to see another figure reeling toward him through the night's gloom. His eyes searched the shadowy form for a weapon, but this one was unarmed. As his newest foe drew closer Herrod could see he was too small and thin to be a grown man; he was nothing more than a youth.

The young boy charged forward, blind with exhaustion and grief and rage. Herrod let him approach then struck the young man across the face with the hilt of his scimitar. His foe crumpled to the earth, barely conscious. Herrod reached down, grabbing his opponent by the hair and pulling him to his knees. The boy's face was drenched in blood, his broken nose jutting out at an obscene angle.

Herrod placed his lips against the lad's ear.

"Boy," he hissed, his fist still clutching his young victim's hair, "know before you die that I will return with more men and kill everyone in this village. Those that flee I will hunt down like dogs. They will die in bloody, screaming agony, tortured for days before being slaughtered like pigs. The women will be raped until they beg for death, and only then will we grant it."

What happened next Keegan could not later explain, could not even remember. His head was still swimming from the blow Herrod had given him, his mind covered in a blanket of pain and terror and wrath. He grabbed the Raider's wrist and a blazing blue light engulfed them both.

The Raider screamed in pain, releasing his grip on Keegan's hair. His scimitar's blade shattered into a thousand pieces, Keegan

grabbed the front of the brigand's armor, his fingers ripping through the mail shirt like paper, digging into the flesh beneath like claws. The young lad rose to his feet, lifting Herrod from the ground, and began to shake the Raider violently back and forth like a child's rag doll.

The sound of snapping bones and ripping cartilage was drowned out by Herrod's shrieks and wails. A vicious crack ended the howls as his neck was broken. And still Keegan shook the body with a primal fury, the elemental power of Chaos surrounding the young wizard and his dead enemy with raging blue flames.

The townspeople found them the next morning: Gerrit's body, mercilessly hacked by the Raider's cruel sword; Keegan collapsed upon his father's corpse, shivering and sobbing and nearly comatose with shock, grief, and exhaustion. A short distance away lay the body of the Raider, his face twisted in a gruesome mask of agony, his limbs projecting from his body at grotesque, unnatural angles, dislocated and broken.

The Raiders had been defeated, not a single one had escaped the well-laid trap. Five of the townsfolk had died in the battle, including their beloved mayor, but the hundred-odd other men, women, and children knew they owed their lives to the young man who now lay recovering in the home of Elimee.

Within the confines of the Smiling Drake Tavern, Willan Coburd spoke in a voice so low the other members of the council had to strain to hear him. "What do we do about Keegan?"

Elimee snorted loudly. "You speak as if he means to harm us, Willan. He saved us all and he lost his father in the process. He sacrificed everything so that the rest of this town could live."

Willan glanced quickly around the inside of the tavern, as if he expected Keegan to appear in one of the corners.

The old woman continued, her voice filled with anger and contempt. "Quit your sneaking, Willan! He is barely able to raise his head, let alone come here!"

"But he does not have to be here to see us," the nervous man hissed back. "He has the Sight! He has the Gift!"

Elimee laughed. "Yes, Willan, he does. He could hear your very thoughts if it comes right down to it. Although I suspect right now he is too exhausted to call upon the Chaos flowing through his veins."

Chastened, Willan resumed speaking in a normal voice.

"Very well, you are probably right. But we still must decide what to do about him. What happened to the Raider in the field was unnatural." Willan's voice lowered once more as he added, "The expression on his face . . . he died a horrible death!"

"I wish I had been there to see it," Adrax proclaimed loudly in his wavering voice. "He deserved no better!"

Murmurs of agreement rippled through the council. Willan nodded, but held up his hand for silence.

"Of course I agree. But what happened out there was wizard's work: an unleashing of Chaos. We cannot help the boy with his power, and I doubt he can control it. The Sight is one thing, the Gift quite another. He cannot stay here."

"No," Elimee agreed, "he cannot stay here. But where can he go? Surely we cannot just send him off as if he were banished."

"We could send him to the Order," Willan suggested. "They could teach him to control his . . . talent. They would be most anxious to have one of his obvious power join their ranks."

Elimee shook her head. "No. His father did not want that life for him, and I doubt Keegan wants it for himself. Besides, he is too old. The Order will no longer take him."

"And even if they did," Adrax added in a thin whine, "the boy will never learn to see as the Pilgrims do. They will pluck out his eyes and leave him blind."

"We could give him to a lord's mage," Willan declared, smoothly switching tracks. "He has the Sight, he has the Gift. He would be a boon to any court in the Southlands. Perhaps even the King's own mage will take an interest in him."

"Yes," Elimee agreed contemptuously, "the mages of the nobility

are known to welcome those who would supplant their own position with open arms. You might as well put the poison in his drink yourself, Willan."

"You are too harsh," Willan chided. "There are many rumors of apprentices who meet suspicious ends, I admit. But we both know most of these rumors are spawned by the Order to discredit the mages. And Keegan needs the guidance only a lord's mage can give or his power might destroy him—and us."

Before Elimee could counter with her own arguments, Adrax spoke up once more.

"This discussion is pointless," he wheezed, exhausted at having taken such an active part in the meeting. "We are simple folk. None of us would even know how to contact a lord's mage."

There was a long silence as the truth of the old man's words sank in, finally broken by Willan.

"Then what are we to do with Keegan?"

A new voice spoke from the rear of the tavern. "I will take him."

The council reacted with surprise and alarm, spinning to face this strange intruder. The doors were locked, the windows shuttered. Yet somehow the speaker had managed to sneak into the council meeting undetected.

The visitor stepped from the shadows and into the light, and the mystery of his sudden appearance was instantly explained. The black skin of the man's face, bare chest, and arms was covered in brightly colored paint and tattoos. His long dark hair was twisted into countless uneven braids. He wore half a dozen necklaces of animal teeth and bones; a few of the charms had been shaped and carved, though most were still rough and irregular. Three gleaming gemstones, each on its own separate golden chain, dangled from the lobe of his left ear, and his belt was heavy with all manner of odd curios and bizarre ornaments. The skull of some ancient, long-extinct beast perched on top of the heavy black staff clenched tightly in his right hand.

The Chaos mage crossed the room slowly but surely, not using his walking staff for support but gently thumping it on the floor as he came. The charm bracelets that covered his left arm from elbow to wrist jangled with each measured step.

"I will take him," the intruder repeated, his voice deep and strong.

"Your L-L-Lordship," Willan stammered out, "we are honored by the presence of a mage in our humble town." Willan's mind, numb with surprise and fear, reverted to the ingratiating patter he adopted with any social superiors he wished to please. "How may we be of service to such a noble guest?"

"Keegan," the Chaos mage replied. "The young wizard. I have listened to your conversation, and what you say is true. He must be taught to control his power. I will take him to be my pupil, to study and learn the arts of magic. He will leave with me tonight."

"How did you hear about him?" Elimee demanded, stepping forward. "How did you get here so soon?"

The Chaos mage gave her a withering glare, but she refused to back down.

"I have been searching for an apprentice for a long time," the wizard said, his words slow and overly patient, as if explaining to a child. "I have cast spells of seeking; I have studied the augers and signs. They led me here."

"They couldn't have led you here in time to save his father?" she asked.

"I cannot change the past," the mage said with a shrug, "but I can offer him a better future than any of you here."

"Forgive her, Your Lordship," Willan said, ushering Elimee to the side. "I think I can safely speak on the boy's behalf when I say he would be honored to serve as an apprentice to the great wizard . . . ah . . . the most renowned . . . the famous mage . . . ?"

The wizard smiled at Willan's predicament, his painted teeth a sickly rainbow of color.

"Rexol," he said at last. "My name is Rexol."

Chapter 19

KEEGAN'S EXHAUSTED BODY fought against itself as consciousness slowly returned. His thoughts groggy and muddled, he was only aware that he didn't want to wake up. Not yet. Stubbornly, he kept his eyes closed as scattered images flitted through his mind then vanished, bits and pieces from half-remembered dreams.

But they weren't dreams. They were visions. And they came true.

He knew if he concentrated he could piece together most of what had happened. But he felt no desire to make the effort. It was all meaningless except for one thing: His father was dead.

Aware of the fact but refusing to fully acknowledge it, he forced his mind to another problem.

Where am I?

Though his eyes were still closed, he could tell he wasn't in his own bed. The mattress was firmer than what he was used to. The scents and smells lingering in the air were different from his own room's—not better, or worse; just different.

It was hot under the covers. He was clad in both shirt and slacks. The feel of the clothes was familiar against his skin—comfortable and well worn. But they were ripe with the odor of sweat, as if he had been wearing them for many days.

For several minutes he lay completely still, eyes still clenched tight, hoping the darkness would take him again. But now that he was awake, his body refused to let him ignore its basic needs. An urgent pressure mounting on his bladder eventually won out, and he finally opened his eyes.

He was in a large, square chamber. Through the small, solitary window high on the wall at the foot of his bed he could see it was night outside. A single candle flickered on a table in one corner, casting just enough light to allow him to make out the rest of the details of the room. The walls were stone, gray and unadorned. There were two small beds—the one he lay in, and another on the far side of the room. In the far corner was a large wardrobe; the only other piece of furniture was a single wooden chair next to the table with the melting candle. Someone had set out a plate of food and a large cup. The only exit was a heavy wooden door, closed tight.

Am I in a prison somewhere? Did they lock me away after what I did?

The room didn't actually look like a prison, but Keegan's mind was still trying to sort things out as he rolled out from under the covers. Fortunately there was a chamber pot beneath his mattress, and he took the opportunity to make use of it.

As soon as he finished relieving himself, his stomach began to grumble. Keegan placed the lid on the chamber pot and pushed it back under the bed with his foot. Then he slowly shuffled his way over to the table and sat down. He took a few bites of the bread and cheese on the plate. The bread was plain, but it wasn't stale or hard—it had to have been put out recently. The cheese was sharp and strong, and he reached for the cup to wash it down. The water was warm, but clear and clean in his throat.

After several more bites the worst of his hunger abated, and he made his way back over to the bed. Instead of crawling under the covers, however, he simply sat on the edge, staring down at his hands clasped in his lap.

When he heard the door open a few minutes later, he glanced up to see a young man of roughly his own age step through.

"You're awake," the young man said as he closed the door behind him. He glanced over at the half-finished meal on the table then added, "And you're eating. That's good."

Keegan didn't reply; he had no intention of speaking at all. His curiosity was drowned out by his weariness and the grief of knowing his father was dead. But as the other boy drew closer, he couldn't help but notice the greenish-brown tinge of his skin.

"You're a Dweller!" he barked out in surprise.

The young man's nose crinkled in disgust. "I am one of the Danaan," he said. "*Dweller* is a word we find . . . distasteful. My name is Vaaler."

Vaaler waited a few moments, as if expecting Keegan to offer his own name, or perhaps an apology for offending him. Neither was forthcoming. The shock of seeing one of the legendary Tree Folk had startled him from his grim silence, but he had no intention of speaking again.

"I'm sorry about your father," Vaaler finally said.

Again, Keegan made no response. The Danaan youth shrugged and made his way over to the other bed.

"I'll leave the food there in case you get hungry during the night," he said as he stripped down to his underclothes and climbed beneath the covers. "The candle will go out on its own."

Keegan peeled off his filthy shirt and pants and crawled under the covers of the bed again. With his stomach satiated and his bladder empty, exhaustion took him quickly off to sleep.

When he woke next the sun was shining through the small window. The table had been cleared and Vaaler was gone. Keegan once again used the chamber pot; just as he was finished the door opened and Vaaler came in again. He was carrying a tray with breakfast— a plate covered with eggs and bacon, a knife and fork, and another large cup, though this was juice and not water. He set it down on the table, then turned to go. At the door he paused and glanced back over his shoulder.

"If you need to empty the chamber pot, or you have other business, I can show you where the lavatory is."

"Maybe after I eat," Keegan muttered.

The Danaan raised an eyebrow in surprise at hearing him speak. Instead of leaving, he watched Keegan make his way over to the table.

"I lost my father, too," he said once Keegan had settled into the chair.

"When?"

"Long ago. Before I was even born. I never knew him."

"It's not the same," Keegan said between mouthfuls.

"No, I guess it's not."

Keegan attacked his food, suddenly ravenous. He stuffed it into his mouth as fast as he could, washing it down with great gulps from the cup. The juice was from some type of sour fruit—tangy and bitter, but still tasty. When he was finished, he finally felt up to asking some questions.

"Where are we?" he said, starting with the most obvious. "Is this a prison?"

"Not the way you mean," Vaaler answered, then shook his head. "This is Rexol's estate."

"Rexol?"

"A great wizard. I'm his apprentice. You are, too, now."

"What if I don't want to be his apprentice?" Keegan asked.

"Would you rather have the Order find you?"

Keegan shook his head, his mind still trying to process everything. Despite his grief over his father's loss, he couldn't help but feel a flicker of excitement at what he'd just been told.

"What's it like?" Keegan asked. "Being a wizard's apprentice?"

Vaaler shrugged. "I make the meals. Tend the grounds. Clean the manse. Rexol's strict, but he's not cruel."

"Is that it? Doesn't he teach you how to use magic?"

"Most of the time he's up in his study, doing research. I might not see him for days. And even when I do, he rarely has time to teach me anything himself. Usually he just gives me something to read. Most of what I've learned has come from the books in his library."

"Are you sure he's actually a wizard?"

"Magic isn't as interesting as you think," Vaaler warned him. "It's not like the stories and legends. Real wizards don't run around shooting fire from their eyes and calling lightning down from the sky.

"Chaos is dangerous. You have to be careful before you call on it. It takes weeks—maybe even months—just to learn how to cast a proper spell.

"First, you have to study the rituals and incantations that summon and control the Chaos. You need to say the right words and draw the precise symbols on your flesh to protect yourself. You have to practice them over and over again—hundreds of times—until you have them completely memorized.

"Get one little thing wrong and the Chaos will break free and destroy you. You can't make any mistakes. You have to be flawless. Perfect.

"And even then," Vaaler added, his voice dropping as if he was speaking more to himself than Keegan, "nothing happens."

A long, awkward silence followed. Eager to break it, Keegan finally asked, "How many other apprentices are there?"

"Just me," Vaaler replied. "I've been studying under Rexol for six years, and until now I was the only other person on his estate."

"Sounds lonely."

"It is," the young Danaan admitted. "It is."

Gazing into a small mirror mounted on the wall of his study, Rexol carefully traced the outline of the protective glyphs onto the skin of his face. The hot tip of the metal stylus burned his flesh as it left an indelible trail of ink across his cheeks and around his eyes, but the fresh glow of the witchroot coursing through his system numbed him to the pain.

He was eager to begin training his new apprentice—he'd felt his power; he could already sense the Chaos that burned within his core. But he understood the need to move slowly. The boy had lost his father; pushing him now might cause him to resent his training. Better to wait until he had come to terms with his father's death.

In another day, maybe two, he would go see his newest charge. Until then, he'd continue his studies of the ancient Danaan texts, searching for more information about the Talismans that had given the Slayer the power of the Gods.

He'd left Keegan under Vaaler's care. The two were the same age, and the Danaan prince was far more empathetic and less intimidating than Rexol. He would help ease Keegan into accepting his new life.

Initially, Rexol knew, the boy would cling to the remnants of his past; they were a link to his father. In time, however, the names and faces of the people from his village would fade. Ultimately, they would be swept aside by the all-consuming hunger that would come when Keegan learned to tap into his latent talent. As he became more engrossed in the arts of sorcery and magic, such plain, common folk would cease to have any meaning or significance to him. He'd barely remember them at all, just as Rexol couldn't even be bothered to recall the name of the town where he had found the boy.

Of course, the villagers had already forgotten about their unexpected visitor by now. To keep the Order from seeking Keegan out, Rexol had invoked a powerful incantation to alter their memories when he'd spirited Keegan away. As far as the simple townsfolk were concerned, the Chaos mage had never been there. In their minds, Keegan had perished along with his father in the brutal Raider attack.

Applying the finishing touches to his tattoos, Rexol turned his attention to the manuscript lying open on his desk—a collection of children's stories presented to one of Lassander the Second's daughters. A book of myths and fables. But myths were often echoes of history; there was truth if you knew what to look for.

He'd found several mentions of the Talismans in the leather-bound book's illustrated pages already. Earlier today, for the first time, he'd stumbled across an actual description of what the Talismans were . . . and what they could do.

The Gods bestowed upon the Slayer three Talismans, each forged in the Sea of Fire. The Crown gave him wisdom; by its power he could see across the entirety of the mortal world, peering even into hearts and minds, that he could keep vigil against the Chaos Spawn. The Sword gave him strength; by its power he could defeat any foe, that he might lead the mortal armies against the Chaos Spawn. The Ring gave him magic; by its power he could call upon the raw essence of Chaos, that he might banish the Chaos Spawn from the mortal world.

Rexol's mind reeled with the implications. A Crown that granted omniscience. A Sword that made you invincible. And, most interesting of all, the Ring. Summoning and channeling Chaos was one of the most difficult aspects of any spell. A ring that could draw Chaos directly from the Sea of Fire itself had the potential to grant a wizard almost infinite power . . . providing he knew how to control it.

The pieces are coming together, Rexol thought as he began the soft chant that would once again temporarily transform the strange symbols on the book's pages into words he could understand. The Crown, the Sword, and the Ring—gifts from the so-called Gods. Talismans imbued with the power of Old Magic. Ancient relics, lost for centuries, just waiting to be found by someone strong enough to claim them.

Rexol understood the ways of Chaos. He knew that discovering this passage now, in the wake of finding his new apprentice, was more than mere coincidence.

The wheels have been set in motion, he thought as the arcane words fell from his lips. *Chaos is gathering.*

Chapter 20

THE STREETS OF Callastan's market square were always crowded, but during the high summer merchants and travelers swelled the river port's population to nearly twice its usual size. Scythe didn't mind the summer crowds, even though their humid heat made her already tight-fitting garments cling to her clammy skin.

She was used to the smell: the acrid stench of sour sweat from a thousand unwashed bodies mingling with the thickly sweet fragrance of a hundred varieties of perfume to form a heavy, noxious cloud that crawled slowly through the overstuffed city streets.

Besides, more people meant more purses, and the sheer number and variety of foreigners congregating in the square meant there was always something interesting to be lifted from an unwary shopper's belt or spirited away from a careless merchant's stall. There was no doubt in Scythe's mind: Summer was the best time of the year in Callastan.

People of all types filled the square. There were many in the crowd who shared Scythe's slight build, olive skin, and jet-black hair: The blood of the Islands was strong in Callastan's people. Because of this few gave her even a second glance as she made her way through the square, making her job that much easier. Besides, there were many things far more interesting to look at than an eighteen-year-old woman, attractive though she might be.

The square teemed with sailors on shore leave, men who drove the economy of the great port, each desperate to make the most of his brief time on land. Clad in colorful, billowing silk shirts accented by flaming red or yellow scarves, green- or purple-dyed hair, enormous glittering hoops of gold dangling from their ears, and the bejeweled cutlasses they kept strapped to their hips, the sailors would have stood out in any crowd—except in Callastan.

Here competition for the eye was far too fierce to be drawn by mere gaudy attire. Bare-chested jugglers danced in and out of the teeming masses, tossing glittering blades back and forth high above the heads of the constantly moving spectators. Acrobats painted in a mishmash of tribal, religious, and decorative tattoos flipped and tumbled and rolled in and among the shoppers and merchants, occasionally upsetting a fruit or bread cart in their reckless performance. Wandering minstrels strummed or blew or thumped their instruments, each valiantly struggling to be heard above the cacophony of the constantly haggling crowd. Of course, all of the street performers gave a wide berth to the snarling, club-wielding Enforcers: soldiers in the service of the city who constantly roamed the square in twos or threes, looking for any excuse to start smashing heads.

Witches and alchemists hawked philters and potions in the street, shouting above the incessant clamor of barter, many of their wares illegal anywhere in the Southlands but here in Callastan. Robed magicians conjured towers of fire in the palms of their hands or summoned sparkling crystal showers from the sky to demonstrate their command of Chaos, though Scythe knew how to perform similar theatrics with the right mix of powders, a deft hand, and a gullible audience.

Scythe herself had lost all but a cursory interest in the so-called wonders of the square. She had seen the darker side of Callastan; she understood how the city consumed and devoured people. The sights and sounds of the square meant little when you were starving, or living in the filth of a back alley. For many who dwelled here, life was a grim, never-ending battle. And only the strong survived.

Scythe was one of the strong. She moved through the crowd with confidence, seeking out marks among the merchants and shoppers while at the same time keeping an eye out for other thieves looking to stake their own claim on a likely victim. And though bored with the familiar, she still kept one eye open to appreciate the truly rare sights that materialized from the crowd from time to time.

Last year had seen an abundance of Dwellers in Callastan, brave explorers seeking adventure among the human cities far to the south. One young male had been particularly intriguing, tall and elegant with unfathomably deep sorrow in his violet eyes and striking features. She could still remember the cool feel of the smooth, hairless skin of his bare chest beneath her trembling touch, and the way the dying light from the fire in the corner of his room had brought out the pale green hues of his skin.

Her exotic lover had promised to take her back to his home in the North Forest, a wondrous city built high among the branches of the trees. But Scythe knew better than to believe such pillow talk. She imagined that even among Dwellers promises made in the afterglow of lovemaking vanished with the coming morn. She had slipped away while he slept, taking only her clothes and the memories of their passion, despite a wealth of interesting treasures scattered about his room. And now she couldn't even remember his name. Had she ever known it?

Earlier this morning she had spotted a small cadre of mercenaries in cobalt-blue chain mail, the weeping eye on the crests of their armor proclaiming allegiance to some unknown master in a distant land. As they marched past she had recognized the blond hair and square jaws of the Northern provinces in their faces. The seriousness of their expression had intrigued her, and she had started the day by discreetly following the armed men to discover what business they had in Callastan. And then she had spotted *him,* towering over everyone like some magnificent titan.

In all the time she had lived in Callastan, Scythe could never remember seeing a barbarian from the Frozen East among the crowd before. She had instantly decided he would prove far more interesting than the sober mercenaries in blue, and she had been following him ever since.

Scythe glided through the crush of humanity with a natural grace and ease that had came from several years of practice, her lithe form making subtle twists and turns to get her through the sea of bodies with a minimum of physical contact. The man she followed was not so skilled.

He lumbered through the throng bumping, shoving, and literally bowling people over as he rumbled along. The fact that he stood well over seven feet and had to weigh nearly four hundred pounds didn't make a smooth passage through the crowd any easier—though it did keep the people he knocked over from cursing him in anything louder than a whisper.

Tracking her target through the crowd was simple for Scythe. His enormous height and girth were not the only things making him stand out from the rest of the disparate crowd. It was blatantly obvious to everyone in the square that the enormous man was a savage from the Frozen Lands, even though most of them had, like Scythe, never seen an Easterner before. His style of dress was that of an uncultured brute, for starters. He wore no jewelry and sported no tattoos, nothing to adorn or accentuate his gruff and simple appearance. A tough leather jerkin that covered his torso but left his enormous arms bare, a short leather apron that came down to just above his knee, and a pair of hard leather boots were his only articles of clothing.

The giant's hair was a fiery crimson tangle, cropped to shoulder length but unstyled and wild atop his massive head. His face was all but hidden behind a thick bushy beard of the same color. The relentless summer sun of the Southlands had turned his skin to a blistering, angry red. Large chunks had peeled away, revealing ugly splotches of a pale and sickly white beneath the outermost layer of his sunburned flesh.

The hulking traveler was the lumbering embodiment of every Southland stereotype of the Eastern barbarian—large, brutish, beastly, wild, rough, uncultured, and unmannered. The only thing missing was a weapon, a great axe slung across his back or a heavy broadsword sheathed at his side. But as far as Scythe could tell, this particular savage was unarmed.

She had been following him for nearly half an hour, ever since spying him on the far side of the square and staking her claim with a series of quick hand gestures, a secret code used by the thieves in Callastan to communicate without drawing attention to themselves. The other pickpockets and hustlers who worked the area had acknowledged her claim, steering well clear of her mark. Scythe had earned their professional courtesy two years ago by killing a pair of thugs who had tried to move in on her fledgling pickpocket business.

The men had confronted her with knives drawn, demanding a half share of the day's take. She had paid them without protest, but the next day their two corpses were found naked in the street. Their throats had been slit, their eyes gouged out, their ears sawn off, and their privates removed. Scythe left it to public speculation as to which injuries had been inflicted before death.

The effects of the lesson had been immediate and enduring. Even now, two years later, Scythe had not had any trouble with the other operators in Callastan who also earned their living on the far side of the law.

The barbarian was lost, she decided. He wandered without purpose or any clear sense of direction. He would stop or change direction suddenly, wreaking havoc among those unfortunate enough to be caught in his path and leaving a wake of angry glares and crude but silent gestures directed always at his back.

Scythe didn't think there was much profit to be made from the savage. She hadn't seen a purse or money pouch yet, though it was possible he kept one stuffed deep inside his leather jerkin or tucked beneath the leather kilt. But she suspected he wouldn't be carrying more than a handful of silver, at best. The Frozen East wasn't known for its wealthy merchants. As far as Scythe knew they didn't even use currency in that forsaken land. What good was a gold coin when tracking a herd of elk across the tundra?

But she found his strange appearance and great size intriguing. She followed him out of a sense of curiosity, merely to see where he would go. She couldn't imagine him having business with the merchants within the city, and he didn't have the look of an ambassador or emissary seeking the ear of a bureaucrat or public official. The only logical assumption was that he was looking for the Pleasure District.

Everything was for sale in Callastan, including human flesh. Large, small, dark, light, male, female—whatever one desired could be found, for the right price. Most of the prostitutes congregated in the Pleasure District for the simple convenience of their customers, though there were always a few wandering up and down the busier streets of the square.

Scythe felt a twinge of sympathy for whatever unfortunate girl ended up servicing the giant beast of a man. Three years ago she had emerged alone and vulnerable from the Western Seas. With no coin in her pocket and no one to turn to for help she had been an easy target, and it wasn't long before she had found herself working in the infamous brothels and whorehouses of Callastan simply to survive. Though only fifteen at the time, she had been old enough to service the needs of the depraved men—and occasional women—who sought carnal fulfillment for a fee. From personal experience, she could well imagine the repulsive appetites of this brute from the frozen edge of the world. The savage would stink of sweat and herd animals; she could imagine him mounting his terrified harlot like a rutting bull.

Or perhaps he reveled in the kind of sexual perversity that had made Scythe finally decide she would prefer the life of a thief to that of a whore—acts so vile and brutal Scythe had realized she would rather die in a city jail or starve on the street than subject herself to such torture and degradation ever again. The pattern of scars across her breasts, hips, and back suddenly burned beneath her clothes, angry scourges of a metal-tipped whip that would never heal. Unbidden, her hand went to the razor-thin, almost invisible scar running the length of the left side of her jaw. Reminders of what she once was.

She shook her head and pushed these thoughts away. Callastan had taken much from her: her youth, her innocence. But in exchange it had made her hard and ruthless; it had taught her to survive. And for Scythe survival meant never dwelling on the past.

Only after the giant had ignored several courtesans who had been brazen or desperate enough to approach him and offer their services did Scythe admit to herself that her original guess had been wrong. He continued on his unpredictable path, unintentionally wreaking havoc among the other pedestrians with every change of speed or direction. He seemed oblivious to the events around him. Scythe recognized the bemused look; she had seen it on the faces of more than a few villagers who suddenly found themselves overwhelmed by the relentless sights, sounds, and crowds of the thriving metropolitan streets of Callastan.

A pair of club-carrying Enforcers made their way slowly through the crowd toward the giant. They stopped him and began to speak, casually using their clubs to point at the ever-increasing crowd of angry victims the man's great bulk left in its wake. Someone must have filed a complaint against the foreigner and his clumsy progress.

Bumping people in the street couldn't get you arrested, no matter how frequent the transgression. But a handful of coins in the right hands could buy a vicious beating. Scythe guessed someone had taken their anger toward the barbarian a step farther than glares and offensive gestures.

The savage was speaking to them now, responding to their questions. If he felt intimidated by the soldiers and the none-too-subtle implication of the clubs in their hands, he gave no sign. Of course, Scythe thought, if she was as big as he was she might not be afraid of them, either. She wanted to hear what was being said, but she didn't dare move any closer. It looked as though a fight was imminent, and she didn't relish being close enough to get caught up in the action when the brawl inevitably spread through the crowd. She expected the savage to put up a good fight, though—something worth watching.

Scythe backed away so she could safely watch the action unfold. But to her surprise, nothing happened. The soldiers were nodding their heads in unison, agreeing with whatever the giant was saying. One of them pointed to the far corner of the square not with his club but with his free hand. The giant nodded in response, the mound of unruly hair atop his head flopping with the exaggerated bobbing of his head. And then they left him alone.

Strange. The Enforcers had gone over with the intention of starting a fight, Scythe was sure of that. Somehow the barbarian had talked them out of it. Or maybe up close they realized just how big he really was and thought better of starting something they might not be able to finish. In any case, Scythe was even more intrigued. And a little disappointed. She needed to get closer to this strange visitor if she wanted to figure him out.

Just then Scythe noticed a young man moving stealthily through the crowd toward the barbarian. She flashed a quick hand signal: *Back off. He's mine.* The young man, little more than a boy really, ignored her. Another quick gesture from Scythe. *I claimed him. He's my mark.* No reaction. Maybe the boy was too intent on his potential victim to notice her slight gestures through the crowd. Or maybe he just didn't know the local sign language of the street.

She didn't recognize him; he wasn't one of the regular operators who worked the square. Now that she was closer she could see he had the broad nose and wide, round eyes of the Mosama Islands, though he was dressed so as to better blend in with the Southlanders in the crowd. A common enough story: A young man signs on with a ship's crew and discovers life at sea can be unbearable. Rather than endure the tyranny of his captain, he jumps ship at Callastan but finds the city a cruel and hard place for foreigners with no money. Hungry and desperate and scared, he turns to petty thievery to survive.

New operators were always welcome to ply their trade so long as they followed the rules and respected the claims of others. For the good of her profession, Scythe felt it was her duty to teach the young man a lesson about Callastan's underworld etiquette he wouldn't soon forget. With casual indifference Scythe reached down inside the top of her boot and slid the razor-sharp blade strapped to her calf free from its sheath. She cupped the small knife in her left palm to keep it hidden from view.

The man was an amateur, she decided as she slowly approached— a onetime cabin boy who knew nothing about the trade. The mere fact that he had targeted the barbarian was a sign of his inexperience. *Never steal from the poor* was a lesson most thieves learned rather quickly. And his technique was an embarrassment: clumsy, awkward, and impatient. He was already standing nervously behind the barbarian, his guilt as obvious as the red bandanna wrapped around his neck. It was a wonder the big man hadn't already noticed him and his reckless rush through the crowd to reach his current position.

Scythe realized he wasn't working alone. Scattered among the nearby crowd were three other Islanders wearing red bandannas identical to that of the young pickpocket. They affected a casual stance, but she could tell by the way each man had a hand wrapped around the hilt of his cutlass that they were taking an unnatural interest in the unfolding crime. Probably shipmates who had defected with the cabin boy, the muscle he'd need to protect his ill-gotten gains and stake out his turf. A regular crime ring in the making.

Scythe continued her casual approach through the crowd, keeping the overeager young thief always in her sights. His armed companions changed things somewhat. It would be harder to intimidate a group of four than a single man. She might have to kill the boy for them to really take her point.

She was still a fair distance away when the young man reached forward, blindly slipping his hand beneath the savage's leather apron in the hope he would stumble onto a hidden purse or pouch beneath. The barbarian spun around, moving far quicker than Scythe would have thought possible for a man of his size. The pickpocket was caught completely off guard as one huge paw seized his not-so-innocently placed hand. The young man screamed in surprise then pain as his fingers were crushed in the barbarian's monstrously strong grip, and the brawl Scythe had earlier expected finally broke out.

The three Islanders in the red bandannas whipped out their cutlasses and leapt to the aid of their partner. The one closest to the giant brought his blade around in a tight slashing arc, carving a deep gash in the big man's left forearm and causing him to break his grip on the mangled digits of the shrieking pickpocket. He leapt back an instant after delivering the blow, but he couldn't quite get beyond his foe's unnaturally long reach.

The barbarian's fist smashed into the side of his head and he crumpled to the street, where Scythe lost sight of him through the suddenly panicked crowd. Pandemonium had erupted in the square. Half the people were rushing toward her, fleeing the sudden violence. The other half surged forward, eager to get a better view of the fight—or to join in. As she squeezed her way among the frantic bodies, Scythe noticed several of the club-wielding Enforcers pushing through the mob toward the battle, eager to restore order with a flurry of hard blows delivered to anyone careless enough to get within range.

Scythe forced her way to the edge of the tight circle that had formed around the combatants and instantly appraised the situation. Within the ring of shouting, screaming spectators the fallen Islander lay on the street, the red blood leaking from his ears and nose nearly the same color as the cloth around his neck. From the unnatural angle of his jaw Scythe knew it was broken. Beside him the failed pickpocket knelt with his mauled hand clutched against his stomach, rocking back and forth. High-pitched moans and whimpers escaped his lips, barely audible above the excited shouts and cries of the surrounding crowd.

The other two pirates were engaging the barbarian more cautiously than their unconscious friend. They feinted and dodged, making halfhearted stabs and aborted thrusts toward the crouching giant that drew nothing but air. Neither man was willing to come quite close enough to feel the wrath of those meaty fists, much to the dismay of the bloodthirsty onlookers.

Without warning another pirate launched himself from the crowd and onto the barbarian's broad shoulders. He clung there like a child getting a piggyback, the savage flailing his great arms around in a desperate effort to dislodge this newest foe from his perch. Unlike the other pirates this one wore no bandanna. Simply a man coming to the aid of his fellow Islanders, Scythe decided as she dropped unnoticed to the street beside the whimpering pick-pocket.

"Please," the young man mouthed at her, tears of agony stream-ing from his eyes as he caressed his mangled hand.

With a single fluid motion Scythe sliced the razor hidden in her left palm up across his right cheek, then down along his left, leav-ing two thin but deep cuts that began to well up with blood an instant later. She had spared him his eyes; maybe she was going soft.

Those eyes now looked at her with horror and shock. She didn't say a word, but delivered a sharp strike to his throat with the edge of her unarmed hand. If the boy was smart he would understand the lesson he had just been given. If not, the next time he violated the unwritten code of Callastan's operators someone would prob-ably kill him.

It would be several minutes before the gasping pickpocket would be able to get enough air to even think about getting up, so Scythe turned her attention back to the battle.

The barbarian's arms and legs were slick with the gore oozing from a dozen cruel but superficial gashes on his meaty limbs. The Islanders must have seized the opportunity to bring their cutlasses to bear while the savage had struggled with the Islander on his back. But now they had retreated to a safe distance, their faces a mix of terror and anticipation at what would happen next.

Somehow the big man had gotten ahold of the attacker on his back. The unfortunate Islander squirmed and struggled in the un-breakable grip, his feet kicking and dangling a full foot off the ground. The crowd screamed for blood and Scythe thought the savage would surely give it to them. She half expected the barbar-ian to rip the limbs from the Islander's sockets one by one and hurl them into the crowd. At the very least she though he would break the man's neck.

Instead the Easterner slammed his forehead into the man's face, breaking his nose in an explosion of blood that matched the bar-barian's tangled mane and bushy red beard. The Islander convulsed once then went limp. The barbarian let the unmoving form slip from his grasp onto the ground then carefully stepped over his defeated, but still very much alive, opponent to face the two now reluctant Islanders still standing against him.

The circle of hollering spectators suddenly scattered as the first Enforcer arrived, his club swinging indiscriminately at everyone around him. A moment later a second soldier arrived to aid in the pummeling. Several careless bystanders went down before one of the pirates was dropped with a sharp blow to the base of his skull. The other was tripped up as he tried to escape into the fleeing crowd, and one of the Enforcers was on him before he could scramble to his feet. A savage smash across the elbow disarmed him, and he howled at the agony of his shattered bone as he rolled around helpless on the ground.

Two more soldiers arrived and the four men charged the bar-barian simultaneously, trying to overwhelm him with sheer num-bers. For a second they buried him under their surge, dragging him to the ground beneath their combined weight. But they couldn't keep him down. In the scrum the fists and kicks of the barbarian inflicted more damage than their pounding clubs and a few sec-onds later he was up again—though two of his attackers couldn't achieve the same feat.

Of the two soldiers still standing, one managed to scuttle backward to safety. The other was seized by the enormous warrior and hurled through the air like ballast launched from a catapult. He hit the ground with a dull thud and didn't even try to rise.

The barbarian scooped up the club from one of the fallen combatants and glared over the crumpled and writhing bodies of his many victims at the lone soldier still standing. In his massive hand the Enforcer's weapon looked like a child's toy. The smaller man wisely turned to run only to find himself face-to-face with Scythe—though in truth she just came up to his chin.

She drove her knee hard into his groin. Scythe had never been one to miss an opportunity to extract some measure of revenge on the Callastan police for the many beatings they had given her friends and fellow operators over the years.

The Enforcer's eyes bulged and his club clattered onto the street as his hands involuntarily clutched at his mashed testicles. Ever so slowly he sank to his knees. Over her opponent's shoulder Scythe saw the barbarian's blood-smeared face break into a wide grin.

There was something infectious in his grin, and despite herself Scythe gave him a coy smile in return. Then she delivered a spinning back round kick to the side of the Enforcer's head. The savage laughed as the soldier went down, the imprint of Scythe's heel barely visible in the soft flesh of his temple. The barbarian's deep booming chuckle echoed down the suddenly all but deserted street.

The mob that had gathered to watch the fight had thinned considerably. People always vanished when the Enforcers started to arrive—where there was one there were soon many, many more. Even now Scythe could see a half a dozen of the soldiers gathering at the far end of the street, debating if they should move in to apprehend the barbarian or wait for more reinforcements to arrive.

She suspected they would take their time. There was nowhere in Callastan the barbarian could go that they wouldn't find him. No inn, no tavern, no shop, no street, no alley where a seven-foot-tall mountain of peeling, sunburned, foreign flesh clad in a brown leather apron could hide.

"Come with me," she said, not even sure if the Easterner could understand her.

"Where?" he asked, his accent so thick she could barely make out the single word.

She glanced back at the Enforcers. Instead of six she now counted eight. Eight men huddled a block away, still waiting for a little more backup.

"Just come with me," she ordered.

He shrugged amicably, dropped the now unnecessary club to the ground, and followed Scythe around the nearest corner and into a narrow alley. She paused to consider whether his enormous girth would make escape impossible. It would be a tight fit, she decided, but doable.

"In there," she said, pointing at a sewer hole built into the stones beneath their feet.

He bent down and pulled the heavy iron grate covering the dark passage aside with ridiculous ease, then recoiled at the stench wafting up from below. He gave her a skeptical glance, but she met his unspoken inquiry with a firm nod. It wasn't likely the Enforcers would follow them into the reeking tunnels beneath the city; their wages were good, but not that good.

"In," she said again, as if speaking to a small child.

The savage gave her another of his wide grins, sucked in his massive gut, and lowered himself into the sewers of Callastan. Scythe took a last look to see if anyone had followed them into the alley. Once sure the coast was clear, she disappeared into the sewers after him.

Chapter 21

"*Tasre feim yinl maouk.*"

The words of the Old Tongue still felt strange in Keegan's mouth. Each one fell from his lips with an awkward thud.

"You're trying too hard," Vaaler offered. "Thinking about it too much."

The Danaan prince was lying on his back in bed, staring up at the ceiling with his hands clasped behind his head. Keegan was sitting at the small table in their shared room, head bowed over the parchment containing the words of the spell he was trying to memorize for tomorrow's trial.

Keegan nodded, took a deep breath, and started over.

"*Tasre feim yinl maouk.*"

"Try to let the words flow," Vaaler said, interrupting him again. "Don't think of them each individually. There's a natural cadence to the spell. Like this: *Tasre feim yinl maouk.*"

As he spoke, the words rolled into one another, blending in a smooth, unbroken rhythm.

Easy for you, Keegan thought. *You've been practicing for years.*

He knew better than to say what he was thinking out loud. In the two years since he'd come under Rexol's charge, Vaaler had done everything he could to help Keegan adjust to life as a wizard's apprentice. He considered the young man a friend—maybe his only real friend—and he didn't want to hurt him with the truth.

Despite Vaaler's long tenure under Rexol, the Danaan had never successfully summoned Chaos. He understood the theories of magic and sorcery; he had memorized the incantations for several dozen spells. Yet for all his study and practice, he would never become a wizard—he lacked the essential spark of power burning inside him.

Keegan had sensed its absence soon after he began his own studies. When he had asked Rexol about it, his master had carefully avoided giving him any kind of real answer. *The incantations and charms help us focus. They are tools to channel and control the Chaos. They augment our abilities, but the source of our power comes from within.*

He suspected that, on some level, Vaaler knew his training was futile. But that hadn't stopped him from helping Keegan with his own studies.

"The witchroot will help tomorrow," Vaaler assured him. "It makes it easier to let go. You'll stop trying to control things, and just let them happen."

He knew Vaaler was right. Under Rexol's supervision, Keegan had been taking regular doses of the drug to build up his tolerance to its effects for several months. Wrapped in the witchroot's euphoric glow, it was almost impossible to feel hesitant or nervous.

But here and now, on the night before his first attempt at summoning Chaos, he was plagued by doubts.

"What if something goes wrong?" he wondered aloud, turning in his chair to face his friend. "What if I make a mistake?"

"There's an old Danaan saying," Vaaler replied. "*A student's failure reflects on the teacher.* If you're not ready for this, its Rexol's fault for pushing you too fast."

"I don't think he'd see it that way."

"Probably not," Vaaler admitted, sitting up on the edge of his bed. "But its not like he's going to send you away if you forget the words to your first spell and nothing happens."

"That's not what I'm worried about," Keegan said after a moment's hesitation. "What if I summon the Chaos and I lose control?"

Vaaler laughed. "That's why you're afraid of it? Honestly, that's the last thing I'd be worried about."

But I'm not like you.

Vaaler didn't know about Keegan's Gift. He hadn't told him about his prophetic dreams, or about how he'd unleashed Chaos to kill the raider who murdered his father. Vaaler studied the lessons because he wanted to prove himself to his mother and his people. But Keegan's motivation was different.

He'd felt the raw power of Chaos surging through his body. He'd killed another man. He'd almost killed himself. He understood magic in a way Vaaler never would. Its devastating potential terrified him, but it also exhilarated him. If he didn't learn to control his power, he was convinced it would kill him. But if he was able to master it—to bend the Chaos to his will—he would never have to be afraid of anyone or anything again.

"I wish I could be there tomorrow," Vaaler said. "For moral support. But I guess Rexol doesn't want you to have any distractions."

Or maybe he's afraid of what might happen to you if something goes wrong.

"I should practice some more," Keegan said, turning his attention back to the words on the page.

"Are you ready?" Rexol asked.

The words seemed far away to Keegan, muffled as if he were hearing them from underwater. The small doses of witchroot he'd been taking over the past months hadn't prepared him for the massive dose Rexol had given him in preparation for the trial.

They had gathered in a small clearing in the gardens at the back of the manse's grounds. Keegan was standing inside a small circle of white stones, each painted with arcane glyphs. Rexol stood outside the circle, a dozen feet away and slightly off to the side. Across the clearing was a stone pedestal; like the stone at his feet it was painted with powerful runes of warding. Atop the pedestal was a small pile of twigs.

"Are you ready?" Rexol repeated, slamming the butt of his gorgon's-head staff sharply down on the grass at his feet. It gave off a sharp crack, drawing his apprentice's attention.

Keegan looked over at his master and nodded.

"Remember your lessons. There is power in the charm, but it is only a conduit. It will channel and augment your spell, but it is you who must control the Chaos that is summoned. Look to your own power . . . the charm is nothing without it."

The apprentice clutched the charm tightly in his fist. It was a small, jagged crystal: a frozen giant's tear. The rough edges bit into the skin of his palm, the pain helping him focus.

"Recite the words of the spell exactly as you have learned them. The incantation will shape and bind the Chaos. Without it the magic will fight against you; you will exhaust yourself battling to contain it.

"Whatever happens, do not step out of the rune circle," Rexol sternly reminded him. "The inscriptions on the stones at your feet will keep you safe if something goes wrong. Step beyond the wards and the fires of Chaos will devour you."

This time Keegan didn't nod, but only shuddered. A cold fear clutched at his stomach. Memories of the night his father died leapt unbidden to his mind, images floating in the fog of the witch-root: fire, the Raiders, his father's broken body, a storm of power and destruction . . .

"Concentrate!" Rexol snapped. "Focus! Put all other thoughts aside. Reach out with your mind and let it touch the Burning Sea. Draw its power to you."

Keegan did as he was told, and the Chaos began to gather.

Rexol felt the air tremble as his apprentice tapped into the source of all magic. His staff thrummed in his grasp, the glyphs carved into the shaft responding to the gathering Chaos. Keegan was strong. Far stronger than any of his previous apprentices had been, except maybe the girl Cassandra. He had sensed the young man's power from the first day he had brought him here, numb with the horror of his father's death and reeling from the shock of the Chaos he had unleashed to avenge him. Even in that ravaged, grief-stricken mind he had felt the potential and realized he would have to be careful with this one. Keegan was a true wizard, with power that might one day rival Rexol's own . . . if he dared to use it again.

The boy had witnessed his father's death; he had felt the awesome fury of Chaos unbound surging through him. He knew firsthand the horrors it could bring. From the very start, Rexol had known he would have to bring him along slowly. Even in the best of circumstances, the transition from mortal to mage was not an easy one.

Fortunately, Vaaler had been there to make the transition easier. He had helped Keegan in ways a master never could. Rexol needed to remain aloof; he needed to maintain an aura of mystery, authority, and even fear to properly instruct the young wizard. He could offer no comfort to his charge. Vaaler, however, was an equal and a peer: two apprentices housed together in the otherwise empty servants' quarters of the manse.

The young men had much in common. Neither had any siblings; both had a parent they had never known. Both had lived lonely, isolated childhoods: Keegan because of his father's frequent moves, Vaaler because of the burden of his impending ascension to the throne. And both found themselves in the service of a cold and distant master, with little outside contact. It was inevitable a bond would form between them.

The Chaos was building quickly. Within the rune circle, his apprentice was surrounded by swirling blue flames, though the glyphs kept him safe from harm. The roaring power echoed in Rexol's mind, and beneath the rumble he heard Keegan begin to recite the arcane words of the spell that would tame the wild power of the magic.

He spoke with a clear confidence Rexol recognized; he had

heard it before in Vaaler's recitations. Not surprising, given that the Danaan had been helping Keegan with his lessons. Though he didn't possess a single drop of Chaos in his blood, Vaaler was an excellent student of the mage's art. He easily grasped the complex theories behind magic and sorcery. He compulsively studied the intricate rituals of summoning and controlling Chaos, perfectly memorizing spells he would never be able to cast.

Obviously, he had passed his own knowledge on to Keegan. Rexol had suspected as much and allowed it, up till now. At least the prince's knowledge would not be wasted. For while Vaaler had neither the Gift nor the Sight, Keegan was strong in both. Like Cassandra had been, long ago. She had been taken from him, lost to the Order before he could fully explore her power and potential. This time Rexol had no intention of letting anything come between him and his pupil.

Which was why he would have to send Vaaler away soon. The prince was a born leader, intelligent and charismatic. He would make a fine king, should the Danaan ever chose to accept his rule. But he was no wizard; he had no place in Keegan's future training or life.

Over the past two years his apprentices had become like brothers; each would give anything to help the other. But an apprentice's only allegiance should belong to his master. It was time to make Keegan understand this.

The world had taken on a haze, as if seen through a cloud of cerulean smoke.

Keegan recoiled as the blue flames licked at his skin: an instinctive reaction only, for the fire didn't burn. But even though he flinched, he continued the mystic chant flawlessly, the strange words tumbling effortlessly from his lips.

The talisman burned hot in his hand, but he dared not let it go. He could feel the Chaos spiraling around him, *through* him. It seeped down into his pores; his blood began to tingle, then boil.

But still he felt no pain. The Chaos was his to control, bound by the strength of his will and the power of his words. Slowly, he raised his head, still reciting the arcane litany. His eyes pierced the blue haze and focused on the small stone pedestal across the court-yard. He could just make out the twigs and tinder piled on its surface; they blended in with the runes inscribed across its surface.

Keegan lifted his hand. The Chaos swept around his arm, climb-ing up and shooting out from his upraised palm. It arced across the courtyard in a single bolt of heat, striking the kindling just as he uttered the last words of his spell. For a brief moment he saw the wood burst into flame and felt the heady rush of accomplishment. And then his world exploded in agony.

Rexol smiled to himself as the Chaos leapt from Keegan's hand across the courtyard to its target, knowing what the outcome would be. But his smile vanished when the flames engulfed the rune-covered pedestal. The dry sticks vanished into ash; the stone cracked from the intense heat, then began to sag and droop as the fire turned the slab into molten rock.

The glyphs of warding echoed the power of Keegan's spell, shooting a blast of fire back onto the young wizard, enveloping him in the searing blue flames. He screamed and dropped to the ground, tumbling out of the rune circle . . . which should have been impossible.

Rexol thrust his staff to the heavens, shouting out a desperate counter-spell of his own. The fire leapt up in response, twin col-umns ascending from Keegan's crumpled body and the bubbling pool that had once been a stone pedestal. The surging flames crashed together above the gorgon's skull, then dove down into Rexol himself, instantly snuffing out the fire wrapped around his apprentice's unconscious form.

The wizard staggered back as the Chaos slammed into him. He felt it raging inside, tearing him apart. Never had he felt such pain; never had he felt such power! Only decades of training allowed him to focus his will in the face of such blissful agony. He spat out harsh words to batter the flames, yanking them out of his body and hurling them into his staff. The eyes of the gorgon's skull blazed with unholy blue light; the staff trembled and shook, the Chaos trapped within threatening to burst it into splinters and dust.

Spinning the staff above his head, he shrieked out a spell to unleash the Chaos upon the world. It poured forth like a great wind, rushing up to disappear high above the clouds. For an instant all was still; then the sky exploded in a storm of thunder, lightning, and rain. Within seconds Rexol was soaked to the bone, but he ignored the downpour as he rushed over to kneel beside Keegan's huddled form.

He was unconscious, but not seriously injured. Rexol cursed himself as he picked his apprentice up and carried him back inside the manse, showing far more strength than anyone would have expected from his lean frame. Even after a year of studying Keegan, of subtly pushing and testing the limits of his power, he had underestimated him. The Chaos had reflected back from the pedestal as he had intended, but instead of a brief and painful flash to scare his apprentice, it had become an inferno.

Keegan had nearly died today; they both had. A second more and Rexol himself would have been consumed by the surging Chaos; he had been forced to unleash the unbound magic out upon the world to survive. Who knew what consequences the backlash of that savage storm would bring?

With hardly any effort, he climbed the stairs to the servants' quarters. Disaster had been narrowly averted, but all was not lost. The lesson had been far more harsh than he had intended, but it was a lesson Keegan was not likely to forget. The Chaos had nearly devoured him, and only the intervention of his master had saved his life.

Outside the storm still raged.

Chapter 22

SCYTHE STUDIED THE small one- and two-story buildings of the town with disdain as the storm pelted them with cold, stinging drops. Her horse walked with its head down, beaten into submission by the relentless rain, plodding slowly through the thick mud of what passed for the main road in the hamlet.

"There." Norr's deep voice cut through her thoughts.

She glanced in the direction he pointed at the faded sign of the Singing Dragon Inn and simply nodded. They had eaten just after dawn, barely two hours ago. Had they known this town was so close they would have ridden on last night instead of making a rain-soaked camp in the surrounding forests. But this burg was too small to even warrant a mention on the map they had purchased at the last town they had stayed in.

The weight of their recent breakfast was still heavy in Scythe's stomach, but at the sight of the inn Norr was ready to eat again. She had come to realize in their year together that he ate whenever the opportunity presented itself. The barbarian was at least three times her size, so it was only natural he would eat far more than she—and far more often. And she didn't expect him to change. Norr's girth was as much a part of him as his long red hair, bushy, fiery beard, or perpetually sunburned skin. Her lover was a tribesman of the Frozen East; a savage, a barbarian; wild, free, and given to lusty appetites—in all things.

She had learned this their first night together, after she had rescued him from the Enforcers in Callastan. Hidden safely away in Scythe's secret refuge beneath the city streets their coupling had been primal and furious, raw animal heat. But Norr could be gentle, too. Later he had entered her again with an almost shy tenderness, his beard scratching softly against her neck as his parched, cracked lips kissed her scarred shoulders. His callused hands had caressed the marks left by the whips and knives on her back and thighs, and his wide blue eyes had welled up with tears.

Norr never asked her about her wounds, the deforming scars that marred her naked beauty. He hadn't even asked her name that first night. It was she who had offered it, though why even now she couldn't say. He was not the first stranger she had lain with, not the first exotic foreigner to share a night of pleasure with her. But he was the first she had ever given her name, whispering it like a profession of love into the darkness while he had slept beside her: "Scythe."

Between his heavy snores he had grumbled "Norr" in return.

Maybe that was why she was still with him. He accepted her for what she was now, in the present. He cared nothing about her past. He had never once asked her about it, as if it didn't matter. As if she had been born again, freed from her own history by their first night together.

The barbarian's own past was as much a mystery to Scythe as hers must have been to him. He had told her once he would never return to his homeland but hadn't elaborated. She was briefly tempted to ask him why; she suspected it had something to do with the fact that he never wore a weapon at his side. But in the end it didn't matter. They were together now, and life was good.

Good, but not easy. Their partnership was not without its trials, though Scythe had never considered leaving her lover. She was irresistibly drawn to Norr: his great size, his exotic appearance, his unknown past. But it was more than curiosity that drew her to him. Around Norr, she didn't always have to be on guarded edge. When they were together she could feel the tension in her shoulders slipping free and the sharpness of her ever-alert gaze giving way to half-lidded eyes of dreamy contentment.

It wasn't that Norr made her feel safe; Scythe could take care of herself. She had done so ever since she had escaped the brothel she had been forced to work at on her arrival in Callastan. If anything, Scythe felt she was the one who had to protect Norr when they were together: He seemed so innocent, so naïve about the often ruthless culture of the civilized Southlands and its people. Scythe was tough and strong and hard and she didn't need any man to make her feel safe. But Norr didn't make her feel safe, the barbarian made her feel . . . soft.

Scythe had been given her first glimpse of what future awaited her and Norr while still in Callastan. No one had died in the brawl in the streets but the Enforcers had been humiliated and they were determined to apprehend those responsible so they could make a harsh lesson of them. The reward for Norr's capture had been substantial, and his description had spread quickly through the city. Even in the cosmopolitan culture of Callastan, the big man was impossible to overlook.

The darkest, dankest corners of Callastan's underworld slums couldn't keep him from being discovered. With the reward being offered Scythe knew the thieves and cutthroats she counted as her friends wouldn't think twice about betraying the savage's location to the authorities. The unspoken trust among those who operated on the far side of the law in Callastan didn't apply to Norr; he was a stranger, a foreigner, an interloper.

And so they had left, together.

A tip from a young harlot Scythe had once saved from the hands of three drunken soldiers on leave gave the pair just enough warning to pack some meager belongings, steal a pair of horses, and ride out under the cover of night before a score of guards had descended on the hidden sewer sanctuary they had been living in beneath Callastan's market square.

There had been no regret in leaving the city behind, not on Scythe's part. And Norr had been eager to move on, too. He had arrived seeking work as a guard or hired mercenary and instead had been assaulted by civilians and the authorities alike. They had ridden off side by side, laughing together at the rush of adrenaline as they escaped into the concealing mantle of the night, determined to make a new start somewhere else in the Southlands.

But their new life had been much like their old. Scythe was afraid the Callastan authorities would send messages via their court mages to the Seven Capitals and any other city of note, so they had avoided the larger metropolises of the Southlands. But the smaller cities came with their own dangers.

Everywhere they went she and Norr were treated with suspicion and mistrust—it was impossible to hide her Islander heritage, or his Eastern blood. Thinly veiled prejudice and not-so-thinly veiled hatred often greeted them. In smaller towns their presence was tolerated for a few weeks at most before stores and inns simply refused to serve them. In some cases they had been driven out by threats or armed vigilante mobs eager to rid their tiny community of the barbarian in their midst. Once or twice things had gotten ugly, if more so for the townsfolk than for Norr or Scythe. Even though he carried no sword or axe the barbarian was more than a match for as many as a dozen untrained farmers and store owners wielding wooden planks, farm implements, and other makeshift weapons.

Usually Scythe would stay back and let Norr have his fun with those mobs foolish enough to take him on—the fighting seemed to take away some of the big man's sting at being driven out like a diseased beggar. Yet on those few occasions when Norr found himself overmatched or overwhelmed through sheer numbers Scythe would have to intervene—much to the ultimate dismay of the vigilantes.

Norr fought with his fists and bare hands; to him it was little more than a roughhousing game. Scythe fought with weapons, her razor-sharp daggers used to injure and maim, though Norr had asked her not to kill anyone if possible. So far she had been able to fulfill his wish, though the price of an ear or an eye had been paid many times over in the small farming communities Scythe and Norr had passed through.

The larger towns were better. Cities where strangers were many and travelers were common allowed Scythe and Norr to blend into the transient population—as best Norr could ever hope to blend in, anyway. People in the larger cities tended to mind their own business, with few of the residents going out of their way to make trouble for the odd pair walking their streets.

Often they could stay several weeks in such a place. Norr would seek work as a laborer, a soldier, a mercenary, a bodyguard; all in vain. Nobody respectable would hire him, convinced he was little more than a beast; an animal in human form. Scythe knew the intelligence behind his brutish exterior. He had learned the common language of the Southlands in only a matter of months, though he still spoke with a gruff, thick accent. And she knew how it tore at his insides to be rejected day in and day out, denied a chance to earn his living, barred from earning his way through honest sweat.

At least Scythe could find work in the cities. She would work the crowds of the local markets, deftly removing purses and pouches from unsuspecting marks. Norr had once suggested he work with her but like all the others she had refused him.

His mere presence would draw attention, make people suspicious, and put them on guard. He had pointed out he could provide protection in case she was ever caught in the act but Scythe was never that careless. The only protection he could give would be against the groping, grabbing hands of the dirty old men who sometimes pawed at her from the anonymity of the crowd. And even these Scythe preferred to handle on her own with a sharp chop of her fist that could easily numb the fingers or break a thumb.

Besides, Scythe suspected Norr wasn't comfortable with her chosen profession. Barbarians had little use for theft, constantly surrounded by the members of their own tribe. The tribe was family; you didn't steal from your family. The possessions of other tribes, Scythe imagined, would be the spoils of war. You earned your claim by right of the sword, not by stealth and cunning. Theft had no place in such a culture.

So she would support them with her ill-gotten gains while Norr tried in vain to find legitimate employment. She knew he hated that life, but Norr never complained. He never turned his frustration or anger toward her.

Eventually, Scythe would draw the attention of the local operators. Sometimes they would give her a warning: Join them, or leave town. But she knew the cut the established operators took from newcomers was in itself a crime. She had paid her dues long ago, and even though that counted for nothing outside the borders of Callastan, professional pride wouldn't let her hand over four-fifths of her take like some green cutpurse.

Sometimes the local underworld wouldn't give her the courtesy of a warning. The first attempt on her life was inevitably sloppy, an amateur sent to earn a reputation by disposing of the troublesome newcomer. Scythe was a survivor; she had an instinct for traps and danger. It was only because of her promise to Norr that the would-be assassins managed to escape with their lives to report back to the higher-ups.

Scythe was brave but she wasn't foolish. She knew better than to stay in a city long enough for a second, well-planned attempt to be made on her life—or on Norr's. And so inevitably they would be forced to leave the larger cities just as they were always forced to leave the smaller towns.

It had been that way ever since that night they had fled Callastan together, but Scythe wouldn't have traded a minute of it for anything. In Norr she had found something she hadn't even known she was missing, and the travel and the danger only made things more interesting. And if Norr didn't like it, at least he didn't complain.

They were nearly at the inn when a matronly woman poked her head out of a nearby door to get a better look at the strangers riding through the storm and into town. Scythe, ever aware of her surroundings, turned in her saddle to meet the townswoman's eye with a challenging gaze.

To Scythe's surprise the woman didn't duck back into the safety of her home, but instead met the challenge with a smile.

"A wet and goodly morning to you," the lady called out cheerily, "welcome to Praeton."

"We're just passing through," Scythe answered quickly. "Trying to ride out the storm. Do you know if there's any room at the inn?"

"Always room for guests at the Singing Dragon," the woman replied. "Good food, clean rooms, and fair prices."

When Scythe didn't bother to say anything in reply, Norr chimed in with his deep baritone. "Your kindness is much appreciated."

"Think nothing of it. We have a saying in Praeton—*Kindness is free and plentiful, so spread it around.*"

Scythe struggled to keep from rolling her eyes, but Norr laughed heartily.

"A fine saying."

"One we take to heart," the woman assured him. "Hope you find Praeton to your liking. Could use a strapping lad like you around here during harvesttime, if you decide to stay awhile."

Much to Scythe's surprise, Norr said, "Maybe we will."

Chapter 23

A HEAVY CRACK of thunder woke Cassandra. She lay motionless on the thin sleeping mat in her otherwise empty room, peering up at the ceiling through the total darkness with her mystical second sight as the rain fell and lightning split the sky above the Monastery.

This was no ordinary storm; at its heart she could sense the sinister echo of the Chaos that had spawned it. The dark clouds had swept across the Southlands, causing massive flooding. Like many of the other Seers, she had seen the cataclysmic aftermath of the storm in her dreams as it approached—crops and even homes washed away by rivers that had jumped their banks; bloated corpses of drowned livestock left rotting in the fields as the waters receded. But tonight her sleep hadn't been plagued by visions of the flood. Tonight she had dreamed of her old master and a wondrous crown.

Dreaming of Rexol wasn't unusual—it happened so frequently she no longer attached any real importance or meaning to it. But the crown was new. There was something special about the crown. Something significant. It wasn't forged from gold or precious metal—it was made of iron. Simple and plain, but it burned with a radiance so intense it had blinded her to everything else.

She rose from her mat and crossed to the door of her room, her steps confident and sure despite the darkness.

Interpreting dreams—even her own—was not her responsibility. She had to tell the Pontiff. He had the wisdom to help her understand the vision.

I must tell him about Rexol, too, she thought as she made her way slowly down the halls of the Monastery's barracks. *He was part of the vision. His presence may be significant.*

Her arm began to itch and she scratched at it absently, unaware of the invisible mark the wizard had left upon her.

The door to Nazir's chamber was closed; a purely symbolic gesture. Had she wanted to, Cassandra could have easily reached out with her second sight to peer beyond the wooden portal. However, doing so would have been a gross violation of the Pontiff's privacy. Instead, she curbed her awareness at the threshold and knocked instead.

"Come in, Cassandra," the Pontiff's voice called out from the other side.

She pushed the door open and allowed her awareness to extend into the room. Only then did she realize the Pontiff wasn't alone—Yasmin was with him. The elderly head of the Order sat cross-legged on the floor, his features a mask of eternal calm. The Prime Inquisitor towered over him, her face twisting into an expression of contempt as Cassandra entered the room.

"What do you want?" she demanded.

Cassandra hesitated for a second, wondering if she should address her or the man she actually wanted to speak to.

"I seek interpretation of a dream," she said pointedly. "As is my right as a Seer."

She had learned long ago that calling on the ancient customs and traditions of the Order was the best way to blunt Yasmin's rage. With a curt nod of her bald, scarred head, the taller woman deferred and stepped back.

"Tell me of your vision, Cassandra," the Pontiff encouraged, motioning for her to approach.

She came farther into the room, scratching at her arm. Her earlier resolve to tell the Pontiff everything about her dream wavered.

Yasmin already considered her to be tainted from her time under Rexol's charge. Mentioning his presence in her vision would only give fuel to the fires of her mistrust.

Rexol isn't relevant anyway, she thought. *The crown is what's new. The crown is the important part.*

"I saw a crown," she said. "It was made of iron, but it glowed with the power of Chaos."

"That's it?" Yasmin said with a sneer. "A glowing crown?"

The Pontiff held up a hand to silence her.

"A crown can represent many things," he said, speaking slowly as if choosing his words with great care. "It can signify a king, or a general. Any type of leader or authority figure, really . . . even me.

"Was there anything else significant about the dream?" he pressed. "Were there any other details?"

Cassandra opened her mouth, determined to tell him about Rexol despite her misgivings about Yasmin. But to her own surprise, she promptly shut it again and remained silent. Rubbing her arm, she gave a shake of her head.

"I'm sorry, Pontiff. All I saw was the crown."

"While the storm looms over the Monastery, we are under the veil of Chaos," the Pontiff said by way of reassurance. "Much is obscured or hidden.

"I will speak with the other Seers," he continued. "If your dream was fractured by the storm, others may have seen pieces that will help make the vision whole."

"The storm can also twist and corrupt the power of those who are weak," Yasmin chimed in. "While it persists we must be wary of false prophecies that will lead us astray."

"My visions are pure," Cassandra declared, clenching her teeth but keeping her voice calm.

Again the Pontiff held up his hand, cutting off any further argument.

"The storm will pass soon," he reminded them. "Once it is gone, Cassandra may dream of the crown again. She may see her vision more clearly.

"Or perhaps the vision will simply fade away when the storm recedes, and we will know the crown was a meaningless fragment spawned by Chaos.

"But there is nothing to be gained by arguing over it now," he concluded.

Realizing she had been dismissed, Cassandra nodded in acceptance of his wisdom and turned to go, closing the door behind her.

After Cassandra left, the Pontiff could sense Yasmin's blind gaze hovering on him. She was his right hand; she knew him better than anyone, and she was trained in the arts of detecting lies and half-truths. She sensed he had been holding something back.

"You think there is meaning behind her dream," Yasmin declared.

I think the Chaos of the storm has heightened her powers, the Pontiff thought. *I think she senses the Talisman locked away beneath the Monastery.*

"Cassandra is one of our strongest and most reliable Seers," he said aloud. "I would be a fool to dismiss her visions out of hand."

Yasmin did not know about the Crown. That knowledge—the Talisman's power, its potential, and how to safely use it—was reserved exclusively for the Pontiff. When Nazir's reign ended and the True Gods called him home, his successor would learn of it through the archives of his personal writings, just as he had learned of it when he unsealed the archives of his predecessor upon ascending to his current position.

I've assumed that successor would be you, Yasmin, he thought, his attention focused on the tall woman with the bald and badly scarred scalp. *But maybe this vision is a sign that Cassandra will be the one to eventually take my place.*

Cassandra was young, but so was Yasmin. They both had the strength to one day lead the Order, though Nazir knew they would do so in very different ways. With the Legacy weakening, he'd thought Yasmin's fierce zealotry might be needed to lead them to victory in a war against the Slayer's followers. But maybe Cassandra's quiet resolve would serve the cause better. Perhaps the Legacy could be preserved and war avoided altogether.

"This storm has blinded the Seers," Yasmin noted, interrupting his train of thought. "All they can see is floods and destruction. So why is Cassandra still having other visions?"

"Do you think Cassandra is lying?" the Pontiff wanted to know. "Do you think she can no longer tell the difference between a true vision and a regular dream?"

These were serious accusations to level against a Seer, and Yasmin was quick to back away from the implication.

"I am not making any formal charge," she insisted. "As always, I defer to your wisdom, Pontiff. I only ask that you remember the source of this storm when you consider her vision."

The Pontiff sighed. "We have no proof Rexol is responsible."

"But if he was, it would make sense that his former apprentice would be the only Seer able to see beyond it."

"You overestimate the wizard's influence on Cassandra," he said. "She has been with us far longer than she was ever with him. Her only connection to him now comes through your suspicion and accusations."

Though it's possible she has some connection to the Crown. Is it calling to her? Is that why she saw it in her vision? Will she be able to master it and use its power in ways even I never dared?

"As Prime Inquisitor it is my duty to question," Yasmin reminded him.

"But the final judgment is mine," he countered. "Cassandra's loyalty is not in doubt. You should focus your attention on a real traitor."

"Jerrod," Yasmin said, the name dripping with bile and venom.

"That is why I summoned you," the Pontiff reminded her. "We have reports from Pilgrims in the North. Someone is spreading the heresy of the Burning Savior in the Free Cities."

"So he's finally crawled out of his hole," Yasmin said with a predatory smile.

"Not him, but new disciples he has recruited to his cause. Their numbers are growing."

"I will send Inquisitors to the North," Yasmin declared. "We will hunt down these heretics and crush them. We will root out every one of his followers until one of them leads us to him.

"With your permission, of course, Pontiff," she hastily added.

"On the matter of Jerrod," the old man assured her, "we are in total agreement."

"This time," Yasmin vowed, "the traitor won't escape."

Chapter 24

KEEGAN WATCHED VAALER packing his belongings with a powerful mix of emotions: sorrow, regret, guilt . . . and relief. A score
of Danaan guards were waiting in the courtyard to escort Vaaler
home, and though he was sad to see his friend go, Keegan knew his
departure would put an end to the tension that had been growing
between them.

Six weeks ago Keegan had unleashed the power of Chaos on the
mortal world. And even though he had lost control of the spell and
nearly been consumed by the terrible blue flames, he recognized it
as the single greatest moment of his life.

He'd felt the touch of Chaos before: in his dreams, and in the
primal release of fury that had killed the man who murdered his
father. But in those instances the Chaos had come unbidden and
uncalled—he was little more than a conduit for its power.

Rexol's trial had been completely different. Through the incantation of the spell, he had summoned the power and bent it to his
will. Before the spell overwhelmed him, he had sensed the infinite
potential in his grasp. In that instant, he'd known for the first time
who and what he truly was. He was a wizard—a mage who would
one day control the very fires of creation.

He'd tried to explain that sensation to Vaaler. The heat of the
fire that didn't burn; the rush of Chaos ripping through him; even

the terror and searing pain when he lost control had all filled him with a sort of mad ecstasy. It was hard to imagine a more horrible way to die, but it was impossible not to want to try it again.

It sounds like some type of madness, Vaaler had replied, and Keegan realized that he'd never understand. Empty words couldn't do justice to the euphoria he'd felt. And from that moment, there had been a distance between them, subtle yet undeniable.

Rexol had warned him this would happen.

You have the Gift, Keegan; it sets you apart from other men. They will never truly know you; they can never understand the power you wield.

You are touched by Chaos. You are marked. Yours is a destiny beyond the comprehension of ordinary mortals, and in time they will resent you for it.

Even Vaaler, though he will one day rule a kingdom, is beneath you. A true Chaos mage has no friends and no equals, save for another mage.

It wasn't that Vaaler was bitter or jealous. Not overtly. When he had learned of Keegan's success, he had been genuinely pleased for his friend. But at the same time it was impossible not to sense his frustration and disappointment with his own failure. The prince had come here as a young boy, sent away by his mother and his people in the hope he would return a wizard. He had dedicated years of his life to this cause, and made no progress whatsoever. Keegan's success stripped away the illusion that Vaaler's failures could ever be overcome.

Looking at his friend, he couldn't help but feel pity for him.

"It's going to be boring here once you're gone," Keegan said, desperate to break the somber silence that hung over the room.

"I'm sure Rexol will keep you busy," Vaaler replied with a shrug as he continued to pack. "You'll be working so hard you won't even know I'm missing."

There was some truth in what he said. Since that day, Rexol had increased Keegan's studies and responsibilities tenfold. In addition to memorizing several new spells, he was now studying translated versions of the Danaan manuscripts that had been the price of Vaaler's tutelage. In time he would learn to use magic to decipher the words himself. But for now, his master just wanted him to become familiar with the legends and histories of the Danaan people.

Rexol had also instructed him to keep a dream journal: Each morning he had to record every detail he could remember from the night before. Initially, Keegan had objected to this as pointless: Most of the time his dreams were just like anyone else's, a mix of the bizarre and insignificant. And when his dreams gave him glimpses into the future—something that hadn't happened since he'd foreseen his father's death—the images were vivid and unforgettable.

The visions you remember are simply the strongest manifestations of Chaos, Rexol had explained. *But there could still be prophetic hints buried in the dreams you don't remember.*

As you continue your training, Rexol had added, *your mind will become more focused on the Gift. Your waking mind will become more adept at summoning and controlling Chaos. As a result, your Sight will grow weaker, and it will be more difficult for you to recognize Chaos speaking to you through your subconscious.*

Keegan had eagerly accepted the new terms of his apprenticeship. He knew the extra work, while daunting in volume, would help him master his potential and become a true Chaos mage. However, there was one condition he had to agree to: Rexol had forbidden him from studying with Vaaler anymore.

He's not a wizard. His understanding of Chaos will always be limited to the superficial—the words of the incantation, rather than the true source of a spell's power. Working with him now will only hinder your progress.

Keegan wasn't even allowed to discuss his new training with his friend, and the secrets had further widened the distance between them. And now Rexol was sending Vaaler away.

"It's not right," Keegan grumbled. "You shouldn't have to leave. Not like this. Not because of me."

"This isn't your fault," Vaaler assured him, stuffing the last of his things into his pack. "Things are going to be hard enough without you carrying a bunch of misplaced guilt.

"Besides," he added, sitting down in the room's lone chair to take a break, "there's nothing here for me anymore. Rexol's done with me."

Keegan shook his head. "It just doesn't seem fair. Even if you can't . . . you know . . . he can still teach you things."

"He taught me things," Vaaler replied. "I know the history and politics of the Southlands. I have a better understanding of their culture, and of how humans and Danaan can get along. And I even learned a lot about magic.

"I may never be a wizard, but I understand the theory and practice of the mage's art. I can pass those teachings on to the sorcerers in my mother's court."

Assuming they'll listen to you, Keegan thought but didn't say aloud.

"This is for the best," Vaaler insisted. "I've been away from my home too long. It's time I get back to my own people."

"Maybe I can come visit you once you become king," Keegan joked. "You could let me sit on your throne and show me all the secrets of the Danaan Forest."

"Sure," Vaaler replied with a sly smile, "but then I'd have to kill you. One of the responsibilities of being the Danaan King."

Keegan rose to the bait. "You could try. But no king is a match for a wizard." He regretted the words as soon as they were out of his mouth.

Vaaler didn't say anything, and the melancholy gloom settled over the room once again. Keegan cursed himself for his stupidity.

"I'm sorry, Vaaler. I didn't mean that."

The Danaan prince nodded in mute acceptance of the apology. He seemed about to say something, then stopped. Keegan waited, letting him gather his thoughts.

"Don't let Rexol turn you into him," the prince finally whispered. "He's arrogant. He's selfish. He uses people. He doesn't care for anyone or anything unless he thinks it can help him in some way."

"He took me in when nobody else would," Keegan replied, feeling the urge to defend his master.

"He took you in because of your Gift and your dreams. He thinks you're a key to unlocking the mysteries of the Old Magic. Just like he agreed to teach me only because of the ancient knowledge he hoped to uncover in the books my people gave him. He's obsessed with power; he'll do anything to get it."

"That's easy for you to say," Keegan countered. "One day you're going to be a king. Most of us don't have that luxury. We aren't born into power—we have to take it!"

"That sounds like something he'd say."

The implied condemnation in Vaaler's tone shocked Keegan into silence, and another awkward silence settled over them.

"There's one thing Rexol didn't teach me," Vaaler finally said. "A lesson my mother made sure I understood as soon as I was old enough to talk. Power comes with a price. It's a burden. It demands sacrifice.

"For all his intelligence and wisdom, your master doesn't understand this. He never did and he never will. When I ascend the throne I will have the power of life and death over all my subjects. When you learn to unleash the Chaos within you, you will have that same power over everybody. But a king must answer to his people. Who does a wizard answer to?"

Keegan wasn't able to think of a suitable reply.

"You're destined for great things," Vaaler added. "I may not have the Sight, but even I can see that. You have to be careful, though. Rexol's ambition will be his downfall; don't let it become yours, too."

"So what are you saying? I should leave? Go off on my own? Tag along with your escort until we reach the Free Cities?"

The prince shook his head. "No, your place is here for now. You have to learn to master your Gift. Stay with Rexol. Let him keep teaching you in the ways of magic. But don't become him."

Vaaler stood up and tossed his pack over his shoulder. Then he crossed the room and reached out, offering his hand. Keegan clasped it in a firm grip.

"You're a good person, Keegan. Don't forget that . . . brother."

"I won't, brother," Keegan replied.

And with that they parted ways, both knowing their divergent paths would likely never cross again.

Chapter 25

"MASTER, I FOUND something! A passage in one of the manuscripts!"

Keegan's tone was breathless, though whether it was from his discovery or from running down the long flight of stairs from the library to the lab to share his news was difficult to say.

Rexol pulled his attention away from the assortment of oddly shaped stones he'd been examining. He'd been hoping to find the petrified remains from a griffin or some similar Chaos Spawn in the collection, but so far had come across nothing save mundane rocks shaped by the forces of wind, rain, and time.

"What did the passage say?" he asked his apprentice.

The young man shook his head and rubbed the back of his hand across his sweating brow, smearing the faded outline of the glyphs painted on his skin.

"I . . . I couldn't make it out. Not entirely. But there was mention of one of the Talismans."

Rexol didn't speak right away. Instead, he studied his apprentice carefully. The young man's dark eyes were glazed and sunken, his face drawn and tired.

It had been almost a year since Rexol had sent Vaaler away. Since then, Keegan had slowly been learning the spells that would enable him to read the obscure languages of the ancient Danaan texts.

And though he worked hard at his studies, he still struggled with the complicated ritual.

His mind is not as quick as Vaaler's, Rexol reminded himself. The Danaan prince had a unique gift for memory and comprehension; he would have made an excellent mage if only he had been touched by Chaos.

"You're certain it mentions the Talismans?"

"The Crown," Keegan insisted. "Something about it being taken or stolen. I thought you would want to see it yourself."

What Keegan lacked in his craft, he more than made up for with raw potential. Even with imperfect technique, he was strong enough to pull important words or phrases from the texts, which he would mark so that Rexol could review them in more detail. And he had an uncanny knack for finding references to the Talismans among the thousands of Danaan manuscripts—even from the dusty pages of centuries-old books, the Old Magic called to him.

"I will review it tonight," Rexol assured him.

"Should I keep searching the other texts until then?"

It was impossible not to hear the eagerness in Keegan's voice. Like Rexol—like all wizards—once he began calling on Chaos it was difficult to stop. But it was obvious he was nearing the physical limit of what he could endure.

Keegan was a valuable tool, but one that had to be employed carefully. His power far outpaced his ability to command and control it. The accumulation of witchroot he'd been taking over the past week would compromise his judgment, make him reckless and overconfident in his abilities. Rexol had to be careful not to push him too fast or too hard.

"Enough studies for today," the wizard declared. "Rest up, then go into town for supplies. I'll expect you back in three days."

Endown was a city of a few thousand inhabitants a day's ride to the northwest of Rexol's tower, the closest settlement of any significant size. Keegan had visited regularly every couple of months over the past year to purchase supplies for the manse, though he suspected Rexol was also using the trips as an excuse to force him to take breaks in his training.

He didn't like putting his studies on hold, but he'd learned to appreciate the brief respites from his grueling apprenticeship. While in town he had no responsibilities: He didn't have to study, he had no chores, and he didn't have to make any meals or clean the premises.

And, unlike the empty manse, in Endown there were other people he could talk to. People like Kayla.

"Here you go," the pretty young barmaid said as she set the flagon down in front of Keegan.

"Thank you," he said, his voice wooden and dull as his mind struggled to shake off the fatigue of the day's ride and the last lingering effects of the witchroot.

For almost a week he'd been taking large doses each morning to enable his spells of translation; it would be another day or two before his system was fully cleansed of the drug.

Instead of disappearing back into the tavern crowd, Kayla hesitated. When he realized she was staring at him, Keegan flicked his gaze up from her low-cut blouse to meet her eyes.

"You look tired," she said.

"I've been working too hard," he answered, his eyes shifting down to the floor.

He hoped she would ask him about what he was doing. He couldn't tell her his true calling—he had to keep his association with Rexol hidden so the Order wouldn't find out. But he'd devised a solid backstory in case anyone ever questioned him when he came into town.

If Kayla asked, he would tell her he had come from Parssia, a city three days' ride away—close enough to be heard of, but far enough away that few in Endown would know much about it in the way of specific details. He'd explain that he was a scribe's apprentice, an occupation that would suit his slight frame and pale skin. Scribes were rare, they made good money, and sometimes they met with nobility: That would account for his simple but well-made traveling clothes and the courtly style of his dark, shoulder-length hair.

He'd tell her that his recurring visits to Endown were to meet with a wealthy client in the area he wasn't allowed to mention by name; and since goods in Endown were less expensive than the city, his master had instructed him to purchase supplies before heading home.

It was a good story—simple, and tinged with a hint of mystery. Unfortunately, Kayla didn't ask.

"I'll come back and check on you in a few minutes, Keegan," she promised, giving him a warm smile before turning to deal with the other customers.

Keegan thought he sensed something more than simple friendliness in her smile. He felt an actual connection with her, something he hadn't felt in a long time—not since Vaaler had left. And she'd actually remembered his name from the last time he was here; obviously he'd made some kind of impression on her as well.

It was almost twenty minutes before she returned; the tavern seemed unusually busy this evening. Instead of another flagon of ale, however, she dropped a sweet-smelling cup of what appeared to be green tea on the table in front of him.

"If you're tired, this will perk you up," she explained.

Keegan took a tentative sip, then curled his lip at the unexpected bitterness of the drink.

Kayla laughed. "Small sips," she told him. "Trust me.

"Can't have you slipping off to bed early tonight," she added. "You'll miss the show."

"What show?"

"We've got a wizard in town!" she gushed, her eyes gleaming with excitement.

Keegan's heart skipped a beat before he realized she wasn't talking about him.

"A wizard?"

"He rode in yesterday," she said, speaking quickly. "I wasn't here last night, but they say he did some magic right here in the tavern!"

"You mean a magician," Keegan said, suddenly understanding. "Not a wizard."

Keegan didn't like magicians. Sleight of hand and flashy effects were often used to simulate the effects of Chaos by hucksters and charlatans. Some used their art only to entertain, but the less scrupulous were not above portraying themselves as actual mages to reap adulations and privileges they didn't deserve. He had seen the terrible power of true Chaos unleashed, and whenever he witnessed parlor tricks passed off as magic it left a foul taste in his mouth.

"What's the difference?" she asked, genuinely puzzled.

"It's—never mind," he said, cutting himself off mid-sentence. Explaining the difference between a magician and a real wizard could draw the kind of attention Rexol wouldn't approve of.

"He's over there," Kayla said, tilting her head toward the center of the room and speaking in an excited whisper. "I'm hoping he gives us another show tonight!"

"I'd be shocked if he didn't," Keegan muttered. "What wizard could resist showing his awesome power for the chance to get free drinks?"

The young barmaid gave him a curious look before turning away and heading back into the crowd. Keegan let his eyes follow her swaying hips as she made her rounds, while at the same time trying to get a glimpse of the so-called wizard in their midst. A small crowd of patrons had gathered around the large table in the center of the tavern, but they were pressed in too tightly for Keegan to see the trickster who had beguiled them.

"Kayla, come here and watch this," one of the men at the table called out, frantically motioning with his arm.

The waitress scurried over quickly, eager to see what was going on. She stood unnaturally straight and tall at first, keeping herself slightly withdrawn from the rest of the huddled crowd, her body tense with nervous anticipation. As the hidden wonder unfolded she slowly bent in closer and closer to watch.

A few seconds later there was a sudden burst of light and a sharp crack, and everyone jumped back with a start. Kayla gave a squeal of surprise then laughed in delight. A small puff of red smoke curled up from the center of the table. When it cleared Keegan finally got a look at the portly charlatan who had conjured the effect.

At first glance he actually did have the look of one who possessed the Gift. His hair was braided in the style of mages, though it was much more orderly than most. A few basic, but accurate, warding symbols had been painted onto his face, though the ink was faint and fading, as if it had been done many days ago. His heavy cloak and thick robes were finely tailored and dyed in rich hues—nothing like the coarse but serviceable clothing Keegan or his master typically wore, though that didn't necessarily mean anything. Rexol preferred to dress in a way that accented the wild, untamed appearance of a Chaos mage for the effect it had on more civilized folk. But a lord's mage often dressed in more cultured and refined fashions to blend into the noble courts where he served. To complete the picture several strings of animal teeth and bones hung from the man's neck.

But even from across the room Keegan could sense that the necklaces were nothing more than bits of ordinary teeth and bone taken from some mundane creature. Relics of the Chaos Spawn tingled with power; an invisible but unmistakable aura surrounded them: the buzz and hum of stored energy waiting to be unleashed. The strings dangling from this man's neck were dead and lifeless, a sham prop to fool his gullible audience.

The audience applauded heartily for several seconds before most of them wandered away, still chuckling over the performance. Four of the more curious spectators pulled up chairs at the table, joining the man who had performed the show with hopes that a steady stream of ale might pry loose some dark and wondrous magician's secret.

"Did you see the show?" Kayla asked when she circled by Keegan's table again.

The young man shook his head. "Too crowded."

He was feeling more alert than before, sharper. Whatever concoction she had given him had done the trick.

"He might do some more magic later," Kayla said. "I bet nobody would mind if you squeezed in at the table to watch."

"I'll pass," Keegan said glumly.

"Come on," she pressed. "It's not every day we get a wizard here in Endown."

"He's no wizard," Keegan snapped. "Colored smoke and flash powder are only good for amusing the ignorant masses!"

Kayla took a step back, her eyes wide with surprise.

"Well," she said coldly as she regained her composure, "I happen to enjoy magic, thank you very much!"

Keegan tried to think up a quick apology, something to thaw the sudden chill. But before he could come up with anything the serving girl had turned her back on him and stamped off to tend to the other patrons in the bar.

For the next hour Keegan watched the magician holding court in the center of the tavern. The tricks were simple: coins appearing and disappearing; mugs levitating or dancing across the table at the magician's command; illusions punctuated by flash powder and colored incense to give them the false trappings of true power.

Every time Kayla brought the man a drink he would perform a caper for her amusement. A tiny flower would unfold in his hand; a glittering cloud of dust would shower down over the table. And each time Kayla giggled in delight and paused in her rounds to talk with the man, smiling and laughing at everything he said.

Occasionally she would head in Keegan's direction and drop another flagon of ale on the table. He tried to make small talk, but she brushed him off, still smarting from the remark he had made earlier. Each time she came by, Keegan guzzled down his drink and quickly signaled for another, knowing it was the only way to keep her from ignoring him completely. It wasn't long before the alcohol combined with the traces of witchroot in his system to wrap him in a comfortable warm glow.

You're drunk, he thought. *Better go sleep it off before you do something stupid.*

He motioned for Kayla to come over so he could settle his tab.

"That fellow's not just some magician, you know," she hissed at him when she got close. "He just got a posting as a lord's mage in one of the Free Cities on the border of the North Forest."

In his inebriated state Keegan could only refute the ridiculous claims by snorting out a derisive laugh.

Ignoring him, she added, "His name's Khamin Ankha. He says he studied under the most powerful wizard in all the Southlands: a man named Rexol!"

Keegan didn't recognize the name, but he had seen enough from the charlatan to know the pompous ass had never studied under his master. He'd probably heard Rexol's name somewhere and was using it to attract attention; Rexol's reputation was well known among the rulers of the Southlands. Dropping Rexol's name was probably how he'd conned some low-ranking noble into give him an official posting.

"I haven't seen any true magic from that trickster yet tonight," he declared with a bravado born of too many ales. "Khamin Ankha is nothing but a fraud. You can tell him that from me."

Kayla gave him an angry glare, then locked her jaw in determination. She spun away and marched directly over to the portly magician. He greeted her with a smile and a laugh but his expression changed as she spoke to him in a hurried whisper too faint for Keegan to hear across the room.

When she finished the magician peered into the corner, but Keegan knew he wouldn't see anything other than a silhouetted figure sitting alone in the shadows. The man pushed his chair back from the table and stood up. Keegan half suspected his rival would come over to confront him but instead the man climbed on top of the table, drawing amused gasps from the other patrons.

"Ladies and gentleman," the man called out, "it seems a challenge has been put forth. Apparently there are some in this bar who doubt my power. There are some who think I am nothing but a charlatan."

High atop the table he was clearly illuminated in the light of the tavern's central fire, and every eye in the building had focused on the man, including Keegan's own. If nothing else, he knew how to work a crowd.

"Gather around, friends," the man continued, "and I will give you a demonstration of true Chaos shaping the likes of which you have never seen."

At the invitation the crowd quickly formed a circle around the magician, eager to get a glimpse of his next performance. Even Keegan got up and approached, though he kept himself on the fringes of the crowd. He had studied the man all night; he had examined and analyzed him thoroughly. He had detected none of the faint glimmer of Chaos clinging to the man and knew him for a fraud. And now he was about to expose him.

The man probably suspected Keegan was nothing but a jealous local who didn't like Kayla paying attention to the newly arrived stranger. Perhaps he thought he would give a demonstration of false Chaos shaping that would cow his rival into silence and win an evening of pleasure with the pretty barmaid in one fell swoop. If so, he was in for a cruel surprise.

"Look closely," the man instructed, drawing a small pouch from within his robes. He opened the leather bag and withdrew a bundle of cloth. Knowing the audience was enraptured with his every move he slowly unwrapped the material to reveal a small glass vial. He held it up for everyone to see.

"Witchroot," he proclaimed, his voice suddenly somber and serious. "The essence of the mage's power," he added, his tone hinting at the dangerous secrets trapped within as he gently removed the stopper from the bottle.

Maybe he's not all smoke and flash, Keegan thought. *Maybe he actually does have some small touch of the Gift.*

The man tipped the vial to his lips and let three small drops spill onto his tongue, then carefully stoppered the vial and placed it back beneath his cloak.

"Until now I have entertained you with minor conjurations and simple spells," the magician said. "But now I must ask for complete silence, for I am about to summon dark and powerful forces!"

There was an apprehensive murmur from the crowd. Keegan knew the magician was stalling, giving time for the witchroot to enter his system. The magician held up his hand to quell the whispers, and then his face twisted into a mask of intense concentration. In a soft voice he began a slow, rhythmic chant—words Keegan recognized from one of the earliest incantations Rexol had taught him. A spell not to destroy, but to mislead.

Slowly, Keegan felt the power of Chaos beginning to gather. But though the magician was reaching out to the Sea of Fire, what came through was a mere trickle. The young wizard held a hand up to his mouth to stifle a giggle at the pathetic display, aware that the rest of the crowd was enraptured by what was unfolding.

He glanced over at Kayla, but her eyes were focused intently on the magician standing on the table. Her face wore an expression of awestruck wonder, her cheeks flushed with excitement.

On a sudden impulse, Keegan began to focus his will. Without a charm to draw on even a simple spell would be difficult, but he wasn't actually trying to summon Chaos. Speaking in a barely audible whisper, he echoed the magician's chant while reaching out with his mind. The similar spells intertwined, allowing Keegan to simultaneously draw on and amplify the other man's power.

A cloud of purple mists began to shift and swirl on the table beside the man, coalescing into the vague outline of a large wolf. Slowly the creature's form began to solidify. The mist became flesh and hair and teeth, though the animal's fur was a purple hue not seen in nature and the creature's eyes were black wells with no pupils. Throughout the conjuration the crowd ooh-ed and ahh-ed. Keegan continued to echo the magician's chanting words, concentrating intently as he subtly twisted and turned the Chaos in another direction.

As the magician finished his chant the wolf completed its transformation from incorporeal mist to physical creature and appeared to come to life. It crouched low to the table, hackles rising as it let out a low growl that rumbled over the mesmerized crowd.

The nearest patrons took a step back, and the magician laughed.

"Never fear," he assured the people, "the beast is incapable of harming you. Though it looks as real as you or I, it is still no more dangerous than mist—a shadow creature of no real substance."

He reached out his hand to demonstrate. To the magician's horrified surprise his hand didn't pass through the wolf as he expected but instead struck against the thick fur of the purple beast's heavily muscled shoulder.

The wolf shied away from his touch then turned to fix its growling gaze on the magician, its indigo lips curled back to reveal long black teeth. The magician took a half step in retreat, his eyes wide with horror.

"Be gone!" he commanded, waving his hand in a wide arc in an effort to dispel the beast.

For a second the wolf's skin shuddered as if it was about to disappear once more into wisps of purple smoke. But the Chaos that Keegan had added to the spell had created a phantasm too strong to be dispelled by the other man's insignificant power.

"No . . . this isn't possible," the magician gasped, dropping to his knees before the snarling beast.

The wolf barked and snapped at the man, and someone in the crowd screamed. The magician threw himself backward to avoid the harmless jaws of the illusion that he now believed to be real, tumbling off the table to land heavily on the floor amid the scattering crowd.

Still atop the table, the wolf tilted its head back and howled. The patrons began a mad dash for the exits, knocking over tables and chairs and one another in their panicked haste to escape. Kayla,

Keegan noticed, hadn't moved—she stood paralyzed only a few yards away from the fallen magician and the snarling illusion.

Fighting his way through the fleeing crowd Keegan stepped forward, a glowing ball of cold blue fire encircling his upraised fist.

"I banish you back to the Shadowlands, foul creature!" he shouted, drawing the attention of the fleeing audience. Even a true Chaos mage had to know how to work the crowd.

He hurled the blue globe at the beast, striking it full in the chest. There was a brilliant turquoise explosion and a crack of thunder that drowned out the rising howl of the wolf. The animal burst into a million purple sparks that showered down harmlessly over the crowd, their cool touch soothing the patrons' fear and calming their panic.

Keegan glared down at the magician still lying on the floor. The cowering man's face was a mix of confusion, humiliation, and slowly fading terror.

"Stick to your magician's tricks," Keegan said, loud enough for the entire tavern to hear. "Chaos is best left to those with the power to control it. If you were truly Rexol's pupil you would already know this."

Without another word Keegan turned and strode through the doors leading to the street, stepping over the fallen magician with haughty disdain. The crowd pressed back to clear a path for him, none of them eager to make contact.

Keegan hadn't gone more than a dozen paces down the street when he heard the tavern door slam open behind him. He didn't turn around, only stopped in the street. His heart pounding, he stood rigid as stone, letting the night air cool the hot sheen of sweat on his brow.

"You're a wizard," Kayla gasped from behind him. "A true Chaos mage! Please, Your Lordship . . . wait for me!"

Khamin Ankha rode slowly down the dark road, slinking away from Endown like a thief in the night. He had spent several weeks traveling south from Torian, the northernmost of the Free Cities, just so he could show Rexol what an important man he had become. Now he had decided not to go visit his mentor after all. All he wanted was to leave the scene of his humiliation behind.

He was about to become the preeminent lord's mage of Torian! He was a man of power and influence. He was a man worthy of respect. He had been a fool to think these Southlanders would understand that. They were beneath him. All of them barely worthy of his contempt. Yet they had dared to laugh at him as he had lain on the floor of the tavern, quivering in fear.

He pressed on through the darkness, driven by his burning shame, the only sound the steady *clip-clop* of his horse's hooves. But in his heart Khamin Ankha silently cursed the young man who had done this to him, the face of his tormentor forever burned in his mind. And he swore one day vengeance would be his.

Chapter 26

AFTER THE SLAYER'S fall, the Crown was given to the defenders of the true faith, that they could use its wisdom to guide the people in the absence of the Gods themselves.

It had taken hours for Rexol to translate the short, two-line passage Keegan had marked for him. The text was written in a dialect he hadn't encountered before, and unlike most of the manuscripts the Danaan had sent him, the contents of the leather-bound tome were protected by powerful wards transcribed onto the pages themselves. The wards cast a veil over the words, making it difficult for Rexol to grasp their meaning even with the help of his translation spell.

It was impossible to know who had created the wards, or why. They could have been a safeguard of the original author, or something the Danaan sorcerers added to the manuscript before sending it to Rexol. But their mere existence forced him to revaluate Keegan.

Rexol had assumed his apprentice's inability to translate the passage was a sign of his imperfect technique, but the fact that Keegan had been able to glean anything at all from the warded document was a testament to his growing strength. He'd underestimated his pupil again, just as he had during his first trial almost a year ago. It was a dangerous mistake—as powerful as Keegan was, even the simplest of his spells could result in strange and unexpected consequences in the mortal world if the backlash of Chaos wasn't properly contained.

Vowing to be more careful with his young apprentice in the future, Rexol shifted his focus back to the brief passage he'd been able to translate.

After the Slayer's fall, the Crown was given to the Defenders of the True Faith, that they could use its wisdom to guide the people in the absence of the Gods themselves.

The phrase *Defenders of the True Faith* was almost certainly a reference to the Order. For seven centuries the Pontiff and his followers had influenced the history and politics of the Southlands; the success of their machinations was easier to understand if they had the aid of the Talisman that supposedly allowed them to see across time and space.

But from what Rexol had read of the Crown, it was also supposed to allow the wearer to see into the hearts and minds of friend and foe alike. If the Order actually possessed it, then why hadn't they discovered Ezra's subterfuge earlier? How had Jerrod evaded the Inquisitors for so many years? And why hadn't the Order sent a summons for Rexol to stand trial for recruiting Keegan?

Maybe the Crown isn't as powerful as the legends claim, Rexol thought. *Or maybe after centuries of trying to halt the spread of Chaos, they've forgotten how to unlock its full power.*

There was a third possibility as well—perhaps the Order didn't have the Crown after all. But Rexol wasn't willing to consider this alternative. Believing the Crown was locked away somewhere inside the impregnable Monastery walls was far preferable to thinking he still had no idea where to find any of the Talismans after so many years of research.

The only way to be sure, however, was to get inside the Monastery—close enough to feel the Crown's presence. A decade ago he'd been on the other side of the black stone walls, but he'd been too focused on his confrontation with the Pontiff to listen for the call of Old Magic. Now he knew what he was looking for.

Getting inside the Monastery, however, was a problem. The Order was too suspicious of him to grant an audience. And even if he somehow convinced them to let him in, taking the Crown and getting out again was a task bordering on the impossible.

But magic was all about making the impossible happen. Now that he knew where to find one of the Talismans, Rexol was determined to claim it as his own . . . no matter what the cost.

Keegan woke screaming, thrashing off the covers and struggling to rise from the deep mattress he was drowning in. Nightmare visions still filled his head, mingling with the unfamiliar surroundings to form vivid scenes of gruesome death.

The terror quickly faded as his conscious mind took stock of his surroundings, though his heart was still pounding and his breath was coming in quick, ragged gasps. Light from a full moon spilled through the open window, enough for him to make out the furniture of the room he'd rented for his stay at Endown.

Only then did he notice the shadowy form of Kayla, naked and huddled in the corner. Seeing a semblance of calm had come over him, she stood up and slowly approached the bed.

"Keegan," she whispered, "can you hear me? It's Kayla."

"I'm . . . I'm okay," Keegan answered, though he was only half paying attention to her.

Concentrate. Remember the details before the dream fades.

"What happened?" Kayla asked, reaching out to put a soft hand on his bare shoulder. "One moment you were sleeping, then all of a sudden you started screaming."

The Order. Inquisitors. They were torturing me for information.

"I tried to wake you, but you just kept screaming. Then you started flailing around. I . . . I thought you were going to attack me."

No. They're not torturing me. It's someone else. A woman.

"Please, Keegan—I'm scared. Is something wrong? You can tell me."

All the pieces fell into place as the terrible truth dawned on him. He'd been an idiot; a fool. Rumors of his performance at the tavern would spread quickly; it wouldn't take long for the Order to hear about the dangerous display of Chaos magic.

They'd send someone to investigate, seeking out the rogue wizard's identity. They'd learn about Keegan; they'd discover Rexol had defied the Pontiff by taking another apprentice. He had to warn his master. Their only hope was to flee before the Inquisitors came for them.

But he and Rexol weren't the only ones in danger. Too many people had seen Kayla leave the tavern with Keegan. The Order would want to question her.

Kayla was brave. She was loyal. The night they'd spent together was more than just sex—she cared for him. She'd try to protect him. The Inquisitors would sense her feelings for Keegan, and they'd know she was lying to them. They'd torture her for the truth: whipping her soft, pale skin; cutting and maiming her pretty features; burning her most tender and private flesh. And when it was over they'd execute her for consorting with a rogue wizard— he'd seen it in his dream.

Your dreams don't always come true. You saved Tollhurst from the Raiders. You can save Kayla.

She began rubbing her hand gently on his shoulder.

"Keegan? Please talk to me, Keegan. I want to help you."

He slapped her hand away and shoved her, sending her staggering back.

"Get off me!"

By the moonlight through the window he could see her eyes go wide with shock and confusion.

"I . . . I don't understand."

"Shut your mouth, you dirty whore!"

She raised a hand and reached out to him tentatively, his unexpected venom leaving her mind reeling.

"But . . . I don't . . . why?"

"I know your type," Keegan spat. "You think I haven't slept with dozens of women who try to win my favor by spreading their legs?"

"No," she said with a shake of her head, still trying to grasp the inexplicable change in Keegan's attitude. "It's not like that. I . . . I thought you were nice. Sweet. Kind."

He barked out a laugh, harsh and cruel.

"Did you think you were special? You're even stupider than I thought."

He laughed again; an ugly, contemptuous sound.

"I'm done with you, whore. Grab your clothes and get out."

In an instant, Kayla's expression changed. Her eyes narrowed and her jaw clenched, her lip curled up and her chin thrust forward.

"You bastard!" she snarled. "You son of a Chaos-spawned bitch!"

Keegan sprang to his feet and lunged at her, grabbing her elbow before she could react. He hauled her toward the door, propelling her along so that she had to scramble to stay on her feet.

"Let go of me!" she screamed, slapping at his face with her free hand.

Ignoring the assault, Keegan yanked open the door and threw her out into the hall, still naked. She stumbled and fell onto her hands and knees, then turned over and crawled backward away from him until her back hit the far wall.

As she sat there on the cold stone—naked, angry, frightened, and humiliated—Keegan scooped up her clothes from the floor and threw them at her, then slammed and locked the door.

Knowing he had to warn Rexol as soon as possible, Keegan quickly dressed. Kayla started banging on the door just as he finished.

"I hate you, you bastard!" she shouted from the other side. "You'll pay for this! I hope the Order burns you alive!"

Good, Keegan thought as he hastily packed his things. *When the Inquisitors show up, tell them everything you know about me. Curse my name and let them see how badly you want revenge. And if you're lucky, they might just decide to let you live.*

Chapter 27

THE PONTIFF SENSED the young blond woman waiting patiently outside the door of his chamber, but he did not call Cassandra in immediately. Instead, he remained on the floor, his legs crossed over each other and his feet tucked away beneath him as he sat on his meditation mat. He took a long, deep breath, holding it for a full minute before slowly releasing the oxygen from his lungs, allowing the outrushing air to cleanse his troubled mind.

This should have been a time of exultation and triumph—only an hour ago he had received word from Yasmin that Jerrod had been captured. He had been taken in Saldavia, one of the Free Cities. Even now the Prime Inquisitor was bringing him back to the Monastery to stand trial for his heresies . . . and to reveal the identities of his fellow conspirators.

There was no doubt that Yasmin would get the names; Jerrod was strong enough to resist her for days, maybe weeks, but in the end he would talk. She always made them talk. The Pontiff hoped that when the truth came out, the numbers of those who had sworn allegiance to Jerrod's cause would add up to only a handful. But he feared the corruption went far deeper.

Yet this was not what troubled him. This was not why he hesitated. He had summoned Cassandra because he had seen her in a vision—a vision even he did not yet understand. A vision eerily similar to the one Cassandra had reluctantly told him about many years ago: monsters at the gate; the Monastery in ruins; the broken bodies of the faithful strewn about the courtyard.

"Come in," the Pontiff finally said.

He took another long, slow breath, trying to find harmony within himself as he rose to his feet and turned to acknowledge Cassandra.

"Do you know why I have summoned you?" he asked her.

"The reports from Endown," she guessed. "The rogue wizard who unleashed Chaos on the town. He is Rexol's apprentice, isn't he?"

"The Inquisitors I sent to investigate believe so," the Pontiff confirmed. "But why would I call you here for that?"

"You are going to summon Rexol to stand trial for heresy," she continued. "He was my master for a time. It would only be natural for you to wonder about my loyalty."

She thinks I want to test her, he realized.

Not surprising, given Jerrod's recent capture. Rumors and speculation as to who might be a traitor were running wild through the Order's ranks.

"I was blind to Jerrod's deceit," he admitted. "But I have watched you closely over the years. I know your faith is strong. I know your allegiance is true."

Cassandra bowed her head in acceptance of his praise, then asked, "So why did you summon me?"

For a moment he considered telling her what he had seen. Like Cassandra long ago, he had seen the destruction of the Monastery and the death of the Order. But in his vision, there was something new: a single survivor. In his dreams he had witnessed Cassandra wandering alone in a frozen wasteland with the Order's most precious treasure.

Instead, he asked, "Have you had any more dreams of the iron crown you told me about before?"

The young woman shook her head. "Not since the storm almost a year ago."

The Pontiff frowned. His vision had shown him a glimpse of a possible future, but whether it was a warning of what to avoid or what had to be done he couldn't say. He'd been hoping Cassandra might have had a vision of her own—a reflection of her destiny that might guide him down the proper path. Instead, he would have to continue on blindly.

"Does the iron crown have something to do with my old master?" Cassandra wanted to know.

"I was hoping you could tell me," the Pontiff answered with a rueful smile. "Are there any other details of your dream? Anything you left out?"

The young woman closed her eyes, reaching back to call up the memory of her vision as she scratched absently at her arm.

"I've told you everything I am able to," she said when she opened her eyes, and the Pontiff sensed she spoke the truth.

"Jerrod is the one who found me for Rexol," Cassandra noted, bringing up a point the Pontiff had already considered. "It's odd that he would be captured at the same time Rexol's defiance of your decree has been exposed."

"The forces of Chaos are gathering," the old man explained. "Threads are being drawn together. This is a dangerous time; the Legacy is fragile. Now we must be at our most vigilant."

"Do you think Rexol will answer the summons?" she wondered.

"I think so."

"Why wouldn't he try to run?"

"His mind is clouded by witchroot and Chaos," the Pontiff reminded her. "It makes him arrogant. He probably thinks he will be able to bargain his way to freedom once again."

"By giving his apprentice to you," she muttered. "As he did me."

"It was the True Gods that brought you to us, Cassandra," the Pontiff assured her. "Not Rexol. He was only an instrument of their will."

"Of course, Pontiff," she said. "And I am grateful for what happened."

Even though he knew she was speaking honestly, it was obvious that talking of her past troubled the young woman. There was no need to make her uncomfortable; she had told him everything she could.

"If you dream of the crown again, you must tell me right away," the Pontiff said, then nodded to the exit, signaling an end to their conversation.

The young woman dipped her head in a sign of respect and left, closing the door behind her.

Alone, the Pontiff's thoughts shifted to the Talisman still locked away beneath the Monastery. The Crown had the power to help him: It would allow him to peer into the minds of Jerrod and Rexol; it would give him the wisdom he needed to walk the righteous path. But the Crown wasn't an option.

The last time the Pontiff had dared to call on the Talisman's power he had felt their immortal enemy on the other side of the Legacy, watching and waiting for his chance to return. It had taken all his effort to keep the Slayer at bay. He wasn't strong enough to risk using it again.

But what if Cassandra is? Maybe that's why I saw her with the Crown in my vision. Maybe she is destined to be the next Pontiff!

He could teach her the techniques to shield herself from its devastating power; he could show her how to contain the Chaos. If she learned to control it, the Talisman would clarify her Sight, purifying her visions to guide them down the proper path.

And if she can't control it, its power will overwhelm her and the Slayer will return.

Was that the meaning of the image of the Monastery in ruins? Did it symbolize the collapse of the Legacy and the failure of the Order?

The old man shook his head, weary with the conflicting implications of what he had seen. Try as he might, he had no way to know if bestowing the Crown on Cassandra was the key to their salvation, or their doom.

Chapter 28

FROM HIS VANTAGE in the thick foliage high above the human camp, Vaaler studied the intruders. He had been watching for several minutes, trying to determine if any of the group were missing: out hunting game or making water in the bushes. No, he decided at last. They were all present in the camp; there would be no latecomers to this encounter.

Eight horses and six humans. Two of the humans appeared to be scholars of some type, probably cartographers. One male, one female. The other four—all large, rough-looking males—had probably been brought along to tend the horses, set up the camps, carry equipment and supplies, perform all the manual labor, and provide some protection from the dangers of the forest. On the last count, Vaaler knew, they would fail.

The camp was at least a full day's ride from the nearest trade route, and it was obvious they had been here for some time. These were not lost travelers; they were here in direct violation of the Free Cities Treaty. The humans knew the North Forest was banned, yet still they came. Some were drawn by legends of fabulous Danaan treasures hidden within the thick woods. Others sought the fame and fortune they imagined would come with the discovery of the fabled Danaan cities. And still others came simply because it was forbidden.

Vaaler shook his head in bewilderment, trying to understand their alien mentality. Despite the grave risks, every month there were more explorers and more adventurers seeking the legendary metropolis hidden within the trees. Fools, each and every one. The Danaan cities were hidden by more than leaves and branches. Ancient magics from the time of the Cataclysm veiled the Danaan capital, remnants from a time when his people were still strong enough to weave Chaos into a shield against the eyes of outsiders.

Maybe, Vaaler thought, the magic was unraveling. During his studies under Rexol he had never learned even the meanest feat of Chaos shaping, but he had learned as much as any Danaan sorcerer about the theories of magic. It existed only in opposition to everything—nature, life, even itself. When a spell meant to obscure a city began to dissolve, the backlash of the escaping Chaos would tend to draw curious explorers in like moths to a flame. Such were the ironies of magic.

Perhaps that was why the last century had seen such a dramatic increase in human trespassers on forbidden Danaan lands. Or maybe it was simply the burning drive of the humans to explore, to spread, and to conquer—a natural instinct in their race that had been long extinguished in the Danaan people, if it had ever even existed at all.

He sighed; a sound so soft it could not possibly have been heard by the humans camped far below. But the archers under his command would have heard it, even those who had crept through the treetops to the far side of the camp to cut off any chance of the invaders' escape.

Vaaler hated that it had to be this way. This isolation was slowly killing the Danaan kingdom. No matter how much they tried to push the world back to the edge of the forest, it refused to stay outside their borders. But he knew there was no choice to be made here. The duty of the patrols was clear; the punishment for venturing from the well-marked trade routes was known to human and Danaan alike. Not even the crown prince could change that.

Not that Vaaler would have ever suggested making such a change.

The history of the patrols stretched back as far as the Danaan kingdom itself, an honored and noble tradition. In the human lands it
was commonly believed the power of the Danaan came from the
many wizards that served in the royal court. But Vaaler knew the
real strength of his people came from the small bands of elite soldiers who guarded and protected the forest.

He wasn't the first crown prince to serve on patrol, though it
wasn't a common practice among the royalty. It was seen as a badge
of honor for any who successfully completed the rigorous
training—an honor worthy of even a king. Perhaps that was why
he had been so eager to join after his return from the life of a wizard's apprentice.

At first, the Queen had opposed the idea. She had protested that
he was too old; most began the training in their early teens. It went
unspoken that Vaaler had wasted those years trying to become a
mage. He had left as a boy, but returned as a man . . . a man lacking
both the Sight and the Gift.

Vaaler suspected that was the real reason his mother objected:
her fear that he would fail, disappointing an entire kingdom once
again. Fortunately, Drake had spoken up in his defense. Before becoming captain of the Queen's Guard he had served three tours of
duty on patrol and he had offered to help Vaaler with his training.

That had been a little over a year ago, and since then the prince
had made remarkable progress. Though cruel fate had cheated him
of his father's mystical Sight, he seemed to have inherited the King's
renowned martial skills. Under Drake's tutelage Vaaler had quickly
mastered archery, fencing, and horsemanship; his skills equaled
those of any man or woman who served on the patrols. He even
liked to think that Drake himself, the finest swordsman in the
kingdom, found him a worthy opponent whenever they sparred.

After six months of training and another three spent serving
under one of the other patrol captains, he had been appointed
leader of his own patrol, a position more suited to the heir to the
throne. But though he had been given command of his troops because of his royal blood, it wasn't his lineage that had won him

their loyalty. That had come only after he had proven himself in the field. Vaaler knew they no longer had any reservations about following his orders.

As the patrol leader, it was both his right and his duty to take the first shot. Vaaler made sure he didn't miss. The arrow buried itself in the chest of the male scholar with a wet, heavy thud, spinning the man around as he clutched at the shaft protruding from his breast. A second arrow fired by another of the patrol pierced his throat, cutting off his scream. Before his corpse had even hit the ground, two more arrows had embedded themselves in the back of the woman standing next to him.

The massacre had begun. The air was thick with the thrum of bowstrings and the hiss of arrows hurtling down from the canopy overhead onto the defenseless humans and their mounts, the patrol choosing their targets with random yet lethal efficiency. A few brief screams of defiance, terror, and pain were the only resistance their foes could muster to the attack.

And then it was over. Fourteen arrow-ridden corpses—six human, eight equine—littered the forest floor. The eight archers of the patrol had unleashed three score of arrows in just over a dozen seconds, and only a handful had failed to find their mark.

His patrol slipped away through the treetops with no more noise than a soft rustle of leaves, vanishing as invisibly as they had gathered for the lethal ambush. Vaaler would meet up with them at the rendezvous point where they had left their own horses later.

Now, however, he nimbly climbed down through the branches to the forest floor forty feet below to investigate the scene. And check for survivors. One of the horses kicked as he approached, by some miracle still breathing despite the seven shafts jutting from its blood-soaked haunches. Pink froth sprayed from its lips as it tried to whinny in fear and pain, though only a faint whooshing gurgle escaped its throat. Vaaler drew his thin sword and sliced it across the animal's neck in one quick and graceful motion, ending the beast's suffering. The others were all dead.

He began to gather evidence for his report to the Queen.

- - - -

"You are sure these were not simply merchants who had become lost?" Andar asked once Vaaler had finished his report.

In reply he tossed the sack of heavy metal cartographers' tools he had taken from the camp onto the floor at the councilor's feet.

"And the bodies?" Drake asked.

"I left them there as the terms of the Treaty dictate. No burial."

"Good," he replied. "Maybe their corpses will serve as a warning to other would be explorers who stumble across them."

Vaaler knew that wasn't likely.

"This is the third time since the harvest moon that our patrols have come across an exploring party, my Queen. The sixth such group since last year. Surely we cannot continue on like this."

"And just what would you have us do, Vaaler?" the Queen asked her son, her voice heavy and tired.

Looking at the weary expressions of the others in the room— Andar, Drake, and the rest of the Queen's privy council—Vaaler realized they must have been in deliberations for several hours before he had arrived and requested this audience with his mother. That could only mean one thing: They were discussing her recent visions. Realizing he was intruding on something he could never understand, he hesitated.

"If you have something to say, then say it," his mother commanded.

"The humans grow and prosper, my Queen. Their empires expand ever outward." Vaaler spoke slowly, emphasizing each word, trying to give his arguments weight and authority so he would be listened to this time. "The forest will not keep the humans from our cities forever."

"The humans know the penalty for trespassing on our domain," Andar said. "If the treaties we have signed with the Free Cities cannot keep them from straying off the trade routes then the swift justice of our patrols surely will."

"The patrols protect our domain as best they can," Drake cautioned, "and they enforce the terms of the Treaty without mercy. But the trade routes are long, and the patrols cannot be everywhere at once."

"These cartographers are far from the first," Vaaler reminded the council. "Maps of the woods around the trade routes can be purchased in the Free Cities and the Seven Capitals of the Southlands, if one knows who to ask. Not only have humans explored the borders of our kingdoms, but many have lived to tell about it."

"Are these maps accurate?" the Queen asked her son.

"They are. As accurate as our own—though they were obviously written in a human hand."

"There could be another explanation," Andar suggested. "It is possible the information was sold to the humans by one of our own."

Vaaler was not surprised. The Queen's sorcerer was always the first to stand against him.

"I will not discount that possibility," the Queen assured him, though everyone in the council chamber knew it was a far-fetched theory.

The Danaan people were loyal to their kingdom and their Monarch. The petty feuds, squabbles, and betrayals of the human nobility were foreign to Danaan politics. The descendants of Tremin Avareen had ruled the Danaan people in an unbroken line since the Cataclysm, and such stability could only be achieved through the absolute will and consent of the people.

"If the humans will not honor the terms of the Treaty then we must close the trade routes," Andar declared. "Cut off all trade with the Free Cities and make it a capital crime for any human to enter the North Forest under any circumstances. And forbid our own people from visiting the Southlands, just to be safe."

The deep-rooted isolationism of the Danaan people always evoked the same reaction in Vaaler when it reared itself up in the supposed wisdom of the privy council. He bit his lip to keep from screaming.

"Remember your dreams, my Queen," Drake said, throwing his

support behind Andar's suggestion. "Perhaps your visions of fiery destruction are a warning of what will become of our people if we continue our association with the violently unstable kingdoms of humanity."

Vaaler loved Drake; the man was the father he'd never had. But sometimes he was as much a fool as the rest of them.

"What do you think the humans will do if we cut off all trade with them?" Vaaler demanded angrily, asking the question of no one in particular. "If we suddenly sever our few diplomatic ties and ban them from entering the forest they will think we are preparing to invade!

"The Free Cities would appeal to the Seven Capitals for help, and an army would amass at our borders."

"Surely when we did not invade they would realize their mistake and disperse their troops," Andar argued.

"You do not understand the humans as I do," Vaaler cautioned. "Once they have an army at their disposal they will use it."

"If they invade we will drive them back," Drake said with confidence. "We have done so before. In all the history of our people no foreign army has claimed victory against the Danaan in the forest. We remain an ancient and undaunted race."

"We are a dying race," Vaaler spat. "The human tribes that invaded our land five centuries ago were the primitive scouts of petty warlords. I have seen the glory of the Southlands. I have seen how their population covers the earth like flies on a bloated corpse. The standing soldiers of the Free Cities are a mere fraction of the army the Seven Capitals can raise in a single month's time!

"The human kingdoms grow and spread and flourish, while we fester and rot in our isolation. For now, the forest holds the humans back. But not for long. Another generation, maybe two . . . and then they will devour us!"

"For one who does not possess the Sight you claim to see a stark vision of our future," Andar said, making no attempt to hide the disdain in his voice.

There was silence, Vaaler momentarily stung by the open admis-

sion of what was normally treated as a terrible, unmentionable secret. Andar himself was flushed at his bold words. He seemed about
to apologize to the prince then shut his mouth as if realizing an
apology would only draw further attention to Vaaler's handicap.
Drake coughed but only stared pointedly at the floor.

Vaaler glanced at his mother to judge her reaction, but the
Queen would not meet his eye. Her right hand had gone up to
caress the simple gold ring she always wore on a chain around her
neck, the symbol of the royal House's power and right to rule.
Vaaler had noticed she always reached for the ring when she felt
uncertainty or indecision, as if she could draw solace and strength
from an inanimate object. She had worn it ever since her husband
had died; Vaaler could not remember ever seeing her without it.
When he used to sneak into her private chambers at night as a
little boy seeking the nighttime comfort of his mother the ring had
dangled from the chain around her neck even as she slept.

"I may not have the Sight," Vaaler finally replied, tearing his gaze
away from the plain gold band. "But I am not blind. During my
years under Rexol I studied their history and politics. And I have
made over a dozen trips to the Free Cities. I have walked among
them; I know how they think. I know them better than anyone in
this chamber.

"We must become an ally of the human kingdoms if we are to
survive. The trickle of commerce we share with the Free Cities is
not enough. We must increase our trade with the Southlands. We
must establish formal diplomatic relations and have permanent
embassies within the courts of the Seven Capitals. And we must
open our borders to the humans.

"The forest will not keep them at bay forever. One day they will
come, and we can only hope they come as friends and not enemies."

Vaaler could see his words had little effect on the Queen or her
council. His words never did. He was the crown prince, heir to the
throne—but he did not have the Sight. Dreams and visions were all
the Danaan advisers cared about; ancient magic they couldn't even

explain guided their actions. But Vaaler knew he was right in this. He had to convince them.

"Your visions, my Queen," he said, addressing his mother, a sudden inspiration forming in his mind.

"What of them, my son?"

Her hand dropped from the ring at his words, as if she suddenly realized she was clenching it in her fist and was ashamed to have him catch her in the act.

"You have seen the destruction of our people in your dreams. Perhaps you are foreseeing the coming of the humans. Perhaps your visions are a warning that we must abandon our isolationism and strengthen our relations with the Free Cities and the Southlands or suffer the inevitable consequences."

"No, Vaaler," the Queen said wearily, "I dream of fire and the utter destruction of our capital in a blaze of burning Chaos. I dream of the coming of the Destroyer of Worlds, not the coming of a foreign army. I have foreseen a second Cataclysm, not a political upheaval."

"But maybe—"

"No!" she cut in, her voice sharp. When Vaaler questioned her about her dreams she inevitably became angry with him. As if it were his fault he had been born without Chaos in his blood. "You don't understand the Sight, Vaaler! You couldn't possibly understand."

"Of course, my Queen." Vaaler's apology was stiff and cold.

"Your input during council is always welcome," the Queen said to him in a softer tone. "But once it is given, you must be content to let us make of it what we will." She gave another weary sigh. "You are dismissed."

There was nothing more he could do but bow respectfully and leave the chamber.

His attendants were waiting for him as he stepped out into the hall, as they always were within the confines of the castle. He hated their presence. Though they obeyed his every order without question, Vaaler suspected they were loyal to him only because of the

Queen. She was the leader of their people, the successor to an unbroken line of prophets who had guided the Danaan race since the Cataclysm. For keeping the kingdom strong and safe and prosperous they owed her their lives, their homes, and the lives of their families. But to the Sight-less heir to the throne they owed nothing.

At least they didn't accompany him out on patrol, or whenever he joined one of the merchant caravans traveling to the Free Cities. He had argued that attendants would undermine his authority on patrol, and they would draw attention to himself in the human lands, making him a target. Far safer to travel alone under the guise of a simple merchant, he had insisted. The Queen had granted her son this one concession, albeit reluctantly. The freedom from the ever-present shadow of his attendants was one of the reasons the prince's expeditions to the human kingdoms were becoming more frequent.

Freedom from the watchful eyes of his attendants had also been the best thing about his apprenticeship under Rexol. He could only imagine how much worse things would be for him now if his mother had insisted on sending someone with him. How much less would they think of him if they had seen him fail not only at the Sight, but at the Gift as well? And not just fail, but fail miserably?

However, despite his inability to master Chaos in any measure, Vaaler knew the importance of those years. Human history, the culture of the Southlands, the politics of the Seven Capitals— Rexol had made sure Vaaler studied and learned as much as possible about the strange, exotic peoples who lived beyond the borders of the forest. The mage had recognized an intelligence in Vaaler, a hunger for knowledge and an ability to study the patterns of the past and learn from them. And through his studies the prince had come to understand that it wasn't necessary to have the Sight to be a visionary.

None of the kings in the Southlands had the Sight, though they all employed the prophets of the Order in their courts. But the dreams and visions of the Seers were only one factor to be considered when decisions had to be made. Prophecy had to be weighed against reason and facts and the opinions of councilors, and the strongest rulers among the humans were those wise and intelligent enough to analyze all the evidence to reach the most logical decision.

Here in the Danaan court everything was backward. Here it was the Monarch who presented the visions and it was the councilors who provided the countering arguments of facts, circumstance, and reason. At least, that was how it had been in ancient times. Vaaler had read many descriptions of those ancient Danaan courts in the texts Rexol had often asked him to help translate. But somewhere the Danaan people had lost their way. They came to rely solely on prophecy, and instead of offering arguments to balance the visions of their Sighted rulers, the councilors' role evolved into one of interpretation—trying to find the meaning behind the often cryptic or symbolic images of the Monarch's dreams.

So far it had worked. The Danaan kingdom had known almost five hundred years of uninterrupted peace. But times were changing. Vaaler knew he would be the perfect ruler should he come to the throne. He would base his decisions on rational analysis, and the future of his people would be guided by logic and common sense—not obscure nightmares of burning Chaos and the return of a long-dead enemy of legend.

But would the Danaan people ever accept him as their king? He glared back over his shoulder at his attendants. "I'm going out on patrol," he told them.

"We shall follow you to the stables, my prince."

He nodded, anxious to be rid of them but content in the knowledge that once he had horsed up they wouldn't follow. On patrol, he was spared the burden of their company. Out on patrol, he commanded respect.

And, most important, out on patrol nobody cared that he was blind to the Sight.

Chapter 29

"GO PREPARE THE horses," Rexol ordered his apprentice. "I want to leave within the hour."

Keegan hesitated, and the mage knew what he wanted to ask. *Why are we answering the Pontiff's summons? Why didn't we run when I told you what happened in Endown?*

But the young man knew his master well enough to understand that if Rexol had wanted him to understand, he would have already explained it to him. Instead, the young man swallowed his question and left to see to their mounts.

Even after his apprentice was gone Rexol did not allow his grim expression to slip. It was important for Keegan to believe that he was upset at having to answer the summons. If the young man suspected the truth, the Pontiff would likely sense it and Rexol's gambit would fail. But if he could maintain the ruse then the Crown—an artifact imbued with the power of Old Magic—could soon be his.

The Talisman was calling to him. How else to explain the events of the last few weeks? After years of researching the Talismans the Slayer had used to elevate himself to the status of a God, Rexol had suddenly stumbled across information suggesting that the Crown had once been given to the Order and locked away inside the Monastery. Then, even as Rexol wondered how to get inside the impregnable walls, Keegan's actions had compelled a summons from the Pontiff.

It made sense, at least to one who understood the ways of Chaos. And Rexol understood Chaos better than any other living person in the mortal world. The Talisman was an object forged with the power of Old Magic; its power could never truly be contained. The monks sought to keep it hidden away and under control, but by its very nature it would seek to break free of their constraints. The power of the Crown called out to the power within Rexol himself, like calling to like. The backlash of his Chaos-fueled research into the ancient Talismans had culminated in this sudden and fortuitous turn of events.

"Master," Keegan said, interrupting his thoughts upon his return. "The horses are ready."

The mage nodded and motioned for the young man to lead the way.

As he followed his apprentice out to the courtyard and their waiting mounts Rexol still wasn't certain of the exact path that lay ahead. He was certain, however, of where the path was leading. The last time he had entered the Monastery he had gone prepared for war. He had survived the encounter but lost Cassandra. This time he would go in the guise of a man willing to submit himself to the Pontiff's will . . . but he would walk out with the key to becoming a God.

Like most Southlanders, Keegan had heard descriptions of the Monastery before. In his mind he had constructed an image of a massive citadel overlooking the barren desert, an imposing and intimidating edifice: unassailable, unconquerable, eternal. But the secondhand accounts of the Order's stronghold couldn't do it justice, no matter how evocative or detailed.

The Monastery was more than a mere building; it pulsed with power, like a living creature. Keegan had first felt it while they were still miles away, when the fortress was a mere speck on the horizon.

It rolled out across the dunes toward them, a tremor in the ground and a crackle in the air that grew ever stronger as they approached their destination.

Now, as he and Rexol pushed their way through the small but fanatical throng of devoted worshippers camped before the Monastery's entrance, Keegan understood why his Master had insisted they both refrain from taking doses of witchroot during their journey. Even without the drug coursing through his system, his mind was awakened to the immense power of this place. He could feel the supernatural heat emanating from the Monastery's unnatural black marble, buzzing in his skull and clouding his thoughts. If he had been under the influence of witchroot, it might have been too much to bear.

As it was, he still struggled to wrap his mind around the sheer magnitude of what he felt. But this was not the wild rush of fire and flame that threatened to swallow him up whenever he called upon the Chaos. Similar, but not the same. This was the slow burn of Chaos trapped and bound, its fire totally and utterly contained within the dark stone walls.

The worshippers parted grudgingly before them as they approached the building's heavy stone gates. Though both master and apprentice were clad in the fearsome garb of Chaos mages—painted faces; hair in wild, irregular braids; bodies laden with jewelry and charms fashioned from the teeth and bones of mystical beasts—the supplicants refused to be intimidated by them. Keegan wondered if they somehow knew that the interlopers' power was muted without witchroot coursing through their veins; or perhaps their bravery was simply due to the proximity of the Monastery itself.

They reached the gates without incident—a barely visible seam in the otherwise flawless surface of the smooth black stone. Rexol rapped once with his gorgon's-head staff.

"I have answered your summons!" he declared, his voice loud and defiant.

A single bell tolled from inside, and the gates opened inward, causing Keegan to blink in surprise. He had expected the grinding of gears and the groaning of machinery to accompany the movement of such massive slabs of stone, but there was only silence. Rexol stepped quickly through and he hurried to follow, not giving his mind a chance to wonder at what he had just seen.

The Pontiff was waiting for them inside, along with half a dozen other monks gathered in a large courtyard just inside the entrance. Their faces were calm but even beneath their loose-fitting robes Keegan could see their bodies were tensed for action. Though he still couldn't hear them he could feel the gates close behind, sealing them in.

"Rexol," the Pontiff said by way of greeting, delivering his words with the timbre of an official proclamation, "you have been summoned because you have defied a direct decree from the Order.

"By right and law, all children in the Southlands touched by Chaos belong to the Order. By taking an apprentice from among them, you have defied the authority granted to us by the True Gods.

"For your actions you are being charged with the crime of heresy. If found guilty, you will be burned alive at the stake in accordance with the ancient laws."

The Pontiff paused, waiting for Rexol to reply. Much to Keegan's surprise, his Master remained silent.

"I did not know if you would come," the Pontiff finally said. "I wondered if you would try to run to save your life."

"My life is only forfeit if I am found guilty," Rexol reminded him. "Or is this trial to be nothing but a sham?"

"You will be given a chance to answer these charges," the Pontiff promised. "But only after the Inquisitors have finished with you.

"Take them to the dungeon," he said with a sharp nod of his head.

The monks closed in, and rough hands seized Keegan by the shoulders. Instinctively he began to summon the Chaos trapped in the charms adorning his body, though without the glow of the witchroot it would be difficult to draw upon their power. But a quick shake of his master's head stayed Keegan's hand.

Now is not the time to panic. Do not start a war we cannot win.

In accordance with the Pontiff's orders Rexol and Keegan were taken down to the dungeons. In a tiny preparation room they were stripped of their jewelry: the necklaces and rings unceremoniously removed by the monks, the braids and feathers in their hair roughly combed out. They allowed Keegan to remove the ornaments from the pierced holes in his skin himself, though they watched him with a determined vigilance as he did so.

There was nothing they could do about the tattoos, but Keegan suspected they had little reason to worry. Here in the bowels of the Monastery they were surrounded on all sides by impregnable black stone. The young man could feel it pressing in all around him, smothering his Gift, making even the tiniest shaping of Chaos all but impossible.

Divested of their talismans the prisoners were led down a dark hallway. Keegan stumbled several times. He briefly wondered how the guards could be so sure-footed, then recalled their sightless eyes. The monks would have no use for torches or lanterns. The guards marched them through the blackness for about fifty paces then ordered them to stop.

Keegan heard the sound of a metal key and a heavy door swinging open on rusty hinges. A hard shove in the back sent him sprawling forward, and he collapsed to his hands and knees. An instant later he heard Rexol grunt as he, too, was forced into the cell, though somehow the mage managed to avoid tripping over his prone apprentice.

Keegan took a few seconds to make sure he was uninjured, then carefully stood up and tried to gather his bearings. He was surrounded by impenetrable darkness; there wasn't a single sliver of light in the cell. He couldn't even tell if someone else was in the cell or if he and Rexol were alone.

A disembodied male voice nearby answered his question. "So

this is your new apprentice. I wonder, Rexol—does he show as much potential as Cassandra?"

"How did the Inquisitors find you, Jerrod?" Keegan recognized his master's voice, though he had no idea who the other speaker—this "Jerrod"—might be. "Did you became careless? Or were you finally betrayed by one of your own?"

"As you betrayed me?" their mysterious cellmate asked.

Rexol gave a dismissive snort. "*Betrayal* puts too fine a point on it. We were allies of convenience, nothing more. You understood that as well as I."

"Coming here was a mistake," Jerrod replied, seeming to suddenly change topics. "The Pontiff will try you for heresy. He will burn you at the stake."

"Don't be so sure," the mage countered. "We haven't even begun the trial."

"I am a prophet of the Order, Rexol. Listen to me and know your fate: You will die here in flames of agony. I've seen your ashes in my dreams."

It was impossible to keep track of time in the stone cell. Had they been here minutes or hours? Keegan couldn't say. He had tried to speak once to ask Rexol any of a dozen questions. Who was the man imprisoned with them? How did they know each other? How long would they be here in the cell? Was there any chance of escape? Rexol had shushed him after the first word. Since then, the three prisoners—assuming there were no others sitting silently with them in the darkness—had passed the time in silence.

Keegan tried to make himself comfortable on the cold stone floor only to find it all but impossible. He crawled forward slowly, feeling his way until he found the wall, then tried sitting with his back to it. Better, but not by much. He was still sitting there, knees pulled up to his chest, when the door opened and the blinding brightness of a single lantern caused him to squint his eyes shut in reflexive pain.

"Let me speak with them alone," a female voice said. Once more there came the sound of the door closing.

Curious, Keegan dared to open his eyes a crack, letting them adjust to the soft light that now filled the cell. His master was seated against the opposite wall.

Another man—Jerrod, no doubt—was sitting cross-legged in the middle of the floor. He looked to be about forty. Average build, with light brown hair and a short beard running the length of his chin. He would have been completely unremarkable if not for the dead orbs where his eyes had once been.

But Keegan barely paid any attention to either Rexol or Jerrod. After a quick glance at his fellow prisoners his full attention was turned to the young woman who stood before them, the lantern dangling casually from her left hand.

She looked to be about Keegan's own age. She was small—a few inches over five feet and slight of build—yet she carried herself with the confidence of all who served the Order. In contrast with the shaved heads of the Inquisitors, she had pale blond hair that hung down to her shoulders. Her aristocratic features were undeniably attractive, though her eyes were the expected dull and lifeless gray.

"Do you recognize me, Rexol?"

"Of course, Cassandra. The years may change your appearance, but I will always recognize you. We have a bond. We always will."

The woman seemed to shiver at his words. "I am a servant of the Order. You are a servant of Chaos. Whatever bond we might once have had is long since broken."

"If that is true then why are you here?" Rexol asked.

There was a long silence, and the woman's expression became one of confusion before quickly giving way to anger.

"I didn't come here for you," she said.

To Keegan's surprise, the woman reached out a delicate hand and pointed a finger directly at him.

"You still have a chance to save yourself," she said. "Rexol and Jerrod will be found guilty of their crimes. As Rexol's apprentice, you will suffer his fate . . . unless you renounce him and testify against him."

Rexol laughed, cutting Keegan off before he could answer.

"Now I understand. You see a reflection of yourself in Keegan— a poor, helpless waif led down the wrong path by the evil wizard."

"Let him speak for himself!" Cassandra snapped.

With a shrug, Rexol turned toward Keegan, waiting expectantly for his answer.

The choice was easy for Keegan to make. Rexol had taught him how to harness the power of Chaos; the Order could offer nothing that would ever come close. And he knew his master well enough to understand that Rexol wouldn't simply surrender himself to his enemies. He had a plan.

"I won't betray my master," Keegan declared.

She opened her mouth to reply, but never got the chance as Rexol suddenly leapt to his feet. Moving more quickly than seemed possible, the wizard seized the young woman by her left wrist. Keegan half imagined he saw a tiny golden flash when his master wrapped his fingers around Cassandra's smooth skin. She cried out in surprise and leapt back, breaking free of his grip.

"Do that again and you will pay with your life," she warned him while rubbing her arm, causing the lantern in her hand to cast wildly dancing shadows across the walls of the cell.

Keegan noticed a faint mark on her skin resembling the tattoos Rexol had often painted on his own body. After a second it seemed to fade, seeping into Cassandra's flesh and vanishing beneath the surface.

"Why are you helping them do this to me?" the wizard demanded of the young woman who had once been his apprentice. "After all I have done for you, why do you hate me so?"

"After all you have done for me?" Her voice grew cold and she stopped rubbing her arm, as if she had forgotten about the sudden flash of pain she had just experienced. "What, exactly, have you ever done for me, Rexol?"

"I cared for you when no one else would," he answered. "I took you in. I kept you safe. Perhaps you were too young to remember."

"I may have been too young to remember but the Pontiff has told me the truth!" Cassandra hissed. "You only cared about me for my talent. You only wanted to exploit my visions! That was why you hid me from the Order. That was why you stole me away when my family sent me to join the Monastery!"

"Your parents never wanted you to join the Order," Rexol replied. "They tried to send you away to the Western Isles to hide you. But the Order found you anyway. The Pontiff was the one who was going to steal you from your family. I saved you."

There was a long moment of silence before she angrily replied, "Why do you think I would believe you, wizard?"

"Rexol speaks the truth," Jerrod said softly. "The Pilgrims came for you, Cassandra, but I was there first. Together you and I fled across the river and into the desert. I brought you to Rexol. What he says is true."

"I trust the Pontiff far more than I trust either of you."

Keegan thought he could sense uncertainty in her voice now.

"Try to remember, Cassandra. You clung to my back and we swam across the river. Surely you must have seen this in your dreams."

A brief flicker of doubt crossed her face, but she quickly masked it with a resolute determination.

"My loyalty is to the Pontiff and the Order! Had I not come to the Monastery I would never have learned to control the terrible power within me. It would have destroyed me."

"You do not control your power, Cassandra," Rexol countered. "You deny it. The Order has done nothing but hold you back and keep you from your true potential."

"Enough!" she spat, then took a deep breath to calm herself.

Turning her attention back to Keegan, she said, "I had hoped you would see reason. But if you will not testify against your master, then you will share his fate."

With a regretful sigh and a somber shake of her head she turned away and rapped once on the door of the cell. It was opened from the other side and she disappeared through it, taking the lantern with her. The door slammed shut behind her and their prison was cast into darkness once more.

Chapter 30

CASSANDRA WALKED QUICKLY through the Monastery's halls, rubbing the spot on her arm where Rexol had grabbed her. He hadn't hurt her, but he had surprised her. There was no bruising from his grasp, no evidence he had even touched her at all. Yet she could still feel his fingers tingling on her skin.

She had hoped the young man with them would accept her offer; as Rexol had said, she recognized something of herself in him. Had she not been liberated from the wizard's clutches, she might be the one facing execution now. But he refused to see his master for what he really was. Cassandra, however, knew better. She had no doubt that Rexol had only taken her in because he hoped to exploit her power.

Yet despite this, she found it difficult to hate him. She didn't remember much of the years she spent as a young child with him, but the memories she had weren't necessarily bad.

Her wrist began to itch, and she scratched at it absently.

Rexol had never been cruel to her. He had never been dishonest with her. For several years, he had raised her and cared for her. And despite her insistence to the contrary she knew there was still some bond between them. She had felt it when Rexol had grabbed her wrist.

There had been magic in the wizard's touch, of that she was

certain. Some lingering spark, a small remnant of his past power over her. But what was the result? Nothing, as far as she could tell. Which meant there was no reason to tell the Pontiff about it.

Rexol's fingers tingled faintly, a response to the magic he had unleashed. The sensation was so slight he wasn't sure if it was real or if his mind merely conjured it up to give him some false hope in an otherwise hopeless situation.

It had been over a decade since he had placed the spell of binding on Cassandra. He'd sensed the glyph beneath her skin, but would the spell still be potent after such a long dormancy? Would it be strong enough to compel one of the Order to betray her brothers and sisters?

It had been many days since Rexol had consumed witchroot; only the faintest traces of it still lingered in his blood. And the monks had stripped him of his charms before throwing him in prison, so there had been no way for the wizard to augment the power of his original spell.

"Master?" Keegan asked, his voice emerging like a ghost from the absolute darkness of the cell. "What do we do now?"

The young man might have noticed the faint flash of magic. He might suspect that his master had some kind of plan. But he himself had no part to play in it. There was no point in telling him anything. Not yet.

"We wait."

He had felt the burning sting of Chaos when he had triggered the rune. He knew he had planted the seed. But would the enchantment take root and grow?

Cassandra marched quickly through the halls, heading back toward her room. Despite her efforts to focus on something else—anything else—her mind kept drifting back to Rexol and the others in the dungeon.

They brought this fate on themselves, she silently assured herself. *They chose the path they are on. Just as you chose to join the Order.*

But did she really choose the Order? Had she not been taken from Rexol, would she have been as foolishly loyal to the wizard as his stubborn young apprentice? Were it not for the whims of fate that had brought her to the Monastery, would she now be the one on trial?

Fate does not turn on a whim, she reminded herself, calling upon the wisdom of the Order's teachings. *We serve the True Gods; we are instruments of their will.*

The Old Gods are dead!

The blasphemous words sprang into her head unbidden; she could hear Rexol's voice as if he were standing beside her, whispering in her ear.

Glancing quickly from side to side to assure herself she was alone, she hurried to her room. Once there, she quickly seated herself on the mat on the floor, legs crossed. Taking slow, deep breaths she sought solace in the act of meditation.

But instead of peace and tranquility, her thoughts were embroiled in images of fire and flame. In her mind's eye she watched as Jerrod, Rexol, and the young apprentice were burned alive, screaming in agony as their skin bubbled and boiled from the terrible heat.

Cassandra leapt to her feet, the vision so real the sickly sweet stench of melting flesh still lingered in her nostrils. For several seconds she struggled to keep her stomach from disgorging its contents before she finally lost the battle and retched up her last meal.

Heretics deserve no mercy! she reminded herself, though for some reason the words lacked conviction.

Nobody deserves to die like that. Once again the voice in her head was that of Rexol.

Cassandra shook her head to dispel the unwelcome presence, staggering backward as her world began to spin.

Something is wrong. I must warn the Pontiff.

Still on unsteady feet, she turned to the door of her chamber. In that instant she became acutely aware of her wrist: The itch was growing worse; it was driving her mad. It felt as if something was writhing beneath her skin, and she dug into the flesh in a desperate effort to burrow it out.

Her nails carved deep red furrows into her pale skin. A second later a single drop of blood welled to the surface and Cassandra's mystical sight was momentarily blinded by a brilliant flash.

In that instant it all became clear. Rexol was right. Everything he said had been true. The wizard hadn't stolen her from her parents: It was the Order that had tried to steal her. The Pontiff had lied to her all these years, he had betrayed her. He was a man without scruples, a man without mercy. Rexol, Jerrod, even the young apprentice were going to be burned at the stake. Unless she saved them.

Cassandra opened the door of her room, moving with quick, sure steps toward the lower levels of the Monastery where the prisoners were kept.

She knew the guards had been given strict instructions to limit all access to the cells holding the prisoners. But they knew the Pontiff had granted her permission to speak with them so she could appeal to Rexol's apprentice. They'd already let her see the prisoners once—they wouldn't hesitate to let her see them a second time.

At her request the two guards at the top of the stairs lit a lantern and accompanied her down into the dungeon, as they had before. At her signal, they opened the cell without a second thought.

As soon as the cell door was open she drove her fist into the soft flesh behind the first guard's ear, a simple move known to all the monks and one easily countered. But surprise gave her the advantage, and he crumpled silently to the ground. The second guard wasn't caught so unawares, however. He blocked her next attack, the still-burning lantern falling to the floor.

Even as he was taking the breath to cry out an alarm Jerrod crossed the cell and fell on him from behind. There was a sharp crack as the man's neck broke.

"You didn't have to kill him!" Cassandra admonished in a loud whisper.

Ignoring her, Jerrod bent down and broke the neck of the unconscious first guard, then scooped up the lantern. Rexol sprang up and hauled his apprentice to his feet.

Cassandra stumbled back as the three men shoved their way past her and out of the cell into the freedom of the hallway beyond. Slowly her mind began to clear, the shock of seeing two of her brothers mercilessly slain breaking the insidious spell that had worked its way into her mind. Her arm still burned but the feeling was rapidly fading now that the enchantment had served its purpose.

"What have I done?" she muttered through the lifting fog.

The words were barely out of her mouth when Jerrod was in motion again. He grabbed her by the waist, spun her around, and shoved her into the far corner of the now empty cell. The door slammed shut, trapping her inside.

They were free. Sort of. Though released from the cell Keegan was smart enough to understand that they were still deep within the bowels of the Monastery, and neither he nor his master had charms with them. The absence of charms, combined with the lack of witchroot in their blood, made even the simplest of spells a trial. If they were going to escape the fortress it would have to be through nonmagical means.

"We have to act before the Pontiff realizes we're free," Jerrod warned. "Follow me."

With the monk leading the way the three fugitives scurried down the dimly lit passage, their hunched forms and Jerrod's swaying lantern casting eerie shadows on the stone walls.

They climbed the stairs leading up from the dungeon. At the top they found a heavy iron door. Jerrod handed the lantern back to Rexol then used both hands to push against its smooth surface.

The door opened grudgingly, the creaking of the hinges sounding unnaturally loud in the heavy silence surrounding them.

Three members of the Order, two men and one woman, were waiting on the other side.

Keegan froze when he saw them, knowing their escape was over. Just in front of him Rexol began the incantations of a spell, but Keegan could sense only the faintest trickle of gathering Chaos—far too little to have any real effect.

Jerrod held up a hand to stay the spell before Rexol could unleash his feeble magic.

"How did you escape your cell?" the woman asked, though not with the anger or fear Keegan would have expected in the question.

"Cassandra set us free, though I don't think she can be considered an ally to our cause. It seems I was not the only one who staged my capture just to plan an escape."

Keegan's mind was quick; it only took him a moment to piece it all together. These monks were Jerrod's allies. They must have been coming to release him from his cell. For some reason he had allowed himself to be captured, knowing his hidden followers within the Order would free him before his trial. Except that Rexol's spell over Cassandra had freed them first.

One of the men fixed his blind eyes on Keegan. "Is this the savior?"

"Yes," was Jerrod's simple reply.

The monks bowed briefly toward the young man in a show of respect. Keegan wasn't sure what to say or do in response. Fortunately they weren't waiting for him to reply.

"We don't have much time," the woman reminded Jerrod, handing him a bundle of clothes from under her arm. "The others are preparing your mounts. Your only hope is to be miles away from here by the time the Pontiff realizes you are gone."

"We will do what we can to delay their pursuit of you," one of the men continued, "but we are outnumbered by twenty to one.

Even with the element of surprise it won't take long for Yasmin's Inquisitors to overwhelm us."

The clothes turned out to be robes of the kind worn by all those who served the Order. With the hoods pulled up, and from far enough away, the three of them would look like any of the other monks within the Monastery. At first Keegan wondered if the disguise was enough to fool the strange second sight of the Order—then he realized it must serve some purpose. If not, they wouldn't have bothered with any disguises at all.

His mind was reeling as he pulled the cloak over his head. It was obvious there was some kind of rebellion or uprising going on in the Monastery, and Jerrod seemed to be at the center of it. Clearly he had let himself be captured, but Keegan couldn't understand why.

And why had they referred to him as the savior? The savior of what? There were too many things he didn't understand, but he was smart enough to realize that now was not the time to start asking questions. The answers could wait until they were safely away from the Monastery . . . assuming they survived.

"If we are careful we can reach the stables without being seen," Jerrod said, turning his attention back to his fellow prisoners. "But we have to go right now."

Rexol, who hadn't said anything since they had escaped the cell, simply shook his head. "No. I'm not leaving without the Crown."

"What Crown?" Jerrod demanded, but Keegan knew what Rexol meant: The Talisman was somewhere here in the Monastery.

"I know it's here," Rexol said. "Ezra knew, too, didn't he? Somehow he learned of the Pontiff's great secret. But he warned you never to tell me about it."

Several seconds of uncomfortable silence passed before Jerrod spoke again. He didn't bother denying the mage's accusation.

"Do you realize what is at stake, Rexol? Whatever ambitions you might have, they must be set aside until we are beyond the Pontiff's reach."

"No. I came here for one reason: to claim the Crown for myself. I will not allow my purpose to be swayed by any plot or scheme of you and your followers."

"Even if the Crown is here," Jerrod hissed, "it is hidden away where no one can find it!"

"I can find it," Rexol said with certainty. "It is calling to me. I can feel its presence."

"Then go find it," Jerrod said with a shrug. "But do not expect us to wait for you. You are inconsequential, anyway." He pointed at Keegan. "He is the one we came for. The savior."

Arrogant rage flashed across the wizard's features, an expression Keegan had seen many times before. "Damn your prophecies! He is not your savior, he is my apprentice! And my apprentice will go with me!"

"You are going to your own death," Jerrod said without a hint of malice or anger. "Your apprentice has a greater destiny awaiting him. He must come with us."

Rexol gave a cunning smile. "I believe that decision lies with him."

All eyes turned to Keegan. The young man felt as if his knees were about to give out.

"I . . . I don't understand what you're saying," he told Jerrod. "I'm no savior."

"There isn't time to explain," Jerrod told him. "A simple choice: Whom do you trust? But whatever your decision, it must be made quickly."

He knew little about the Order, and even less about this rogue monk and his followers. Rexol, on the other hand, had been his master for a full year. He understood the wizard, and he knew why he was here and what he was after. He wanted the Crown; he wanted to possess the power of the Talisman. True, he had risked Keegan's own life to put himself in a position to acquire it. But the young man would have expected nothing less from his master.

The monks wanted to help him. Or seemed to, at least. But what would they expect in return? And what could they offer? The one thing he wanted—the power to bend and shape Chaos to his will—could only come from his master.

"I will stay with Rexol."

Jerrod sighed. "Then I must go with you two, as well." He turned to address his followers. "Let the others know what is happening. Try to keep our escape secret as long as you can. Make sure our horses are ready."

"And have someone find our charms," Rexol added. "Especially my staff. They were taken from us when we were thrown into the cell."

Jerrod nodded. The three ran off to carry out their new instructions.

"I have agreed to help you with this only because I see no other way to ensure the safety of the savior," he warned the wizard. "But once this Crown is discovered, we must flee this place and the Pontiff's wrath."

Rexol gave a short, dark laugh. "Once I possess the power of the Crown we won't have to."

The wizard muttered a few quick words, and Keegan sensed the faint whisper of Chaos as it bubbled up into the mortal world.

"Follow me," his master ordered.

Rexol took the lead, Keegan and Jerrod fell in behind. They moved at a brisk, purposeful walk to avoid attracting attention. The members of the Monastery were still unaware that anything was amiss; the halls within the building were largely unpopulated. Those few who did see them were always at a distance, and took no notice of the three robed figures.

Focused intently on maintaining control over his spell, Rexol didn't speak. But his steps never wavered, and he never hesitated on his chosen path. Even with his power dulled by a lack of witchroot and charms, his spell was still strong enough to follow the Crown's call.

He led them to a staircase near the back, then down into the Monastery's lower levels. This time they weren't going into the dungeons, but rather the Order's fabled libraries: room after room after room of shelves piled with books dating back to the Cataclysm itself. Under normal circumstances Keegan knew his master would have marveled at the manuscripts they passed. But even the ancient knowledge contained within their brittle, yellow pages had not deterred Rexol from his all-consuming goal.

The Monastery's libraries were massive beyond all comprehension. Keegan had heard it said that all the knowledge of man was contained within these archives, and as they had marched past the seemingly endless array of books he had begun to believe such a claim might be true. They went ever deeper into the archives, turning and twisting through the maze of shelves, descending staircase after staircase until Keegan was certain they must be hundreds of feet below the earth.

The deeper they went the heavier the air became. Inches of dust, the accumulation of centuries, could be seen on the books and shelves of the lower levels. Their feet stirred up gray, choking clouds from the floor as they walked. Even those who had sworn their lives to preserving the knowledge and worship of the True Gods did not venture this far down into the labyrinth of documents. Keegan wondered how long it had been since anyone, even the Pontiff himself, had been through here.

His wondering was cut short when he felt the first wisps of the Crown's power reaching out to him. Rexol's spell had been woven around the mage; it hadn't included his apprentice. The fact that Keegan could now sense the Talisman's presence must mean they were getting close.

It was faint at first: a half-imagined hum, a zephyr wafting across his consciousness. But it grew steadily stronger. Soon the Chaos made his blood tingle, the same sensation he felt when he ate witchroot or channeled the energy from one of his charms. By the time they had reached their destination Keegan's head was pounding and his body was sweating from the Chaos boiling within him. He couldn't even imagine the intensity of what Rexol was feeling with magic heightening his awareness.

Their way was barred by a heavy iron door.

"The Crown is just beyond here," Rexol whispered through tightly clenched teeth. His body was trembling, the veins on his head and neck were bulging out, and tears were streaming from his wide, wild eyes.

"Don't do this, Rexol," Jerrod begged one more time. "If you are right and the Talisman is here then it will destroy you. Remember: I have seen your death in my dreams."

Rexol let loose a sound that was half laugh and half scream. "You said the Pontiff would burn me at the stake! You saw me die in flame and fire! Your dreams are worth nothing."

He pushed on the heavy door, but it didn't budge. He staggered back, his trembling hands clutching his head as if his mind was about to tear his skull apart.

"Quickly, Keegan. Open the door."

Without question the apprentice did as he was told. It was a simple matter to shape the magic now, even without the witchroot in his blood. The very air was alive with the power of the Crown; all he had to do was draw on it. He crafted a simple shaping designed to shove the door ajar just enough to break the lock holding it shut. Focusing his mind, he released the spell.

Instead of a gentle push, the metal ripped from the hinges as the door exploded free and was hurled into the room. It smashed into the wall with a deafening clang, a warped and shredded piece of metal.

Inside the room the Crown sat on a small pedestal, glowing fiercely with its own light. Rexol staggered forward as if he was drunk and seized it with both hands. He fell to his knees and placed the Talisman atop his head.

Rexol's mind exploded with the knowledge of infinity. A million voices screamed out, the thoughts of every living being in the world rising in a single unbearable cacophony. The span of history trailed out behind him, a vast landscape stretching back to the Cat-

aclysm and beyond, to the very dawn of time itself. The multiplic-
ity of infinite futures fanned out before him, ever shifting, changing,
dissolving and re-forming.

It overwhelmed him, crushing him beneath the unfathomable
scope of pure Chaos rushing in to fill the empty void of what had
once been a human mind. His mortal self was engulfed by the
flood of knowledge, his very identity drowned out like a flickering
candle doused by all the oceans of the world at once.

A minuscule corner of what had once been Rexol clung briefly
to his identity, a single star resisting the pull of an infinite universe.
And within that tiny grain of self Rexol knew he was going to die,
utterly devoured by the untamable power of the Talisman's magic.

Rexol's last sensation before he was swallowed by the Chaos Sea
was the curious realization that he was not alone.

Daemron felt it like a hot knife thrust into the back of his skull; a
searing pain alerting him to the fact that a passage had been opened
to the mortal world. His body collapsed as he cast his consciousness
out, determined not to miss his chance again.

He saw it flickering in the infinite chasm like a beacon of blue
fire. He marked it: latching on, seizing it so he would not lose it
again even as he let his consciousness return to his physical form.
His connection to the mortal world would not be severed this
time.

"No!" Keegan screamed as the blue fires of Chaos engulfed his
Master. Instinctively he lunged forward, but Jerrod held him back.

"Do not interfere," the monk declared in a solemn voice. "This
is his destiny."

Rexol's skin swelled and split, and a bubbling blue liquid oozed
out from a thousand tiny rips and tears in his flesh. His back arched
as he shrieked in agony, and then his body exploded. The flames
flared up, vaporizing the spray of blood and bone instantly—then

suddenly the fire was snuffed out. The Crown clattered to the floor amid a small pile of black ash: all that remained of the greatest wizard of the Southlands.

Keegan stood paralyzed with horror and disbelief at what he had just witnessed. His mind numb, he didn't object when Jerrod grabbed him by the arm and pulled him away.

"Every person in the Monastery will have felt that Chaos surge. We have to get out of here right now."

The monk ran through the archives, winding his way back up to the surface and dragging the still-dazed Keegan behind him. When they burst forth from the library half a dozen of Jerrod's followers were waiting for them. Three other monks—no doubt those loyal to the Pontiff—lay dead on the floor.

"This way," they shouted, leading Jerrod and Keegan through the halls.

The sounds of fierce battle all around him managed to pierce the veil of confusion that clouded Keegan's mind. "We'll never make it," he mumbled.

"We're outnumbered but we're better organized," one of their escorts reassured him. "The others still aren't sure what's happening, they can't tell friend from foe. It won't take long for the Pontiff and Yasmin to rally them, though."

They encountered several small pockets of resistance in their flight, but only ever two or three monks at a time. The six-person vanguard surrounding them made short work of this disorganized opposition while ensuring neither Jerrod nor Keegan was ever in danger. They never even had to break stride as they ran, the bodies of those foolish enough to get in their way left broken and quivering in their wake.

And then they were at the wide-open Monastery gates. Another six monks were waiting for them there. At least a dozen cowled bodies littered the courtyard. A pair of horses stood saddled up and ready to ride; another pair had been loaded with provisions. Keegan could clearly see Rexol's gorgon's-head staff, wrapped in a blanket and strapped lengthwise across one of the packs, among the supplies.

"The four fastest mounts in the Monastery," the woman holding the reins explained as Jerrod and Keegan climbed into their respective saddles.

"They'll follow us," Keegan said in a dull, faraway voice.

It was a stupid comment but his mind was still struggling to grasp the full implication of everything that had just happened.

"They'll have to follow on foot," the woman replied, her voice grim. "I hobbled all the other horses in the stable. They'll have to be put down."

"Close the gates behind us and hold them off as long as you can," Jerrod shouted, spurring his mount toward freedom.

The other animals, including Keegan's own horse, instinctively leapt after the leader. It was all the dazed young man could do to hold on as they charged out into the moonlit desert night, scattering the small knot of sleepy and confused supplicants gathered outside the gate.

Chapter 31

DAEMRON MADE A final inspection of the bloodstained inscriptions on the rock. All seemed right; the ritual was ready to begin. The nine he had chosen waited impatiently nearby, separated from the crowd by the arcane symbols scrawled across the ground.

These nine were the strongest, the most ruthless, the most cunning of his people. He had chosen them to be his Minions, chosen them to return to the mortal world. After an eternity of banishment into this blighted realm these nine alone would be sent back. They were his heroes, his champions—and the ones he most feared.

He ruled through strength and strength alone. His generals bowed down to his power, not to him. The effort of maintaining his recently forged connection with the mortal world had cost him much of this power. Bridging the gap across the chasm would further tax what remained. After the ritual he might seem vulnerable, a target for rebellion.

Not the small pockets of resistance that plagued his kingdom now; they were mere nuisance, rebel insects to be crushed at his leisure. No, this would be a real rebellion, a true threat to his thousand-year reign. An uprising of mortal armies against an Immortal King, the armies led by a champion who thought to seize the power of a God for himself. Daemron knew all too well that such a thing was possible. But with these nine gone, the greatest threat to his rule would be sent across the chasm, through the roll-ing mists of the maelstrom to the mortal paradise placidly adrift in the Chaos Sea. And should all go as planned, the Minions would prepare the way for his own return.

The Legacy of the Old Gods was fading; the Gods themselves were dead. The veil hiding the world of the mortals had grown thin, allowing the brief surge of the Crown's magic to momen-tarily tear the gauze aside, revealing a beacon to show him his es-cape from this nether realm.

He himself could not return to the mortal world. Not yet. He had tested the Legacy, found its weakest points. But even these he could not yet cross. Not without the power of his Talismans to aid him. The Old Gods had woven their enchantments with special care to keep their fallen champion imprisoned in the shadow world Daemron had escaped to after the Cataclysm. But he was strong enough to send others through.

It would be difficult, but he could do it. They could find the Talismans and bring them back to him. With his rightful power restored, he would break free of this prison and return to rule the world he had once claimed as his own. And this time, the Old Gods would not be there to oppose him.

Still, fear held him back, made him hesitate. Sending the nine across the chasm was a calculated risk, but a risk all the same. If he failed the Chaos would devour him, swallowing up his very es-sence. No mortal feared death as he did, for no mortal could truly understand what a God had to lose.

Had his hesitation been noticed? Daemron scanned the crowd nervously. Were the usurpers who would overthrow him watching from within the crowd, plotting against his life, knowing he was soon to be weakened and drained by the awesome magic he was about to wield?

The misshapen features of his followers watched intently, some licking their fangs, others grinning from ear to ear across their pig-like snouts. Those with wings flapped them softly in anticipation. Once his people had been beautiful, but a millennium trapped in this prison world floating in the Chaos Sea had deformed them beyond all abnormality. Daemron had created this world as a refuge; but unlike the mortal world fashioned by the Old Gods, the boundaries of his realm could not hold the effects of Chaos at bay.

Here the Chaos Spawn walked the land unchecked, ravaging the wastes and wilderness and any foolish enough to venture from the high walls of the lone city Daemron had constructed. And with each generation, with each new birth, the physical manifestation of Chaos became more predominant among his people, twisting, changing, and transforming what had once been human followers into nameless abominations.

With relief he realized his hesitation had gone unnoticed. These mutants, these disfigured demons that bowed down to him, were not focused on their leader. Right now they cared nothing for the Immortal King who had once promised their ancestors all that the mortal world could offer. The eyes of his people were focused solely on the Minions, the nine chosen to go back.

This barren, blasted land Daemron and his followers had escaped to was a world devoid of all hope save one: the chance to one day escape this forsaken realm and return to the mortal world. The Minions were fulfilling that hope, and offering a chance for all the others to return as well. Those left behind studied the chosen nine, their pale eyes filled with hate, resentment, envy—and silent prayers for a successful mission.

Reassured, he began the ritual. From his scaled lips came whispered words of power. His clawed hands wove slow patterns in the air. His black leather wings twitched ever so slightly.

The sky began to churn slowly. Rumbling thunderclouds formed overhead. A chill filled the air, and those in the crowd without fur began to shiver. The symbols on the ground began to pulse with an eerie light. The Chaos began to gather.

His voice became louder, his hands began to move quicker. The thick muscles beneath his crimson skin began to flex and strain. His wings beat in staccato bursts, lifting his hooved feet several inches off the ground.

A glowing arch formed in the air; pale at first, then intensifying in brightness. Fearful moans and growls came from the watching crowd as they slithered and crawled farther away from their liege.

His wings beat furiously now, raising him twenty feet into the air. Lightning flashed from the sky, striking his form and engulfing it in fierce white light.

High above the crowd he threw back his horned head to the godless heavens and screamed out the sacred profanities. His form twisted and writhed in the white light, calling down a rain of arcane magic from the torn sky. With each convulsion a searing bolt of lightning surged down into the crowd, incinerating the demons it struck in a blinding blaze of heat. The panicked spectators scattered across the empty field, fleeing the unholy Chaos storm.

The Minions stood frozen as statues. Protected by the mystical runes carved into the bloodstained rock beneath their feet, they had no need to fear the spell their master was invoking. The reek of charred flesh filled their muzzles, causing them to salivate hungrily, but they kept their eyes averted from the crowd, focused on the glowing arch.

Daemron shrieked the words of the incantation, the white heat tearing through him, ripping him apart inside with a terrible, wonderful agony. His mind reached out, grasping, flailing, desperately searching to bridge the chasm of infinite space and time separating him from the mortal world. The pain intensified; his racked body dropped from the sky, plummeting to earth and crashing on the ground, still bathed in the blazing white light. The crack of an Immortal's breaking bones echoed across the dead plains—but Daemron was oblivious to the carnage wrought upon his physical shell.

The precipice of madness loomed before him; his disintegrating mind teetered on its edge. One final time he reached out . . . and grasped the edges of the mortal world. Clinging on with the tattered remnants of his sanity, he began to will the passage to form. His claws clutched spasmodically at the earth, carving gashes in the stone.

The Minions watched the portal.

His body began to spasm, and in a corner of his battered, broken mind Daemron began to draw strength from those around him. Only the Minions were shielded from his hunger. From his crumpled form tendrils of red smoke poured out, racing across the landscape in pursuit of the fleeing crowd. The fastest and strongest escaped, but those in the rear were swallowed up by the red clouds, their screaming bodies melting into pools of bubbling liquid.

Daemron fed on their suffering, drawing strength enough to complete the passage, to open the portal. The glowing white arch turned blue, then green, then clouded over like fogged glass before clearing to show a landscape of endless white sand beneath a star-filled sky.

The first Minion leapt forward into the doorway, disappearing through the arch. The others followed quickly, less than a second separating each one. Their master's crippled body jumped and twitched and shook on the ground, every muscle taut with the strain of keeping the portal open. The seventh Minion was through when the light surrounding Daemron vanished and the arch collapsed, slicing the eighth minion in half as he tried to cross over.

The ninth Minion stared at the severed remains of her companion lying on the rock—one arm and leg, half the torso, most of the head. Black ichor oozed from the corpse, seeping into the ground. The lone Minion turned away, sickened. Now she saw the remains of the crowd, many of them wounded and dying, trampled in the mad rush to escape the terrible power of the Chaos her master had unleashed upon them.

Her lord rose slowly to his feet, charred and smoking body hunched over in pain and exhaustion. His left leg jutted out at an odd angle, but Daemron ignored his injury to turn his full fury on the Minion before him.

"You should not have hesitated," he whispered.

The Minion threw herself on the ground before her master. "My lord, I had no chance. The portal collapsed even as Aeschel tried to cross."

Daemron made no reply but held out a single claw, burned and scarred as the rest of his body. Red fire flashed out from his eyes and engulfed the Minion. Her scream was cut off as her form was consumed by the flame in less than a second.

He began to move toward the injured in the crowd, standing a little straighter than before, the red flame flashing again and again among his followers who lay helpless on the ground, taking what remained of their wounded essence. By the time he was done his broken bone had mended, his burned flesh was completely healed, and none of the injured was left alive.

An infinity away, across the Chaos Sea, darkest night settled in on the sweeping dunes of the Southern Desert. Invisible beneath the faint stars and moonless sky, seven twisted forms made their way across the sand of the mortal world.

Chapter 32

THEY WERE GONE, like fugitives into the night. Running like the thieves they were. Rexol had paid for his crimes; in her mind Cassandra had heard the screams of her former master as the Chaos consumed him. But the others—Jerrod and the apprentice—had escaped.

Cassandra stood in the courtyard staring up into the blackness of the night sky. Two days ago, the ground had been littered with the bodies of her fallen brothers and sisters, slain by Jerrod and the traitorous monks who followed him. The actions of the rebels were punishable by death; treason was a capital crime among the Order. Not that it mattered. None of the dissenters had surrendered. They had given their lives to aid Jerrod's escape, willingly sacrificing themselves to buy him and his companion a few more precious seconds to get farther beyond the Pontiff's reach.

By the time someone had come to free Cassandra from the dungeons that night, the brief rebellion was already over, put down by Yasmin and her Inquisitors. They were gone now, too—setting off within hours of the battle's end to pursue Jerrod on foot. And though the traitors had a head start, Cassandra knew it was inevitable they would be caught.

Messenger birds had been sent out ahead to all the Pilgrims and servants of the Order scattered throughout the Southlands and the

Free Cities, warning them to be on the watch for Jerrod and the young man traveling with him. Wherever they fled, Yasmin would soon get word of their presence. Eventually, she would find them. And when she did, their punishment would be swift and just.

As for her own punishment, Cassandra knew she deserved no mercy. She had aided Rexol and Jerrod's escape; she had been the catalyst for all the death and carnage within the Monastery walls. The Pontiff had no choice but to charge her with heresy, and she had no intention of disputing the charges.

"Cassandra."

The voice at her shoulder startled her; she hadn't noticed the Pontiff's approach amid her guilt and self-loathing. She didn't bother to turn her dead eyes toward the speaker, didn't even dare to use her Sight. She was blind, alone in the darkness. A just punishment.

They were coming to take her back to the dungeons, where she would remain locked up until her trial. She had expected this; she was surprised it had taken them this long.

"I'm sorry for my part in this," she said in a soft whisper, her voice on the edge of tears. Not an excuse, nor a plea for mercy. Just the truth. But even as she said the words she knew how hollow they sounded. "I'm sorry for what I have done."

"What has been done here cannot be undone," the Pontiff said, though his voice was bitter. "And the consequences may be far greater than you can imagine. A second Cataclysm is coming and I am powerless to stop it."

Cassandra felt the hot sting of tears down her cheeks, her eyes no longer able to detect light or shadow but still able to weep in grief.

"It was my fault. I was weak. I should have fought against the wizard's spell."

The Pontiff made no offer to console or comfort her. "What you have done—what you were a part of—carries a terrible sentence."

"I . . . I'm ready, Pontiff." She hated herself for the tremor in her voice, for being weak in the face of her imminent execution. She took a deep breath and added, "I can bear the weight of my crimes."

"I hope you can, Cassandra. For all our sakes, I truly hope you can."

Something in his voice puzzled her. She let the black veil slip from her senses, allowing the Sight to make her aware of her surroundings. The Pontiff stood alone behind her, his gnarled hands gripping the reins of a magnificent black horse.

"Is he injured?" she asked, her supernatural awareness sensing that something was wrong with the animal.

"The heretics hobbled all the horses in the stables. This mount was always strong, and I have used my power to heal him as best I can. This is the best ride I can offer, it will have to make do."

"Ride? I . . . I don't understand."

"The wizard has opened a door to another world, Cassandra. A great evil has come through—twisted servants of our ancient enemy.

"They seek to tear down the Legacy so that the Slayer may return. But to do this they need the power of Old Magic. I have seen them in my visions, crossing the desert far to the south, heading toward the Monastery to claim one of the ancient Talismans."

"The Crown," Cassandra gasped. "The one I dreamed about!"

The Pontiff nodded. "For centuries we have kept it hidden here in the Monastery. But Rexol's actions exposed our secret. The Slayer's Minions know the Crown is here, and I fear we are no longer strong enough to defend it."

"Let me stand with you when you fight them!" Cassandra declared, her own recent betrayal of the Order forgotten in the sudden passion she felt welling up inside her. "We will destroy them or dispel them or banish them back to the world they came from!"

The Pontiff shook his head.

"The Minions are creatures bred in a world where Old Magic still reigns and the Chaos Spawn walk the land. Their bodies are born from Chaos itself; it thickens their blood and strengthens their bones. They wield magic not seen in the mortal realm since the Cataclysm.

"The battle with Jerrod's followers thinned our ranks, and Yasmin and her Inquisitors are too far away to return in time to reinforce us. And even if they were here, I doubt we'd have the strength to withstand the coming siege."

Cassandra noticed that the Pontiff carried a saddlebag slung over his shoulder. With her Sight she saw food and water packed inside . . . and something else. Something that burned so bright it made her mystical vision recoil. The Crown.

"Then you must flee!" Cassandra insisted. "Take the Crown and go, take it where they will never find it."

"Not me," the Pontiff replied, handing the saddlebag to her. "I am too old for such a journey. My limbs are weak with age. No, Cassandra. It must be you."

"But . . . but I am not worthy!" she protested. "I betrayed the Order! I helped release this evil! I have brought ruin upon the Monastery."

"You are linked to the Crown," he told her. "Its power kept it hidden for centuries. In all that time, no Seer ever sensed its presence . . . until you dreamed of it.

"Since then," he added, "I have had visions of my own. I have seen your flight, the Crown at your side. Only now do I understand what those visions foretold.

"Your fate is entwined with that of your old master I thought I could free you from that curse, sever the bond linking your destiny to his. In that, I failed you.

"Rexol is dead, but his actions have begun a series of events that have the potential to destroy us all. It is up to you to try and prevent this, Cassandra. You must atone for what you have done. It was not clear to me before, but now I understand: You alone can stop the Cataclysm."

She nodded slowly, her mind spinning out of control. But she put her faith in the Pontiff and his wisdom, accepting what he said as absolute truth. "What must I do?"

"The Minions will come for you, once they learn the Crown is not here. They will seek you out with their spells and hunt you down with their foul magic. For the sake of the mortal realm, they must not find you."

"Where will I go?"

"East," the Pontiff replied. "East to the ends of the earth. Seek the Guardian beyond the mountains at the end of the world. Let your Sight be your guide, Cassandra. The Crown will direct you through your dreams, but do not be so foolish as to put it on lest you suffer the same fate as the wizard."

She bowed her head in supplication, knowing further argument was merely a waste of valuable time. The Pontiff's decision had been made. She secured the saddlebag in place on her steed and swung herself up into the saddle.

"I will go at once," Cassandra said, her mind a mix of guilt, fear, and a fierce determination that threatened to overwhelm her. "I will not fail you!"

"We will hold out as long as we can," the Pontiff promised. "But we will surely fall. We are giving our lives to protect the Crown. Do not let our sacrifice be wasted."

There was a crack like thunder, and the ebony gates of the Monastery flew open. Cassandra spurred her mount through the opening, racing off through the desert night with the terrible words of the Pontiff ringing in her ears and tears of desperate shame streaming from her eyes.

Chapter 33

"WE'LL STOP HERE," Jerrod said, pulling his weary horse to a halt. "It will give us a chance to decide what to do next."

The mounts had been bred to travel long distances in the harshest conditions, but their prolonged flight had reduced the beasts to a slow walk at best.

Keegan slid from his saddle and nearly collapsed onto the soft desert sand. They had ridden north for three days with hardly a break. The Monastery was at least a hundred leagues behind them, but they wouldn't leave the desert wastes behind them until sometime tomorrow.

During their desperate flight, Jerrod had barely spoken to him. The long silence had given Keegan a chance to sort things out for himself. Rexol, his master, was dead. He didn't feel grief, exactly—not like when his father had died—but there was a definite sense of loss. And now he found himself a fugitive from the Order, a heretic fleeing with a man he had just met and knew almost nothing about . . . apart from the fact that he was crazy. That wasn't surprising; the religious fanatics who served the Order were all a bit mad. But Jerrod seemed to suffer from a very particular and specific delusion: one in which Keegan was supposed to be some kind of savior.

"Have something to eat and try to rest. We can only stay a few hours before we have to start moving again."

"Are you afraid the Inquisitors will catch up with us?" Keegan asked as he rummaged through the supplies on one of the pack horses. He found bread and cheese in one pocket, a bottle of wine in another.

"No, but not all the servants of the Order are within the Monastery," Jerrod explained as he unrolled a pair of trail blankets. "Once we reach the borders of the Southlands, the Pilgrims will be searching for us as well. Though not as dangerous as Yasmin's trained killers, they are still formidable foes."

Keegan took the food and drink from the saddlebags and sat down on one of the blankets. He tore a chunk of bread from the loaf and passed it to the monk as Jerrod sat down on the blanket beside him.

"I realize this must be confusing for you, Keegan. I'm sure you have many questions. Ask them, and I will do my best to answer them for you."

For a minute, the young man wasn't sure what to ask. He chewed thoughtfully on the bread, then washed it down with a swig from the wine bottle.

"How did you and my master know each other?"

"We used to be allies, of a sort. He wanted a worthy apprentice: a child touched by Chaos. I needed to find a champion—someone with the strength to stand against the armies of the Slayer when the Legacy crumbles."

"Meeting you in that cell wasn't just coincidence, was it?" Keegan asked.

"No. I had seen a vision. I knew the Pontiff was going to summon Rexol. I knew he would answer. I knew he would bring you with him. So I allowed myself to be captured."

"You let the Inquisitors imprison you just so you could meet me?"

"You are the champion we have been waiting for. In my visions, I saw that your master would die in a blaze of fire within the Monastery's walls. I thought the only way to save you from a similar fate was to be there myself."

"So you arranged for your own capture, knowing you had loyal followers who would help you escape?"

The monk nodded. "It was a gamble, but one I thought was necessary. I have searched too long for a savior to let you be burned as a heretic."

"And what, exactly, am I supposed to be a savior of?"

"Everything, of course."

Keegan snorted and took a bite from the block of cheese. This time he didn't offer any to his companion.

"A time of great danger is drawing near, Keegan. The Legacy is fading, and an army of monsters will soon pour forth from the Flaming Sea to overrun the land."

"The Chaos Spawn are extinct," Keegan said matter-of-factly. He had studied under Rexol long enough to realize what the monk was talking about. "They died out long ago. All that remains are their bones."

"Not extinct, merely banished by the power of the True Gods. One day soon they will return. For many years I and my followers have been preparing for this day," Jerrod explained. "We have been searching for a champion: a mage with the power to stand against them. For a long time Rexol was helping us in our search, until we went our separate ways."

"Why didn't you just ask Rexol to be your champion?"

"The wizard was strong," the monk admitted. "But much of his strength came from knowledge and study. He had mastered his craft, but his talent had reached its apex. He did not have the raw ability; he lacked power to stand against our enemies.

"We knew there were others. As the Legacy has weakened children have been born with Chaos in their blood. Children with the ability to go far beyond anything Rexol could ever hope to accomplish. Children like you.

"But Rexol could never accept this. We wanted him to train our champion, to create a savior for the entire world. But Rexol did not believe in our cause. He only wanted power for himself. He was dangerous; his selfish ambition was a threat to our plan."

"Is that why you let him die?" Keegan asked the question without bitterness. He was too tired to be bitter.

"I tried to warn him. I tried to tell him that I had foreseen his death in a blaze of fire, but he would not listen. His pride destroyed him. There was little I could have done to change that.

"In the end it didn't matter. I did not come for him. I came for you. The savior."

The young man just shook his head. "I'm no savior. I'm just an apprentice."

"Chaos is strong in your veins," Jerrod assured him. "You have the Sight, you have the Gift. All you need is to learn how to unlock your potential."

"And how am I supposed to do that now that my master is gone?"

The monk was silent for a time, trying to come up with an answer. "Rexol had other students before you. Many of these completed their training and now serve in the noble courts. Perhaps they can help."

"Sure. All we have to do is head to the nearest of the Seven Capitals and ask the resident court mage to finish my training so I can save the world. I'm sure they won't mind."

The monk reacted as if he hadn't noticed the sarcastic tone of Keegan's suggestion.

"No, the Order holds too much power in the Southlands. We cannot look for help there."

Keegan gave a weary laugh. It all sounded so ridiculous, so unbelievable. He was no savior. But what other options did he have? He wasn't stupid enough to even think about going back to Rexol's manse: The Order was probably already there waiting for him. He was a heretic now, a fugitive with no home and no one to turn to but this crazed fanatic. Whatever else he might think of Jerrod, the monk was his only hope of survival.

"Where, then? You're obviously the one in charge here. You tell me where we should go."

"The Free Cities. They have no love of the Order; I stayed there often while I was in hiding from the Pontiff and his followers."

"That'll take weeks," he protested. "We'll have to cross the entire breadth of the Southlands!"

"Yes," Jerrod agreed. "And the Order will be hunting for us the entire way. We'll have to avoid the larger settlements and the more traveled routes so that reports of our passing are not relayed back to the Pontiff."

"We do make a rather conspicuous pair."

The robes they were still wearing from their escape were plain enough, but Rexol's staff destroyed any illusion that they might be simple travelers. It was strapped to one of the pack horses, the empty eyes of the gorgon's skull staring out and marking at least one of them as a wizard to any who saw it.

"We can always hide the staff," Jerrod said, as if he were reading Keegan's thoughts. "And I have learned to alter my own appearance in subtle ways." His unmistakable eyes shimmered and slowly transformed into a common brown. "A simple illusion that helped me conceal my identity during my years in hiding."

"Magic?" Keegan asked in surprise. "I thought the Order disapproved of such things."

"You will learn that I am more tolerant than most of my kind on this subject," Jerrod replied with the hint of a smile. "In any case, my skill is a simple alteration of myself. The power comes from within, and it is wholly contained. My talent is far more limited than the act of unleashing Chaos upon the world."

"Which is why you need a wizard like me to be your champion," Keegan said, slowly wrapping his head around Jerrod's mad reasoning. "Even if you had the power, you don't know how to unleash it."

"You need to sleep," the monk said by way of reply. "We have a long journey ahead of us."

Keegan lay down, burrowing his body into the soft sand until it shaped itself to the contours of his body. He closed his eyes and immediately felt sleep overtaking him. Before he slipped away he managed to ask one final question.

"You still didn't tell me where we're going," he mumbled. "Which of the Free Cities?"

"We'll go to Torian," came the reply. "One of Rexol's former students was recently given a prominent position there. A man I met once long ago, though only briefly. A man named Khamin Ankha. Hopefully he will help us."

Chapter 34

STORMS WERE RARE in the desert, but this was no ordinary thunderhead. The winds carried the scent of destruction. The unnatural clouds crawled over the desert sand until they hovered above the Monastery like a dark ceiling. The air seethed with an almost palpable hatred as the green sky boiled above. A crack of thunder and a flash of blue lightning arced down to strike the ebony walls, scorching the invincible rock—a test of their strength, a warning of what was to come.

The members of the Order stood undaunted along the battlements, gazing with their second sight into the eerie darkness, seeking in vain for any sign of their enemy beneath the black clouds. A dozen monks manned each of the south, west, and north walls. The remaining members of the Order within the Monastery, a group of a mere two dozen led by the Pontiff, had gathered in the courtyard to guard the east wall should the enemy somehow breach the massive gates.

The rest of the monks, along with the supplicants who gathered outside the walls, were gone. The Pontiff had sent them out as Pilgrims to spread the word of the coming Cataclysm, to hunt down the traitor Jerrod, to choose a new Pontiff—and to keep the Order alive when the Monastery inevitably fell.

Beneath the rumble of the storm an endless litany of rhythmic chanting could be heard, an ancient ritual of the Order, the same one used to bind the Chaos within the Monastery walls. But now the chant was directed out and upward, forming an invisible shield of power overhead to ward off the evil of the storm.

The monks were armed with staves inscribed with mystic symbols and ancient glyphs of power copied from texts that predated the Cataclysm. They wore no armor to protect them, but instead had donned simple cloaks adorned with runes of protection designed to negate, absorb, and shield against the Chaos their enemy would unleash.

Over the past days similar markings had been carved into the interior walls surrounding the Monastery, to strengthen the latent energy within them. Even the ground had been etched with symbols to ward off the spells of the Minions, the Pontiff drawing upon the vast resources of the Order's library to uncover the knowledge of a lost age to help defend the sacred fortress. But it would not be enough.

The Minions were out there, hidden by the power of the storm they had conjured. And soon, the Pontiff knew, they would lay siege to the stronghold of the Order.

The sky boomed with the thunder of Chaos, and the clouds looming dark above the Monastery erupted in a spectacular explosion of blue lightning. Searing electrical strikes knifed down toward the monks defending the walls, only to be deflected by the invisible barrier. The will of the monks within shuddered but held; their chanting continued in an endless refrain.

The deadly bolts flashed down again and again, until the earth outside the Monastery walls began to smoke and smolder from the constant barrage of blue lightning. But inside the Monastery all was calm; the blue fire from the sky could not enter. The collective will of the Order had held firm against this first assault.

As suddenly as it had started, the lightning stopped and the clouds burst. Sheets of rain pelted down. The monks' magic only protected against that which was harmful, so the rain passed unhindered through the barrier. Within seconds they were all drenched through their cloaks with the chill waters of the storm.

From the clouds three winged Minions swept down, becoming visible to the Pontiff's second sight as soon as they left the concealing power of the storm. All three were humanoid in appearance, but eons of exile in the Slayer's blighted realm had mutated them into perverse monsters. Generations of ancestors subjected to the terrible whims of Chaos had turned the three into hideous creatures, each unique and alien to the mortal world.

The first had the head of an alligator; green scales covered its body from the ends of its clawed feet to the tips of its taloned hands. Its leather wings flapped in a slow rhythm, keeping its reptilian form aloft. The second flew on the wings of a great eagle, but had the body of a man. The body may have been human at one time, but now was hairless and withered as if it bore the age of a thousand years. The skin was drawn tight against the bones of the skull; the lips had receded to reveal a savage rictus of sharpened fangs. The joints protruded prominently beneath the dry, desiccated flesh that covered its limbs, and the ribs could be seen on its sunken chest. Its naked skull was adorned only by a pair of hollow eye sockets; the nose had long since rotted. Its skin was the sallow color of a mummified corpse.

The third Minion was barely more than a shadow, even to the magical second sight of the monks watching from the battlements. Jet black from head to toe, its wings made no sound as it glided on the currents of the storm. The dark, naked body was in the form of a beautiful woman, but her head was that of a giant bird, the mouth extending into a cruelly hooked beak. Its eyes, two flaming red points set into the black forehead of the beast, pulsed with sinister power.

The macabre trinity hovered over the monks, the heavy beat of their wings audible even above the sounds of the storm. But these were creatures of Chaos, its foul power ran thick in their blood, and they could no more pass the Order's shield than the bolts of blue lightning. In unison they howled to the sky in rage and frustration, piercing the torrential downpour with their screams. Blood trickled from the ears of many of the monks, but they kept their will firm. As one voice the Order chanted the mystic words of power that banished and rejected their magic, and the Minions could not enter.

Outside the gate four more Minions approached across the rain-soaked sand—the Pontiff could see them in his mind's eye, his second sight penetrating through the dark walls of the Monastery. They marched forward in pairs, the first two identical twins except that one was dark blue and the other was bright red. Like their airborne brethren this pair were humanoid, but they scuttled on all fours, crawling across the sand on freakishly long arms and legs, the muscles of their limbs flexing as they scrambled forward. They had the heads of boars, but they were completely hairless and had no ears. On reaching the gate they paused and rose up, waving their claws in the air, sniffing the wind with their snouts.

The pair behind them did not scuttle forward, but walked upright through the mud that minutes earlier had been desert sand. The one on the left was eight feet tall, its body a bizarre cross between a gorilla and a bear, its fur the brownish red of dried blood. Two short horns grew from its forehead, and a long whip-like tail trailed behind it in the sand. Its serpent tongue flicked in and out with each step, and its tail swished from side to side.

The other Minion stood only slightly taller than an average man, his body cloaked in a heavy cloth cape wrapped close about his form. His skull was hairless, too long and too narrow. His features were bat-like, his ears pointed and pinned back, his nose small and sunken, his thin, lipless mouth lined with too many sharply pointed teeth. Yellow cat's eyes peered out hungrily from his chalky complexion. He reached a long thin hand out from his cape to signal the others above, inch-long nails gleaming at the ends of his long, elegant fingers.

The three in the air flew down to meet their companions at the edge of the east wall. The Pontiff could not sense if there were

more than these seven hidden somewhere within the clouds. The
Minion in the dark cape spoke briefly with the shadowy flier, revealing two rows of pointed yellow teeth. Their conversation was
a mixture of human speech and animal grunts and squawks. These
two approached closer to the gate—the dark bird-like creature
leaving no footprints as it glided over the wet sand half a pace behind the pale, thin man. After several seconds the caped Minion
spoke in a loud, clearly human voice.

"I am Orath, right hand of Daemron. The dark one is Raven,
chief counselor to our lord. Give us the Crown and we will spare
your lives. This is my promise."

The Pontiff made no reply—none needed to be made. The
Order understood the Slayer's true nature; none among them
would willingly surrender to such an evil, even though none of
them expected to survive the coming battle.

For several seconds there was silence; then Raven whispered
something to Orath. Again he called out, flashing his tiny, sharp
fangs as he spoke.

"Raven holds great sway with our master. Surrender and she
will see you are rewarded when our master comes again to reign
over this world."

The Minions would ultimately destroy the Monastery and everyone inside. The Pontiff knew this, as did all the monks. They
fought not to win this battle, but to buy time for Cassandra. Again
the Pontiff made no answer, though he raised a single hand high in
the air. At his silent command the monks focused their spirits, further reinforcing the shield along the perimeter of the Monastery
that was sustained by their ceaseless chanting.

Orath at last realized no reply would be forthcoming. He turned
back to his followers, speaking again in the strange half-human,
half-animal language. Raven remained by his side, but the other
two winged Minions took to the air, circling high above the Monastery walls, darting in and out of the obscuring clouds of the
storm.

The crawling twins circled around to the west side of the fortress, shuffling back and forth eagerly at the foot of the wall, held at bay by the Chaos barrier emanating from the dark stone. The gorilla-bear lumbered off to stand at the base of the south wall, its tail swiping back and forth, its tongue darting in and out in anticipation.

Orath and Raven linked hands and raised their arms to the sky as they began to speak a slow litany of mystic syllables. Above their heads a small ball of sickly green light formed—the gathering of Chaos. As the chant continued the ball grew in size and intensity. The winds began to howl, turning the driving rain into sheets of water that fell sideways. Cracks of thunder drowned out their foul words of evil sorcery. The ball of summoned Chaos was now nearly five feet across. Still, they chanted.

The floor began to tremble beneath the feet of the monks guarding the still-sealed gate of the east wall. The faint rumblings increased into powerful tremors; the earth heaved and buckled, throwing many of the monks to the ground. The very walls of the Monastery began to sway as the earthquake gained force and spasms swept across the desert sand like waves over a storm-tossed sea.

The Pontiff could do nothing but focus his will on trying to maintain the protective shield around the Monastery, channeling the power of the entire Order through him in a futile effort to resist the increasing magic of the two Minions beyond the gate.

Raven and Orath stood motionless but for their chanting mouths, unmoved by the earthquake that rocked the foundations of the Order's stronghold. The ball of Chaos above them swelled to twenty feet across, burning with the intensity of a green sun. Moving in perfect synchronicity the two wizards threw their upraised arms downward, then dropped to their knees. The burning ball of Chaos dove into the ground.

The sky erupted into deafening peals of continuous thunder; a huge fissure appeared in the ground, running from the feet of the two Minions to the wall of the Monastery. The east wall burst asunder, the stone gates twisting and melting and tearing apart with a sick, wet sound.

The shield was breached, the spell of protection broken, the force field surrounding the Monastery instantly dissolved. The Minions on the ground leapt onto the Monastery walls, using their claws to scale the perfectly smooth surface even as the night exploded in brilliant blue and white lightning. Bolts of fire shot down from the clouds, striking the monks atop the battlements.

Those who were strongest were only knocked from their feet, their cloaks smoldering from the lightning's heat as they resisted the terrible powers of Chaos. Those who were not strong enough to resist—well over half the monks atop the battlements—were consumed by the bolts, their bodies exploding into ash and cinders.

The reptilian Minion dropped from the clouds onto the south wall where only two monks had survived the initial assault. A second later the deformed gorilla clambered over the battlement as well, the inhuman howls that rose from its jaws drowning out the heavy beat of the other's bat-like wings.

One of the surviving monks rose to his knees, his staff spinning above his head in preparation for the coming combat. The reptilian Minion stepped forward, mystic words of power falling from its scaled lips. The monk tried to rise to his feet, but could not move his legs. The Minion's words continued and a second later the monk was frozen in white marble—a statue with a scream of horror etched on its face for all eternity.

The second Minion on the wall, the great gorilla-beast, lashed out with its tail, driving the poisoned tip deep into the throat of the second monk before she could bring her runed staff to bear. Her body tumbled lifeless from the battlement, crashing to the stone floor of the Monastery fifty feet below. The creature leapt from the parapet, landing on all fours on the Monastery's interior grounds. The reptilian Minion followed, gliding down on its bat-like wings.

On the north wall three monks fought desperately against the Minion that had descended like a macabre angel from the heavens to confront them, its desiccated body reeking of musty death. The monks charged their emaciated foe, their staves spinning, whirling blurs as they attacked. Each time a staff struck the battlement wall a chunk of stone dissolved into dust, disintegrating instantly when struck by the devastating power channeled through the glyphs etched upon the shaft of the monks' weapons. But their enemy was elusive: The Minion ducked and dodged, leaping over one attack while sidestepping a second blow. The air was filled with putrid feathers shed from its decaying wings; they fluttered and spun crazily in the wind before settling gently to the stone floor.

The Minion chanted and wove its withered hands in the air as it danced away from the deadly blows of the monks' staves. The stone floor of the battlement melted into mud, and the surprised monks sank up to their ankles before they realized what had happened. And then the floor became stone again, trapping them in place.

Their enemy began another chant, his atrophied arms raised to the dark sky above as he slowly backed away. The monks struggled desperately to free themselves as an inky mist floated down from the black clouds above. The Minion watched in silent satisfaction as the mist settled on the helpless monks. Safely outside the toxic cloud it listened to the screams of the humans as the mist ate away their flesh, stripping away their skin and muscle, turning their blood into thick red steam. Seconds later three skeletons collapsed, the bones of their feet and ankles still encased in the stone floor.

To the west the crawling twins climbed over the battlements. The four surviving monks rushed to attack them, but a ten-foot wall of ice materialized to block their path. The monks lashed out with their will, the ice melting as they dispelled the Chaos. But the delay as they unbound the magic of their foe gave the twins time to invoke a powerful channeling of Chaos. Even as the ice wall melted away a gust of enchanted wind swept the monks from their feet, tossing them like dry leaves before the hurricane. Their bodies were hurled from the battlement and thrown across the courtyard, slamming into the far wall of the Monastery. The echo of the crash masked the sound of shattering bones and cracking skulls.

Raven and Orath rose to their feet, still linked hand in hand. At a signal from the Pontiff, the monks guarding the east wall rushed forward through the breach to attack. Bolts of black fire shot from Raven's eyes and drove them back. The monks managed to throw up a magical shield to deflect the dark and deadly flames, a localized variation on the shield used to protect the Monastery earlier. But some were too weak to withstand the sorceress's spell and were instantly consumed by the arcane flames ripping through their personal protective barriers.

Orath threw back his head and bellowed to the sky. The monks closest to him fell to the ground upon hearing the ghastly sound, their bodies racked by convulsions and seizures as their brains melted into gray pulp within their skulls.

None of the monks manning the battlements was left alive, and of the two dozen guarding the east gates almost half were dead or dying. The survivors fell back and surrounded the Pontiff in a desperate attempt to protect their leader. But before they could mount a counterattack, the Minions fell on them.

Orath and Raven stayed back as the other five engaged the monks in a short but bloody melee. The monks were too slow to use their staves against the unearthly quickness of the Minions. The creatures swept through the crowd of helpless mortals, ripping and tearing with claws, talons, and teeth. Within seconds the ground was littered with writhing monks, many of them disemboweled or dismembered by the fury of their inhuman foes. The ground was stained with great pools of the Order's blood that even the torrential rain could not wash away.

In a matter of minutes the entire force of the Order had been wiped out, the monks reduced to carrion by the savagery of their enemies. The Pontiff alone still lived, but he could only watch, powerless. His body was frozen by one of Orath's incantations—he had been paralyzed at the start of the brief but brutal melee, unable to come to the aid of his dying brothers and sisters. The Minion had simply brushed aside the Pontiff's efforts to defend himself against the Chaos, laying the most powerful member of the Order bare and vulnerable to the effects of his spell.

Orath approached the slaughter, surveying the scene of his victory with a twisted smile on his dark blue lips. "Ermus, Cerus—the survivors are yours." The crawling twins scuttled forward and picked their way through the carnage, using their pig-like snouts to systematically tear out the throats of any monks that still twitched or showed any signs of life in their mangled bodies.

While Ermus and Cerus finished off their enemies, the other Minions were breaking the enchanted staves of the monks, causing flashes of bright light as the Chaos burst free. They captured the released energy, drawing it into themselves and feeding on the magic contained within the rune-etched wood. The Pontiff, held fast in the powerful spell of their leader, could do nothing but watch. Orath's spell would not even allow him to close his sight on the gruesome scene.

"Enough," the leader of the Minions finally called out. "Time grows short. Gort, Draco—find the Crown."

Draco, the reptilian Minion, and Gort, the gorilla-bear, set off to search the Monastery for the ancient Talisman. Ermus and Cerus, the crawling twins, continued their grim executions while the others waited expectantly for Draco and Gort to return with their prize.

Despite the complete and total defeat of the Order, despite being held powerless in the grip of his enemies, the Pontiff felt some satisfaction. The Minions would not find what they searched for; all that remained was a pile of cinder and ash in the small room at the bottom of the library.

It was nearly an hour before they returned, empty-handed. "It is gone," the alligator hissed. "Even the library is destroyed. They set fire to all the manuscripts. Everything is burned." If he had been able, the Pontiff would have laughed out loud.

Orath approached the Pontiff, his drawn features twisting into a frown as the pupils of his yellow eyes narrowed. "Your attempt to thwart our search will not save you—our master's return will not be so easily halted. Scirth will find out what we need to know." His voice was a whisper filled with menace. Orath motioned for the emaciated Minion with the angel's wings to come closer.

Scirth approached and placed a single bony hand on the Pontiff's throat. With the chilling touch the Pontiff could feel his life force, his very essence, being drained out of his body. His spirit was drawn from him, sucked into the gaunt, skeletal arm of Scirth. And with his spirit went his thoughts and memories.

"They once had the Crown here, but it is gone." Scirth's voice was soft and rasping. "Sent away even as we approached, taken east by one of the Order. This battle was only an attempt to stall us."

The Pontiff fought against Scirth's magic, gathering his own will to hold on to his knowledge, to hide from the Minions those secrets they must not know.

The mummified man trembled, his diseased wings quivering slightly. Scirth laughed, a truly cruel and evil sound. "He fights me, General. He knows much that is hidden."

"Continue the interrogation," Orath commanded. "He must know the location of the other Talismans. That was why they burned the library, to stop us from learning where they are hidden."

The Pontiff could feel Scirth's grip tighten around his neck, could feel the probing thoughts of the Minion slicing through his psyche. And he could feel his body growing weaker, withering and aging beneath Scirth's touch.

"There is another. A monk, though he is no friend of the Order. And with him a young wizard of great power. They aided the one who was consumed by the Crown."

Orath nodded. "It is as Daemron foresaw. A champion has arisen from among the mortals; a child touched by Chaos; the catalyst for the master's return. What else? Where did he send the Crown?"

"His mind is strong," Scirth admitted. "Much is still hidden. I must go deeper."

Scirth's mental invasion continued; the Pontiff could sense his thoughts being raped by Scirth's mind even as he fought to keep the most vital secrets from being exposed. In desperation the Pontiff lashed out with his will, trying to destroy that which was destroying him. Scirth gasped and recoiled as if he had been stung, releasing his hold on the Pontiff's throat. The Pontiff's body, now that of an old, old man, collapsed on the ground.

"What is wrong?" Orath demanded.

"His mind is strong," Scirth explained again. "He has worn the Crown. He is no longer a mere mortal; he has been touched by the magic of the Old Gods. This will be difficult, it will take some time. Have patience, my General."

Orath frowned. "The more time we spend, the farther ahead of us the escaping monk gets."

"I cannot rush," Scirth cautioned. "I would not want to damage his mind, or destroy it. It must be carefully picked. He knows the locations of all the Talismans—I could sense it. We do not need the library; we will have all the information we need from this one, in time. But he shields himself and guards his secrets well. I must rest before I try again."

Scirth lowered himself to the ground, curling his scrawny body into a tight ball then folding his moldering wings over his body. Orath watched impatiently; the others began searching the bodies of the monks, looking to scavenge anything of value or worth. No one paid any attention to the decrepit form of the Pontiff lying on the ground.

Slowly, careful not to draw the notice of his enemies, the Pontiff gathered what remained of his strength, delving deep into the well of latent power that resided within him. They knew he was strong in the Sight, but they did not suspect he also possessed the Gift. It had never been strong within the Pontiff, and he had never developed this unholy ability. He had never even tried to use it since joining the Monastery many decades ago. But the Gift was a part of him, however small.

He gathered the Chaos in minuscule amounts. The scene around him dissolved into darkness as the Pontiff lost the magical ability of second sight—he was channeling all of his energy into another task.

Orath began to pace, anxious to resume the interrogation. Angrily he kicked the huddled form of Scirth, sending the frail body sprawling over the dirt. Scirth cast a hateful glare at the more powerful Minion, then slowly rose to his feet.

"Very well, I will continue."

He approached the quivering, wrinkled form of the Pontiff, prepared to resume stripping the mind and soul from his captive. But as he reached out with an eager hand he felt something, and paused. "General, he is gathering Chaos."

Before Orath could react the Pontiff struck. He unleashed the Chaos in a single focused bolt of lethal energy. He directed the attack not at his enemies, for their power was too strong, but at himself. Within his chest his heart exploded, bursting with an audible pop. The Pontiff died instantly, taking his knowledge of the Talismans with him.

Orath leapt forward, seized the withered body of the Pontiff, and lifted him up from the ground. His yellow fingernails biting deep into the dry flesh of the atrophied biceps, he flooded the corpse with the power of Chaos in an effort to reverse the lethal injury. But as great as his magic was, the Minion could not resurrect the dead. After several seconds the Pontiff's body began to steam and smoke; the skin cracked and blistered, and foul, putrescent liquid began to seep from his wounds. In disgust Orath let the lifeless body collapse to the ground.

"Scirth," the leader of the Minions said simply, "you have failed."

Scirth dropped to his knees, his hands held before him in supplication. "Please, my General. It was not my fault." His soft, raspy voice now squeaked with terror. "Give me another chance, I beg you . . ."

Scirth's pleas died on his lips as Orath placed his hand on the kneeling Minion's head. A globe of white light enveloped them, briefly blinding the other Minions to the scene. When the light faded Orath stood alone, his hand resting on a heap of dust, which was quickly scattered in the howling wind.

Orath turned his back on what had once been the Minion known as Scirth, pulling his cape close once more about his naked blue body. "Raven, I know you will not fail. Go east. Find the monk that flees with the Crown."

Raven made no reply but simply took to the skies, her shadowy form disappearing into the dark storm clouds that still loomed above the Monastery.

"Destroy this place," Orath ordered the others. "Raze it to the ground. Nothing must survive; not a single stone of these walls may remain intact. Unleash the Chaos trapped within the walls, scatter the dust of this place to the wind. We will wipe its very memory from existence, just as we will destroy all who oppose our master's return.

"Then we begin our search for the other Talismans."

Chapter 35

CASSANDRA HADN'T SLEPT—TRULY slept—since the Pontiff had cast her out of the Monastery. Her flight had been constant. She only paused long enough to commandeer a new horse whenever the one she was riding threatened to keel over from exhaustion, or to get more food and water to sustain her on her journey.

Otherwise, she hadn't dared speak to anyone; not even when she had sensed a fellow Pilgrim in the vicinity. After the betrayal by Jerrod's faction, she couldn't be sure a member of the Order would prove her ally.

She checked her horse to a slow trot, trying to conserve its strength. New mounts were easy to acquire in the Southlands. Those who saw her took one look at her sightless eyes, recognized her as part of the Order, and invariably gave her what she demanded without question. But now the Southlands were behind her.

This morning she had passed across the border of the last province that bowed to the Seven Capitals and entered the Frozen East, land of barbarians and savages. The bleak tundra stretched out miles before her, devoid of buildings or habitation. The only people she would meet out here would be nomadic hunter tribes who had no allegiance save that of their chieftain—and no respect or use for the Order or the mission of its emissary.

Here she was truly alone. This horse had to last.

The steady *clop-clop-clop* of the hooves soothed her, and she let herself drift into a deep meditation as she rode. But meditation was no substitute for what her weary body craved. Her meditation became deeper; the semiconscious state of her trance slid into the warm darkness of true sleep. And Cassandra dreamed.

She was standing in the sands of the Southern Desert, the Monastery under assault from an army of mutated demons. The mantle of the sky was torn asunder, and thousands upon thousands of the twisted creatures poured through the rift, overwhelming her brothers and sisters, devouring them, swallowing the Monastery itself in savage bites that tore the indestructible stone apart piece by piece.

And then the Chaos army swarmed out from the Monastery like a spreading plague, covering the Southlands, killing, ravaging, destroying as they came. The Slayer himself walked among them—a pillar of fire in her dream, a hundred feet tall. He strode across the land, leaving smoldering ruin in his wake. Cities burned and crumbled into lifeless ash at his passing. Chaos had been unleashed upon the mortal world. The second Cataclysm had begun.

The desert disappeared, and Cassandra stood alone in a burning field against the countless thousands of the Slayer's army, the ancient Crown of the Old Gods perched atop her head. With quiet confidence she raised her hand, and a wave of yellow light poured out from her palm to wash across the burning plain, quenching the Chaos fires. The demon army was swept away in the magical flood, their screams drowned out by the sound of a roaring ocean storm.

Even the Slayer himself could not escape the power of Cassandra's dream. The golden wave of light circled his ankles and tendrils of luminescence shot up from the glimmering depths. They entwined his legs, the magic binding her enemy in a deadly grip as it crawled up and around his massive limbs. The Fallen One screamed his defiance but was unable to escape, rendered helpless by the power of the Crown that Cassandra had unleashed. The yellow vines of magical light grew thicker and longer, wrapping themselves over his torso and chest. They bound his arms; they twisted around his neck and head until he was barely visible beneath the thick golden cords of living Chaos.

Cassandra clenched her fist and the snake-like tentacles of her spell began to constrict, crushing the very life from the flaming pillar of Chaos that was the Slayer. Her enemy screamed and collapsed to the ground, shaking the earth as he fell.

In triumph, Cassandra raised both her hands above her head, calling upon the ancient magic of the Old Gods contained in the Talisman atop her head. She felt the Chaos gathering, swelling to an unimaginable crescendo—

And then she woke up, jarred from her dream by a slight stumble of her horse on the uneven ground. She could feel the weight of the Crown that had been entrusted to her by the Pontiff in its nondescript sack as it bumped against her thigh with every step of her mount. She could feel it calling to her, urging her to seize the power of Old Magic.

The second Cataclysm was coming, but with the Crown she would have the power to stop it. She could stand against the Slayer, and destroy him once and for all. She could become the champion Jerrod's prophets had seen—the fate that would have been hers had Rexol been allowed to train her into adulthood!

Cassandra shook her head to dispel the insanity that had momentarily gripped her. Her dream had been no Seer's vision; these were the fevered imaginings of a wizard. She half imagined she could sense Rexol's presence in her mind, urging her to such madness; it was as if she were still poisoned by the lingering effects of her old master's spell over her. The magic of the Crown was beyond her ability to control. The Chaos within the Talisman would consume and destroy her—as it would any mortal who dared to use it.

Even Rexol, for all his knowledge of magic and ancient power, had not been able to control the Talisman. Instead, he had given the Slayer a bridge back to the mortal world. In his quest to become a God, Rexol had set in motion the events heralding a second Cataclysm.

The Pontiff had understood this. He knew the Talisman must be taken to one who would never use it. One with the power to protect it against the Minions. The Guardian. She had seen the Guardian during her recent meditations. Not the exhausted flights of fancy she had just experienced, but true visions. The Guardian was calling to her, speaking to her through her Sight, giving her guidance just as the Pontiff had promised.

East, her visions told her. East across the frozen waste ruled by savage barbarian tribes who would slaughter her on sight. East through the deathly chill of ice and snow that awaited beyond the line of endless winter. East over the impassable mountains towering at the edge of the world. And there the Guardian would be waiting for her, the last of the Old Ones, the only one of the Chaos Spawn who had not joined the Slayer in his war to overthrow the Gods.

Cassandra had sworn to her Pontiff to deliver the Crown to the Guardian, and in doing so she would be released from this burden. She would fulfill her oath and free herself from the ever-growing temptation to seize the Talisman's omnipotent but uncontrollable power . . . if she survived the journey.

Chapter 36

IT HAD BEEN three weeks since the night of Rexol's death. Three weeks of constant flight, with only the briefest of rests. Jerrod had insisted they avoided the main roads and only stopped at villages long enough to acquire more provisions, and he refused to stay at an inn. Instead they slept in makeshift camps in the woods.

The routes they followed couldn't even be called roads; most were overgrown trails long abandoned by any respectable travelers. Some, like the one they were on now, seemed to cut right through the thickest parts of wild, untamed forest. The uneven ground and overgrown roots made the horses stumble along the path, and Keegan's hands and face were covered with cuts and scrapes from low-hanging branches and encroaching shrubbery. Despite all this they were making good time. Though they had seen no hint of their pursuers, Jerrod pushed the pace like a man possessed. Like a fanatic.

Which was exactly what he was. Neither man was much for conversation, but during their endless journey Keegan had realized that much about his traveling companion. He was utterly convinced that Keegan was destined to be the savior of the world. And mad as that might seem, Keegan understood his companion's unshakable conviction. Jerrod had the Sight, and he had seen Keegan's future in his visions.

Keegan also had the Sight. He could appreciate how vivid and powerful a vision felt; it burned with an intensity that dwarfed the waking world. It was easy to understand how the visions could have driven the monk to devote his entire life to a single cause despite all opposition.

But Keegan had also seen visions that did not come to pass. He understood that the future was malleable. And through Rexol, he had learned enough about Chaos to understand that what seemed to be so clear and real was often a confusing mess of symbolism, hidden meanings, and obfuscation.

Despite Jerrod's insistence, Keegan didn't see himself as the heralded savior. But the prospect didn't seem quite so ridiculous now as it had three weeks ago. Chaos was strong in him; even Rexol had admitted he had the potential to be the greatest wizard the Southlands had ever known. If the Legacy were to fall, how much more power would Keegan have? Maybe he really would be able to stand against the Slayer and his invading horde.

He laughed softly to himself, reflexively ducking and turning his head to avoid a twig that seemed determined to put out his eye. These were the thoughts of an unbalanced mind. The product of travel fatigue and the effects of the witchroot he had started taking again the day after their escape. The root was stronger than he was used to; he had found four vials of Rexol's distilled extract among the mage's possessions on one of the packhorses. He'd been taking a few drops with every meal; dangerous, but if the Order ever caught up to them he wanted to be able to unleash his full power. He just had to be aware of the potential side effects: reckless inclinations; delusions of grandeur; the belief that he really was a savior.

He brushed away the thorns clawing at his legs as his horse bravely pushed its way through a thick wall of gorse that had grown across the path, then suddenly spat out, "I'm sick of this!"

"Sick of what?" the monk asked calmly.

"Crashing our way through bushes and brambles and trees! Sleeping on the cold, hard ground. Going weeks without a chance to bathe."

"Would you rather spend your time shackled to the wall in one of the Pontiff's dungeons?"

Keegan ducked to avoid another branch then cursed as it scraped along the back of his neck, leaving a burning furrow. "That's a chance I'm willing to take. I'm tired and dirty and I think I'm losing my mind. I can't keep this up!"

The monk considered his request.

"Perhaps I underestimated the toll this is taking on you. I can sustain my own mind and body as I ride through my meditations, but you have not shared in that training. And there isn't time to teach you. I suppose for your sake we could risk a single night in a small settlement."

There were some benefits to having a companion who thought you were destined to be the savior of the world, Keegan mused, rubbing the welt on the back of his neck. It made him much more willing to listen to your suggestions.

"If I remember correctly there's a small village only a few hours' ride away," Jerrod said. "We can stay there tonight."

"What's it called?" Keegan asked, throwing up his arm to protect himself from a tangle of leaves and vines that suddenly appeared before him.

"I believe it's called Praeton."

"Can I get you anything, Scythe?" Julia asked.

Scythe glanced past the young barmaid and over at the group of five men standing together leaning on the bar. She couldn't hear them across the crowd of patrons, but she could clearly make out her lover through the haze of the fire. Norr's frame towered above the others in the group as he laughed and shook his shaggy head back and forth in comic disbelief. From experience she guessed Herrick was regaling the group with another of his ridiculous tall tales about his latest trip to Argot, the nearest of the Seven Capitals. Either that or Gil was sharing another of his bawdy ballads in his painfully out-of-tune voice.

On the bar beside her lover was a heavy tankard, drained of its contents and flipped upside down—an Eastern custom Norr hadn't yet broken himself of.

"I think we'll be going up to our room soon," Scythe answered.

Julia gave her a wan smile. "Don't count on it." She tilted her chin down toward the tray of foam-topped ales she was carrying. "One of these is his, and he's already told everyone he's buying the round after this one."

"I think I'll just go out for some air," Scythe replied, giving the young woman a smile of her own.

Julia nodded and vanished into the crowd, artfully maneuvering the overbalanced tray through the crowd that always seemed to gather at the Singing Dragon, the undisputed centerpiece of social life in Praeton.

It had been almost a year since she and Norr had stumbled across the sleepy little town, and over the past months Norr had become a regular feature at the tavern. The rooms they rented were on the floor just above, so it was common for the barbarian to come staggering up the stairs several hours past midnight— invariably waking Scythe as he blundered into the room, too drunk and clumsy and big to have any hope of sneaking into bed unnoticed.

Amazingly, the small town of Praeton was able to provide Norr with everything he had looked for and failed to find in cities twenty times its size. Here the big man had found work and a chance to earn some money. During the harvest he'd been in constant demand, doing the work of three regular-sized men. And when he wasn't busy in the fields, he did odd jobs around the inn. Sometimes he helped Herrick with his inventory. Occasionally he worked with Yusef in the smithy. Norr's easygoing nature, his willingness to share a drink, and his ability to work hard from sunrise to sunset without complaint were fast making friends among the men of the town.

Not town, she silently corrected herself. Praeton was little more than a village. Less than a hundred people lived in and around the small cluster of buildings the nearby farmers referred to as "the city." The population and size of Praeton hadn't significantly changed in almost a hundred years, the townsfolk had proudly told her once when she had been foolish enough to ask. Most of the residents were fourth or fifth generation: sons who inherited the family farm or business, local girls who married the neighbor's son. Almost everybody living here was born here. Nobody ever moved to Praeton.

Yet strangely, the community was anything but closed. As both Scythe and Norr had learned that first day, the town welcomed strangers with open arms—no matter who they were or where they might have come from. A few days after their first arrival, Scythe had suggested to Norr that the hospitality was the result of everyone being sick of seeing the same faces day after day after day. Her lover had just given her a disappointed look and countered by saying, "Maybe they're just good folk."

It turned out Norr was right. Praeton was nothing if not "good folk." Norr hadn't just found work in the hamlet. He had found tolerance and acceptance. They didn't mind his pale skin or his flaming hair. They couldn't care less about his thick accent. They didn't see him as a brute or savage. They considered him a friend, a part of their community. Scythe had been accepted just as easily, despite her own exotic appearance. Islander, Easterner: All seemed welcome in this quaint little village.

As she watched Norr laughing and drinking with the others at the bar, Scythe realized he could build a life here in Praeton. He could settle down and raise children and go to the festivals and celebrations and spend his days working and his nights here in the tavern with his neighbors; good, honest folk each and every one.

Scythe hated them all.

She shoved her chair back from the table and sprang to her feet, desperate to get some air. A barrage of friendly greetings, pleasant waves, and warm smiles assaulted her as she pushed her way through the crowd of men and women between her and the door to the outside. It seemed the entire town was here tonight, and they all seemed to know her name—though she had made a point to learn as few of theirs as possible.

She nodded and waved and smiled in return, though if any of the town had looked deep into her eyes they would have seen an emptiness that revealed how hollow her gestures were. But people saw what they wanted to see, and a pleasant manner and bland smile could hide the seething hatred beneath the surface.

She had learned the art of affectation long ago, during her days selling herself in the streets of Callastan. As stupid as she knew it sounded, that was what she felt here in Praeton. Only now she wasn't selling her body, but her soul. And every day she stayed in this tiny village she felt a small part of her spirit die.

Where Norr saw peace, she saw only boredom. Where Norr saw comfort, she saw only complacency. Where Norr saw security and a possible future, she saw a trap of mind-numbing monotony.

Survival. It was all about survival. Scythe prided herself on being a fighter. She reveled in the daily struggle to survive; the constant hum of mortal danger in the background invigorated her. Life was a brutal contest where the weak were left dying in the street, a knife blade snapped off in their belly for the simple mistake of getting caught with their hand wrapped around a mercenary's coin pouch. Growing up on a ship sailing the Western Isles and her years in Callastan had honed her survival instincts to a keen razor's edge.

Now she was losing that edge. Praeton was dulling her senses little by little, bit by bit. And as she lost that edge, she was losing her identity as well.

The night air was cool against her skin, and the wind blowing through town smelled sweet with the scent of freedom and mystery and opportunity.

She had told Norr nothing of her feelings. He was happy here—happier than she had ever seen him. And he had never complained once while they lived the life of vagabond thieves, though she knew he hated it. It was only for him that she had stayed as long as she had. But she didn't think she could endure this torment much longer.

There wasn't even anybody to steal from here. Scythe had no qualms about stealing from the people she exchanged banal small talk with every day. She had no feelings toward them but contempt, anyway. But she knew Norr would object to robbing their new neighbors, so she hadn't even brought it up. Not that there was anyone in Praeton wealthy enough to make the effort worthwhile anyway.

Any travelers passing through the town had been relieved of a few minor items, just for the sake of practice. A small relief to the boredom Scythe felt constantly dragging her under. But travelers were few and far between, and it was difficult to keep herself from succumbing to the depths of despair with such sporadic relief.

She did her best to hide her feelings from Norr. She wanted him to be happy. But lately he had begun to sense that something was wrong. It wouldn't be long until her misery began to ruin his own blissful mood. And then she would have two choices: ask him to leave his life in Praeton behind and come with her, or slip away in the night alone. She honestly didn't know which was worse.

The faint clopping of horses' hooves snapped Scythe out of her black mood. She peered into the dark streets, anxious to see who was on the road at this late hour. Probably one of the local farmers making his way to the Singing Dragon after finishing some repairs on his barn. Nothing to get excited about.

Her heart began to pound with exhilaration when two strangers on horseback materialized out of the night's gloom. She moved forward to greet them, eager to scope out these potential marks.

"We need lodging for ourselves and our horses," Jerrod said to the exotic young woman who emerged from the shadows beneath the sign of the Singing Dragon Inn. "I hope you have room for us."

The monk's eyes had taken on the illusion of a completely normal appearance. Rexol's staff had been covered in tightly wrapped cloth and tied onto one of the supply packs. It looked like nothing more than a large bedroll, and the pair of them looked like simple traveling merchants.

"I don't work here," the woman replied, perhaps a bit more sharply than was necessary. Then, in a much more pleasant voice she added, "But I think there are rooms available. And I can guarantee that the beds are clean and the food is fresh. Take your horses around back and tell the stable boy Scythe sent you. I'll go inside and let Gavid know he's got a couple of customers."

She slipped away through the tavern door as Keegan and Jerrod slid from their saddles.

"She seemed quite helpful for someone who doesn't work here," the young man commented.

"A little too helpful," Jerrod replied. "And did you notice? She was an Islander." Keegan had, in fact, noticed. "Islanders don't usually venture this far from Callastan. Normally the Southlands aren't tolerant of foreigners."

"She didn't have an accent," Keegan pointed out. "Maybe her father was a merchant from this town who married a woman from Callastan, then came back here to settle down."

"Perhaps," Jerrod conceded. "But there is something dangerous about her."

Keegan smiled. "Are you saying she's a spy for the Order?"

"No, probably not," the monk conceded. "But I sensed a hunger in her. She may have grown bored with the men of this village. She might be looking to share the bed of a young merchant this evening."

Keegan wasn't sure if he was joking. Truth be told, he found himself strangely drawn to the olive-skinned girl with the dark hair. There had been an unspoken challenge in her gaze and a defiance in her stance that demanded an answer. That had intrigued him as much as the lean, hard beauty of her body.

As if sensing the direction of his thoughts Jerrod added, "We are here to rest. Do not do anything foolish. Remember what happened the last time you gave in to your carnal passions."

This time the young man knew his companion was being gravely serious. He made himself a mental note to always be aware of the witchroot in his blood. He didn't want to do anything he might later regret.

They reached the stables at the back and a tall young lad of maybe fifteen came out to meet them.

"Evening, m'lords," he said with an earnest, awkward bow.

"Scythe said you would look after our horses for us," Jerrod said.

"Of course, m'lords. Take what you need and then I'll water and rub them down for you."

Keegan grabbed a few essentials from the packs. He briefly considered taking everything, but looking at the simple, honest eyes of the stable boy he couldn't imagine that anything he left with the horses would end up missing. He didn't even bother to grab the roll of blankets that hid Rexol's staff, though out of habit he did grab a single vial of the witchroot extract and the small bag containing a few minor charms. Not that he would have any need of them in this place.

"You can go in through the back way here. Just head up to the bar and talk to Gavid to get the keys for your rooms."

They did just that, and within ten minutes they were standing at the doors of their respective sleeping chambers.

"We can have dinner downstairs," Jerrod said "We might as well conserve our supplies. But we can't spend long in the tavern. Early to bed; I want to be gone at daybreak."

"Give me twenty minutes to clean up and I'll meet you downstairs."

Jerrod nodded, then opened the door to his room and went inside. Keegan did the same.

As the young woman had promised, the room was clean, if a little small. A single bed, a chair, and a tiny table had been jammed into the tight space. A small washbasin and a pitcher of water rested on the table. There was a small window in the corner, shuttered against the chill of the night.

Keegan splashed some water on his face, the cool liquid washing away the dirt and grime of the road. From the pouch at his belt he withdrew the small vial of witchroot and let a few drops spill onto his tongue, scowling at the bitterness. Hopefully by the time he went down for his meal the aftertaste would be gone.

He went over to the bed and collapsed on it with an audible sigh. The mattress was firm, but compared with the hard ground he was used to it may as well have been stuffed with handpicked down from the geese of the wealthiest lord in all the Seven Capitals.

He lay there for several minutes, struggling against the urge to let himself drift off into blissful sleep despite his rumbling stomach. His eyelids fluttered and suddenly he was dreaming in a fitful doze. Not a vision, but a simple, ordinary dream of the young, olive-skinned woman they had first met sitting naked astride him.

Her taut muscles flex in rhythm to his own as she rides him, her skin sheened with sweat; soft moans of passion escape her lips. Her back arches, her moans rise in pitch, she bucks and grinds against him . . .

And suddenly he was awake again. He laughed and forced himself to sit up before he drifted off again. The witchroot was to blame, of course; it stirred up the passions. But though the witchroot had caused it, there was no significance to the dream. It was nothing but a lustful fantasy . . . and as close as he would get to a woman tonight.

He took a deep breath, savoring one last time the erotic mental image of her naked body against his own bare flesh, then got to his feet. He couldn't have slept long—a few minutes at most. Any more and Jerrod would have come to check up on him. But if he didn't hurry down the monk might come up to see what was taking so long, and Keegan had no desire to get on his bad side tonight.

He briefly considered taking the leather pouch with his charms, then decided against it. Rexol had taught him that a wizard should never go anywhere without something that could augment the power of a hastily formed spell, but he had a small bit of giant's bone on a necklace beneath his shirt in the unlikely event he needed to summon Chaos. He also decided against taking the vial of witchroot he had with him. He placed it in with the charms, then stuffed the small bag beneath his pillow, left, and locked his room.

The monk was already seated at a table in the corner; he could just make him out through the crowd. As he crossed the room he caught sight of an enormous man with ruddy, sunburned skin, flaming red hair, and a thick, red beard, but his mind was too tired to care what an Eastern savage would be doing here, of all places.

He took his seat next to Jerrod. "I don't see the young woman we met at the door," he said casually.

"I saw her earlier speaking with that rather large barbarian," Jerrod informed him. "I believe they are more than just friends. Yet another reason to be suspicious."

Jerrod was obviously on edge. The line of his jaw was set hard, as if he was expecting trouble.

"You worry too much," Keegan said, hoping to calm him.

It didn't seem to help. He supposed it was inevitable the monk would see conspiracies and treachery everywhere he looked; it was part and parcel of being a fanatic. That didn't mean they both had to worry about it, though.

Even so, he couldn't help but cast a quick glance over at the giant savage. His arms were as big around as Keegan's thigh. The lingering images of his erotic dream were swept away by a vivid picture of the barbarian catching Keegan and his lover in the act, then ripping Keegan's limbs from his torso in a jealous rage.

Even the haze of the witchroot wasn't enough to make him risk the wrath of the living mountain leaning against the bar, and he quickly pushed all thoughts of the Island girl from his mind as he raised his hand to call the waitress over.

Chapter 37

SCYTHE WIGGLED AND twisted and turned until she finally managed to slip her small form through the tiny window of the second-story room. She stood in the darkness for a minute, letting her eyes adjust to the gloom and trying to catch her breath. Scaling the wall had been easy, but the tight squeeze through the window had been a struggle.

But there was no need to rush. The merchants were in the tavern downstairs enjoying their supper, giving her plenty of time to search their stuff for anything worth stealing. And if they should unexpectedly try to return to their rooms Norr would create a compelling diversion. It was a tactic the two of them had used many times in towns other than Praeton, and it hadn't failed them yet.

It was just like old times—except for the disappointment in Norr's eyes when she had quickly whispered to him what she planned to do. Had they been alone he might have tried to talk her out of it, but in the crowded confines of the Singing Dragon's tavern he could only give her the disapproving stare. Then at last, he had nodded.

The older of the two men had already been down in the tavern when she spoke to Norr. She could sense him staring at her and Norr, but she quickly dismissed it as idle curiosity—Islanders and

Easterners were unfamiliar sights this deep into the Southlands. When she heard the young man coming down the stairs to join his companion, she had quickly slipped out the door, then made her way around to the back of the inn.

Her eyes had adjusted to the darkness of her surroundings, so she began a methodical and thorough search of the first room. It was hardly worth the effort. They had left their saddlebags with the horses, and what had been brought up wasn't worth stealing. She turned her attention to all the usual spots people tried to hide their wealth—under the mattress, stuffed beneath the pillow, tucked away above the doorjamb—but her search turned up nothing save dust and a few dead insects.

When she saw the men it was obvious they weren't carrying much in the way of actual goods, but the extra pack horses had given her some hope that they were wealthier than they appeared. She'd guessed they were traveling merchants looking to purchase inventory they could bring back home and sell at a profit. If that were true, they'd be carrying substantial portable wealth in order to purchase enough stock to make their journey worthwhile. So where were the gems, jewelry, and gold coins she had expected to find?

She bit her lip in frustration, then smiled when a sudden hope hit her. There were two men; maybe they had stored all their valuables in the second room. With some difficulty she wriggled out through the tiny window and back onto the second-story ledge, then shuffled her way along to the next room's window.

Here, she thought to herself, she'd find something more interesting.

Norr was only half listening to Gil's out-of-tune singing. He had to keep an eye on the two strangers, to make sure they didn't head up to their rooms until Scythe was done. He dreaded to imagine what might happen if they caught her going through their things.

He wasn't worried about Scythe; she could look after herself with the razor-sharp knives she always kept hidden somewhere on her person. But if she overreacted—an all-too-common occurrence with his hot-blooded love—one of the merchants might end up lying in a pool of blood on the floor. And that would be it for their life in Praeton.

Norr now wished he hadn't agreed to her plan. But Scythe needed this; the simple life in Praeton was unbearable to her. She hadn't said anything, but Norr could see it in her eyes. She endured Praeton for him and him alone. The least he could do was allow her a chance to play the cat burglar from time to time.

And it wasn't like these men were friends or people who knew them. These travelers weren't like the rare folk of Praeton who welcomed Norr into their fold despite his foreign ways and appearance. These were strangers, the kind of people who hated and despised him because of his Eastern heritage. Or so the barbarian kept telling himself over and over.

He kept one eye on the table; the other's focus was split between Gil and the door he kept praying Scythe would stroll in through. He hoped the men wouldn't get up to leave before she came back. He hoped they wouldn't force him into a confrontation. He hoped it wouldn't come to that. But of course it did.

Not twenty minutes after they had sat down to eat the strangers were done. Leaving a few coins on the table to pay for their meal, they rose from their chairs and began to cross the room. Fortunately, their path would bring them right past the main bar where Norr and his companions were gathered.

The big barbarian turned his back to the strangers and raised his half-full flagon in one massive hand. He picked up the reflection of the advancing pair in the polished ornamental shield that hung on the wall behind the bar and waited until they were right beside him.

He spun suddenly, an overexaggerated turn with the arm holding his drink extended far out in front of him while loudly asking, "Where's Scythe?" to make it appear as if he was turning to scan the crowd for his lover. His arm slammed into the chest of the

younger of the two men, and Norr made certain the entire contents of his ale poured down the front of his shirt.

The man gave a cry of surprise as the cold, foamy liquid drenched
his clothes and the skin beneath. His shout drew every eye in the
tavern, which was suddenly and shockingly silent.

Herrick good-naturedly bellowed, "Damn clumsy barbarians!"
and the patrons laughed, dispelling the tense silence.

Norr silently cursed his friend. It was hard for him to start a bar
brawl at the best of times—for some reason people were reluctant
to take a swing at a man a foot taller and several hundred pounds
heavier than they were. And if the good-natured Herrick was
going to defuse the situation, provoking these merchants would be
all but impossible.

But there were other ways to keep them from reaching the top
of the stairs.

"I'm so sorry," Norr exclaimed, reaching out to paw at the dripping clothes of the young man in a futile attempt to mop up the
stain.

The young man didn't react, he just stared at Norr with wide,
slightly terrified eyes. It was obvious he wasn't about to start anything.

Fortunately, his companion reached out and slapped the meaty
paw away.

"Don't touch him," the older man said quietly. The threat in his
voice was unmistakable.

His eyes weren't angry, but there was something definitely dangerous in them. This one wasn't about to back down from anyone.

"I'm such an oaf," Norr apologized, letting a sheepish grin
spread across his face. He turned his attention to the older man
now, placing a beefy hand on his head and tousling his hair: a seemingly friendly gesture that was at once humiliating and often en-
raging.

"Let me buy you both a drink to make it up to you."

"Just leave us alone," the older man insisted, snapping his head
away and trying to shove past the barbarian blocking his path.

The merchant could have taken a full run directly into Norr's mountain of flesh and not budged him an inch, but at the slight shove Norr stumbled back and pinwheeled his arms as if to keep his balance.

"Hey!" Gil exclaimed, quickly jumping to Norr's defense. "It was just an accident! He said he was sorry!"

He might have said more, but the man turned his cold gaze on him, instantly killing any further words in the would-be bard's throat.

"Look," Herrick said, playing peacemaker once more, "nobody wants any trouble. If you don't want to accept our apology, you're free to go."

Norr would have none of that. He reached out a huge paw and dropped it—hard—onto the younger man's shoulder.

"No hard feelings, buddy!" he loudly declared, even as the merchant's knees crumpled beneath the enormous weight of the barbarian's mitt and he gasped in pain.

As he had hoped, the older man jumped in to intervene, moving much more quickly than Norr expected. Even more quickly than he would have thought possible. He seized Norr's wrist with both hands, twisting it back and away from his younger companion's shoulder. And then the brawl the barbarian had been looking for finally began.

The man lashed out with a kick to Norr's calf, knocking the big man off balance. Without breaking his grip on Norr's wrist, he turned his body, stepped in close, and tossed him over his hip. The move yanked the barbarian from his feet, flipping his body high in the air to land with a crashing thud on his back, the force of his impact cracking the wooden floorboards beneath him.

Norr stared up at the ceiling with stars in his eyes, gasping for breath and trying desperately not to laugh. He had seen Scythe use a similar move on her opponents, but she had assured him he need never worry about it. "Even with leverage, size makes a difference," she had explained. "You're too big to flip." He'd have to tell her how wrong she was.

The sound of screams and crashing furniture jarred him back to the present, and he managed to half sit up so he could see what was happening. Herrick was lying dazed on his back amid the splintered remains of one of the tavern tables, likely the victim of the same move used against Norr. Gil was crumpled on the floor clutching at his groin, his face an ugly shade of purple. Standing in the middle of the carnage in a fighting crouch was the older man. The other had retreated off to the side, hiding himself in a corner while he let his companion—probably his paid bodyguard—deal with the angry crowd.

The barbarian struggled to his hands and knees as Petr, one of the men Norr had worked with in the smithy, rushed the stranger. A flurry of fists and elbows staggered the burly laborer and a jumping back round kick to the chin finished him off. Petr's eyes rolled back into his head as he slumped to the ground.

The barbarian opened his mouth to warn his friends not to interfere. He knew he himself was in no danger—he was too big and too experienced to get seriously hurt in a fistfight, even against a foe as obviously skilled as this. But before the words left his mouth the man took a quick shuffle step back and delivered a sharp kick to Norr's windpipe, somehow aware the big man had managed to get to his knees even though he was facing in the complete opposite direction.

Norr fell forward, choking and gasping for air as his hands reflexively clutched at his throat. His unprotected nose slammed against the hard floor beams; he heard the crunch of cartilage as it broke. He tried to scream a warning to the others but only managed a faint rasping caw, further muffled by the gurgling blood gushing from his nose.

Still lying facedown on the floor, he wretched and coughed, hacking out a shower of thick crimson fluid—but he was rewarded by a rush of welcome air into his lungs. He began to pant heavily, drawing in oxygen until he had the strength to push himself up to his knees once more.

He blinked and wiped away the blinding tears welling up from the blow to his nose. Including Herrick, Petr, and Gil, half a dozen townsmen were incapacitated on the barroom floor. But there were a dozen more encircling their common foe, just gathering up the courage to rush their opponent in unison. A few of them would fall beneath a storm of savage punches and kicks, but the rest would inevitably drag him down beneath the sheer mass of their numbers.

It was impossible for one unarmed man to overcome such overwhelming odds, no matter how skilled. Norr forced himself to stand. When the rush of humanity came he wanted to be in on it, to use his massive bulk to bowl the man over and pin him helplessly to the ground. And to shield him from the angry blows of the villagers once he was down. Norr had provoked this fight; he didn't want to see his opponent get seriously beaten.

The younger man was still standing in the corner; from the corner of his eye Norr saw his lips moving rapidly and his hands weaving strange patterns in the air.

There was a shout from one of the townsmen and the charge began. Norr took a single step forward just as a fist-sized ball of blue light launched itself from the younger man's hand, hurtling toward the fray. And then the room exploded.

Scythe chewed her lip, uncertain what to make of the leather pouch she had found tucked beneath the pillow in the second room. She'd felt a brief satisfaction when she discovered it, but it turned to dismay when she poured the contents out into her hand. No gold, no gems, no expensive jewelry—only a small vial of brownish liquid and a few dozen strange trinkets carved from what appeared to be bone and crystal.

She had seen such objects before; you could buy them on every corner in Callastan. Men and women proclaiming themselves magicians or witches hawked such charms, promising love, luck, fortune, and good health to any who bought them. Scythe was smart enough to recognize a scam when she heard one. If the charms really delivered on their promise, they would cost a lot more than a single piece of silver.

But maybe these were different? Maybe the merchants were heading toward the Free Cities and beyond. Maybe they planned to take one of the trade routes into the North Forest, to deal with the Danaan. It was said the Danaan people had strange and ancient magic, real magic from a time before the Cataclysm. Was it possible these seemingly worthless trinkets actually had magical properties?

And if they did, did she really want to steal them? Scythe was an expert in the cons and swindles of magicians, but she knew almost nothing about true wizards. How much was this stash worth? And if she did take something, where would she even sell it?

There were other concerns, as well. Were these relics safe to take? What kind of power did they possess, and what effects would it have on her if she took them? What if there were some strange protective magic guarding them against theft? She hated to walk away empty-handed, but she wanted to be sure the payoff was worth the risk.

Her deliberations were cut short by a thunderclap from the tavern downstairs. The blast rocked the room, bowing the floor beneath her feet upward. The concussive shock slammed Scythe against the wall and she collapsed on the bed, stunned.

As she lay there, momentarily dazed, the truth hit her with nearly as much force as the blast that had knocked her off her feet. The men weren't merchants—they were wizards! And she had set Norr against them!

She jammed the leather pouch and its contents into her belt and scrambled to her feet. She unlocked the door to the hall and raced down the stairs into the tavern. Instinctively she had drawn the throwing dagger she always kept in her boot. She wasn't about to trifle with wizards; if she saw the opportunity to kill them she would. She only hoped it wasn't too late.

The scene that greeted her was one of mass destruction. Every table in the place was overturned, most of them broken. The chairs were splintered and cracked and jumbled in heaps against the walls, blown out from the center of the room by the force of the explosion. Forks, knives, and cracked mugs were scattered everywhere. The ceiling beams were twisted and bent and cracked, though it looked as if there was no immediate danger of the roof collapsing.

The two strangers were nowhere to be found. The men and women of Praeton were slowly picking their way through the wreckage, just now recovering from the effects of the Chaos unleashed in their midst. Cuts and bruises and huge welts were common in the crowd. Several people limped noticeably, others cradled injured arms as they shuffled through the mess.

Norr was crouched on the floor near the center of the carnage beside a motionless body, along with several other men of the village. Scythe dropped her throwing dagger at the foot of the stairs and rushed over, her stomach lurching as she noticed the grim shock etched on the faces of the battered townsfolk.

Gil lay on the ground, his sweat-covered face a mask of agony and his breath coming in short, quick gasps. The sharp white of bone jutted out from the thigh of his left leg; Scythe could see his right was shattered in at least two places below the knee. His ashen pallor and glazed eyes made it obvious his injuries had sent him into shock.

Despite this, nobody was doing anything. They simply huddled around him, their faces a mix of bewildered disbelief and paralyzed horror. Norr held his hand, as if trying to send him strength and comfort through the connection. Scythe knew he needed more than that.

"Find me several pieces of wood, straight and about two or three feet long," she ordered. When nobody moved she snapped, "Herrick, go! Hurry, if we want to save his legs."

Herrick leapt up and began to scour the wreckage for boards to make a splint. The rest of them also sprang into action, yanked from their numbness by Scythe's take-charge attitude.

There was no healer in Praeton; the town was too small to warrant one. Taking Gil to a witch was out of the question—he wouldn't survive the trip, and Scythe doubted the townsfolk would let another Chaos user within their borders anytime soon. That left it up to her.

Methodis had taught her the basics of field surgery during her years on the *Dolphin,* though among the sailors amputation was the quickest and most common cure. But with Gil there were other options. If she could set and splint the bones he might even one day walk again, though he'd probably have to use a cane for the rest of his life.

She wasn't able to look across the wounded man at Norr, for fear of the accusation she would see in his eyes.

"You'll have to help me," she said to her lover, not taking her eyes from Gil. "It's going to hurt, he's going to fight and scream. But you have to hold him still, no matter what. Do you understand?"

"Yes."

There was no emotion in his voice, nothing to give her a clue as to how he felt toward her one way or the other.

Herrick returned with the boards. She gave them a quick examination to make sure they would work. Satisfied, she slipped her largest knife out from its hiding place beneath her belt. Herrick's eyes got wide in surprise, but Scythe didn't even bother coming up with a lie to explain the blade's presence.

"Herrick, you stay. Grab two more strong men. We might need them to help hold Gil still while I operate. And clear everyone else out: This isn't going to be pleasant."

Once the tavern was clear, Scythe took a deep breath to steel herself. "Let's begin."

Gently she felt along his shattered lower right leg until she had some idea of how the bones had been broken and twisted beneath the skin. With even the faintest touch of her fingers, Gil moaned and trembled. Confident she could reset the leg so it would be reasonably straight, she placed both hands where the end of bone jutted up, bulging beneath the skin, and prepared to push.

"He's going to scream," she warned Norr and the other men holding him down.

And scream he did.

The pounding of their horses' hooves was like thunder in Keegan's ears. Part of him wondered he could still hear at all, after the blast from the explosion he had unleashed within the tavern. He had only meant to create a small wall of force, a field of energy to push the townspeople away from Jerrod before the monk killed one of them. Instead he had nearly brought the entire building crashing down on their heads.

It had been the witchroot. The higher doses he had been consuming made it easier for him to draw power from the charm at his neck, and he had gathered more Chaos than he could control. That, and the adrenaline rush of the fight. Which shouldn't have happened at all.

"What were you thinking?" Keegan shouted out at the rider ahead of him. "Why did you attack those people?"

"I had to protect you," the monk replied in a calm, even tone.

Keegan briefly wondered how he could hear him over the crashing sound of their flight, then realized it must be yet another manifestation of the Order's power.

"But why did you have to react so violently?" Keegan pressed, not finding Jerrod's reply to be any kind of real answer. "We could have talked ourselves out of that situation without drawing all this unwanted attention. We could have spent that night sleeping in beds instead of riding nonstop until dawn!"

"You did not seem so intent on a peaceful resolution when you unleashed the thunder of Chaos in the center of the tavern," Jerrod reminded him.

"I panicked," Keegan admitted, then in his own defense added, "but it would never have come to that if you hadn't overreacted in the first place."

"You assume the barbarian could have been reasoned with," Jerrod replied. "But this is a time of great uncertainty. I sense the convergence of many prophecies and visions, and not all will come to fruition. There are forces at work in the world that would destroy you and the destiny you embody. The Order, for one. Perhaps other, more sinister enemies.

"My brothers and sisters have already given their lives for you, and I have sworn an oath to do the same. I will protect you with relentless vigilance, lest the sacrifice of those who have fallen before be in vain."

After a brief pause while he let Keegan consider the significance of his words, Jerrod continued his explanation.

"Was it not strange to find an Islander and an Eastern savage there, in the tavern of that small town? I cannot believe that such a remarkable occurrence is mere coincidence. Something or someone manipulated events so that you and the barbarian would encounter each other at the bar."

"Backlash," Keegan called out, not sure if Jerrod would understand the reference.

"Backlash from Rexol's attempt to use the Crown. Yes, I have considered that." Obviously the monk was familiar with the concept. "But there could have been other explanations. Perhaps a Pilgrim who serves the Order had discovered us, and hired the barbarian to hunt you down. Had I hesitated, the giant might have killed you with a single hard slap that snapped your neck. Prophecies are often undone with such a sudden, unexpected blow."

"But you had no way of knowing if that barbarian was an assassin," Keegan countered. "You don't even know for sure that he meant to harm me at all."

"I cannot take that chance," Jerrod replied.

"So what if I hadn't interfered?" Keegan wanted to know. "Would you have killed everyone in the tavern?"

"I did not kill," the monk reminded him. "I disabled and neu-tralized. The only casualties from the fight will be from the Chaos you unleashed."

That nearly cowed Keegan into silence. But he felt responsible enough to add one more thing.

"There will be some kind of backlash from my spell," he warned. "We could end up fighting more innocent people. Promise me you won't hurt them."

"I can't promise that," Jerrod replied. "You are the savior of the world. I would sacrifice a thousand innocent men, women, and children if I believed it was necessary to protect your life."

The monk's words, delivered in a voice so simple and matter-of-fact he might have been discussing the weather, chilled Keegan to his bones. He had no reply to such a mad statement, no way to reason or argue with such blind and ruthless devotion to a cause. True, the monk was on his side . . . but Keegan was no longer sure that was a good thing.

It would be several hours before Norr returned, Scythe figured. After the surgery, he and Herrick had constructed a stretcher to carry Gil back to his home. Likely both men would stay for some time, to make sure Gil was comfortable and to try to offer some solace to his wife.

She hadn't been forced to amputate; for that at least Scythe was grateful. But the break in the thigh had been bad. Very bad. It was doubtful it would mend cleanly. Even if it did, Gil would never be able to properly use his leg again.

And it was all her fault.

Norr hadn't spoken to her since the surgery. Partly because he didn't want the others to know the brawl had been part of Scythe's plan to steal from the travelers and partly, Scythe suspected, because he was too hurt and angry and disgusted with her to even know what to say.

When he got back, it wouldn't matter. Because she would be

gone. She couldn't stay here, not after what she had done to these people. Norr could build a life here without her; she didn't deserve to be with him. Not anymore. She was leaving, and she would never come back.

If she left tonight she could still pick up the trail of the two men who had come into the town posing as merchants. She knew now they were nothing of the sort. Mages, warlocks, wizards: It didn't matter to Scythe what name they called themselves. And it didn't matter why they had passed through Praeton. All that mattered was they would pay for what they had done.

If she rode hard all night, she figured she could catch them in a day or two. Wherever they were—the next town, a camp in the woods—she'd wait until darkness. Until they went to sleep. And then she'd make sure neither of them would ever wake up again.

She packed quickly, taking only what she absolutely needed. And then, as she had so many times before with so many other men, she slipped soundlessly away into the night to abandon her lover.

Norr was outside waiting for her. She looked up into his eyes, but couldn't read them through the darkness.

"You're leaving?" he asked in a sad whisper.

"I can't stay here," she replied, wishing she had been quick enough to avoid this confrontation. "Tonight was my fault. You even tried to warn me, but I wouldn't listen."

The barbarian sighed, but didn't say anything.

"I'm not meant for this life, Norr. If I stay, something even worse might happen. And that will be my fault, too. I have to leave. To-night."

Norr dropped to one knee so that their eyes were almost level. Inside them she saw not hate or anger or rage, but only sadness. Sadness and something else. Determination? Resolution?

He wrapped his huge arms around her and pulled her close against his chest.

"Then we leave together," he whispered. Just that, nothing else.

And for the first time since they had met, Scythe cried.

Chapter 38

THE BLACK SILHOUETTE gliding silently across the starless night sky moved in wide, slow circles, carefully scanning the earth below. Even from several hundred feet above, Raven's glowing, demonic eyes could pick out every detail of the frozen wasteland beneath her. But what she sought wasn't visible to the naked eye.

And then she felt it, a ribbon of pure Chaos winding its way eastward—a trail left by the one who fled with the Crown. Burning lust flared up within the cold darkness of Raven's twisted soul; a tangible hunger to possess and consume the Talisman's power seized her heart. But she knew to be cautious; she would not underestimate her prey's power, as Scirth had underestimated the Pontiff during his interrogation back at the Monastery. These mortals were not as weak and helpless as Daemron had led them to believe. Some, like the Pontiff and the one she hunted, had true power. Chaos was strong in their blood.

Had it not been so, she would have caught her quarry already. But during her hunt she had been led astray several times by false trails. Numerous times she had sensed tendrils of Chaos spiraling off in various directions. Eager to make the kill, she had raced after them, only to reach a dead end and realize she had followed a false path designed to lead her away from the Crown.

It was impossible to know if the one she followed was intentionally throwing her off the trail, or whether this was some type of instinctual defense mechanism conjured by the mortal's subconscious. In either case, though, the implications were undeniable: The one she hunted was drawing on the Crown's power.

Raven's wings ached with the twinge of exhaustion as she swooped down to examine this latest find; flying hundreds of wasted leagues chasing the false bait had taken their toll. She was strong, the strongest of the Minions except for Orath. Chaos bubbled and boiled beneath her ebony skin, giving her a physical endurance far beyond the mortal creatures that lived in this world where the Legacy made Chaos almost nonexistent. Its power had been bred into her magnificent body over countless generations—but even the Minions had their limits. And she was beginning to approach hers.

She landed silently on the snow, her naked female form crouching low to the earth as her majestic wings wrapped around her to give some shelter from the cold. Her avian head tilted to the side so that she could focus one of her glowing eyes on the trail. Now she was wise to the tricks and deceptions. She could be fooled by the magic no longer. She studied the trail for many minutes, weaving her own spells over the glowing traces of the Crown's passage, probing, testing, verifying until she was very, very sure.

This time, she knew with certainty, she had found her prey. It was many days since the Crown had passed; the taste of its power had already begun to fade from this place. But it had been here. Of that there could be no doubt. Now the hunt would begin in earnest.

Raven tilted her head back to scream her victory to the sky, the harsh call from her beak shattering the silence of the night.

Cold. So very, very cold.

Like all members of the Order, Cassandra could sustain her body through the most extreme environmental conditions. She could march for days in the blazing heat of the desert sun or through the frozen wastes. She could survive without food or water for weeks at a time . . . provided she was able to focus her power to do so.

But hunger and cold were the least of her concerns right now. She was being hunted. She knew that. And so she had instead channeled her energy into creating false trails, powerful illusions to throw her pursuers off course. She didn't fully understand how she did it: It had come to her in a dream.

The Crown was part of it, she understood that. Something inside the Talisman was alive on some level, a divine spark of the True Gods themselves, perhaps. This spark had reached out to her as she dozed; it had shown her how to create the false paths. But doing so required her to focus her energies outward, leaving her body vulnerable to the ravages of climate and physical suffering.

And so she had known the unfamiliar pangs of hunger on her journey through the wastes of the Frozen East, foraging for nonexistent plants to sustain her when her supplies had run out. She had known exhaustion and fatigue when her horse had finally died and she had continued on foot. She had known pain as her feet blistered and bled. She had known fear while cowering in a frozen ditch to hide from a roaming barbarian tribe. She had experienced a thousand different pains and sufferings as she trekked over the empty, windswept plains. But when she had crossed into the icy plains at the foot of the mountains, every other sensation had given way to the cold.

She had lost two fingers to the numbing chill. The skin was black and cracked and hard over the useless digits, and with her vision she saw rotting gangrene below the surface. Her toes were worse, her boots so encased in frozen ice they had fused with the flesh of her doomed feet. The lobes of her ears were gone, and the tip of her nose would soon follow. She had lost all feeling in her body, the chill seeping through her bones into her very core. Yet somehow she persevered.

It was the Crown. Packed away in the saddlebag she carried slung over her shoulder, its magic somehow sustained her through all her suffering. Her frozen corpse would have collapsed long ago, but the power of the Talisman animated her frost-ravaged limbs and she soldiered on.

She was aware of only three things. The cold. Her ever-nearing destination. And the insistent, insidious whisper telling her she could end her misery by simply placing the Crown atop her head. The Chaos could banish the cold and restore her lost body in a single, glorious flash of magical fire. If she wanted she could banish the endless winter and transform the Frozen East into a lush garden paradise. She could defend the mortal world against the Slayer and his Minions. She could stop the coming of the Cataclysm.

Somewhere in the depths of her mind a small part of Cassandra still existed, clinging to a single unshakable belief. This vision was a lie, the tempting lure of flawed and desperate Sight corrupted by her old master's teachings. She had been ensnared once by Rexol's trickery, and it had brought ruin on the Order. She would not yield to lies again. She would find the Guardian and deliver the Crown.

From many, many leagues away she heard a shrill scream, its inhuman caw echoing across the snow-covered plains. It sounded like the piercing shriek of some monstrous bird of prey, a sound that couldn't possibly be human, a sound of pure evil. Cassandra knew the beast that made that terrible cry was hunting her. There was nothing she could do but press on.

Chapter 39

"THE DREAMS ARE stronger now," the Danaan Queen told her council, "the nightmares worse. More vivid. I see the terrible fires of Chaos devouring our city and its people. I see the Destroyer of Worlds walk among us. I can no longer sleep, for fear of the visions. The time of the second Cataclysm draws close."

There was silence as the privy council digested her words, trying to find something useful in them. Searching for some hint, some clue that might guide the Danaan people through this dangerous time. Each of them hoping the Queen knew something more than what she was telling them, but all of them too afraid to ask.

It was Andar who finally broke the silence. "What must we do, my Queen?"

Rianna Avareen, proud ruler of the Danaan people, shook her head in a reluctant admission of defeat. "I cannot say. My visions have shown me nothing but death and destruction. I have not seen how the Cataclysm may be averted."

"Perhaps it cannot be," Andar offered.

"I will not believe that." It was Drake who spoke now, defending her against hopeless despair over the fate of her people. "Destiny is malleable and ever changing. Prophecy and vision have always guided our Monarchs. We have averted catastrophe and tragedy in the past. The history of our kingdom is proof the visions are glimpses of what may be, not what will be. We all know the future is not yet written."

"The Cataclysm is different," Andar argued. "Maybe there is no other future."

"No! I will not accept that. If the Queen's vision only shows what must inevitably be, then what is the purpose? Why would she glimpse what cannot be changed? There is no logic to it. It makes no sense."

Andar shrugged. The Queen's sorcerer wasn't anxious to argue with the well-respected consort of his ruler, but neither was he willing to back down. "Such is the way of Chaos. It is not bound by logic or reason or predictability. We have seen stark evidence of this in the shortcomings of the prince."

The Queen stiffened at the insult to her son, but once more Drake was there to defend her and the young man he had all but raised as his own son.

"You are a fool, Andar!" he shouted, unable to contain himself. "Vaaler is a capable, intelligent young man. He commands the respect of all who serve on the patrols—they would give their lives for him! He is smart, he is strong of character, he is brave of heart. Vaaler is a born leader!"

The council shifted uneasily, uncomfortable in the face of Drake's righteous anger. But still Andar would not be cowed.

"Yet he does not have the Sight."

The Queen kept her silence, watching the confrontation play out between her two most trusted advisers. Both men were in the right, both men spoke the truth. Vaaler was everything Drake said and more—and yet he possessed the one unforgivable failing that none of his other talents would ever compensate for. This was why the council would not heed her son's warnings of a slowly spreading malaise through the Danaan culture and kingdom. This was why they dismissed as foolish and reckless his calls to open their borders and their society to the humans.

How could they trust decisions of government to one who did not have the vision? It was like letting a blind man lead you across a narrow ledge. And the Queen wondered once more whether her son would ever be allowed to claim his throne.

"No wonder Vaaler spends all his days with the patrols," Drake was saying. "You have already judged him unfit, Andar. You and all the rest. Out there his worth is noticed."

"Perhaps that is because his worth has more value as a leader of the guard than as a king."

Now the Queen had no choice but to intervene.

"Andar, your words come dangerously close to treason," she warned in a cold, hard voice. "Vaaler is the rightful heir, descended in an unbroken line from Tremin Avareen himself. He will one day rule this kingdom, and you will one day bow to him . . . or lose your head."

"Forgive me, my Queen," Andar said, genuflecting as he spoke. "I was caught up in the heat of the argument. I have sworn my loyalty to you and your royal House, and I would sooner lose my life than break my oath."

Loyalty to me and my royal House, the Queen thought, *but not to my son.*

Out loud she said, "Your apology is accepted, Andar. But you had best not speak such things beyond the walls of the council."

She had no choice but to forgive him absolutely. He was only speaking what everyone else was thinking. And if she punished him for speaking out here, the others would begin to guard their tongues. They would cease to be valued advisers and become fawning sycophants. She needed their true and honest counsel. Now, more than ever.

"The Cataclysm is coming. The Queen has seen it," Drake proclaimed. "That is what we must focus on here in council: the Cataclysm and the possible destruction of our people. We must set aside talk of the prince and return to the issue at hand."

His words were greeted with verbal assent from all present, but in their faces the Queen could clearly see they all believed Vaaler's flaw was very much part of the issue at hand.

The debate continued long into the night, but it was as fruitless as all their previous discussions. Her vision was powerful, but completely useless. It showed her a terrible fate, but not how to avoid it. It was said the ancient Monarchs had possessed the power to bend the Sight to their will, to force the Chaos in the royal blood to show them what they commanded be revealed. If so, that power had long since been lost.

The Queen had no control over her dreams. She was but a conduit for the Chaos to manifest itself; as her husband had been, and the Monarch before him, and the Monarch before her. Perhaps this was evidence that the Sight had been steadily growing weaker within the Avareen line. Perhaps Vaaler's condition was not as unforeseeable as they all wished to believe.

It hardly mattered anymore. The council would argue, the Queen would listen, and nothing would be decided. At night she would sleep and dream of fire. And soon the Destroyer of Worlds would come.

Unconsciously her hand strayed up to the ring dangling from her neck, her delicate fingers wrapping tightly around it as if they could draw reassurance from the plain gold band.

Chapter 40

FOR THE FIRST four days after their hurried escape from Praeton, Jerrod increased their already exhausting pace. Keegan wasn't about to complain about the redoubled rate. It wasn't retribution from the simple villagers they feared, but rather word of their actions reaching the ears of any Pilgrims who might happen to be in the area.

News of their exploits would spread quickly. Using the messenger birds of the noble Houses they served, the Pilgrims could communicate with one another much faster than horses could ride. Their recent location would soon be known, and from there it wasn't hard to guess they were heading north to the Free Cities. They had to reach Torian before the Order could assemble an army to block their way.

Keegan was even more eager to avoid a confrontation with the Order than before. In their flight, he'd left his charms and the vial of witchroot behind—he was basically defenseless now. Vulnerable. If something happened, he'd be totally reliant on his companion to save him.

He hated admitting his own weakness, but he consoled himself with the knowledge that it was only temporary. Once they reached Torian he'd stock up again on supplies. And in the future, he'd be careful to always carry some witchroot and an assortment of charms with him.

On the fifth day of their flight they crossed the Larna River on the northern edge of the province, and Jerrod finally allowed their pace to slow. Technically they were in the borderlands now, and beyond the Pontiff's official reach. It would take at least another week until they reached the city of Torian itself, but the Order had few agents in this territory and little sway with local rulers, so any pursuit would likely come from behind.

They had successfully escaped the Southlands. Now the only question was whether Khamin Ankha, Rexol's former student, would help them.

The name seemed somehow familiar to Keegan, though he wasn't sure why. Perhaps Rexol had mentioned him? Maybe the fact that he recognized the name was a good sign. His master rarely referred to his former students by name; maybe this Khamin Ankha had been someone special enough to warrant such a mention.

And if they didn't find what they needed in Torian there was always one more option: Vaaler. They were drawing ever closer to the North Forest, forbidden domain of the Danaan. And Keegan just happened to know the heir to the throne. Surely Vaaler would help him . . . providing they weren't killed making their way through the forest to reach him.

He hadn't mentioned the Danaan prince to Jerrod yet. He was afraid to. If the monk knew of such a potentially valuable ally he might insist they try to reach him no matter what the cost. During their time together under Rexol, Vaaler had told him many vivid tales of the Danaan patrols and what they did to any humans foolish enough to wander into their lands. Given the graphic nature of these tales, Keegan would rather not risk such a journey unless it was their last hope.

He decided to keep his secret a little longer. At least until they had tested out the hospitality of those in Torian.

- - - -

Scythe was up first, as usual. When Norr slept, he slept hard—throwing himself into his slumber with reckless abandon. Instead of waking him, however, she left him snoring away while she scouted ahead to pick up the trail once more.

The false merchants they followed weren't making any effort to hide their progress, but Scythe was city born and bred. It took her a long time to find even the most obvious sign of their quarry's passing. Sometimes she never could find the trail, and she would have to go back and wake Norr. The barbarian was a hunter; he could track the men easily. But she hated to wake him. And she hated to admit defeat.

Not that the trail mattered much, anyway. They were heading almost due north, deviating only to avoid the cities and well-traveled roads. Often they went directly through the sparse birch forests that grew in the wilds of the upper Southlands, cutting through streams and fields with no regard to any existing path. At first Scythe thought her prey were trying to throw off pursuit, but later she came to realize it was simply a matter of taking the shortest, most direct route possible. The wizards were trying to move quickly, and they were succeeding.

After the first few days Scythe had nearly given up. The trail was getting colder as they fell farther and farther behind, despite only sleeping a few hours each night. It was as if the men they followed needed no sleep at all. She had even considered the possibility that they were using strange magic to replenish themselves and their mounts. After what she had seen in the Singing Dragon's tavern, it didn't seem out of the question.

She still had the pouch she had stolen from the wizard's room tucked safely away inside her belt, though she herself had no use for the magical trinkets or the strange vial of liquid. If she remembered Methodis's lessons, the vial was probably witchroot—a powerful drug wizards used to unfetter their minds. And the trinkets were probably charms; bits of teeth or bone from long-extinct creatures thought to embody the power of Chaos itself.

Scythe hoped these were the mages' only source of power; without them they might be defenseless and vulnerable. But she knew it was likely they had more of their arcane supplies stashed away somewhere on the pack horses.

Despite this, she refused to turn back. It was as much a fear of returning to life in Praeton as her unquenchable burning lust for revenge that drove Scythe onward.

Once they passed the Larna River they had finally begun to gain ground. Norr had noticed it first, of course. But now even Scythe could see the signs that they were getting closer. They began to run across abandoned camps, something they hadn't seen before. Norr showed her where the men had slept, the weight of their bodies bending and breaking the soft undergrowth they had lain on. He was even able to tell her how long they spent at each campsite, and after their initial sleepless run Scythe was relieved to learn that even wizards needed a full night's rest at some point.

Norr had even been able to tell her what order the men had taken their watch in, deducing who had woken whom for the next shift by the faintest of footprints in the soft ground. This merely confirmed what she had suspected, but a posted watch didn't worry her. She could slip past any guard unseen in the darkness of the night—or slit his throat before he could make a sound. At least they weren't using some fell Chaos magic to ward their camps. Scythe didn't know if she'd be able to circumvent anything like that.

For her and Norr posting a guard wasn't an issue. For one thing, they had no one to fear. They weren't being hunted, and the chance of a random encounter this far from the main roads was minuscule. Too, Scythe was a very light sleeper. Anyone trying to creep up on them unawares was likely to find themselves staring down Scythe's blade as soon as they got close enough to try anything.

So she and Norr both slept comfortably the entire night. Unless they woke up to make love. Ever since she had realized they were gaining on their targets Scythe had felt an exhilarating flush, the heat of anticipation. Norr felt it, too, the long-forgotten thrill of the hunt. Energized by the adrenaline pumping through their bodies and the untamed surroundings, their sex was primal and wild. Even feral. She clawed at Norr's chest and back, her raking nails leaving bright red trails across his pale skin. He thrust into her madly, like an animal in heat until her screams of pain and pleasure tore the night's canopy. They would lie motionless in the aftermath, limbs entwined, the cool night air bringing goose bumps to their naked flesh as their sweat evaporated. And maybe, just maybe, Scythe hoped Norr didn't regret leaving Praeton behind.

A broken branch caught her eye. She had found the trail once more. Satisfied, she tore a larger branch from a nearby shrub and jammed it into the ground by the sign of her quarry's passing so she could easily find it again after she woke Norr.

Scythe didn't know what would happen when she and Norr caught up to the two wizards, but not knowing didn't worry her. In fact, she reveled in it. Unlike the monotonous predictability of Praeton, their future was once more unwritten and unknowable.

Unaware she was smiling, she returned to camp with a spring in her step, eager to wake Norr so the hunt could resume.

Chapter 41

Torian, like all the Free Cities, was surrounded by an enormous wall fifty feet high and twenty feet thick. The cracked, gray stone attested to the age of this formidable defense. The fact that it was still standing after so many centuries and countless attacks upon the city gave testament to its strength.

From his studies under Rexol, Keegan knew the Free Cities—sometimes called the Border Cities—had earned their name through the blood and suffering of their peoples. In the wake of the Cataclysm seven hundred years ago, the entire Southlands had been a collection of a hundred independent city-states evolved from primitive nomadic tribes that had chosen to settle and build rather than continue their ceaseless wandering. The settlements had been ruled by descendants of the tribal chieftains, and the towns were constantly involved in skirmishes and clashes with their neighbors.

Petty warfare was the norm; small raiding armies marched the Southlands, burning and ravaging everything in their path. The battles were crude, the weapons simple but effectively lethal none-theless. Valuable fertile farmland was fought over and changed hands on an almost yearly basis, until the endless struggle left only a blighted, blasted stretch of sterile soil. Entire generations of young men were lost to the slaughter. Population growth and cultural evolution ground to a halt as the Southlands wallowed in the mire and misery of constant, ceaseless warfare.

And then, after nearly three centuries of stagnation, came the Unification. Seven of the strongest and most powerful warlords joined their armies and began a war of conquest and subjugation throughout the Southlands. The tiny would-be kingdoms were swallowed up into the ever-expanding empire, their ancient rivalries and conflicts forgotten as their leaders were ousted and executed by the Alliance of the Seven.

The banners of the Alliance were first seen in the middle lands, but within two decades its rapidly spreading borders had pushed south until they reached the desert, east until they reached the Frozen Wastes, and west until they reached the Great Sea. The foundations for the Southlands as it existed today were laid as the warlords divided their spoils into the provinces known as the Seven Kingdoms, each claiming the grandest city in his region as his territorial capital.

The great Southland Empire had been constrained on three points of the compass—south, east, and west—by geography and nature. So the warlords turned their land-hungry armies to the north, where they expected their massive forces to conquer everything until they reached the forests of the Danaan. Instead, for the first time, they found pockets of true resistance and an enemy they couldn't sweep away with the sheer numbers of troops at their command: the Free Cities.

Legends of the wars against the Free Cities were well known among the Southlands, and were even more famous in places like Torian. Tales of sieges lasting twenty years, with a few hundred soldiers holding the great walled fortress towns against ten thousand armed foes camped around the gates. Myths of brave City Lords who refused surrender, fiercely clinging to their independence against overwhelming, impossible odds yet somehow succeeding in the end. Epic sagas of the Southland generals crashing their forces against the walls with the relentless fury of pounding waves battering the shore cliffs, only to have their charge and spirits broken time and time again by the stalwart courage of the defenders on the other side.

Of course not all the stories from the Free Cities' Wars were heroic. Dark rumors of cannibalism evolved out of whispers that those trapped within the walled towns could not have survived without devouring their own kind, but Rexol had taught Keegan that this was mostly Southland propaganda. The sieges were not proper sieges. Each of the Free Cities had been built against the very edge of the North Forest, their walls actually extending back into the tree line. When the Southland armies came, they found it impossible to totally surround the walled towns. The north gates within the woods were not blockaded, giving the citizens an escape and a back door to bring in supplies and food.

Not that the Southland generals hadn't tried to cut off this access route. But each time soldiers had been forced into the forbidden woods to try to encircle their enemy, they never returned. It was never proven or admitted, but most historians suspected the Danaan were responsible for the vanishing troops. Either overtly or covertly, they had supported the efforts of the Free Cities, anxious to maintain a buffer between their own lands and those of the expansionist human empire to the south.

In the end the Southlands had admitted defeat, and turned from warfare to diplomacy to try to bring the unbreakable walled towns into their fold. The result was a collection of semi-autonomous cities, strongly allied with the Seven Capitals yet able to resist many of the compromises and political capitulations the rest of the Southlands had to bow to, including the decrees of the Order.

During the Purge, the Free Cities had resisted the Order as they had resisted the Southern warlords before, with similar success. Here the Pontiff had little influence and even less power. Here Keegan and Jerrod might find sanctuary against the death sentence imposed on them by the Monastery, appealing to Beethania the City Lord through her court mage Khamin Ankha, Rexol's former apprentice.

They were nearing the southern gate now, Keegan and Jerrod

and a hundred other travelers along the massive road. The pair had joined the crowd about a mile back, diverting from their previous plan of staying on the lesser-used paths. There was only one way into Torian from this side, and that was through the massive, heavily guarded gates.

Despite the crush of people around them, Keegan knew they would stand out. Jerrod had decided they would make no effort to hide who or what they were. In fact, he had insisted that Keegan adorn himself in full battle regalia: bare-chested, his body covered in painted glyphs and wards, and Rexol's gorgon's-skull staff held in his hand.

The monk wanted to make an impression. He wanted to draw the attention of the city authorities. He wanted everyone to know a fierce Chaos mage was in the city; he wanted Rexol's former apprentice to come to them.

Keegan could feel the eyes of everyone on him as they passed through the enormous walls and into the borders of the city. He disdained to return their gaze—as a Chaos mage, the commoners were beneath him. Yet from the corner of his eye he saw a runner scurrying away, obviously going to alert the city officials of their presence. Jerrod had what he wanted: They had been noticed.

Torian, once a bastion of military might that had withstood the Alliance of the Seven Warlords, was now a thriving trade center; a bridge between the Southlands and the mysterious Danaan kingdom hidden in the trees beyond the north gate. The Danaan influence was obvious throughout the city. Many of the green-hued Forest Folk walked among the crowd, and in the features and coloration of the general populace Keegan could detect the subtle traces of a not quite purely human ancestry. Anywhere else a child of a Danaan and a human would be reviled as an abomination, a half-breed. But judging by the evidence in Torian, here such offspring were accepted with at least a grudging tolerance.

The clothing and fashions were also markedly different from those in the Southlands. Of course styles varied city to city and region to region, but even among the most disparate trends there was always something familiar, something distinctly Southern about the preferred dress within the provinces: functional, durable garb, and subdued colors.

Here people wore clothes that were loose and flowing. They accessorized with long, delicate scarves that fluttered when they walked or wore diaphanous capes and cloaks atop their outfits. Boots were soft worked leather rather than the hard, cured hide Keegan was familiar with. And everywhere he looked Keegan saw bright tones; red, orange, and green were obviously the colors of choice.

The architecture also reflected the influence of Danaan culture. The squat, square edifices common throughout the Southlands were rare here; instead the town was dominated by tall, elegant towers reminiscent of sketches of the Danaan capital that Keegan had seen in the volumes of Rexol's library. Torian looked less like a city and more like a forest of buildings.

The main thoroughfare was crowded, but no more so than any merchant city in the Southlands. The towers were widely and evenly spaced, creating an orderly grid of broad crisscrossing roads that made moving about the city a simple, almost enjoyable task. And the streets within Torian were, to Keegan's surprise, remarkably clean. The stench and grime associated with major urban centers was all but absent; the congestion and filth of overcrowding that seemed to be a common trait among the Seven Capitals had not yet settled into Torian's character.

Keegan was able to take in the look and feel of the city at his leisure, as Jerrod had slowed their pace to a crawl. He wanted Torian's officials to find them. By now, Khamin Ankha had to know that another wizard had arrived in the town. And, Keegan thought, if Rexol's old apprentice chose not to approach them—if he chose to keep official channels closed—they could simply venture onward into the Danaan lands.

They were still heading north on the main thoroughfare, which would eventually lead them to the much smaller gates of the northern wall. There, Keegan knew, they would have to pay a toll to cross into the Danaan lands. Likely, the guards would warn them not to stray from the well-defined road.

If they followed the trade route it would eventually lead them to the Danaan town that had sprung up at the intersection of all the trade routes from all the Free Cities, a nameless community created solely for the purpose of exchanging goods between the human and Danaan peoples. There merchants could buy or sell their wares before returning along the trade routes to the Free Cities that led back into the Southlands.

It was common knowledge the Danaan tolerated merchants and visitors in their domain only so long as they stayed on the trade routes. Anyone straying from the designated areas would be sentenced to immediate execution should their transgression be discovered by a Danaan patrol. And yet there were those who dared to leave the trade routes. Explorers trying to locate and map the hidden Danaan cities. Foolish or brave adventurers seeking long-lost treasure rumored to be hidden beneath the thick branches of the North Forest. Emissaries determined to bypass the restrictions of the Danaan monarchy so they could try to establish diplomatic relations with the forbidden kingdom. Very few of these who left the road, for any reason, ever returned alive.

They had already passed the midway point of the city when they were finally greeted by an official presence. A cadre of banner-carrying footmen marched in tight formation through the streets toward them, the crowd parting before their progress. Behind them were several mounted knights, their lances fluttering with the same flags the footmen carried—a single white tower on a deep blue background, the symbol of Lady Beethania, Torian's current City Lord. Behind the knights rode a man Keegan could only imagine was Khamin Ankha, the most important lord's mage in Torian.

In general, Keegan had little respect for lord's mages. Rexol had once told him that they were often far more skilled in political maneuvering than in the wizard's Gift. Their position was primarily ceremonial; it was rare they could wield magic with anything even approaching the power of a true Chaos mage—or even a village witch or sorcerer.

Keegan had often wondered why those with a true command of Chaos were so rarely found in the position of lord's mage. Perhaps the nobles feared the spellcasters in their employ would overthrow them if they had any true power. Or perhaps those with the ability to shape and control Chaos would not subject themselves to the employ of another, even one as important as a city lord or king. Keegan knew Rexol would never have sworn fealty to anyone but himself.

He had expected Khamin Ankha to be the exception to the rule. He had, after all, studied under Rexol. However, his first impression reinforced his previous experiences rather than dispelled them. This was a man with only the slightest hint of Chaos in the aura about him.

Despite the many cultural differences between Torian and the Seven Capitals, his uniform of office was remarkably similar to that of the lord's mages Keegan had seen in the Southlands. He wore heavy purple robes that completely covered his rather ample frame, the tower of Lady Beethania emblazoned prominently on his chest. His hair was neatly combed, his body almost devoid of tattoos or piercings. His only visible ornamentations were a pair of small earrings, a few necklaces dangling down, and several rings on his plump, fleshy fingers. His skin had a pale hue and seemed to gleam with a strange sheen, though that might merely have been the sun reflecting off the rivulets of sweat running down the fat man's brow.

The man looked vaguely familiar to Keegan, even though he was sure they had never met. After a few moments, he dismissed it as unimportant. The man looked like any other lord's mage in any of a dozen courts in the Southlands. Why shouldn't his appearance seem vaguely familiar?

As the company drew close the footmen stepped to either side to form twin lines along the edges of the road. They raised their banners in unison as the knights pranced their mounts through the line, then assumed their places beside the footmen. Next came the lord's mage, slowly riding forward to greet them. The pomp and ceremony of his arrival left a bitter taste in Keegan's mouth.

"I am Khamin Ankha," the man proclaimed in a booming voice that surely carried several blocks in every direction, "I welcome you to the Free City of Torian. I am honored to extend an invitation to you and your companions on behalf of Lady Beethania. I have come to escort you to her mansion."

"I am Jerrod, and this is Keegan—a student of Rexol, your former master," Jerrod replied in a much lower voice.

"We were beginning to think you wouldn't show, Khamin," he added. "We certainly did our part to let you know we were coming."

"It took much convincing on my part," the man explained in a much quieter voice than the one he had used at his first greeting. "Lady Beethania was reluctant to give you an audience: You have been declared heretics by the Order."

So news from the Monastery had already reached beyond the farthest borders of the Southlands. Keegan wondered how Jerrod would respond to the accusation, but the monk said nothing.

Obviously uncomfortable with the silence, Khamin Ankha tried to further explain his position.

"Even though the Order holds no influence here, she was afraid of making a powerful enemy if we acknowledged your presence. But my counsel prevailed upon the City Lord, and she at last came to understand the potential benefits for Torian if we were to give you a more suitable welcome."

The fat man leaned forward eagerly, like a fishwife eager to hear the latest gossip. "Tell me, are the rumors true? Is Rexol really dead?"

Jerrod nodded, then warned, "This is not the place to speak of this, Khamin."

"Of course, of course," he said, sitting up straight once more.

"Where are my manners? Gentlemen, if you would please follow me I shall take you to meet our ruler, the most noble Lady Beethania."

"I don't like this," Norr said again. He had been uneasy ever since it became clear the wizards they followed were heading to Torian. Scythe could guess the reason. Of all the Free Cities, Torian was the farthest east—less than a day's ride from the borders of Norr's own homeland. In the past, it had been common for some of the more war-like barbarian tribes to raid the smaller settlements along the border: pillaging towns; burning farms; killing and raping the defenseless villagers; and leaving only charred, smoldering corpses behind.

In retaliation, Torian would send heavily armed patrols into the Frozen East to extract bloody vengeance on the invaders. Their retribution was swift and gruesome, and at times the icy steppes were dotted with a hundred crucified corpses of Norr's people. Often the victims of Torian's vengeance were not even those responsible for the killing of the Southlanders. The Free City patrols knew little about the vast differences among the many tribes—and wouldn't have cared even if they did. To those in and around Torian, the people of the East were all the same: savages, animals in human skin deserving a terrible, painful death. Killing one was as good as killing another.

And the policy of Torian's patrols was to kill as many Easterners as they could on their excursions, leaving their tortured, mutilated bodies on display as a warning against further raids. Men, women, children—none were spared the ruthless, misdirected justice. Only when they had slain ten Easterners for every single victim of the raids would Torian's officials call off the hunt.

There hadn't been a raid in the area in nearly twenty years— more a result of the Easterners' concentrated efforts to exterminate the most war-like tribes among their own people than the bloodshed of the Free City patrols, according to Norr. Yet there was still a standing bounty in Torian for the head of any savage caught within twenty miles of the city.

But their quarry was heading to Torian, and Scythe wasn't about to let them go. Not now, when she and Norr were only a little more than a day behind them. She had expected to catch up with them much sooner. Three nights ago they had closed to within a day of their prey—and then disaster had struck. Norr's horse had broken down, its foreleg snapping as it tried to leap across a small stream with the massive barbarian atop its back. They had lost several days trying to find a mount large and strong enough to bear Norr's weight for eighteen hours of every twenty-four. And when they finally located the magnificent beast her lover now rode, he had refused to allow Scythe to steal it from the owner's stable. Scythe had handed over a substantial sum of coin—the last of her emergency stash—and Norr had spent a full day working the farmer's field before the owner considered the value of the animal to be paid in full.

It had taken them this long to make up the lost ground, pushing their horses and themselves to the limits of endurance. And now they had come up a day short. The men had camped here just last night, only a few hours away from Torian. The trail led from the camp to the main road into the Free City; no doubt the wizards were even now passing through Torian's mighty gates. And it was impossible for Norr to follow them.

But Scythe wasn't ready to admit defeat. Not yet. Which was why she was going on alone.

"I don't like this," Norr repeated once more.

Scythe realized she wouldn't be able to leave until she had reassured him one more time.

"It will only take me a few hours to reach the city," she said, saddling up her horse in preparation for the trip. "I'll scout things out, see if I can get any information. I'll see if I can find out why they went to Torian, and if and when they'll be coming back to the

Southlands. Once we know that, they're ours. We can set up an ambush and wait for them to walk right into our trap."

"What if they see you?" the big man asked.

"Torian's a big place. I'll blend into the crowd. They'll never even know I'm there."

"What if you see them?" Norr's voice was even more worried now.

She hesitated, uncertain what to tell him. In the end, she decided on the truth. Norr knew her too well for her to lie anyway. "If I see them, I'll kill them."

"Scythe . . . ," her lover began, but she slung herself up into the saddle before he could continue.

"Don't worry, I'll be back tomorrow. The day after at the latest. Stay here, stay out of sight. When I come back this might all be over."

"I want to come with you."

She nudged her horse over to where Norr was standing. Mounted on her steed she was actually taller than he was. Barely. She leaned down slightly and planted a soft, warm kiss on his bearded cheek.

"You can't, my love. It's too dangerous. But I won't leave you. I will come back. I promise."

Norr nodded, a slight bob of the head. As usual, he understood. It had to be this way. He couldn't come with her, and she couldn't simply let the men who had destroyed their life in Praeton get away free . . . even if she had hated that life. That was just the way she was. Norr knew he couldn't change her, and to his credit he had never tried. That was why she loved him and hated to leave him, even if only for a day or two.

She wheeled her horse away and rode off toward the main road. The sooner she reached Torian, the sooner this could all end. And she and Norr could begin once more to search for a life in which they would both be happy.

Chapter 42

"WHY DOES THE Order want you dead?" Lady Beethania asked between bites of braised pheasant. She brought the topic up casually, as if asking how their journey had been.

Keegan wondered how much she really knew. In the Southlands all the prophets working for the nobility were members of the Order. No doubt they would be under strict instructions from the Pontiff not to reveal what they knew about Jerrod's heretical followers lest they find converts among the political elite. But in Torian the Order didn't hold sway. Were Seers common here? Did Lady Beethania have a prophet working for her who had warned her of their coming?

"We have different interpretations of the fate of the world," Jerrod answered slowly, obviously sharing his companion's concerns about how much their host was aware of. His speech was ponderous and heavy, as if every word required careful thought. "Great and terrible times are in the future, my lady. The Order fears to acknowledge the evil that is to come."

Khamin laughed at the coy response. "Come, Jerrod. You think we are ignorant? You aren't the first to speak of a second Cataclysm, you know."

"The way I have heard it told," Lady Beethania slyly suggested, "you and your followers are the ones who will ultimately be responsible for unleashing the second Cataclysm upon us. It makes me wonder who to believe."

"Prophets do not always see clearly," Jerrod admitted. "But I stand against the Pontiff and the Order, and I know they are no friends of yours. That is why we have come to you for help."

With a knowing wink the Lady answered, "The enemy of my enemy is my friend. Or so they say."

Again, Keegan wondered how much she knew. He took a sip of wine, only to have a servant rush to refill it as soon as he placed the cup down. Like many of the dishes in the opulent feast before him, the wine had a strange and unfamiliar taste. But after weeks of nothing but stale bread, cheese, cured meat, and water he was more than eager to gorge himself on whatever was offered. Jerrod was similarly eager to sample the fine exotic fare Khamin's employer had laid out before them.

The heavy meal, the rich wine, and the warmth of the fire were making Keegan sleepy. He struggled to keep his eyes from closing of their own accord and tried to focus on the conversation at hand. The reception they had received had not been hostile, but it was obvious both Khamin and his liege were not eager to incur the wrath of the Pontiff. It appeared it was going to be difficult to secure their help; he needed to pay attention.

Despite his efforts, his mind only hoped that once the supper was over Lady Beethania would offer them each a warm, soft bed for the night.

"You have to help us," Jerrod said in a long, slow slur. "The Legacy is failing. The Slayer and the Chaos Spawn will come again to the mortal world, and Keegan must be our champion to stand against them."

Had his lids not been as heavy as bricks, Keegan's eyes would have popped open in surprise. Why was Jerrod telling them that? It was strange the monk would so willingly divulge so much to someone they had just met.

"Oh yes, I know all about this young man's power," Khamin said as he rose to his feet and slowly walked the length of table toward

Keegan. "We have met once before. Or do you not remember, Keegan? Have you so easily forgotten how you disrupted my display of Chaos magic the last time we met?"

Through the thick fog closing in around his mind it all came back to the young wizard. He hadn't recognized the man in his purple robes, but now there was no mistaking his features or his name. Khamin Ankha—the traveling magician claiming to be Rexol's apprentice at the tavern in Endown. The one Keegan had embarrassed in his efforts to win the affections of a young barmaid.

Keegan tried to leap to his feet but his body wouldn't respond. Across the table he saw Jerrod slumping sideways in his chair.

Khamin Ankha was beside him now, leaning close to whisper into his ear. "The next time you humiliate a man, you had best remember his name. You may have forgotten our last encounter, but I most assuredly have not. And now I shall have my vengeance. Remember this as you burn at the stake for heresy!"

"Don't make this so personal, Khamin," the City Lord admonished, her words sounding muffled to Keegan's ears. "This is merely a politically wise decision. The Order is a powerful ally, one we have too long neglected. This execution will be an excellent first step in securing Torian's new place of importance among the Pontiff and his followers."

"Of course, my lady," Khamin replied, grabbing one of Keegan's wild braids in his beefy fingers and tilting the young man's head back. "A politically advantageous situation must be exploited. My personal vengeance is merely an enjoyable side benefit."

The fat man lashed out with his fist, landing a hard punch on his helpless victim's nose. As the blood streamed from his nostrils, Keegan's drug-addled mind barely had time to wonder at the fact that he hadn't felt the blow. And then the darkness took him.

Scythe knew she'd have little trouble gathering the information she sought. The streets of Torian were much like those of any other city. Wider, cleaner, but still teeming with life, still buzzing with the news of the city if you knew who to ask. From the moment she had passed through the guarded gates, Scythe knew she was in her element.

She thought she'd begin by asking one of the gatemen for information, but she saw no reason to rush her investigation. It was getting dark; she would end up spending the night here in any case. She might as well enjoy it—the sights, the smells, the sounds, the crowds. And besides, she might need some coin to pry the information out of the guards, and she'd spent the last of her funds on replacing Norr's mount.

There were other ways to loosen the guard's tongue, of course. Once she would have considered it a waste to spend coin on something she could obtain with flirtatious banter and a suggestive manner, but since meeting Norr her perspective had changed somewhat. Now her sexuality had value beyond what she could barter it for; it was something special between her and her lover.

And after catching a glimpse of herself in a shop window, Scythe had to wonder if her charms would even be noticeable beneath the thick layer of accumulated road grime. That was another thing she'd need money for: a hotel where she could draw herself a nice, hot bath.

Not that obtaining money proved to be any trouble. She may have temporarily lost her looks, but her pickpocket skills were as sharp as ever. Within an hour she had scouted out Torian's merchant center and successfully acquired an even dozen purses, pouches, and wallets. The coins would be more than enough to buy the information she needed, obtain a luxurious room for the night, and replenish their supplies with enough food to satisfy Norr's enormous appetite for at least a fortnight.

Remembering the dirty, mud-caked waif she had witnessed in place of her own reflection, Scythe decided to start by getting a room and cleaning herself up. Maybe if she was lucky the information she was after could be had from the inn's tavern and she could save herself a trip to the south gate's watchtower.

The innkeeper eyed her filthy clothes and soiled face with suspicion, but his attitude quickly changed when she dumped a pile of gold coins in his lap and demanded the best room in the house. She had given the proprietor at least triple what the room was worth, but she considered the money to be well spent for the effect it had on the attitude of the entire staff toward her. By the time Scythe finished her bath her clothes had been laundered and dried by the fire then laid out on her bed by one of the maids. A small note on the pillow told her an extravagant meal was being prepared especially for her by the cook and would be brought to her room as soon as it was ready.

She'd offered no explanation for her apparent wealth, but given her exotic features and disheveled state on arrival, she could imagine the types of rumors the staff would already be spreading about her. An Island princess on the run from a sibling trying to steal her throne; one of the famed pirate queens who roamed the Western Seas eager to retire from the cutthroat life and live on her ill-gotten fortune; the foreign mistress of a Southern noble fleeing an abusive relationship—any or all could fit. But whatever or whoever they thought she was, they were convinced of two things: She was rich, and she was mysterious.

As she dressed in her once more clean clothes, Scythe briefly considered eating in her room, then decided against it. She wanted to mingle with the patrons at the bar to see if they had any information about the wizards. And making an appearance would add fuel to the wild speculation already swirling about her.

The innkeeper scuttled over as she descended the stairs, a look of genuine concern on his face.

"My lady," he gushed, "I hope there is nothing wrong. Did you receive my note? I assure you, the meal will be ready in a few minutes. I apologize for the delay, but preparing a fine feast requires more time than the simple meals we usually serve."

He spoke with the ingratiating patter of the practiced sycophant, groveling and apologizing with each word. In Callastan she had often heard such speech directed toward wealthy customers wandering the market square, and it never failed to fill her with revulsion and contempt for both the speaker and the snob being addressed. Much to her surprise, she found she rather enjoyed the fawning tone when it was directed at her.

"Everything is fine," she assured the obsequious innkeeper, trying to adopt the haughty, cultured air she associated with the rich. "However, I believe I will dine in the tavern with the common folk. I have traveled long in my journey without conversation and I am eager to learn the news of the city."

The man bowed so low his chin nearly brushed his knees. "As you wish, my lady. Would you do me the honor of allowing me to escort you to your table?"

Scythe did precisely that, slipping her sleek sleeved arm into the crook of the man's elbow and accompanying him down the stairs.

Back in her room later that night Scythe was almost too excited to sleep. The evening had gone better than her wildest imaginings. She had expected a long night of gathering information, trying to track down the men she had been following since Praeton. A long and expensive night. But to her surprise, the bartender had provided her with all the information she needed completely free of charge.

It began when the innkeeper, trying to make pleasant dinner conversation, had asked if she was going to the executions tomorrow. The arrests of the strange travelers were the talk of the city, and the innkeeper was only too happy to answer her questions about the events of the day. It didn't take long for Scythe to determine that it was indeed her quarry that had been captured by the City Lord and sentenced to death.

She had felt a brief pang of regret, knowing she wouldn't have the pleasure of killing them herself. But when the innkeeper mentioned that the men arrested were to be publicly burned as heretics at noon tomorrow, she took some solace in the prospect of witnessing their agonizing end.

No longer burdened with the task of tracking the men down,

she had spent the remainder of the night playing the part of a rich, exotic stranger with a mysterious secret to the full. When she finally retired to her bedchamber, she knew the gossip in the tavern would be as much about the mysterious Island woman staying at the inn as it would be about the coming executions.

As her head hit the pillow Scythe felt sleep quickly overwhelming her. She hadn't realized how exhausted she was. She snuggled beneath the soft, warm covers and couldn't help but feel a little guilt when she thought of Norr having to sleep on the cold, hard ground once more.

Still, she knew he would be pleased to know the hunt was over. He'd be even more pleased when he learned Scythe hadn't killed them herself. As her mind slipped willingly into the darkness of a deep, deep sleep Scythe's last thoughts were of how perfectly everything had worked out.

Chapter 43

RAVEN CIRCLED HIGH in the clouds, ignoring the buffeting winds and shards of ice that pelted her naked flesh. Miles below, her eagle eyes had picked out a small, huddled form moving slowly along a ledge. She knew it was the one she hunted; she had tasted her fear for days now.

Raven could sense the fire of the Crown she carried, a gleaming spark in the pack slung over the mortal's shoulder. Her instincts urged her to swoop down and seize it, plucking it from the pack and tossing the woman off the narrow ledge and into the chasm below.

But something held her at bay. There was another power here. She felt its presence on the wind, but it would be strongest in the earth and rocks beneath the mortal's feet. This was the domain of the Guardian, one of the ancient Chaos Spawn. And Raven knew she was no match for him.

Here among the frozen clouds she was safely hidden from the Guardian's awareness, but if she dove down to the earth he would sense her coming. Was he close enough to stop her from getting the Crown?

It would only take a few seconds. She would plummet from the sky, snatch the pack up in her claws, and fly back to Orath victorious. Or the Guardian would emerge and smite her from the sky, snuffing out her existence.

She circled again, then screamed in frustration. She would not dive down; she would not risk her death in a single desperate act. Her prey had escaped and the Crown was beyond her reach. She wheeled on the currents, turning west, leaving the land of endless winter—and her failure—behind her.

But where could she go now? She dared not return to Orath empty-handed.

Leaving the mountains behind, she continued west for many leagues until she reached the tundra-covered steppes where the barbarian hordes ranged, safely beyond the Guardian's reach. Coming in to land on the ground, she tilted her head back and tasted the air. There was life here—beasts she could hunt for food and mortals she could kill for sport as she waited for the Crown to return.

She coiled herself up into a ball on the ground, wrapping her black wings around her. Her dark skin began to shudder as ancient words of power spilled from her hooked beak. Seconds later her crouching, trembling form was enveloped in an orb of impenetrable black shadow. Within the darkness she screamed as the spell ripped and tore at her flesh.

After many minutes the darkness faded away, leaving Raven transformed. Her avian head and wings were gone; her naked, ebony body had taken on the form and features of an ordinary mortal woman dressed in the hides and skins of the nomadic tribes she had seen from high above.

A faint glimmer of a plan had formed in her dark mind. The Crown could not stay with the Guardian forever. Its power was anathema to him; too long in its presence and he would sicken and die. After a few weeks, maybe a month, the Guardian would be forced to send it away, and the mortal would leave the safety of his lair.

Raven knew she could bide her time until then. She would live among the mortals of the barbarian tribes, sowing the seeds of Chaos and waiting for her chance to strike.

The cold had long since ceased to matter. The numbing pain meant nothing anymore, for Cassandra knew she was going to die. She felt the presence of her enemy high above her as she moved slowly along the ice-covered ledge. She felt it circling, she felt its hate, she felt its fear. It had found her.

She wanted to cry. Not for herself, but for her failure. She would cry for all those who had sacrificed for her, for those who had died for her, for those who had trusted her on this mission. She wanted to weep, but the tears froze at the corners of her eyes, trapping the grief and sorrow inside her.

And then suddenly the presence above her was gone.

Puzzled, she turned her frostbitten face up, exposing it to the savage winds. Slowly she began to feel another presence. But this one did not fill her with sorrow or terror; it did not promise a grim and brutal death. It welcomed her, it called to her. It was close now, closer than she would have dared to believe. Through the blinding, endless blizzard she sensed the opening of a cave. She knew the presence was inside.

This presence offered hope and salvation and . . . and *warmth*.

She redoubled her pace until she stepped off the ledge and into the pleasant heat of the sheltered cave. The Guardian was waiting for her.

Tears of joy rolled down her cheeks as the Guardian wrapped his strong arms around her, drawing her into his heat and away from the cold.

Chapter 44

SCYTHE WOKE FEELING completely refreshed. The weeks of exhausting travel had been swept away by a warm bath, some clean clothes, a good meal, and a single night in a real bed.

The executions were scheduled for noon, she remembered. If she wanted to have a proper view of the festivities, she'd have to arrive early. Reluctantly she climbed from the bed to wash up before leaving the comfort of the inn.

The innkeeper was waiting for her when she descended the steps. His eyes lit up when he saw her. Scythe realized he had developed a crush on her, and she hoped he wouldn't make any inappropriate advances. She wanted to maintain the illusion of a wealthy lady of culture, but if he made a move she'd respond with a knee to the groin and the charade would likely be over.

Fortunately, the innkeeper considered her a true lady and acted with nothing but grace and courtesy.

"Good morning," he said, bowing low. "I trust last night was to your satisfaction."

"I slept very well," she replied. Noticing his desperate, hopeful expression she added, "I always find a good meal and sparkling conversation put me at ease so that I may enjoy a restful night. I thank you for both, good sir."

The innkeeper blushed, and a coquettish giggle escaped Scythe's lips—a reaction suitable to the character she was playing, but one that was unplanned and unwelcome. Bile welled up in her throat, and suddenly she no longer enjoyed the game she had been playing. It conjured up memories of her life among the whorehouses of Callastan: adopting personalities that were not her own, subsuming her own identity into the roles her clients demanded, taking on false mannerisms to please the men—and sometimes women— who paid gold to own her, if even for one night. She hadn't realized how easy it would be to slip back into the old practices, and the realization disturbed her.

"I'll be leaving today," she said to the innkeeper, not bothering with the aristocratic accent anymore.

He was too infatuated with her to notice. "Surely my lady plans to stay for the executions?" he inquired. Before she could respond he added, "There has been a third added to the list."

"A third heretic?" Scythe was suddenly wary.

She'd been convinced the two wizards were acting alone. Was it possible they had come to meet an ally in Torian?

"Oh, no—not a heretic," the innkeeper explained. "Last night the City Lord sent out a number of patrols to scour the area to ensure a smooth execution. One of the patrols stumbled across a barbarian spy hiding in the forest a few hours outside the city."

It took all Scythe's strength to keep from collapsing. She leaned heavily on the railing, trying to support her weight so the innkeeper wouldn't suspect anything was wrong.

"They say he is a giant beast of a savage," the man continued. "He attacked like an animal, using only his bare hands. It took the efforts of a full dozen men to subdue him!"

Gathering her courage, Scythe forced herself to ask a question.

"Where are they holding him?"

"Never fear, my lady—you'll see this monster at the execution. The City Lord has arranged for all three to be burned together. A simple matter, really. They'll just add another stake to the bonfire."

Scythe half stumbled, half ran down the stairs. She shoved her way past the innkeeper as he reached out to help her keep her balance, then raced out into the street. She ran for several blocks, then doubled over and vomited up the remains of last night's supper, much to the disgust of the people passing by.

Her stomach continued to retch up its contents until there was nothing left. She gave her mouth a slight wipe and straightened up. She still felt like throwing up. Or crying. Or screaming.

Instead, she took a deep breath and began to walk toward the town center. She pushed her emotions—guilt, rage, grief—aside for now. There would be time enough for such things later. After she rescued Norr.

The crowd was already buzzing with excitement; they had begun to gather before the soldiers had even finished setting up. In the early hours of the morning the sounds of hammers and saws and commanders shouting out orders had been heard above the drone of the ever-increasing crush of people gathering in the square. Now the construction was finished. In the very center of the square a huge stage had been built of large masonry stones, nearly ten feet high and twenty feet across. Three large, sturdy stakes jutted up from its surface, surrounded by a pile of wood faggots soaked in oil.

Nearby a massive grandstand had been erected, a place for the wealthy and politically important personages of Torian to view the execution away from the unwashed masses pressing up against the wooden barriers set out around the edges of the stage.

Scythe had scouted the area from one side to the other, committing the layout to memory so she might better execute her plan to free Norr. Except she didn't have one yet.

She had initially thought it might be possible to slip him away before the prisoners were brought forth for the execution, but she had since abandoned that idea. The dungeon where they were being held was deep in the earth beneath Lady Beethania's mansion. A score of guards had ringed the building, and only the Gods knew how many more were inside.

Bribing them was another option she briefly considered then

dismissed. If she had more time, she might be able to learn which guards were approachable and open to the idea of accepting a few coins to help one of the prisoners in their charge escape. But as it was she was likely to stumble on one devoted to duty, and she could end up being thrown in prison herself.

The blare of a horn was heard, and the crowd erupted in a wild, bloodthirsty cheer. The long blast announced the arrival of the prisoners; Scythe was out of time. At the far end of the square she saw a caravan of armed guards marching forward through the crowd. Twenty, maybe thirty in all, surrounding a large flatbed wagon. Chained to the wagon were the prisoners.

As the wagon slowly made its way through the throng of spectators, the people hurled insults at the condemned men from the crowd. They spit onto their helpless bound bodies; they hurled fruit and clumps of dirt and manure at them, screaming with the mindless hate of a true mob. The guards did nothing to stop their antics, save for drawing slightly farther away from the wagon lest they be hit by a stray missile.

Scythe shoved and pushed her way through the people, trying to gain a better look at Norr. When she finally got close enough to see the details, she nearly threw up again.

He had been stripped naked, his hands bound behind his back, his ankles tied together, and his mouth gagged. A thick metal chain had been latched onto the heavy collar around his neck and then attached to an iron ring in the bed of the wagon.

His naked body was a mess of dark, purple bruises. Nasty welts and cuts covered his back where they had whipped him; huge welts and angry red lumps covered his arms and legs where they had beaten him with metal rods. His face was nothing but a bloody, lumpy mess. His lips were swollen and split, his nose broken and twisted at a grotesque angle. His eyes were ringed with black-and-blue splotches and had puffed up so badly he probably couldn't even see. The thought of what they had done to him made Scythe want to kill every guard in the city, slowly and painfully. And her rage only grew when she saw the other men.

They were naked and bound as Norr, but had suffered neither whipping nor beating. On the younger of the two, she saw the strange tattoos of sorcery painted on his skin. The other had no markings traced onto his flesh, but she was close enough now to see his eyes. Or lack of them. He had once been a member of the Order, and now he was being tried for heresy.

The cart rolled slowly past her, and Scythe scrambled to keep up. She was able to twist and turn her small body through tiny gaps in the crowd, ignoring the rude comments, angry exclamations, and crude gropes she suffered as she squirmed her way toward the stage.

Despite her desperate efforts to hurry, the press of people slowed her down. By the time she reached the edge of the wooden barriers keeping the mob back, the prisoners had already been unloaded from the wagon and secured to the stakes. Their gags had been removed so the crowd could hear their dying screams.

Norr's head lolled to one side, and his eyes had rolled back into his skull. The nearest guard stepped up and slapped him until he regained consciousness, drawing a fresh stream of blood from the big man's broken nose and an approving roar from the crowd. Scythe marked that one, a tall, dark-haired young man.

Another horn blast silenced the shouts and cries of the crowd, and upon the nearby scaffold Scythe noticed that a platform had been built for a speaker to address the crowd. A woman who could only be Lady Beethania stood atop it, her face a mask of sadistic triumph. Beside her was a man clad in the outfit of a lord's mage, and in his hand he held a long staff with the skull of some strange monstrosity on the top.

Still not even sure what she was going to do, Scythe began to worm her way through the crowd toward those gathered near the base of the grandstand.

"Welcome, my people of Torian," Lady Beethania proclaimed, her voice amplified by some minor enchantment of her mage so that it would carry to the farthest reaches of the square. "You are here to witness the execution of three men. One is a spy from the frozen steppes, an Eastern savage caught lurking in the fields and farms surrounding our great city. The other two have been declared heretics and sentenced to death by the Order itself.

"But the Order does not hold sway here in Torian—we are a Free City and answer to none but our own!" A great cheer went up from the crowd, and the City Lord waited for the noise to subside before continuing. "Before I pronounce sentence on these men I turn to you, the people of Torian, the strength of this Free City, united in heart and spirit and mind. How say you, my subjects? Are these men deserving of death, or mercy?"

A brief hope flared in Scythe's breast, only to be quenched when the crowd began a ruthless chant of "Burn! Burn! Burn!" She tried to shut out the hateful words, forcing her mind to focus on a way to save Norr at any cost.

"The people have spoken!" Lady Beethania declared, her arms raised for silence once more. "The prisoners shall burn!"

She turned her head to the lord's mage at her side. Scythe was close enough to see him draw a vial from his belt and take a sip. He swooned briefly, then smiled and slipped the vial back out of sight. He held up a fist with something small clenched inside and began a quick but intricate series of strange gestures. She could see his lips moving quickly in an arcane litany.

Scythe remembered the vial of witchroot she had taken from the room back in Praeton; it was still tucked safely away in the pouch at her side. She pulled it out, even though it could do little to help her now. She was no wizard.

She glanced over at the stage and saw that the guards had all climbed down. The prisoners stood alone, the oil-soaked faggots piled up to their knees. The lord's mage stamped the butt of his skull-topped staff down onto the wooden platform of the grandstand, drawing her attention back to him. He was sweating profusely and breathing in long, heavy gasps. Whatever spell he was concocting was taking its toll.

He stamped the staff again, and suddenly one of the faggots burst into flame. The fire caught on the oil, and the blaze quickly spread. A look of relief briefly passed across his heavy jowls, and then his face assumed an expression of arrogance and disdain fitting his position.

The crowd erupted in cheers and screams of delight as the mob pressed forward, knocking over the barriers. Scythe was swept along with them, but managed to break free and run over to the grandstand. All eyes, including those of Lady Beethania, her lord's mage, and the guards themselves, were on the quickly spreading blaze.

Clutching the witchroot vial in her fist, Scythe broke through the front ranks of the crowd and rushed the stage. One of the guards stepped forward to stop her, but she ducked beneath his clumsy grab and continued her charge. She leapt up and managed to clutch the edge of the stage with her empty hand, then swung herself up on top before any of the other soldiers could react.

The oil-soaked wood had been arranged so that the fire would burn slowly; just hot enough to cook the heretics over many minutes, giving the crowd ample time to enjoy their dying screams. Even so, the heat from the rising flames nearly bowled Scythe over. A wall of smoke blocked her path to the prisoners, but she threw her free arm across her face to shield her eyes as she plunged into the conflagration.

The low flames wrapped themselves around her legs, scorching her boots and blistering her skin. She ignored the pain and leapt toward the nearest prisoner, the young wizard. She yanked the stopper from the vial and jammed it into his surprised mouth.

"You better save all our asses!" she screamed as she dumped the entire contents down his throat.

For a brief second there was a look of horror on the young man's face, as if what she had done was somehow worse than the execution he was facing. And then he began to convulse and froth at the mouth.

Scythe took a half step back and almost fell to her knees, the heat and smoke from the fire overcoming her. She had failed. Norr was going to die here, as was she. The blaze was higher now; in a minute the flesh of those on the stage would begin to melt and burn, their hair would burst into flames, and they would perish in agony. Ignoring the seizures racking the young man's body, she turned away to find Norr and kiss him one last time before the heat devoured them both.

A great rush of wind nearly swept her from the stage, an updraft that appeared from nowhere and lifted her momentarily from her feet. Instantly the flames were gone, sucked up into the sky, swallowed by an ominous green cloud that had suddenly materialized above the city.

There was stunned silence from the crowd; the guards nearest the stage took a fearful step back. She glanced over at the young wizard: His back was arched, his head tilted up to the sky. His bound body thrashed about in the grip of a great seizure, though his eyes were wide open. He was screaming out an endless string of nonsensical gibberish, blood and spittle spewing from his mouth.

Scythe turned to the grandstand to see if the wizard who had started the fire was about to ignite it again. But the man had collapsed in a heap, trembling in terror. His left hand covered his head as if he was afraid to look, and his right held the staff aloft as if it could shield him from the fury of the growing storm. The staff glowed with its own green light, though somehow Scythe knew that was not the cowering lord's mage's doing.

As she watched, a great crack of thunder erupted and a fork of emerald lightning shot down, engulfing the entire grandstand in an unearthly blue glow.

A collective scream rose up from those gathered on the wooden structure as a million volts seared their innards, cooking their bodies from the inside out. The grandstand collapsed with an audible crash, and wisps of greasy smoke wafted up from the charred corpses in the rubble. The strange staff lay amid the carnage, still glowing and apparently undamaged.

And then the clouds burst and fire poured down from the sky, burning embers falling like drops of rain over the whole of Torian. Panic seized the mob as they broke and ran, screaming and trampling one another in their haste to escape. As if fueled by their fear, the blazing orange drops flared into fist-sized balls of white-hot flame. The deadly hail incinerated everyone it struck, reducing them instantly to piles of smoking ash. Flashes of lightning split the night, arcing down to lash at the great towers of the city. Wherever they struck, the very stone itself was set ablaze with unnatural blue flame. Within seconds, the whole city of Torian seemed to be on fire.

Everywhere, that is, except the stage where only moments before a more natural fire had blazed. Here the wood had cooled to a comfortable temperature. The guards had scattered with the rest of the crowd—at least, the few who had survived the deadly burning rain. All around the stage were piles of ash, as if the storm had been directed by conscious will to wreak its most fearsome havoc among the men who had imprisoned its creator. Except for the four figures on the stage, Torian's square was now empty.

Scythe tore her attention from the destruction engulfing the city and ran over to her lover. Using one of the knives in her belt she cut the cords binding Norr to the stake. Once free he collapsed to the ground, and Scythe quickly inspected his wounds.

His skin had begun to blister from the heat of the flames, but the damage from the fire was the least of his injuries. The beating and bruises he had received would take a week to fade. There didn't appear to be any broken bones, but there were several large lumps on the side and back of Norr's skull.

"Quickly," one of the other men—the older of the two—called out to her, "cut me loose!"

She glanced over at the speaker. He was still lashed to the stake, as was his companion. The convulsions of the younger mage had stopped, and he had lost consciousness. Scythe ignored the man's request.

"Norr," she whispered. "Norr, can you hear me? Norr, you have to get up."

Responding to the sound of her voice, the big man got to his knees.

"There isn't much time!" the man tied to the stake shouted. "Hurry, before the city rallies against us."

Scythe paid him no heed. She had come here to save Norr. If the wizard's sorcery couldn't free them from the stakes, she sure wasn't about to.

"We have to go, Norr," she whispered, trying in vain to haul him to his feet. She gave up the physical struggle and dropped down beside him. "You're too heavy; I can't support you. You have to walk on your own."

Still on his knees, the big man shook his bruised and swollen head. "The others," he croaked through cracked and swollen lips. Scythe noticed that several of his teeth were missing. "Cut them loose."

"Yes, hurry!" the monk exclaimed. "We don't have much time!"

Scythe glanced out and saw that the fury of the terrible firestorm was abating. The flashes of lightning were few and far between, but the blue flames still raged throughout the city, spreading from tower to tower like a forest fire through the treetops. Any survivors of the town guard would be busy all night trying to put out the flames.

"We don't need them," Scythe said to Norr, still refusing to acknowledge the other. "We can sneak away before they find us."

"They saved my life," Norr whispered. "I would have burned. I owe them."

Realizing the noble barbarian wouldn't leave until the men were free, Scythe reluctantly got to her feet. She approached the older man, his dead eyes fixing her with a long, cold stare. She could kill him now. A single cut of her blade across the throat and his life would be over. She could do the same to the unconscious wizard.

Norr would be angry, of course. But she could claim it was revenge for what they had done in Praeton. She could claim the mage had begun a spell and she had panicked. She knew that somehow she could convince her lover to forgive her for her actions, once the deed was done. She could kill them both right now.

Instead she cut the cords binding the monk to his stake. Norr would forgive her if she killed them. But she knew it would destroy a little part of him to do so; it would be one more sacrifice he had to make for the sake of the woman he loved. She had already asked him to make enough sacrifices.

Without a word she cut the bindings on the wizard, the monk catching the unconscious body of the young man as she sliced him free.

"What did you do to him?" he demanded angrily.

"I dumped that bottle of witchroot down his throat," she shot back.

"Where? Show me!"

She didn't like the tone of his voice, but she liked the implied warning in his gray eyes even less. She might have made a mistake in freeing the monk, with Norr as weak and vulnerable as he was.

"Here," she said, scooping the vial up from where it had dropped on the stage and tossing it to him. Still supporting his friend with one arm, the monk's free hand snapped out and plucked it from the air, so quick it was nothing but a blur. Scythe turned her back on them and made her way over to Norr, pretending she neither feared nor cared what happened next.

"Distilled witchroot," she heard the man mumble. She glanced back and met his unseeing eye. "You could have killed him!" he said to her, his tone one of unmistakable outrage.

Scythe wheeled to face him, unable to keep silent any longer.

"You would have all died if I hadn't dumped that vial down his throat!" she snapped. "Instead of lecturing me you might want to thank me for my quick thinking!"

"Thank you for almost killing the savior of the world," he snarled back. "The Gods alone know what kind of irreparable damage you might have done to him."

Any further reply from Scythe was cut off by the feel of Norr's heavy hand upon her shoulder. "It's beginning to rain, Scythe."

All eyes save those of the still-unconscious young mage turned skyward. It was true. A soft but steady rain—of water, not fire—

was falling over the city, quickly dousing the magical blue fire of the terrible spell that had freed them all.

"The Order," the monk said. "They're dispelling Keegan's Chaos storm. Pilgrims must be here in the city. They must have come to witness the execution."

"How many?" Norr asked.

The man tipped his head to the side, as if listening for a sound only he could hear. "I can't say for sure. A dozen. Maybe more. In the panic they were separated and their individual power was not enough to stand against Keegan's spell. But now they have reunited to fight his power. As soon as the fires are out they'll begin searching for us."

"Give him to me," Norr said, offering to take the young wizard from the other man's arms. "We can move faster if I carry him."

When the man made no reaction, Norr persisted.

"We will come with you. Scythe and I. We will help you."

"Why?" There was no mistaking the suspicion in the question.

Norr pointed to the unconscious young man. "He saved my life. I owe him a debt I must repay. It is the way of my people."

The monk hesitated before nodding. "Okay, you may come with us. But you can barely stand yourself, let alone carry someone else."

The monk scooped the young mage up and slung him over his shoulder with surprising ease, then leapt down from the edge of the stage to the ground ten feet below. Moving as if the man over his shoulder weighed no more than a small child, he approached the still-smoldering remains of the grandstand. He bent down and scooped up the skull-topped staff. At his touch the green glow illuminating it vanished.

"Hurry," he called out over his shoulder. "We have to leave now. Before the Pilgrims restore order to the city."

Norr clambered awkwardly down from the stage, his bulk and his injuries making his descent clumsy and inelegant.

"This way," the monk said, moving quickly down an empty side street, using the staff as a walking stick to help offset the imbalance caused by the young wizard draped over his shoulder.

Scythe could only watch in amazement as Norr complied without question or protest. Did he really expect her to do the same? She had a hundred objections she wanted to voice, a thousand reasons they should not join up with this doomed pair. She wanted to grab Norr by the scruff of his neck and slap some sense into him. She wanted to stomp off and just leave them all behind, three naked men fleeing through the streets of Torian. But she wanted to stay with her lover more.

Biting back the insults and protests, Scythe leapt nimbly from the stage to follow in their wake.

Chapter 45

KEEGAN WAS SURROUNDED by the blue flames of Chaos. The fire licked his skin, enveloping him. It covered his eyes, blinding him to everything else. It flooded his mouth and nostrils, crawling down his throat to fill his lungs.

He felt the searing heat surrounding him, he felt it inside him. But there was no pain. He welcomed the heat, embracing the eternal flames as they embraced him. Floating in an ocean of fire, he was at first aware of nothing but the endless fury of the flames all around him.

Slowly memories began to surface: a prison cell, being bound and gagged, being lashed to a stake. The smell of smoke from the smoldering wood. And then the Island girl standing before him, one last beautiful vision before he died.

But he hadn't died. He understood that now. Other memories crashed in. The girl pouring something down his throat. A rush of Chaos, an exploding storm. He was not dead, but he was lost in the haze of witchroot; his mind had broken free from his physical form and now floated free in the Burning Sea, source of all magic.

Suddenly Keegan realized he was not alone. Though he could see nothing through the veil of endless burning blue, he sensed another presence with him. Something that wasn't human; something alien reaching out with its awareness into the Chaos from a great distance, seeking to establish a link with the mortal world.

The Slayer. Ancient enemy of the Gods. A champion who, through the Talismans, became immortal.

Emboldened by the heady rush of witchroot and the Chaos all around him, Keegan reached out to touch the other's mind, completing the bridge between their two worlds. Instantly, he was buried under a tidal wave of images: the memories, dreams, and visions of seven hundred years of existence.

Keegan recoiled in terror, his mortal consciousness unable to process the overload of information. The connection was broken as Keegan's awareness fled down into the depths of the Chaos Sea to escape the horrors he had witnessed in the other's mind. For a moment the other presence flailed about, trying to grasp onto the unexpected intruder. Then it was gone, swept away by the currents of Chaos.

His psyche reeling, Keegan sank deeper and deeper into the Chaos Sea, drowning beneath the weight of all he had seen. In an act of desperate self-preservation, he began to cast aside the images, purging them from his awareness before they dragged him so far down that his own identity would be washed away forever.

Just before he reached the bottom of the infinite ocean of Chaos, he managed to regain some semblance of control. With an act of monumental will, he began to claw his way back to the surface until he finally broke free, his sanity battered but intact.

Most of what he had seen in the Slayer's mind was gone, but he had clung to a few precious pieces of what he had seen. The Pontiff was dead, the Monastery in ruins—the work of powerful Minions the Slayer had sent through to the mortal world. They were seeking the Talismans—the Crown, the Ring, the Sword—that had transformed Daemron into a God.

There was something else Keegan clung to, something he had sensed an instant before the connection had been broken: fear. The Slayer was afraid of him. In their brief moment of contact the God had sensed Keegan's power, and he knew the mortal could destroy him.

And Keegan knew the Minions wouldn't just be hunting the Talismans, now . . . they'd be hunting him, too.

Gil stared out his window, listening. His home was on the outskirts of town, but that didn't stop the wind from carrying the laughter and voices to his window. The people of Praeton were celebrating; the rebuilt Singing Dragon had finally opened for business again.

For many days the mystery of the strange men who'd wrecked the tavern and their relationship with Scythe and Norr, who had vanished the night of their arrival, had been the sole topic of conversation among the citizenry. Friends and neighbors had spoken of nothing else as they came in a steady stream to keep Gil company while he recovered from the terrible injuries to his legs. Though no answers were forthcoming, wild speculation ran rampant. Gil himself even became something of a local hero for those first few weeks, credited with a far greater role in the events of that night by virtue of his wounds.

But as the days progressed to weeks the visitors to Gil's room became less frequent. Life went on; there was business to take care of. Praeton had grown weary of the topic. Talk turned to crops and local concerns. Money was raised to repair the Singing Dragon. Bit by bit Praeton was putting the tragedy behind them. The town's wounds were healing.

As were Gil's own—though far less quickly. He was still an invalid, unable to even leave his bed without help, barely even able to roll onto his side without passing out from the jolts of pain shooting up from his legs and ripping through his entire body. His wife cared for him constantly, though she slept in her own bed because of his injuries. But his visitors became less frequent and stayed for briefer periods, as if seeing him like this was an unwanted reminder of events best forgotten.

Gil understood their attitude. There was a world beyond his bedroom window that hadn't stopped; a world he was no longer part of. His friends and neighbors had to get on with the business of living. But understanding did little to quell the bitter resentment welling up as he heard the joyous shouts and pealing laughter from the Singing Dragon wafting down the street.

He stared wistfully out the window at the darkness beyond. The lamps hung out in windowsills to guide folk home cast strange shadows on the deserted streets. It would be many hours before people returned to their homes. Perhaps one or two would stop by tonight, drunkenly pounding on the door until Gil's wife roused herself and let them in. More than likely they would arrive late tomorrow morning, hungover and eager to regale him with stories of the evening's events.

Tonight Gil had resigned himself to an evening alone, staring out the window at the shadows cast by the lanterns.

Suddenly one of the shadows moved. For a second Gil thought the shadow was that of a man—a man too drunk to stand, for he crawled along the street on all fours. *Not crawled,* Gil realized as a cold finger touched his heart, *scuttled. Like some horrible human spider.*

He blinked and the shadow was enveloped by the darkness. But he could sense it was still there. Afraid even to breathe lest he reveal himself, Gil peered into the night, trying to pierce its black veil. The shadow moved again, but now there were two. Two ghastly inhuman silhouettes scuttling through the streets of Praeton on clawed appendages, noses pressed low to the ground, snuffling like hounds on a scent.

One of the shadows paused, tilted its head back, and gave a screeching howl of evil triumph. The cry rose up on the wind, borne away to the sky—and then the creatures vanished again into the night and Gil felt a cold fist release itself from around his soul.

They hadn't come for him; the monsters were after other prey. And he couldn't help but feel pity for whoever the twisted, crawling twins were hunting.

Chapter 46

THEY HAD FALLEN in with a madman. There was no other explanation Scythe could come up with. She should have expected as much from a heretic. She didn't know much about the Order, but she knew they had been a power in the Southlands for centuries. Anyone desperate enough to openly defy them was dangerously unstable. And only a madman or a fool would have led them into the North Forest, far beyond the forbidden borders of Danaan territory, and then stopped to set up camp.

That was exactly what the monk had done. He called himself Jerrod. The young wizard with them, the one who had saved them by raining fire down on the city, was Keegan. More than this she didn't know.

Jerrod rarely bothered to speak with either her or Norr, and she wasn't eager to engage him in any sort of conversation, either. She didn't trust the blind monk, didn't like the way he was always tense and alert, always poised on the verge of violent action. She had seen such men before, trained bodyguards of important nobles, men willing to sacrifice their own lives for the sake of the one they protected without hesitation or remorse. Scythe couldn't understand such fanaticism, though the way Jerrod always hovered close to Keegan's inert body left little doubt as to whom his devotion was directed toward.

He watched her constantly. Not with his useless eyes, but with that damnable second sight. She felt herself being studied everywhere she went; there was no escape from his vigilance. Even in the dark she could feel his invisible gaze pressing down on her, suspicious and wary. Scythe hated being under constant scrutiny.

Part of her wanted to ask him what he had done to get himself declared a heretic by his own Order, but if she asked it would mean she cared. And she didn't want to give a damn about these men—not even the still-unconscious wizard. It had been three days and he still hadn't woken up yet, though sometimes he tossed and turned or cried out.

"Dreams," Jerrod had said once when Norr had asked about the outbursts. "He has visions. Keegan is a true prophet." She wasn't exactly sure what that meant, but she doubted it could be good.

Unlike her, Norr didn't seem to be the least bit troubled by their companions. It was as if her lover had succumbed to some strange insanity of his own, allowing himself to be guided by some ancient, unbreakable custom of a people and culture he had long since abandoned for the Southlands. For reasons she couldn't understand, Norr was determined to stay by Keegan's side wherever he went. And Scythe was just along for the ride.

She could have left them that first night in Torian, but she wasn't about to turn her back on Norr. Even as strange as he was acting, she still loved him. So together they had followed along.

They had fled the square, Jerrod leading them through the streets while the quenching rains of the Pilgrims doused the city and extinguished the blue flames ravaging the buildings and towers. They had gone straight to the north gate, not even stopping long enough to grab clothes to cover the men's naked bodies.

They had encountered no resistance at all. The city guard had either fled in panic when the storm began, or were off in other parts of the city fighting the fires that threatened to consume all of Torian. The gates were open and unguarded. They had passed through them onto the trade route, still heading due north. Once they passed the borders of the Danaan lands, Jerrod had veered from the path.

She should have objected right then, but at that point she still hadn't realized the man leading them was completely mad. She had expected him to double back to the south at that point; within a few hours they would be back in the relative safety of the human lands. Even that short journey through the forest was risky, but it would have been worth it to escape Torian.

However, their leader hadn't doubled back. He had pressed farther and farther into the forest until they found a small clearing. He had set the unconscious wizard gently on the ground, and laid the strange wizard's staff beside him. And then he had proceeded to set up camp.

By the time Scythe realized he had no intention of leaving the forest it was too late. She was city born and bred; there was no chance of her finding her way back alone through the woods. And Norr had expressed no desire to abandon their new companions and turn back.

At least Jerrod had tended to her lover's wounds once they stopped. Scythe had learned much about the ways of medicine from Methodis but she was unfamiliar with the foul-smelling poultices he'd fashioned from scavenged roots and fauna around their campsite. He'd applied them to Norr's injuries, and almost instantly the swelling went down and his bruises faded. Scythe suspected there was some strange magic underneath the simple folk cures.

She was grateful Norr's pain had been eased, but she couldn't help but wonder if Jerrod's ministrations had other effects as well. Norr didn't seem at all bothered by the fact that for the last three days they had just been sitting here, waiting for a Danaan patrol to find them and kill them for the trespassers they were. It certainly bothered Scythe.

For three days she had waited, and for three days Jerrod had told her nothing. He had spent most of his time tending to Keegan, though it was obvious he could do little more than try to make his comatose patient comfortable.

Scythe tried not to think about Keegan too much. She knew it was his spell that had broken Gil's leg; but whenever she noticed him lying on the ground it was hard to imagine him as a powerful wizard. He looked so frail and weak, part of her actually felt sorry for him.

She suspected that once the wizard regained consciousness they would move on, but who knew how long that might take? They had already spent too much time camped in a place where the penalty for discovery was death. She had already saved Jerrod and Keegan once; they weren't her responsibility anymore. Steeling her resolve, she decided she wasn't willing to wait any longer.

"Norr," she said, rising to her feet. "We have to go. If we stay here, the Danaan will kill us."

"I won't abandon Keegan," he replied, glancing from her down to the helpless wizard. "Please, Scythe. Don't force me to choose between my debt to him and my love for you."

She sighed. How could she argue with that? She turned her attention to Jerrod instead, hoping to have better luck.

"Is there some plan you're not sharing with the rest of us? Is there some reason you led us here?"

"The Pilgrims are still searching for us," he explained calmly. "There are enchantments in these woods that obscure and confuse my Sight—and theirs. Plus, the newly appointed Torian officials will be reluctant to send troops into the forests, knowing the severe penalties awaiting trespassers."

A logical explanation, though it ignored the fact that the Danaan were just as likely to kill them as the Pilgrims or the Torian patrols.

"But why are we just sitting here in one spot? Wouldn't it be safer if we at least move around?"

The monk tilted his head in Keegan's direction. "His condition is growing worse. I have done what I can to offset the damage of the witchroot, but I can only do so much. He is still too sick to move, thanks to you."

Scythe glared at him, but wouldn't rise to the bait. She refused to feel any guilt over the young man's condition. If she hadn't done what she had done, none of them would be alive now. Or so she kept telling herself each night whenever she heard him cry out in the darkness.

"The North Forest is forbidden," she pointed out in case he wasn't aware of the blatantly obvious. She was no expert on the Danaan, but what she was saying was common knowledge among all the human lands. "If we wait here much longer they will find us. And then they will kill us!"

"I won't move him," Jerrod replied. "Not until he returns to this world."

"Returns to this world?" Norr asked. "What does that mean?"

"His mind is adrift in the Sea of Fire. The minds of those who imbibe too deeply of the witchroot can be lost forever in the Chaos.

"But Keegan is not like other men." The monk took a deep breath, as if to convince himself that what he was about to say next was in fact true. "He is strong in the Gift, maybe stronger than any wizard since the time of the Cataclysm. His mind might still find its way back to the mortal world, in time."

"Then we will wait as long as it takes," Norr said, placing a reassuring hand on the monk's bare shoulder.

It was obvious they weren't going anywhere yet. Reluctantly Scythe sat back down, silently cursing the events that had brought her and Norr to this place.

"I found the plants you wanted," Norr said, handing a fistful of leaves to Jerrod as he crouched over the still-inert form of the young wizard.

Jerrod took them without a word. He gently opened the young man's mouth and placed a single leaf beneath his tongue. "These will help his fever break," he explained. "But they won't bring his mind back to us."

"You care greatly for him," Norr noted.

"He is special. He is the savior of the world."

From across the camp Scythe snorted. "Bet you didn't know that when you vowed your life to him," she said to her lover, half joking and half bitter.

"I do not understand," the barbarian said to Jerrod, refusing to acknowledge her snide comment. "The ways of your Order are strange to me. I would know of your history . . . and of what is to come."

"Even among the Southlands few know the real history," Jerrod admitted. "The Order has preserved the truth within the Monastery, but beyond its walls much has been forgotten. Legend and myth blend with history, and truth and fiction are not easily separated anymore."

"Sounds like you're avoiding the question," Scythe accused him, having made her way over from the other side of the camp. She wrapped her arms around Norr's massive waist. At least, she tried to. Her hands only reached three-quarters of the way around his girth. Without even thinking about it the big man reached his arm down and around her protectively, drawing her small body up close against his.

"Norr's vowed to help your so-called savior," she continued. "And where he goes I go. The least you can do is tell us what we're getting into. Or is it forbidden to share your knowledge with an Islander and an Eastern savage?"

"The truth is forbidden to no one," Jerrod replied calmly. "The story of the True Gods is the history of all the peoples: Southlanders, Islanders, the Free Cities, the tribes of the East, and even the Danaan."

He was silent for several seconds, gathering his thoughts. When he began to speak his voice was deep and heavy, as if it held power beyond the mere words.

"The mortal world, like all things—all life, all magic, even the Gods themselves—was born from Chaos. The Gods, the True Gods, shaped and worked the fires of the Chaos Sea to create an oasis within the ever-churning flames. They bounded the north of the world with an impenetrable forest to keep the terrible power of Chaos from drowning the mortal shores. To the east they set an impassable range of mountains; to the south, a vast desert of infinite sand. On the western shore they poured forth an ocean of unfathomable depths, its cool waters quelling the blazing waves battering the tranquil island floating in the infinite maelstrom of space and time.

"In the firmament above they set the sky, the stars, the sun, and the moon. Using the magic of Chaos they breathed divine life into the cold foundation of the earth, and a multitude of creatures sprang forth to cover all the land. And the Gods themselves dwelled among the mortal men and women who praised them for the paradise they had created, while all around the mortal world the Chaos raged, seeking to devour what they had made.

"For though the essence of life and creation is Chaos, the essence of Chaos is destruction and death. And the universe rebelled against what the Gods had wrought. Terrible monsters—dragons, ogres, all the Chaos Spawn—rose up from the depths of the fire. They climbed the mountains, they swam the ocean, they crossed the desert and stormed through the forest, leaving only death and destruction in their wake. The Gods turned their divine power against the invaders wherever they found them, but the monsters were legion, and even an Immortal cannot easily defeat a creature birthed from the Sea of Fire.

"The magic unleashed in these terrible wars ravaged the land, and with each battle the echo of the Gods' own actions brought forth more Chaos Spawn to oppose them. The Gods knew they could no longer dwell within the mortal world, for they themselves were beings of Chaos and it was their very presence that gave birth to the monstrous creatures that crawled forth from the burning sea.

"Yet they couldn't leave their children defenseless, and so a champion was chosen from among the mortals: Daemron, a great warrior-king who would stand against the Chaos Spawn. The

Gods forged artifacts of great power and presented these gifts to their champion to aid him in his battles: a Crown to give him wisdom and foresight; a Sword to give him strength and courage; and a Ring to give him the power of magic—the ability to channel Chaos itself and shape it to his will.

"Armed with the Talismans, Daemron led his army of followers against the invaders from the Chaos Sea, slaughtering the enemy and driving them back into the flames. Trolls and ogres and dragons alike fell beneath his enchanted blade, and in honor of his victories the people of the world gave Daemron the title of the Slayer.

"But with unchallenged power comes unbridled ambition. With the enemy vanquished, the Slayer declared himself ruler of all the mortal world, a king over all other kings. Those who did not bow down to him felt the fury of his wrath, and destruction and death spread once more across the land.

"As long as he possessed the Talismans the Slayer commanded all the power of the Immortals, and none could oppose him; none save the Immortals themselves. And so the Gods returned to our world to wage war against the Slayer. But the enemy did not stand alone; many flocked to his banner. Among his horde were a new generation of Chaos Spawn, united with him in their hatred of the Gods, following the one who had once been the scourge of their monstrous kind.

"In the final battle the full fury of Chaos was unleashed upon the world in a fiery Cataclysm. Blazing meteors rained down from the sky; the ground shook and heaved and erupted in volcanoes spewing burning death. Cities crumbled to dust, kingdoms were reduced to ash and cinders, and the earth itself was rent asunder.

"In the end the Slayer finally fell, unable to oppose the combined will of the True Gods. Stripped of the Talismans, he fled the mortal world to a blighted land of his own creation hidden somewhere in the Sea of Fire."

"We have a similar tale among my people," Norr interrupted. "It talks of Daemron, the warrior-King. It tells of a great Sword he used to smite his enemies. But in our legend he became proud and boastful, and challenged the Gods. They say he fell in the Long Battle that blighted the earth, and the Sword was lost.

"It is said it will reappear in the hands of a chosen warrior," Norr added thoughtfully. "One who will unite our people and lead them to victory when the time of the final battle comes."

"The Talismans were lost," Jerrod agreed. "The Gods scattered them after the battle, lest they give rise to another Slayer."

"Why not just destroy them?" Scythe asked, trying to bring some logic into the conversation.

"They were forged from the essence of the Immortals themselves," Jerrod replied without hesitation. "Even the Gods did not have the power to destroy them. But they were dangerous: Their power was too great for any mortal to control. So they were hidden away."

The monk paused briefly before continuing, as if trying to regain the thread of his obviously well-rehearsed tale after Norr's distraction. "After the battle, the Gods wept and their tears cooled the flames of the Cataclysm. But though the Slayer was banished, there was no peace in the land. Once again the Chaos Spawn walked the earth, monstrous refugees from the Slayer's army who had escaped the spell banishing their liege. Combining their energies the Immortals cast a spell over the world, causing the creatures to fall into a deep sleep, binding them far beneath the surface of the earth.

"Yet even the Gods cannot wield such magic without paying a terrible price. Wounded from the war with the Slayer and weakened by the spell of eternal hibernation, the Gods began to fade away. Their essence was spent; all that they were was returning to the Chaos from which they were born.

"A God dies slowly, and before their passing the creators had one last gift to give—a Legacy to endure beyond their own passing. As their last act the Gods sacrificed themselves to create a shield over the mortal world, an impenetrable barrier to keep out the Chaos Spawn and prevent the Slayer from ever returning.

"Through their ultimate sacrifice the mortal world was saved. Its people spread across the surface. New cities were built, new kingdoms were formed, the races as we know them today came into being.

"Some among the mortals sought to preserve the sanctity and memory of the True Gods: The Order dedicated itself to protecting their Legacy. But for most men and women the importance of their daily, mundane lives far exceeded the great events of a generation . . . then a century . . . and then a millennium ago.

"The horrors of the Cataclysm faded into legend, and the name of the Slayer slipped from the minds of the common folk. Over the centuries the True Gods were supplanted by new deities created to satisfy the needs and desires of the people who worked and toiled and ruled on this island forever floating in the fires of the Chaos Sea. The people abandoned the True Gods, and only we of the Order remembered their history."

Scythe had heard many similar stories during her time in the Southlands. Some of the specifics were different, but Jerrod's tale was basically the same as every other creation myth she had heard. Vague in the details, and set long enough ago that the facts were difficult to disprove. But she wasn't going to be satisfied with the recounting of a mere legend.

"You still haven't answered my question," she pressed. "What does this have to do with your friend?"

"The Legacy is weakening," Jerrod explained. "The barrier that holds back the Slayer and the descendants of those who fled with him is growing thin. In their exile, they have become twisted abominations—like the Chaos Spawn that once ravaged the land. And when the Legacy finally crumbles, the Slayer will return and unleash his unholy army so that he can once more claim rule over the mortal world.

"Only a wizard with the power of true Chaos in his blood can drive the hordes back when they come. In my visions I have seen a champion who can save us all. One strong enough to defeat the Slayer and his army."

"Him?" Scythe asked, raising an eyebrow and pointing at the frail young man lying naked and unconscious on the ground.

"You saw what he did in Torian," the monk reminded her. "Only the wizards of old had that kind of power."

"Fair enough," she conceded, surrendering the point but still unwilling to fully accept Jerrod's story. "But there's one thing I still can't understand.

"Back in Torian they said you were heretics. If Keegan is the savior of the world, why is the Order trying to kill him?"

Jerrod's face darkened, though she wasn't sure if his anger was directed at her. "There are some who do not believe in his destiny. Some, like the Pontiff, refuse to accept that the Legacy is crumbling. They have chosen to cling to it for as long as they can, ignoring the inevitable.

"The Order is afraid of Keegan. They see him as a threat, they fear the power he wields, they believe his magic will weaken the Legacy and hasten its destruction. The Pontiff and those who blindly follow him imagine Keegan as a destroyer rather than a savior."

"I don't understand," Norr said, shaking his head slowly from side to side. "I thought the Order was made up of prophets. How can they ignore these visions you have told us about?"

"That's the problem with visions," Scythe said, trying not to sound too smug. "They tend to be open to interpretation. People can twist them around however they want."

Jerrod didn't allow her remarks to upset him, much to Scythe's dismay. Obviously he was used to dealing with skeptics.

"Believe what you will," the monk told them. "But I have told you everything I know. That is more than the Order could ever say. The Pontiff has hidden much of what he has known even from his own followers. He believes the only way to keep the Legacy safe is to guard its very existence from the general population. He seeks to manipulate and control the governments of the Southlands through his agents, but he would never dare to share the full extent of his knowledge with them for fear of how they might react."

"If the Pontiff keeps everything so secret"—Scythe pounced, sensing another logical flaw in his tale—"then how did you learn all this?"

"Some of what I knew was common knowledge among the Order," Jerrod explained. "Some I learned from my visions and the visions of those who share my belief. Much was passed down to me by Ezra, my predecessor and the one who first understood the need to find our champion.

"The rest I have learned through years of study and research. The Order has tried to keep its secrets by gathering any and all texts that make mention of this in their great library. In the Southlands they have largely succeeded, but in the Free Cities there are still manuscripts to be found that contain the truth.

"I have devoted my life to finding Keegan and preparing him for his destiny," Jerrod added. "But if he dies—or if his mind does not come back to us—then all hope is lost."

The monk turned back to tend to Keegan; he had obviously finished speaking for the time being. Scythe didn't say anything, but waited for Norr's reaction. Unfortunately, it was what she expected.

"We will help you in this, Jerrod," the barbarian vowed. "I have sworn my life into the service of Keegan until the debt I owe him is repaid. Now I offer my life to your champion and his cause."

Jerrod didn't bother to glance up from his worried examination of the young wizard, but he did say, "Your help is welcomed, brother."

Scythe slipped herself free from Norr's grasp, disgusted with them both.

Chapter 47

FLOATING IN THE blue flames of the Sea of Fire, Keegan could sense the mortal world. Someone on the other side of the Legacy was reaching out to him, willing him to return.

Jerrod.

But if he did come back to the mortal world, Keegan knew he would have to face the Minions of the Slayer. They were searching for him; eventually they would find him. And he didn't have the strength to stand against them. Not yet.

The Talismans made Daemron a God. They can do the same for me.

He could still sense the Crown, though its power was faint and distant. But as his mind drifted in the fiery currents, he sensed another Talisman—brighter, stronger, closer. Like the voice of Jerrod, it, too, was calling to him. Its power shone like a beacon, showing him the way to return.

It was for this—not Jerrod—that he began the long journey back. And as he did so, Keegan sent out a call of his own.

Vaaler stopped so suddenly that Naria, his second in command, nearly walked into his back and knocked him from the thick, intertwining branches the patrol was using to traverse the sector.

"What is it?" she asked, instinctively slinging her bow off her shoulder and nocking an arrow in one fluid motion. The other half a dozen archers under Vaaler's command did the same, scanning the leaves above and the ground twenty feet below for signs of danger.

"Did you hear something?" Vaaler asked.

"I heard nothing. What was it?"

"It sounds crazy," Vaaler mumbled, half to himself, "but I think I heard someone whispering my name."

He saw Naria glance back at the others, but they returned only puzzled glances and perplexed shrugs.

"We heard nothing, my Captain."

"Perhaps I imagined it," he muttered, shaking his head.

"Just because none of us heard it, doesn't mean it wasn't there," Naria insisted.

The prince gave her a hint of a smile, grateful for her show of support.

"Let's go check it out," he said. "This way. Keep your bows at the ready, but nobody fire until I give the word."

The patrol set off again, veering to the southwest, heading in the general direction of Torian.

Drake burst into the Queen's chambers without even knocking. He had run the full length of the royal grounds upon receiving her summons, its short but terrifying message spurring him on: *Vaaler is lost to us.*

"Tell me where my son is," the Queen said as soon as he had closed the door behind him.

Her voice was soft, barely above a whisper, yet it still had the timbre of royal command. Drake hesitated before replying, momentarily taken aback by his Queen's ghastly appearance as she sat propped up by pillows in her bed, too weak even to stand. The servants had warned him of her condition, but they could not have prepared him for this.

"He is on patrol, my Queen."

Rianna Avareen had not left her room in a fortnight. Not since she began the fast. The council awaited her summons, but she had not once graced them with her presence. Even Drake had not seen her these past weeks, banished from her bedroom as she had banished all her worldly pleasures. Despite his reservations about her plan, Drake had wordlessly bowed to his Monarch's will.

What objection could he make, when there was nothing he could do? Before she sent him away, the Queen would wake screaming and trembling each night and collapse sobbing uncontrollably in Drake's protective but powerless arms. But the visions came whether he was there or not, and nothing he could do or say would take away her terror and anguish. Finally she had sent him from her bed, and he had not objected—partly because she was the Queen, and partly because he could do nothing for her.

She was convinced her ties to the physical world were obscuring her Sight, and after Drake's banishment she had vowed to do whatever it took to free herself from her earthly bonds. After the first week the servants had begged him to return to her side, convinced he could somehow reason with her. They pleaded with him to defy their own Queen's orders. They feared she was dying. Now that he saw her in person, Drake feared they were right.

Rianna's face was drawn and haggard, her beauty all but invisible beneath a grim mask of exhaustion and starvation. Her skin was sallow and sunken, her eyes bloodshot and dark, her lips dry and cracked. Her long, silken hair was a tangled mass of knots and clumps hanging down past the protruding bones of her shoulders, far more prominent than they should have been. The fast had taken a much greater toll than was possible in such a short time. Something else was at work, devouring her from the inside, consuming her until only this sickly, scrawny shell remained of the woman he loved.

The Queen couldn't sleep and she refused to eat, hoping to purify her body so the Chaos in her blood might gain strength. So her visions might have some meaning, some purpose or clue to guide her will so she might spare her people from the Cataclysm she had foreseen. And her desperate vigil was rapidly destroying her.

"Bring him to me," the Queen whispered, lying back in her bed, as if even the effort of sitting upright was too much for her now. "Bring him to me quickly. I . . . I must see my son."

Drake ushered the servants out with a nod of his head. Alone, he knelt beside the Queen's bed and took her frail hand. The skin was dry and thin as paper, he could see the blue blood of her veins through the surface; he could trace the outline of each delicate bone in her slender fingers.

"Rianna," he whispered, "my love—we are alone. Please, tell me what has happened."

She turned her head on the pillow, her eyes glazing with tears.

"Another vision," she whispered. "Vaaler. He walks with the Destroyer of Worlds in our forest. They laugh together, they call each other friend. Vaaler leads the Destroyer here, and together they will devour our city."

Drake shook his head. "No, my love. You are weak. Exhausted. Your Sight is weary from overuse. You have made a mistake. Vaaler would never betray his people. He would never betray you."

She nodded ever so slightly. She wanted to believe, she wanted to take some solace in the words of her consort. Yet in her eyes Drake could see that she knew his soothing assurances were nothing but false promises against the undeniable truth of her own vision.

"Where is he?" she asked again, the words escaping as little more than a sigh from her parched lips.

"He is on patrol," Drake said for the second time, reaching out to caress her cheek. She flinched away, as if the touch of his hand scorched her—but it was Drake who felt heat, radiating from her skin as if it were on fire.

"I will send word to him immediately," he assured the Queen. "I will tell him to return to your side."

Again she nodded, comforted by his promise. Then with seemingly great effort, she closed her weary eyes and turned her head away from him. He held her burning hand while her breathing slipped into the soft, shallow rhythm of a light doze. He waited, bracing himself in case Rianna suddenly awoke screaming from her dreams.

But she didn't stir. When he felt her drift into a deep and restful slumber he gently laid her hand on the bed and slipped out to tell the servants not to wake her.

For the first time in many weeks she was sleeping peacefully. Drake tried to convince himself it was a good sign. Either that, or she had fallen into an exhaustion and despair so deep even the horrors of the visions could no longer affect her.

Chapter 48

KEEGAN WOKE WITH a gasp. The sensation of returning to his mortal shell was like the shock of plunging into an icy river. The first thing he noticed was how physically weak his body felt: exhausted, drained. But his spirit felt strong. He tingled with energy and power. The witchroot was still coursing through his veins; it would be weeks before it all passed from his body. And there was something else. The very air of this place was thick with magic. He could almost see the ancient spells, enchantments woven many centuries ago but still strong enough to permeate the air around him.

He was acutely aware of his surroundings. They were in a forest: a thick, dense wood with a canopy so lush it blocked out any view of the sky above. He was lying in a small clearing, maybe twenty feet across. Jerrod hovered anxiously over him, drawn by the sudden signs of life. For some reason, the monk was naked.

Across the camp were two strangers. No, Keegan corrected himself. Not strangers. He recognized the young woman from the inn they had stopped at during their journey. The man he also recognized, though that was no great feat. Anyone of his massive size was likely to leave a lasting impression—the red-headed barbarian from the bar; the seven-foot, four-hundred-pound giant of a man who had foolishly picked a fight with Jerrod. Like the monk, he was also bereft of clothes.

Keegan realized that he was naked, too, but he was too weary to be embarrassed.

"Why are they here?" Keegan tried to ask, but his voice was only a cracked whisper in his parched throat.

Jerrod knelt down beside him and gently placed a water-skin against his lips. He tilted it just enough to allow a slow trickle, which Keegan greedily sucked down.

"Why are they here?" he asked again once he had drunk his fill, his voice still barely above a whisper as he tried to piece everything together.

He felt disconnected, out of sorts. He vaguely remembered the big man being thrown to the floor beside him, bound and naked as Keegan himself had been. But he couldn't remember where or why this had happened. He thought he could remember the woman, too: a figure emerging from a haze of heat and smoke and flames. And there were other flames. The fires of Chaos. And a presence . . . something alien, and ancient beyond imagining.

"They travel with us now," Jerrod said, still crouched down beside him. His relief at hearing Keegan speak was obvious. "The man is Norr, the woman is Scythe."

Keegan struggled to sit up so he could get a better look at their new companions, hoping it would help him reorganize his thoughts. Jerrod was quick to slip a hand behind his head and neck to support him.

The man raised a mighty paw in acknowledgment and smiled at him. The woman only glared at him with an expression he couldn't read.

He stared at them from across the camp, his head spinning with a fierce collage of unconnected thoughts and sensations. His brain was a tangled mess of overlapping images. He knew there was something important buried beneath the jumble, but he couldn't sort it out from the mess quite yet.

"I feared you might be lost," Jerrod said. "I didn't know if you could find your way back to us."

Scythe and Norr had made their way over from the other side of the camp to check on his condition. They stood just behind the monk, who was still crouching down to help hold Keegan in a half-sitting position.

"I am glad to see you awake," the big man said. "You saved me from the fire . . . me and Scythe both. For that, I owe you my life."

Keegan wasn't sure how to respond, and before his stumbling mind could formulate an answer the woman cut him off.

"Can you stand?" she asked. "We have to get out of here before the Danaan find us."

"Do not rush him!" Jerrod snapped back angrily. "He can barely sit up. He needs to rest."

"No, I'm okay," the young wizard said, his voice stronger than it was before.

He sat up a little straighter, no longer leaning on the monk for support. The memories of what he had seen were slowly coming back to him.

"The Pontiff is dead," Keegan said flatly. "The Monastery is destroyed."

Jerrod's head snapped back in surprise. "Destroyed? How?"

"The Slayer's Minions have crossed over to this world. They came for the Crown. They laid siege to the Monastery and slaughtered everyone inside. Even the Pontiff."

"And the Crown?" Jerrod asked.

Keegan shook his head. "Gone. Sent away before the Minions arrived. I'm not sure where—it's like something was hiding it from me."

There were several seconds of silence before Jerrod spoke again.

"The Pontiff may be dead, the Monastery may be razed. But the Order lives on," he replied. "The death of Nazir will throw them into confusion for a time, but they will soon regroup.

"As Prime Inquisitor, Yasmin will be elevated to his position. It may have happened already. And she will continue the hunt for us."

"She's not the only one hunting us," Keegan whispered.

"The Minions."

Keegan nodded.

"Look," the young woman—Scythe—interjected, stepping in from where she and the enormous barbarian had been standing off to the side. "I'm not sure exactly what you two are talking about, but it's pretty clear that you have a lot of people after you.

"In my experience," she added, "if you're on the run, then sitting and waiting for someone to find you is a pretty bad plan."

"She's right," Jerrod admitted. "We need to find somewhere to hide. We have too many enemies and not enough allies."

"There is someone who can help us," Keegan assured him. "Someone I trust completely."

"Great," Scythe chimed in, her voice dripping with sarcasm. "Maybe we should send him a message. Let him know we're here."

"I already have. The Danaan are coming for us."

Scythe knew it was pointless to argue; she was dealing with men who were ruled not by logic, but by visions, dreams, and prophecies. But if she couldn't reason with them, at least she could try to make Norr see how mad they were.

"If you think the Dwellers will help us, then I know you're mad!"

She spun to face her lover, turning her back on the other two men.

"Please, Norr," she begged, looking up into his eyes. "Don't you see how crazy this all is?"

He didn't reply, only stared down at her with an expression of despair so deep it made her cringe.

"You don't owe him anything," she whispered. "He saved your life, but I saved his—everybody's even! We can just leave."

He shook his massive head, his eyes beginning to film up with tears.

"I can't, Scythe. This debt is not so easily wiped away." His voice broke for a second, the words sticking in his throat before he could continue. "If you wish to leave, I will understand."

She almost did. Part of her screamed at her to just walk away. But she and Norr had been through too much together. He had given up his life in Praeton so she could pursue her vengeance; that was the whole reason they were here. It was her fault he had become involved in this. She couldn't abandon him now.

She sighed in resignation, reaching up with a tiny hand to grab a fistful of his red beard. She pulled his head down level with hers and kissed his cheek. "I'm not going anywhere. I think you're a fool to stay, but you're *my* fool. So I'll stick around to keep an eye on you."

The smile of relief on her lover's face was almost enough to make everything that had come before worth it. And a small part of herself—a part she still refused to acknowledge—actually wanted to stay.

She turned back to the other two men.

"So how long before the Dwellers find us?"

In a shower of leaves and twigs a man dropped down from the forest canopy twenty feet above, landing with cat-like grace on the ground at the edge of the clearing not five feet from where Scythe was standing.

"Not long at all," the tall Danaan said.

Keegan's calling had been answered, and Scythe supposed she should be grateful. The Danaan had been able to give them some clothes—simple robes for Jerrod and Keegan to cover their naked bodies. Of course, they didn't have anything to fit Norr. In the end they had sliced the stitching out from several cloaks and sewn them back together into a loose-fitting sleeveless shirt that hung down to his knees. A belt around the waist made the outfit at least passable.

In addition to the clothing, the very fact that they had been found and not killed on the spot brought Scythe some sense of relief. It was obvious from the way they had greeted each other that Keegan and the leader of the patrol knew each other.

Upon arriving at the clearing, the Danaan had knelt down by the young wizard's side and clasped his hand in a firm embrace. And then Keegan had introduced him as Vaaler Avareen, heir to the throne of the Danaan kingdom.

That had managed to get Scythe's attention. Out of habit she tended to study and scrutinize everyone she met, but with the Danaan prince she had paid particular attention.

Vaaler looked to be young, about the same age as Keegan. Roughly the same age as her, though she imagined she was far more mature then either of them.

He had the same flawless, pale green hue to his complexion as the anonymous Danaan traveler Scythe had shared a night with many years ago in Callastan, and she found herself wondering if the skin of his arms and chest would be as smooth and hairless as the man she had lain with. The hair on his head was long and fine, hanging straight down to his shoulders. He was taller than her nameless lover had been, and thinner. But his shoulders were broad, and his arms were made of lean, wiry muscle. She suspected there was more strength in him than one would first imagine.

He carried himself with the natural grace of one born into high nobility, but he didn't possess the air of palpable arrogance Scythe normally associated with those of his class. Humans born into such privilege often became insufferably proud, despite the fact they had done nothing to earn their lofty positions. Perhaps it was different with the Danaan. From the way the other members of the patrol acted around him, it was obvious he had earned their respect.

That respect was probably the only reason Scythe and the others were still alive. She had seen the unbridled contempt in the eyes of the archers accompanying the prince. She could feel the tension of racial hatred in every short, curt word they said to the interlopers in their nearly impenetrable accents.

Vaaler must have felt it, too. Why else would he have sent the entire patrol on ahead, leaving him alone with the humans?

Naria, the Danaan woman who seemed to be his second in command, had balked at the order. "We will not leave you alone with these outlanders, my prince!"

"Keegan is like a brother to me," he had assured her. "I will be perfectly safe while we wait for his strength to return. And when he is ready, I will escort him and his companions to the capital to meet the Queen."

His words had done little to calm Naria. "Since the earliest days of our kingdom, no human has set foot in any of our cities . . . let alone our capital," she had objected.

"All the more reason you and the others must go on ahead. This is a momentous event in the history of our people. The Queen must be told of our coming, so a suitable reception can be prepared for these most honored guests."

Naria had obeyed without further protest, leading the rest of the patrol away into the forest to alert the city and the Queen of their coming. But Scythe had read the look in her eyes. The Danaan woman didn't think too highly of Vaaler's "honored" guests. Scythe couldn't really blame her. She herself looked like little more than a common rogue, her clothes smoke-stained and scorched from their escape at Torian and crumpled and soiled from several days of camping in the clearing. Norr looked even more primitive and bestial than usual, thanks to the dark bruising and swelling that still lingered from his recent beatings. Jerrod was obviously one of the Order, and everybody knew they had no love for the Danaan people. And Keegan's skin was still covered with the wild tattoos and strange symbols marking him as a wizard. A thief, a savage, a monk, and a mage: Scythe wouldn't have trusted their group, either.

She watched the Danaan disappear into the forest, and she couldn't deny a sense of relief once the last of them had gone. She briefly considered the notion that they might leave someone behind to watch them from the camouflage of the trees, but she quickly dismissed the idea. Vaaler would probably notice, and even if he didn't Scythe couldn't imagine the Danaan daring to spy on the man who would one day be their king.

"It is good to see you again," Vaaler said, taking a seat on the ground beside the young wizard. "I only wish it could be under better circumstances."

Keegan gave him a tired smile. "I always told you I would one day come to see you."

The Danaan shook his head. "But I never really believed you. You are lucky my patrol found you before any of the others did. You know the penalty for trespassing in these woods."

"We had no other choice," Jerrod said, breaking into the conversation.

Unsure who he should be speaking to now, Vaaler turned his head from the young man on the ground to the blind monk, then back again. "Why *are* you here?" he asked of no one in particular.

There was a long silence before Keegan said, "We can trust him, Jerrod. He can help us."

Much to Scythe's surprise, the monk told him everything. Even more surprising, the prince seemed to be familiar with much of the tale. Apparently, the Danaan prophets saw as much as their counterparts within the Order.

"My people have known the Legacy is weakening for many years," he said when Jerrod mentioned the magical protections the Gods had set up to protect the world against their ancient foe. "In the weeks before I was born one of the Chaos Spawn awoke to ravage the land, shaking off the magic that had kept it in slumber for nearly a thousand years. An entire army was needed to destroy the beast, and a score of soldiers fell in the battle. It took the life of the King . . . my father."

Jerrod recounted the events of his capture and meeting with Keegan, and the death of Rexol.

"I warned you Rexol's ambition would be his downfall," Vaaler said to Keegan, though from his tone Scythe could tell he was troubled on hearing the news.

"You don't find this all a bit hard to believe?" Scythe asked, inserting herself into the conversation.

"I always knew Keegan had a great destiny before him," he said softly. "But even I never imagined this."

Scythe began to laugh. She couldn't help herself, it was all so ludicrous.

"There is little about this that is amusing," Jerrod said sternly.

"I'm sorry," she gasped, bringing the laughing fit under control. "It's all just a bit much to take."

She noticed everyone was staring at her strangely, even Norr. They were all looking at her as if she was the one who was crazy.

"I . . ." Another fit of the mad laughter cut her off. She struggled against it and managed to calm herself down. Jerrod was right; it really wasn't funny. Not funny at all.

"I guess I was expecting some other type of reaction from you," she said to Vaaler. "I just don't understand how you're taking this so well."

The Danaan scratched his chin thoughtfully. "I do not have the Sight, but I know many who do. My mother—the Queen—has seen many visions of the coming Cataclysm. She has seen Daemron's return; she calls him the Destroyer of Worlds.

"In our own way, we have also been searching for a savior. Someone with the Sight and the Gift who can lead us in our time of greatest need.

"Rexol was a mage of great power," he continued. "His magic far surpassed that of all the wizards in my mother's court, even the High Sorcerer. I knew this when I went to study under him."

"Great," Scythe grunted. "Another wizard."

"No," the prince whispered. "Not me."

He took a deep breath, then continued in a more normal voice.

"I used to think my time with Rexol was wasted. But maybe being sent there was part of my destiny after all. Maybe it had a purpose."

He glanced over at the frail young man sitting beside him, then turned back to Scythe and continued speaking.

"While I was his apprentice, I saw only hints of Rexol's power. It was in his bearing: his arrogance, his pride—everything about him gave evidence to it.

"He was a legend throughout the Southlands; he bowed to no man. The Order itself was afraid of him. Nobles, kings, and even other wizards were in awe of Rexol. And Rexol was in awe of Keegan.

"So why couldn't he be our savior?"

Something in the prince's tone made Scythe suspect he was trying to convince himself as much as her. She waited for Vaaler to say something more, but instead it was Jerrod who picked up the tale.

"Rexol refused to accept Keegan's destiny, and it destroyed him. Even he could not deny the savior's power."

"So all of you really believe this?" Scythe pushed. "Even the part about this Slayer sending Minions here to hunt for these magical Talismans? These supposedly powerful artifacts that have somehow been lost for centuries?"

"Not lost," Jerrod clarified. "Hidden."

"The Talismans are real," Keegan insisted. "I've seen the power of the Crown. And I can feel the power of the Ring. It's close."

"You're right," Vaaler agreed. "It's very close. And I know where to find it."

Chapter 49

DRAKE DROPPED TO one knee at the Queen's bedside. He was relieved to see that a hint of color had returned to her face since he had last spoken to her four days ago. The servants had assured him she was eating again, and sleeping. But after his last meeting with Rianna he had almost been afraid to believe their reports. Now that he could see her for himself he knew it was true. Her strength was returning, though slowly. It was as if something terrible had held her in its grip and now suddenly she was free.

She stirred slightly, aware of his presence. Her eyes fluttered open. The glassy, faraway expression was gone, but it had been replaced by a deep, deep sadness.

"I did not summon you, my love," she said softly. "Have you come to check up on me?"

Drake thought he almost detected a hint of a smile pass across her face. It had been so long since she had smiled. The weight of her visions had borne her down into a deep, dark despair; only now was she beginning to climb out. As he prepared to deliver the news, Drake prayed it wouldn't send her spiraling back into the dark place that had nearly killed her.

"I have news about Vaaler, my Queen. The members of your son's patrol have returned."

"My son is not with them." It wasn't a question, merely a statement of fact.

"He sent them on ahead. He follows, with a group of humans. They are his guests. A young woman from the Islands, a barbarian from the East . . ."

"A monk of the Order, and a young Chaos mage," she finished for him, briefly bowing her head.

"Yes, my Queen."

"It is as I have foreseen," she said calmly, as if sorrow and grief were no longer a part of her. Or a part so familiar she no longer cared.

She took a deep breath as if to steel herself.

"Vaaler has betrayed our ancient laws. For this crime, he is forbidden from ever setting foot in Ferlhame again. He must live the rest of his life in exile."

Drake's eyes opened wide, but he didn't protest. There was no point. She had reached a decision; he could see it in her face and her bearing. Something in her visions had been revealed to her, and he was neither proud nor foolish enough to speak out against what she had seen.

"I shall do as you command."

"Take a patrol and intercept them before they reach the city," she commanded. "Tell my son he is banished from the Danaan lands, by my proclamation. Do this yourself, Drake. If he hears it from you he will know it to be true."

"Yes, my Queen." Drake hesitated before asking the question he feared he already knew the answer to. "And if he refuses to obey your edict?"

"My son and those who travel with him cannot be allowed to enter the city. If necessary, you must kill him."

For the past five days Vaaler had been leading his new companions toward Ferlhame. For the patrols, the entire journey would have taken only three days, but the humans couldn't move with the speed of the Danaan, and Keegan was still too frail to push their pace beyond a slow, steady walk. Even at this pace the young mage was forced to lean heavily on Rexol's staff to support him.

None of them spoke much on the journey, which was fine with the prince. He had enough on his mind as it was.

Everything made sense to him now. It had all come together as he had listened to the monk and Keegan tell their story. Vaaler was no wizard, but he had learned much about magic during his years studying under Rexol. He understood Chaos better than anyone in his mother's court, including High Sorcerer Andar. When they mentioned the Talismans, the truth had struck him in a sudden flash. Suddenly the signs were all too clear to him.

Rexol had devoted decades to learning and mastering his craft; however, his Danaan counterparts needed no such study. The Danaan were a people of magic. There were more wizards in Ferlhame alone than in all of the Southlands. Controlling and shaping Chaos came naturally to them; they took it for granted. Vaaler had never understood why this should be, until now.

The ring his mother always wore around her neck—the symbol of the Danaan Monarchs—was one of the Talismans. Forged to allow a mortal to shape the very fires of creation, the power of the Ring had guided and shaped the Danaan nation and its people. It had become a part of them, molding them into a nation of Chaos users.

And now with the Legacy weakening, the full potential of the Talisman was being unleashed. And it was destroying his mother.

That was why she dreamed of fire and destruction: The waxing power of the Ring was twisting her visions and her mind. She had seen the coming of the Destroyer of Worlds and a second Cataclysm for her people, but she had not understood that the means to stand against their enemy was close at hand. None of them had realized it.

He would tell them. He would explain everything to the Queen and her council. He would free his mother from the terrible burden by convincing her to give the Ring to Keegan, that he might fulfill his destiny.

He would bring his people a savior, and his people would finally accept him as the heir to their throne.

Walking a route he knew by heart, he was so wrapped up in his thoughts that he wasn't even aware of his surroundings. Not as aware as he should have been.

"We have company," Jerrod whispered, coming up behind him to place a hand on his shoulder to stop his progress. "Watching us from the branches."

Keegan's physical strength was returning quickly. Each morning he felt more refreshed and alive, despite the miles they had traveled the day before. The witchroot in his veins was no longer at a toxic level. Instead it energized him, made him feel confident and powerful. It drove him onward.

He also felt as if he was drawing strength from the forest itself. The woods were old; many of the trees had survived the Cataclysm; their roots ran deep. They reached down into the earth and touched the well of life below, drawing on the magic the Gods had used to create the world itself. Powerful enchantments had been cast over the forest long ago; the magic of the ancient spells still lingered. Jerrod had said the enchantments obscured and confused his Sight, but Keegan felt his own abilities feeding on them. The magic of the forest was healing and regenerating his Chaos-ravaged body.

But it was more than just the witchroot or the woods. When Vaaler had told them where to the find the Ring, it was as if a spark had flared up within Keegan. He could feel the power of it calling to him even across the forest, just as Rexol must have felt the power of the Crown calling to him in the Monastery. Vaaler was leading them to the hidden Danaan capital, but Keegan honestly believed he could have found the way himself.

Ahead of him, Jerrod reached out a hand and stopped Vaaler in his tracks.

"We have company," he heard the monk whisper. "Watching us from the branches."

Now that he was aware of them, Keegan could see them clearly with his mind's eye—they had walked right into an ambush. There were a dozen of them all told; they were surrounded on all sides.

"What's going on?" Scythe demanded from the rear of the group, her voice tense and nervous. "Why'd we stop?"

As if in answer to her question, half a dozen Danaan descended from the treetops: two behind them, and two each on the left and the right. They had their bows drawn, arrows nocked and aimed. Like Vaaler, they had long, thin swords strapped to their belts. Their uniforms were similar to Vaaler's as well, except that they had the insignia of their own patrol emblazoned over their hearts. The other six remained hidden in the branches above, each taking careful aim at their targets below.

Another Danaan—this one older than the others and wearing a different uniform—stepped from the trees directly in front of them.

"Drake!" Vaaler exclaimed in surprise. "What is the meaning of this?"

Keegan guessed the man to be in his late forties. He remembered Vaaler mentioning him before; after the King's death Drake had taken over many of the duties of raising the young prince. Unlike the others he did not have a bow, but in his left hand he held the hilt of a rapier.

"Vaaler, by order of Rianna Avareen, ruling Monarch of the Danaan people, you and your companions are hereby banished from the Danaan realms. This company is to escort you to the border of the kingdom."

It was obvious to Keegan that Drake took no joy in the proclamation.

"What are you talking about?" Keegan couldn't tell if Vaaler was confused, insulted, or afraid. Probably all three. "Is this some kind of joke?"

"If you do not comply I have been ordered to use any force necessary. Even lethal force." The man hesitated then added, "Please, Vaaler. Don't make it come to that."

"This is an outrage!" the Danaan prince shouted, directing his wrath at the archers training their arrows on the company.

Like Keegan, the others were completely motionless, knowing the slightest movement might trigger a barrage of deadly missiles. Vaaler, however, seemed unable to grasp the danger they were all in. His head turned from side to side, his body twisting round and round as he tried to look at all of their assailants at once.

"Lower your weapons this instant!" he shouted. "How dare you threaten the heir to the throne!"

The archers made no move to comply. From the corner of his eye Keegan saw Jerrod's head give a faint tilt upward. Like him, the monk sensed there were more Danaan than just these in the clearing. The woods around them were filled with enemies.

"Vaaler, you are no longer the heir to the throne," Drake told him. "By order of the Queen you are banished, forbidden from ever returning to Danaan lands."

"I . . . I don't understand," Vaaler stammered. "What are you saying? My mother has disowned me?"

Without even realizing he was doing so, Keegan began to gather the Chaos. "The Queen knows the path you walk," Drake told him. "She knows you threaten to bring destruction on us all. She has seen it in her visions."

"Damn her visions! Damn your blind faith in prophecies and dreams! I have done nothing wrong!"

Keegan's body began to tingle as he gathered his power. The beating of his own heart slammed against the walls of his chest, trying to burst free. It took all his effort to remain still as a sudden surge of Chaos flared up within him, a caged beast hurling itself against the bars so that it might unleash its fury on the world. But somehow he kept it in check.

"You have brought humans to our lands!" Drake spat out. "You're leading them straight to Ferlhame itself! You have violated one of our people's oldest laws! You have disobeyed the will of the council and your Queen!"

There was little chance he would be able to invoke a proper spell. Several of the archers were aimed specifically at him, poised to fire. Any movement from Keegan, a single arcane word, any hint that he was channeling magic through Rexol's staff, and they would let fly.

But as Rexol had told him time and time again, the single greatest tool available to those who dared to call upon the fires of Chaos was the strength of the wizard's own Gift. Ultimately it was the ability of the individual that determined the effects of any given spell. In theory, a wizard who was strong enough in his talent could unleash magic through the sheer force of his will. And Keegan's Gift was stronger than any other mage in the mortal world.

"Please, Drake, you have to trust me," Vaaler begged. "I am bringing salvation to our people."

"You are like a son to me," the older Danaan replied, his voice near to breaking. "Had you become King, I would gladly have bowed down before you. But you do not have the Sight, you cannot see what lies ahead. The Queen has seen the destruction you will bring upon us, and she has sent me to stop it."

"My mother is sick," Vaaler implored. "Her power has become too much for her to bear. It's twisted her mind. You've seen it just as well as I have—something is destroying her. Let me go to her, and I can save her!"

Drake bowed his head, and for a moment it seemed as if the young man's words had reached him. But when he looked up his eyes were hard and cold as steel.

"I must obey the will of my Queen," he said through tightly clenched teeth. He raised his arm, and Keegan heard the creak of the bows as the strings were drawn taut. If they were to have any chance to survive, they'd have to find some way to stop the archers from mowing them down.

"Surrender your weapons to me now, Vaaler, or this will end with blood."

Keegan unleashed the Chaos he'd been gathering. Set free on the mortal world, it exploded outward, the air rippling as a wave of force rolled out across the clearing in all directions, moving faster than thought itself. The ground buckled; the boughs of the trees bent and swayed as the concussive wall ripped through them. The bows and arrows of the archers cracked and splintered, shattered in a single instant by the power of the spell.

A shower of leaves and small twigs rained down from the foliage. The Danaan in the trees above came crashing down to the ground below, dislodged from their perches by the same spell that had destroyed their bows before a single shot could be fired.

Everyone in the clearing staggered, knocked off balance by the invisible wave. But only Keegan, standing at the magic's epicenter, fell to the ground. The effort of casting and controlling the spell with only the force of his will had taken all his strength in a single burst, as if it had been a candle snuffed out by a sudden gust of wind. He collapsed and lay there panting, his body exhausted and utterly drained, Rexol's staff lying on the ground beside him.

For a brief second nobody reacted; the archers simply stared in confusion at their suddenly useless weapons. And then Drake raised his sword. "For the Queen!" he shouted, and the battle began.

Jerrod was the first to react. With three running steps he crossed the distance between himself and the nearest archer, who still stood staring at his cracked bow. Without breaking stride the monk dropped into a somersault, wrapping his ankles around the other man's neck as he tumbled past. Then he twisted his body at the waist, jerking his torso around hard to generate enough leverage through his hips and thighs to snap the neck of the helpless opponent. And then he was on his feet again, already moving to his next victim.

Bereft of their bows, the Danaan drew their swords and fell upon the group en masse. From where he lay on the ground Keegan saw one of the patrol struggling with his rapier, trying to free it from the tangle of his belt and the string from his broken bow. Before he could, Scythe fell upon him. The keen gleam of the six-inch razor in each hand glittered as she slashed relentlessly at her screaming opponent. The Danaan threw his hands up to protect his face, already gashed wide open by the flickering blades. Scythe responded with a series of fluid, rhythmical swipes—forward, back, and forward again, her wrist nimbly turning so that each pass left a mark on the hands of her enemy.

The savage grace of her surgical strikes held Keegan enthralled. The Danaan's fingers and palms were sliced open to the bone, each cut sending a fresh stream of blood splashing across his clothes. The entire sequence had taken less than a second and Scythe wheeled away, her tiny body little more than a blur as she twirled over to the next closest enemy. The man she had carved up fell forward and landed only a few feet away from Keegan, already dead from the deep slit across his throat.

The mage tried to stand but collapsed helplessly back to the ground, unable to support his own weight. A deep grunt caused him to roll over onto his side and look to his right.

Norr had scooped up a large, heavy branch and was using it as a makeshift club to keep one of the soldiers at bay. The Danaan ducked under the wide swath of his sweeping cudgel and tried to move in near enough to bring his rapier to bear. But the barbarian's reach was too great and before the Danaan could get close he was forced to retreat, narrowly dodging another swing of the stout tree limb that would have removed his head from his narrow shoulders.

A second member of the patrol joined the fray and they attacked in tandem, trying to coordinate their efforts so one of them could get inside the radius of the club's wide arc. The first soldier saw an opportunity and darted in, only to be met full in the chest by Norr's massive foot. Neither Keegan nor the unfortunate Danaan had expected such an agile maneuver from the hulking savage, and the force of the kick sent him reeling.

As he stumbled and fell onto his back, Norr leapt forward. The second solider tried to step between the barbarian's charge and his fallen comrade but Norr's massive bulk bowled him over, knocking him to the earth as well. Then the tree limb came crashing swiftly down, caving in the crown of the first soldier's skull, reducing his head to a pulpy, bloody mess. Keegan turned away, but the sickening wet thud told him the second soldier had suffered a similar fate.

The sharp clash of swords drew Keegan's attention next, and he rolled over to see Vaaler and Drake hammering at each other with their blades. The rapiers flickered and danced in quick cuts and parries, the steel moving too quickly for the eye to follow. Drake seemed to be pressing forward; Vaaler was on the defensive. A lunging thrust by the older man got through his enemy's defenses, but Vaaler spun out of the way and the blade caught only air. The unexpected miss caused Drake to overbalance ever so slightly, and Vaaler seized the moment, delivering a sharp counter-thrust to a suddenly exposed flank.

The blade bit deep into Drake's side, drawing a gasp of agonized pain. Vaaler's next strike was even more lethal as he drove the point of his sword through Drake's rib cage and into his heart, killing him instantly.

And just like that the melee was over. None of the Danaan patrol had survived. From where he lay untouched in the center of the battlefield, Keegan surveyed the carnage. Three of the corpses had obviously been slain by Scythe, their skin all but flayed from the skulls by her razors. There were at least four with broken necks, the telltale mark of Jerrod's unarmed combat. Another four seemed to have had their skulls caved in by Norr's club.

Yet in all the slaughter, none of his companions had been harmed. Jerrod stood protectively over him, unmarked despite tackling four trained and armed soldiers without any weapons or armor of his own. Norr and Scythe stood together on the far side of the clearing covered in blood and gore, none of it theirs.

On the other side of the clearing Vaaler stood trembling over the body of the vanquished Drake. Keegan felt he should say something to his friend, but he wasn't sure what. Before he could speak, Vaaler collapsed to his knees.

And then the disowned heir to the throne vomited on the blood-soaked ground.

Chapter 50

IN THE AFTERMATH of the skirmish, Scythe was flush with the adrenaline-fueled thrill of victory. The battle was gruesome, but she had seen far worse while sailing the Western Isles or working the back alleys of Callastan. The violence and gore hadn't disturbed her in the least . . . until she saw Vaaler's reaction.

The young man was doubled over, retching uncontrollably. Jerrod stood over Keegan's prone form, as if awaiting a second wave of attackers. The young mage didn't appear hurt, but it was obvious the monk wasn't about to leave his side.

She glanced up at Norr and he merely shrugged, uncertain what to do. If anyone was going to help Vaaler, it was obviously going to have to be her.

Silently cursing the men for their incompetence she crossed the clearing and crouched at Vaaler's side, rubbing his back until the seizing of his stomach passed. She helped him to his feet and gently walked him over to a clean patch of ground.

"Sit down," she said.

He obeyed without question, his eyes those of a lost little boy.

"Haven't you ever killed anyone before?" she asked sympathetically.

"I have killed more trespassing humans in these woods than I can count," the young Danaan had replied in a dull monotone.

"Any who work the patrols are intimately familiar with death and killing.

"But you've never had to kill one of your own, have you?"

He shook his head.

"Drake was my mentor," he whispered. "He was my teacher. He was like a father to me."

An hour ago the prince had been in high spirits, the prodigal son leading them to the capital of his people. Now he was banished, an outcast with the blood of his mentor on his hands. Scythe knew what it was like to lose everything in a sudden cut of fate's cruel blade; she knew what it was like to suddenly realize you were alone in the world.

"You had no choice," Scythe assured him, hoping at least to ease his guilt. "You were forced into this. It wasn't your fault."

"He couldn't bring himself to kill me," the prince said after a long silence. "Even when he attacked me, he was holding back."

"What do you mean?" she asked gently, hoping to help him work through this.

"Drake was the greatest swordsman in the kingdom. His prowess with a blade was legendary. Everything I knew, every move and every counter, I learned from him," he said slowly, his mind struggling to form coherent thoughts. "I should never have been able to beat him. He *let* me win. He let himself die rather than kill me. Why? Why would he do that?"

"Destiny," Jerrod called out, still poised at the fallen wizard's side. "Keegan is meant to be our champion, he is meant to have the Ring. Those who oppose us must fall."

Scythe shot a wicked glare back over her shoulder at him. The Danaan was in a vulnerable state; his world had just collapsed around him. This was not the time for the monk's stupid prophecies!

Fortunately, the Danaan was stronger than she thought.

"No," Vaaler said, rising to his feet and turning to face the others. "This wasn't about destiny. This was about a good man trapped in a terrible situation."

He took a deep breath and exhaled, collecting himself before continuing.

"Drake knew my mother's command was born from her illness. He knew it was wrong: I could see it in his eyes. But he had been raised all his life to obey the will of the Monarch. Duty was everything to him.

"He could not disobey her command, even though he knew it was wrong. And he couldn't bring himself to kill me, either. For him, death was the only honorable way out."

"Duty and honor are fine things," Scythe commented, "but I can't ever imagine a situation where I'd be willing to die for them."

"I can," Norr said unexpectedly.

She glanced over at him, but he turned away and couldn't meet her eye.

"Is Keegan okay?" Vaaler asked suddenly, noticing for the first time his friend lying on the ground.

Scythe was relieved. The best cure for one's own grief and pain was worrying about the well-being of someone else.

"I'm fine," came the tremulous reply. "Just a little weak. Summoning the Chaos took more out of me than I thought."

"You should know better than to try and cast a spell without invoking the proper enchantments first," Vaaler said, walking over to crouch down and check on his friend. Jerrod stepped aside wordlessly and let him approach. "Even I learned that much during my apprenticeship."

"I figured if I started waving my arms around and chanting strange words those archers would have killed us all."

"Of that I have no doubt," was the grim reply.

The Danaan extended his hand, and Keegan reached up to grab it. Jerrod swooped in to seize the mage's other arm and the two of them helped him back to a standing position. He swayed unsteadily but managed to keep his feet by leaning on his staff for support.

"This changes things," Jerrod said. "The Danaan know we are coming. We can't fight our way through a whole army to reach the capital."

Vaaler frowned, his brow wrinkled in deep thought.

"No," he said at last, "I don't think they do know. My mother would have tried to keep my banishment secret. She believes our kingdom is teetering on the edge of destruction, and she cares too much about her people to make things worse with a public schism between the Queen and her only heir."

"Are you saying nobody else knows?" Jerrod pressed.

"She sent Drake and his patrol because she knew they could be trusted not to say anything to anyone. She must have wanted to keep it secret even from Andar—the High Sorcerer—or she would have instructed him to send some of his war wizards with Drake.

"There may be a few among her personal guard who know of her decree," Vaaler concluded, "but I doubt it is common knowledge, even among the staff of the castle."

"Then there is still hope for us," Jerrod said.

Vaaler nodded.

"But if we enter the city together they are sure to report it to her. There hasn't been a human in Ferlhame since before the Cataclysm."

"But you could go in alone. The prince returning to the castle won't draw any undue attention," the monk pressed. "You could slip in, seize the Ring, and bring it back to us!"

"Hasn't he been through enough already?" Scythe objected, jumping into the conversation.

"He's right," Vaaler said with a shrug in Scythe's direction. "Drake's death changes nothing. Keegan still needs the Ring, and I can still get it for him."

"Don't do this," she pleaded, suddenly certain the plan would be a disaster. "Don't let all this talk of dreams and prophecies turn you against your own people!"

"I'm doing this for my people . . . and for their Queen," he replied calmly.

Scythe found something about the prince's sudden serenity disturbing.

"I have seen what the Ring has done to my mother," he explained. "It will destroy her completely unless I do something. This is my only chance to save her."

"This goes far beyond your mother's fate or the borders of the Danaan kingdom," Jerrod reminded him. "We are on a quest to save the entire world."

Scythe didn't even bother to glare at the monk this time. Vaaler had found a way to deal with his grief; he'd made his choice. And like everything else that had happened since she and Norr had been swept up in this mad quest, there was nothing she could do about it.

Keegan was worried about his friend. In the hours since the slaughter of the Danaan patrol, Vaaler had spoken little, though the wizard knew him well enough to sense his inner turmoil. But there was little he could say to help the prince cope with everything that had happened.

Besides, Keegan had problems of his own. He was still weak from summoning the Chaos. He'd been able to draw upon the power of Rexol's staff in lieu of a charm, but being unable to invoke any kind of incantation to direct the power of his spell, he'd been forced to use himself as a conduit. And while his will was strong enough to withstand the ordeal, the toll on his physical form had been high.

When they found the horses of the patrol tethered a mile away from the ambush, he had been able to ride without slowing the group down, Rexol's staff lashed across his back. By the time they stopped for the night, though, he was ready to collapse from his saddle in exhaustion.

But the weakness of his body wasn't his primary focus. During the ride, he'd sensed that he had been fundamentally changed by all that had happened. He'd been transformed in some subtle yet meaningful way.

The Chaos was stronger in him now. That much was undeniable. He had felt it ever since waking from his coma; the force of the magic he had unleashed during the attack only confirmed what he knew to be true. But he had lost something, too.

The heat of the flames coursed through his veins, but beyond that he felt little else. Part of him sympathized with Vaaler, but he felt no real grief or sadness. His concern for the prince was strangely muted, as if it were coming to him across a great distance.

As he mulled over his altered state he realized that even his reaction toward Scythe had been affected. He still knew the Island girl was exotically beautiful, but it stirred up no emotion in him. No lust, no passion, no desire. Nothing. He felt dead inside; empty; hollow. Numb to everything but the ever-present Chaos burning inside him.

"We're only a league away from the city, and the Queen might have set up patrols around the perimeter," Vaaler said once they had finished setting up the camp. "We'll wait here until nightfall, then I'll go on alone."

Keegan closed his eyes to help himself concentrate, focusing his attention on the strange hyperawareness he had been experiencing ever since waking up in the enchanted forest. Another change, though Keegan suspected this second sight was merely a response to the Chaos that hung like a thick fog in the woods.

He cast his senses out like a net, searching for signs of the Danaan patrols. He scanned the area around them, inspecting every branch and leaf for a full league in every direction. It took him less than a second.

"There's nobody around. Not for miles."

"Then we'll stay with you right up until the edge of the city," Jerrod said. "Your destiny is tied with Keegan's now, Vaaler . . . just like the rest of us. I don't want to separate the group any longer than we have to."

Scythe gave him a strange look but didn't say anything. The prince just nodded.

Once it was dark, they broke camp and pressed on until they were within sight of the city's edge. Keegan sensed their destination long before they actually reached its borders. The magic was

strong in the Danaan people, he could feel the pulse of their collective energy coming from the capital. And he could sense the
Ring, calling to him. Even so, when they emerged from the obscuring tree line he couldn't help but be impressed by what he saw.

Ferlhame had been founded in the center of a large clearing—
or perhaps the clearing had been the result of harvesting the trees
to create the massive city. In many ways the architecture resembled
that of Torian: tall, elegant towers in orderly rows. But the Danaan
capital had a more natural feel to it, as if order and symmetry had
not been imposed upon the city by regulations and building codes
but had evolved organically over the centuries.

Everything in the city was built not from mortar, stone, or brick
but rather wood, furthering the natural aesthetic. To the wizard's
eye the towers and buildings reaching up toward the night sky had
obviously been created with magic, the lumber shaped and reinforced by the power of Chaos during the construction so each
structure would be as stable and secure as any edifice made of more
conventional materials. However, despite the changes wrought by
the spells bound into their surface, the buildings were still unmis-
takably made of wood.

"No human has looked upon this place since it was founded
seven centuries ago," Vaaler said, his voice so soft Keegan thought
he must be speaking to himself. "And now the isolation is broken
by a small group of thieves in the night."

Keegan wasn't sure if his friend sounded resentful or just sad.

"We can go no farther together," he said more loudly. "I can approach the castle without drawing attention. You humans cannot."

"We'll wait here with the horses for you to bring us the Ring,"
Jerrod agreed.

Scythe laughed.

"You make it sound so simple. Like he just has to go into the
Queen's jewelry box and pull it out."

"It won't be in any jewelry box," Vaaler said flatly. "She wears it
on a chain around her neck, even while sleeping. She never takes it
off."

"Even better," Scythe replied. "You really think she'll just hand it over to us? After what happened with Drake? Am I the only one who sees how foolish this all is?"

"I have no choice. The Talisman has taken control of my mother's mind; it uses her own visions to bind her beneath its spell. Unless I free her from it, she is doomed. We all are."

"So how do you plan to get it from her?" Scythe asked. "I've lifted my share of necklaces without getting caught, but this isn't like clipping the chain from an unsuspecting mark in a crowd."

When Vaaler didn't immediately respond she added, "How do you even plan to get close enough to try and steal it? You've been banished—remember?"

"I doubt anyone but Drake and my mother's personal guards knows anything about that," he reminded her. "No one will challenge me when I enter the castle."

"Okay, so you get inside the castle," Scythe conceded. "Then what? How are you going to get close enough to the Queen to pull this off?"

"I know a way," was all he said.

Giving up on the young Danaan, she turned to Jerrod. "Even if he succeeds, what are we supposed to do after we get the Ring? Do you even know?"

"We follow Keegan's destiny," the monk replied. "Keegan's visions will give us guidance when the time is right. For now we must concentrate on the task at hand. Once Keegan has the Ring all will become clear."

She threw her hands up in exasperation and spun to face Vaaler again. "Fine, go ahead. We'll wait here for you. But if you aren't back by morning, I'm gone." She cast a quick glance over at Norr. "Even if I have to go alone."

"I'll be back long before that," Vaaler assured her, before disappearing into the shadows of the nearest building.

Chapter 51

IT TOOK VAALER less than an hour to reach the castle gates. He kept his hood up while walking through the streets to hide his face, not wanting to draw any extra attention. Not one of the citizens he passed recognized the heir to the throne. However, once he reached the gates he knew he would have to try a different approach.

"Who approaches at this hour?" a guard called from within.

Throwing back his hood he said, "Open the gates. Drake is expecting me to meet back with his patrol before the dawn and I have no time for formalities."

It was a plausible lie. He had told himself over and over again that the guards wouldn't know of his banishment yet. All they would know was that Drake and his patrol had left suddenly on an urgent errand. It would make sense that the Queen's son should also be involved in this mysterious business. But these constant reassurances couldn't keep his heart from pounding. If he was wrong—if they knew the truth—they would seize him and throw him in the dungeons . . . if they didn't just kill him.

He heard the sharp twang of a bow being fired and flinched, then realized it had only been the creaking of the gates' hinges as one of the guards opened it up to let him in. The men on watch saluted him and he returned the gesture in kind without even thinking.

"Her Majesty is asleep," one of the guards informed him. "Shall I send a request that one of her attendants wake her, my prince?"

"No time," he replied with a shake of his head. "And no need. Tomorrow, tell her I was here. Tell her I met up with Drake. She will understand."

The guard saluted again and Vaaler turned away, disappearing into the castle's halls. He made his way toward the eastern wing, the seat of the administrative branch of the city's government. Here in the various rooms and chambers the daily business of running the kingdom was conducted. During the day it would have been bustling with functionaries ranging from pages and low-level clerks all the way through to the various ministers, including the High Sorcerer. However, at this time of night the place was completely deserted.

He reached the council chambers and found them empty, just as he had been hoping. He glanced around again to make sure nobody was around then began to feel along the edges of the large tapestry set into the far wall behind the Queen's seat. The tapestry had been sewn to a thick wooden frame, and the frame itself had been set into the bricks and stones of the castle wall.

He picked and worried at the edges of the frame and the seams of the stitching until he was able to pop a few threads loose and work his fingers through to the other side. Then he gripped the tapestry and tore it loose, revealing a small, dark tunnel behind.

Almost every room in the eastern wing had such a tapestry, and behind every tapestry was a long-forgotten tunnel. Vaaler suspected they had once been used to keep tabs on the various branches of government operating within the castle walls. Agents working for the ruling Monarch could spy on any of the ministers and civil servants—there were even tunnels running to and from each of the private rooms of the royal family. But whoever had ordered their construction had also managed to keep them very, very secret. As far as the prince knew nobody was aware of their existence anymore, not even the Queen herself.

Vaaler couldn't remember how he had discovered the castle's

network of hidden passages, but he had used them often as a child. Sometimes he had even crept carefully from his bedchamber through the winding tunnels only to stop at this very room, where he had sat safely out of sight in the hidden alcove behind the heavy tapestry and eavesdropped on his mother and her council. Other times he had crawled to the tapestry of his mother's room, frightened but curious, drawn by her cries and screams as she had suffered through one of her terrible visions.

He had always considered the tunnels to be something special and private; something that had helped make up for the fact that he had been born blind to the Sight. It had been his secret and his alone. One he had carefully guarded.

His secret wouldn't last much longer. In the morning someone was sure to notice the tapestry on the floor and the rather obvious opening behind it, but Vaaler planned to be far away from the castle by then.

Taking a deep breath he stepped into the darkness, the familiar musty smell of the air inside stirring up the memories of all the time he had spent in the dark maze of passages as a little boy. He was a grown man now, and he had to crouch down to avoid the low ceiling. By the time he had gone twenty feet in it was black as pitch and he was forced to move by shuffling slowly forward, feeling with his hand along the wall to guide him. Fortunately, he knew the tunnels well enough to navigate them even in total darkness.

He counted the passages on each side, calling on the mental map he had formed in his head while exploring the tunnels as a child. He turned down the corridor that led to his mother's chambers. He knew he was nearing the end when he saw a faint orange glow ahead, the light from the Queen's fireplace shining through the fabric.

Careful not to make any sound to reveal himself he crept to the end of the tunnel and paused to listen. When he heard the faint, even breathing of his mother coming from the other side he gently pulled the stitching free until he was able to lift a corner of the tapestry back and look through at the scene beyond.

His mother lay in bed, asleep. It had been only a few weeks since he had last spoken with her, and he was shocked at how thin and frail she looked. He had heard about her refusal to eat, but even a hunger strike couldn't have brought about such a startling transformation in such a short time.

It was the Ring, of course. Once she had been able to control its power, but with the fading of the Legacy, the Chaos within the Talisman had grown beyond her abilities. He had known it consumed her thoughts; now it was consuming her physical body as well.

Surely Drake had seen it, too. Why hadn't he listened? Why had he been so stupid and stubborn? Was that part of the Ring's power, too? Was it affecting not only the Queen but also those who served her? Sowing Chaos among the hapless mortals? Could it even be affecting Vaaler himself?

He shook his head to clear away such thoughts. The Ring was destroying his mother; that was all that mattered. He had to take it, not just for her sake but for the sake of the entire kingdom.

Slipping silently out from behind the tapestry, he crept across the floor until he stood over his mother's bed. Up close she looked even worse, her pale skin covered in sweat and her brow furrowed as if she were in great pain. Behind her closed lids her eyes flickered madly with the never-ending visions brought on by the terrible power of the Ring. Though still asleep, her breath came in short, ragged gasps from her sunken chest.

The prince leaned in close, and the sickly smell of fever sweat filled his nostrils. His mother groaned and twitched in her sleep, but didn't wake up. He reached down and carefully undid the clasp of her chain then gently removed it from her neck, taking the Ring with it.

She stirred once more, and Vaaler was certain she would wake this time. But instead she only sighed and settled into what seemed to be an even deeper sleep.

Clenching the Ring in his fist, he leaned forward and softly kissed the Queen on her forehead. Her furrowed brow relaxed, and her flickering eyes became still. She sighed a second time and rolled onto her side, her back to him, her breathing now slow and even.

He escaped back into the tunnel as quietly as he had come in, the Ring tucked safely away in the pocket of his belt.

Rianna woke slowly. For the first time in many months she didn't want to wake up. On some unconscious level she was aware that she wasn't dreaming; she wasn't in the grip of a terrible vision. Sleep was a comfort, a peaceful sanctuary that her exhausted body and mind were reluctant to leave.

But another part of her knew something was wrong. She had longed to escape the torment of the dreams for so long that she couldn't remember what real sleep was even like. It felt unnatural. She rolled and stretched, feeling refreshed but also anxious as she became aware of her surroundings.

Instinctively, her right hand reached up to clasp the ring at her neck. To her horror she found nothing.

Rianna Avareen, ruling Monarch of the Danaan kingdom, began to scream.

Vaaler emerged from the shadows on the southern edge of the city just as the first horn sounded. The Danaan looked back over his shoulder then sprinted toward them.

"Alarm!" he shouted as another horn blast nearly drowned out his words, this one coming from the opposite side of the city.

"What happened?" Jerrod demanded. "Did you get the Ring?"

The prince hoisted himself up into his saddle and nodded. "They must have discovered it was missing."

Another horn echoed its call across the spires and towers of the city. This one was answered by two separate blasts coming from somewhere deep within the woods.

"They're signaling the patrols," Vaaler explained quickly. "The entire army is being mobilized to hunt us down."

A sudden cacophony of noise exploded from deep within the forest as a score of horns answered the call with their own deep blasts. A similar wave of sound rolled out from the city, seeming to shake the very foundations of the buildings.

"Mount up!" Vaaler shouted. "We have to get out of here!"

They could barely hear him above the resounding blare, but he didn't need to tell them twice. With Vaaler in the lead they wheeled their horses around and fled into the forest, making for the southern border that marked the separation between the Danaan woods and the lands of the Free Cities.

Keegan clung to his horse's bridle with his right hand as they charged through the trees, the call of the horns echoing all around them. In his left he clutched Rexol's staff, keeping it close so he could draw on its power should the need arise. It was impossible to tell where the patrols were from the noise, but it seemed as if they were coming from all sides. As they drove on the wild cacophony settled into a steady rhythm of call and response, first one from behind and then one up ahead. It was clear the Danaan were signaling to one another, coordinating their efforts.

The wizard closed his eyes and let his mind drift out, extending the vision of his second sight as far as he possibly could. The swiftness of the Danaan response was amazing. Behind them an army on foot and horseback was already swarming out from the city. Wave after wave of armed soldiers poured into the forest, each squadron led by a pair of Danaan wizards using magic to quickly pick up the trail of the invaders. The squads scattered out in all directions then pressed south, beating the bushes to drive their quarry forward.

To the south, ahead of the fleeing party, were the patrols. There were literally hundreds of them, fanning out in response to the staccato bursts of sound to form a wide semicircle that threatened to cut off all hope of escape.

Even the forest itself seemed to answer the call. The horns had woken ancient magics meant to protect the Danaan and their kingdom; long-dormant spells woven into every branch and leaf had been stirred to life. The trees were shifting and moving, a subtle transformation of the path ahead, funneling them into the heart of their enemy's strength. The trees themselves were leading them into an ambush.

Keegan recognized the hopelessness of their situation in a single instant of revelation. But he hardly cared. There was something else that dominated his vision, a single glowing ember so bright it threatened to blind him to everything else: the Ring in Vaaler's belt.

"Stop!" he hollered when they stumbled into a small clearing. Everyone pulled up their horses sharply, as if the very command of the word had some power they could not resist. "We can't outrun them. We're already surrounded."

Vaaler agreed. "This is the land of my people. We can move farther and faster on foot or through the treetops than you can on horseback. The patrols won't let us get away."

The wall of sound closing in on them made it impossible to doubt his words.

"I didn't come all this way to die in the woods, hunted like some animal!" Scythe snapped. "Come on, wizard. Cast some kind of spell to get us out of this!"

"Magic can't save us," Vaaler said. "Danaan war wizards are among those hunting us. Strong as Keegan is, they would simply overwhelm him if he tried to use the Chaos against them."

"Not if I use the Ring," Keegan said. "They can't stand against the power of Old Magic."

"No!" Jerrod suddenly shouted, much to the mage's surprise. "It's too dangerous. The Crown destroyed Rexol when he tried to use it; its power consumed him. The Ring is just as dangerous."

"What are you talking about?" Scythe snapped. "You're the one who keeps saying Keegan's supposed to save the world! He doesn't stand much chance of that if he dies right here. Let him use the damn Ring!"

"No," Jerrod repeated. "He needs more training. He needs to let his visions guide him, teach him. If he uses the Ring now he will suffer the same fate as his master. He needs more time to learn to control the power of the Talisman."

"I don't think he's got much time left," was her scathing reply.

"Vaaler knows these woods, he knows how the patrols operate," Jerrod said, speaking to Keegan and ignoring the angry young woman. "Use your magic to hide yourself and him. The rest of us will press on and draw the attention of the Danaan while you double back and around to freedom."

"That's suicide," Keegan protested. "The patrols will kill you all!"

"Our lives are meaningless," Jerrod said.

"Speak for yourself," Scythe muttered.

The monk gave her a grave look.

"You may not believe in Keegan's destiny, but he alone can save the world. His life is worth more than any other: yours or mine. The fate of the mortal world hangs in the balance. Keegan must survive. He must be allowed to fulfill his destiny."

Scythe seemed at a loss for words and turned to Norr for support. The barbarian only shrugged his massive shoulders, uncertain what he could say. It was actually Keegan who spoke next.

"No. I won't abandon you. None of you. You deserve better than this."

"What we deserve is not—"

The young wizard cut him off. "If I am to save the world, then I must first be able to save those who stand with me."

He turned to Vaaler and held out his hand. "The Ring. Hurry."

The Danaan hesitated only briefly before surrendering the Talisman.

Keegan took it with a trembling hand. He climbed awkwardly down from his horse, the Ring clenched tightly in his right fist and Rexol's staff in his left, and handed the reins to Jerrod.

"Take the horses and move to the edges of the clearing. I don't want you to be too close in case . . . well, just in case."

There was no time to argue. The sound of the horns continued to draw closer. The others did as he instructed without speaking.

He waited until they had moved as far from him as they could go without completely vanishing into the trees. He hoped that would be a safe enough distance.

Knowing it was time to claim his destiny, Keegan placed the Ring on his finger.

Chapter 52

POWER FLOODED THROUGH the young wizard. Power beyond anything he had ever known. Power unlike anything he had ever imagined. The Ring had torn open a fissure in the mortal world and Keegan had become a mere conduit channeling the raw energy of Chaos. He gasped and dropped to his knees, physically unable to stand as the magic poured through him, Rexol's staff slipping from his grasp and falling to the ground beside him.

His mind was lost amid the Chaos storm. Everything he had done before was but a taste of what he had unleashed, a sprinkling of a few drops compared with the torrent drowning him now. His mind was overwhelmed by the fury of the storm, his will battered and tossed aside by the Talisman's infinite power. Without boundaries or limits, the Chaos exploded out from him into the mortal world.

It flew up to the sky, gathering into a dark and ominous cloud. A sudden wind sprang up and howled around him, a tornado whipping his hair and clothes, tearing at him as if it would flay his very flesh from his bones. It swept up the fallen leaves and twigs in the clearing, surrounding him with a swirling green and brown wall. Arcs of lightning shot down from the thunderclouds, slamming into the ground and trees around him, shattering the branches and splitting the trunks.

His companions were driven back farther from the clearing by the tornado enveloping him. They retreated into the trees, seeking shelter from the unnatural lightning and trying to stay beyond the range of the magical winds.

The power continued to well up inside him, pouring into him from the Chaos Sea far faster than it could escape into the mortal world. He felt as if he were going to burst, the pressure inside him mounting until his skin stretched and began to crack, bleeding out tiny rivulets of molten blue liquid. He threw his head back and screamed in agony.

In response to his cry Jerrod leapt from the forest and rushed toward him, only to be blown back by the ferocious winds within the clearing. The monk was lifted from his feet by the wild currents and hurled against a nearby tree hard enough to crack his ribs.

He grunted in pain, struggled to his feet, and rushed forward again. This time the storm flung him twenty feet through the air to land face-first with a dull thud outside the range of its localized fury. Jerrod rolled onto his side, tried valiantly to rise, then fell back down and lay still.

Keegan could feel the Chaos rushing out from the Ring and through him like a great river that had jumped its banks, wild and untamed, a force of pure destruction. A bolt of lightning struck him, engulfing him in its blue fire. He should have been consumed in that single instant, devoured as Rexol had been when he dared to use the Crown. Only he wasn't.

The pain was excruciating, the heat from the incandescent flames unbearable. His skin was scorched and blistered and burned. But somehow he was still alive. Somehow, he had survived. Clinging to the knowledge that this alone proved he was stronger than his master had ever been, Keegan gathered his will and tried to impose it on the Chaos.

He began to rein it in, building a dam deep inside himself to stem the wild flow, caging the infinite power within the structure of the Ring itself. The magic rushing through him became a mere trickle. The Chaos began to well up within the Talisman instead of him, a great pool he could draw upon as he needed it: a part of him, but separate.

He allowed the reservoir of Chaos that had built up within his own body to seep out into the forest, and the heat and pressure inside him began to subside. With great effort, Keegan rose to his feet.

The storm still raged in the clearing; he couldn't see for all the debris swirling around him. He raised his left hand to the sky and slowly brought his arm down to his side, his fingers closing into a tight fist as he did so. In response to his command the winds died and the lightning stopped, though dark clouds still boiled overhead.

The Chaos was his now: his to control, his to command. The Ring offered him a limitless supply of energy, and all he had to do was draw it out and bend it to his will. He began the slow chant of a dark spell. The clouds above him rumbled and churned, then began to dissipate, spreading out in a fine, black mist that settled slowly down upon the trees.

Keegan continued his chant, closing his eyes so he could see the effects of the Chaos. With his second sight the mage located a single patrol moving swiftly toward the clearing, clambering through the branches high above the forest floor. He set the magic upon them.

The dark mist had become a shadowy fog. In response to his will, it crawled through the forest toward the advancing patrol, wrapping itself around the trunks and branches of the trees, seeping beneath the bark and into the leaves, slithering down into the roots. The trees began to change.

For a brief instant he felt the old enchantments of the forest fighting against him. Powerful wards binding the woods to the Danaan resisted his spell, but he easily brushed them aside and continued to work his spell of transformation.

The patrol leader stopped; she sensed that something was wrong, though she wasn't sure what it was. She crouched down on the branch she had been standing on and reached back to draw her bow. Beneath her feet the branch began to sway. No, not sway: *writhe.*

She glanced down and to her horror saw that the leaves around her feet were squirming like great green maggots. A thin branch slithered out and wrapped itself around her ankle. A swarm of leaves fluttered down to cover her face, leaving a sticky, glistening trail as they crawled across her skin.

She tried to shout out a warning, but another limb lashed out and encircled her neck, drawing so tight her eyes bulged and her mouth gaped. She struggled to draw breath, but the leaves filled her mouth and pushed down her throat, choking the life out of her.

Not that her warning would have made any difference. Behind her the forest had already come alive and swallowed every member of her patrol.

The shadow fog spread south rapidly, working the hideous meta-morphosis on every tree it touched. In his mind's eye Keegan watched with morbid fascination the futile struggles of his enemies as they encountered this unthinkable foe.

The scene was repeated over and over, the Danaan sensing or seeing the fog but not realizing what was wrong until the attack began. Then they slashed wildly at the branches snaking out toward them, hacking the wood in desperation. But the branches they chopped through still slithered forward as if they were alive. And as they looked on in numb horror, vines dropped from the foliage above to entangle their limbs and choke the life from them.

Others panicked and fired their bows into the swarms of leaves falling down to envelop them, to no avail. They vanished beneath a blanket of squirming, wriggling vegetation, their muffled screams quickly smothered.

A few managed to sound their horns before they died, but this was a different note. Fall back. Retreat. The line of the patrols had broken. Those still alive were now in a race for their lives, fleeing before the horrors of the shadow fog, moving away from Keegan and his friends. Satisfied, the mage turned his focus to the north, directing the fog toward the soldiers that had pursued them from the city.

Warned by the horns of the patrols, the city soldiers had already begun their retreat to the relative safety of the city. A few brave wizards stayed behind, combining their power in an effort to halt the spread of the deadly fog. But their spells were useless against Keegan's magic, and they fell screaming as the forest consumed them, unable to slow the relentless advance.

Most of the soldiers were going to make it back to the capital, however, before the spell ever reached them. Realizing this, Keegan dispelled the fog with a simple wave of his hand, breaking the enchantment that had given life and malice to the trees, and allowing them to revert to their natural form.

He was in complete command of the Chaos now. He felt strong, invincible. An aura of blue light shimmered and crackled around him. He had routed his enemies with his magic and he still felt an untapped ocean of power pulsing within the Ring, his for the taking. His ears roared with the sound of victory, his heart pounding with the euphoria of conquest. The battle was over, but he was ready to continue the fight.

The wizard crossed his arms above his head, and the aura around him flared in response. He gathered the Chaos into a ball of light hovering above him, then released it with a single word. Keegan's body began to grow.

He shrieked as his bones cracked and reknitted a hundred times in the space of a few seconds, growing longer and thicker. His muscles ripped and tore, then re-formed, then ripped and tore again. Three times his outer layer of skin split and peeled away as he shed the useless husk of flesh for a new one.

Moments later the transformation was complete. Keegan stood twenty feet tall, a giant towering above the trees surrounding the clearing. Oblivious to the fate of his companions, the wizard set off toward the Danaan capital with a purposeful stride, smashing tree and limb as he went and leaving a path of destruction in his wake.

Those who had escaped the forest were safe, for now. But they could not escape him. He would level the Danaan city completely. And none could stand against him.

Chapter 53

SLEEP. THE IMMORTAL sleep of seven centuries beyond death. The cold sleep of rocks and stones buried in the earth, a spell of such power it cannot be broken. Power. The power of Chaos, the magic of the Gods. The sleeping mountain beneath the earth stirs.

Far to the north of the Danaan capital, in the depths of the forests never seen by human or Danaan since the first Cataclysm, the ground shuddered. Screaming birds took flight, the sound of their beating wings filling the crisp night. Stags and deer and hares crouched trembling low to the ground, paralyzed with fear so great it overwhelmed their instinct to flee.

Slowly, it wakes. And remembers. The wars. Wars against the Gods, led by the one once called Daemron, champion of the Immortals, defender of the mortal world and slayer of the Chaos Spawn. But then the Slayer joins their side and leads them against the Gods to claim the power that is rightfully theirs.

Far below the surface the beast clawed at the soil of the grave from which it was never supposed to rise. Its horned, scaled head burrowed up through the dirt atop its serpentine neck. Powerful foreclaws carved deep furrows through strata of rock and stone; massive back legs kicked as it swam up from the ocean of earth and mud. Its long, thick tail twisted and turned, propelling it ever upward to an escape it was never supposed to know.

It stirs and it remembers the wars. It remembers bitter defeat. It remembers the invincible power of the Immortals. It remembers eons spent frozen beneath the earth, chained by a power too great to resist. Now the power calls it to awaken, and the creature must obey.

The ground erupted in a shower of dirt and stones and uprooted trees as the dragon burst forth. It spread its great leathery wings and took to the sky, screaming its rage and fury at centuries of magical captivity. It swooped and dove and turned, stretching and flexing muscles and limbs that had lain still for seven hundred years. And then it climbed. Higher and higher it soared, clouds of sediment trailing behind in a great plume as the residue of centuries was washed away from its glittering green scales by the rapid ascent.

At the apex of its climb, the dragon twisted its sinewy neck to regard the mortal world far below with black reptilian eyes. It dove down to the earth and spread its massive jaws to unleash a blast of fire that ignited the trees in a blaze of blue flame. The inferno spread far faster than the terrified animals below could flee, racing through the forest in every direction, incinerating all in its path.

The dragon flapped its fifty-foot wings and climbed once more, high above the smoke and the sweet stench of the charred flesh from the animals caught in the fire. Here the air was pure and clean. The scent of power reached its scaly nostrils, the scent of Chaos magic. The beast wheeled in the air, turning to the south, drawn by the power of an ancient Talisman.

From the safety of the trees beyond the clearing Scythe, Norr, and Vaaler watched Keegan's startling metamorphosis.

"What's he doing?" Vaaler asked when the transformation was complete and the now giant mage had turned to the north and strode off through the trees.

None of the others answered him.

"Keegan!" he called out, taking a stride toward the clearing. "Keegan, wait!"

Norr dropped a heavy hand on the Danaan's shoulder, holding him back. "No, don't go after him. It's too dangerous."

Vaaler turned and looked up at Norr's towering form.

"But the horns have sounded a retreat. It's over. We won. Someone has to tell him."

"I doubt he'd even hear you," Scythe said. Like Norr, she had seen the murderous intent in the gigantic wizard's eyes, and she understood what it meant. "You saw what happened to Jerrod."

"That wasn't Keegan's fault," Vaaler protested. "He wouldn't hurt one of us. Not on purpose."

"I agree," the barbarian said, then added, "But he is not himself right now. Let him go."

A soft groan from Jerrod's prone form drew their attention. Norr rushed into the clearing and crouched down beside him.

"He's still alive," he said, surprised. "Scythe, come help him."

Scythe made her way over to the fallen monk, Vaaler following uncertainly behind her.

"I doubt there's anything I can do," she said without even bending down to check him out.

Still crouched over their injured companion, Norr's gaze was now level with her own.

"Please," he said, looking into her eyes. "At least try. For me."

She sighed and bent down to investigate.

"Help me get this cloak off him."

Under the Danaan garment Jerrod's body was badly bruised. Dark purple splotches covered his torso and limbs. Scythe checked for broken bones, but to her surprise found nothing more serious than a few cracked ribs. He had suffered a blow to the head that had knocked him unconscious, but there didn't appear to be any fractures in the skull.

"He'll live," she said. "But he'll be in a lot of pain when he wakes up."

"I'm awake now," Jerrod replied in a weak whisper, responding to her voice. "Where's Keegan?"

Vaaler was the first to answer. "He . . . he left. He was heading north."

"We have to go after him." Jerrod struggled to stand up, but Scythe held him down easily.

"You're not going anywhere. Not with the beating you've taken."

Ignoring her, he turned to Norr.

"Help me up. Hurry."

The big man glanced at Scythe, who rolled her eyes and moved aside. He lifted Jerrod to his feet, then stepped away gingerly, ready to catch the wounded monk if he was unable to stand on his own.

Jerrod swayed but remained standing, though he was nearly doubled over from the pain in his cracked ribs. He bowed his head in concentration and took a long, deep breath.

The bruises on his body began to fade. Scythe had heard tales of the Order's supernatural recuperative abilities, and she had suspected them to be true while watching Jerrod tend to Norr's injuries after their escape from Torian. Now her suspicions were confirmed. Even so, she was amazed at the miraculous recovery happening before her very eyes. Within seconds his healing magic had knitted his bones so that he could stand up straight.

"Now," he said, gasping slightly from the exertion of mending his injuries, "tell me again where Keegan went."

"He went north," Vaaler said. "I think . . . I think he was heading back to Ferlhame."

A shadow passed across the monk's face.

"Are you certain?"

"He's heading to the city," Scythe confirmed. "I'm sure of it."

"I still don't understand why," Vaaler admitted. "We're safe now. I heard the horns blowing their retreat."

Jerrod frowned but didn't answer, and Scythe shook her head in disgust.

"You can't even admit it, can you?"

"Admit what?" Vaaler asked her. "What are you talking about?"

"Jerrod's precious savior is going to destroy Ferlhame."

"No," Jerrod said defiantly. "He would not do that. He is our champion; he is the protector of the mortal world."

"I saw the look in his eyes," Scythe said. "He wanted revenge. He wanted to destroy."

"No," Jerrod repeated. "There must be some other explanation. He must have gone north for some other reason."

"He turned himself into a giant and marched off to destroy the city," Scythe insisted. "What other explanation can there be?"

"Jerrod," Vaaler asked, fear in his voice, "What if she's right?"

"We must have faith in Keegan," Jerrod assured him. "He will stand against the forces of Chaos and destruction; he will not unleash them on us. He is our champion."

"How can you say that?" Scythe protested. "You saw what he did to Torian. He'll do the same to Ferlhame."

"Torian was not his fault," Jerrod muttered. "It was an accident. Chaos is difficult to control. Keegan needs more training to master his power so he can fulfill his destiny."

"You think he's some mystical savior, but you're wrong," Scythe said. "He's just a mage drunk with ambition, a wizard gone out of control. Why can't you admit that?"

It was Norr who answered her.

"Because there is no one else. Keegan is his last hope."

Vaaler turned to the monk.

"Is this true?" he demanded angrily. "Are you willing to stand idly by and let my people be slaughtered?"

"I do not believe Keegan will slaughter your people," Jerrod said without hesitation.

Scythe threw her hands up in exasperation.

"You can't argue with a fanatic," she noted, dismissing Jerrod's opinion. "But you aren't like him, Vaaler. You saw what we saw. And you know I'm right. Keegan is going to destroy the city."

Vaaler didn't want to believe her. He knew Keegan, or at least he thought he did. But he'd thought he had known Drake, too. And the young man he remembered from their days studying under Rexol was not the same man he had seen today. Keegan was a wizard now, and Vaaler knew from his studies that the Chaos left its mark on all who used it. It could have changed Keegan, perverted him into something he wouldn't recognize. It could have turned him into Rexol.

"I can't let him destroy Ferlhame," he said solemnly. "We have to stop him."

"You can't," Scythe said simply. "We've seen him level a city and rout an army with his magic. You wouldn't stand a chance."

"I'm the one who brought him here; I'm the one who gave him the Ring!" Vaaler shouted. "This is my fault, and those are my people in that city!"

"Forget about the city," Scythe snapped back. "We have to worry about ourselves now. I say we get the horses and ride south, away from Ferlhame."

"What about Keegan?" Norr asked. "We can't just abandon him."

"Keegan can look after himself. But we have to get out of these woods before the patrols have a chance to regroup."

"No, we have to go after him," Jerrod said, joining the conversation again. "But not to try and stop him.

"The power of the Ring is limitless, but Keegan's ability to control it is not. Eventually his strength will falter and he will be vulnerable. We must be there to help him when that time comes."

"Then there's still a chance to stop him before he reaches the city," Vaaler said hopefully.

"Right now all the power of the Ring is his to command," the monk said. "Until his will is spent no mortal can stand against him. I do not believe he intends to destroy the city, Vaaler. But if that is his purpose you must understand that he cannot be stopped.

"And you must understand that Keegan is still the only one who can stand against the Slayer's return. Even if he destroys Ferlhame, you must accept that he is our only hope. When you brought us the Ring you made a choice. Do not turn your back on that choice now. Your loyalty must be to the future of the entire world, not just to your people."

Chapter 54

KEEGAN MOVED QUICKLY in his new form, covering the ground in great, loping strides. The earth rumbled beneath his feet; trees were bent and broken as he charged heedless through the forest, oblivious of his surroundings. His mind raged with thoughts of Chaos unleashed upon a defenseless city: images of fire, death, and destruction. But when he emerged from the trees on the edge of Ferlhame the city was already burning.

Confused, he stood on the edges of the inferno, taking it all in. The entire north side of the capital was ablaze, the glow from the fires lighting the night sky. Screams of terror filled the air, though he could barely hear them above the roaring Chaos that filled his head. The smell of acrid smoke and immolated flesh assailed his nostrils as he watched the panicked Danaan fleeing the inferno, tiny figures running through the streets to the sections of the city not yet touched by the flames.

And then, from a thousand feet above, he heard something else: a sound no mortal was meant to hear. The shrill cry sliced through the night, shredding the very fabric of the mortal world. The Danaan fleeing the carnage collapsed and threw their hands over their ears, writhing in pain, their minds ripped apart by the terrible shrieking. But Keegan only turned his gaze skyward.

Vaaler opened his mouth to say something else, then dropped his head and slumped his shoulders in resignation.

Jerrod was right. He had felt the terrible power of the Chaos that Keegan had summoned; he had seen the remarkable transformation of his friend in the clearing. Such things would have been impossible, even for Rexol. Keegan's magic was beyond that of any other mortal; there was nobody else who could wield the power of the Talisman and survive. He gave a grim nod to show he understood the truth of the situation.

Satisfied he had secured the loyalty of the Danaan prince, Jerrod turned to Norr. "Gather the horses. We must move quickly or we will arrive too late."

As the big barbarian moved off to follow the monk's command, Scythe realized her lover wasn't about to abandon Keegan yet, despite all that had happened. Which meant she wasn't going anywhere yet, either.

With a sigh she asked, "So what happens when we get to the city?"

"By the grace of the True Gods we will arrive in time to help Keegan when his strength falters," Jerrod replied. "And I pray we will find that your assumptions about him were wrong."

She didn't say anything, simply leapt up into the saddle when Norr brought her horse around. Jerrod scooped up the wizard's fallen staff from the ground and secured it to one of the mounts. Then they set off toward the city without speaking, easily following the path of destruction Keegan had carved through the forest.

For a brief moment he was mesmerized by the terrible beauty of the creature above, circling so high its forty-foot length was small enough to blot out with a thumb. But even at this distance Keegan recognized the telltale signs of a dragon, greatest of the Chaos Spawn.

The wyrm continued to circle, descending slowly, its eyes piercing the night as it sought out its prey. Its massive body glowed with a supernatural green light, emerald scales not just reflecting the moon but alive with their own inherent illumination.

Keegan knew it was searching for him. He knew it could sense the Ring; the beast was drawn to the well of infinite power contained within the simple gold band. But he felt no fear. The power of the Gods was his to command, and even a dragon was no match for him now.

Never taking his eyes from his enormous adversary, the young mage began another incantation. In response to his spell the sky above began to glow with blue light and jagged, surreal turquoise clouds began to form, coalescing around the still-hovering dragon. The mists thickened and churned as Keegan first gathered the Chaos then unleashed it in a storm of death.

From far below the man who was now so much more watched with morbid fascination as blue lightning struck the dragon from all sides. The clouds opened and poison rain engulfed his reptilian foe. The beast's great body shuddered and trembled beneath the onslaught, but the creature refused to break off its circling descent.

The fury of the storm continued unabated. Wherever the tiny drops of concentrated acid fell on the city they left a scorched hole through buildings, into foundations, and deep into the earth. Hundreds of fleeing Danaan fell victim to the deadly shower, the poison rain turning them into withered husks seconds after burning through their clothes and making contact with their bare skin. But the dragon did not fall.

In the face of his foe's implacable, ponderous circling Keegan's will briefly faltered. And in that instant, deep within himself, he felt something strange. His connection to the infinite well of Chaos contained within the Ring was fading, ever so slightly. And he realized his own power was not so infinite after all.

Surprised, the wizard refocused his will on the storm, drawing on the magic of the Talisman to give his spell more power before his strength faded, channeling ever-increasing amounts of Chaos through him. The lightning intensified, the sky constantly lit up by incandescent blue flashes. The rain became a solid sheet of burning liquid. The torrent of acid dissolved the towers and homes of Ferlhame's central district, melting them like statues carved from salt and thrown into a raging river. Fierce winds rocked the wooden towers, and several buildings—their foundations weakened first by fire and then by the terrible rains—collapsed, toppling still more structures with their falling mass.

But even as the spell grew stronger, Keegan himself was growing weaker. The power of the Ring was being poured forth in an endless gush at the glowing green monster high above his head. Its wings thrashed madly in the currents of the storm, and its body was racked by the lightning and corrosive rain. Again and again he threw more Chaos up and into the storm, determined to bring the monster crashing down to the earth, a victim of his irresistible power. And with each thrust of his spell, his ability to call upon the reserve of magical energy diminished.

Finally the dragon fell. Its wings pulled in tight to its sides as it began to plummet to the earth. Keegan's flush of victory was shortlived, however, as he realized the beast was not falling, but diving. At him.

Frantically, Keegan began the incantations of another spell, one to preserve him from the certain death hurtling toward him. The dragon grew in size as it approached, becoming large, then huge, then monstrous. It spread its wings wide, blotting out the sky. It was close enough for Keegan to see the deep scars and horrible burns on its scaled hide inflicted by his storm, but the wounds weren't enough to be fatal. The beast roared once more, the cry making the earth tremble. And it opened its enormous tooth-filled mouth.

The dragon pulled out of its dive twenty feet above him, shooting a powerful jet of flame from its wide-spread jaws as it peeled away. Keegan barely had time to throw up a protective barrier—a shield of pure Chaos—to deflect the fire.

The intense heat of the dragon's breath dropped the wizard to his knees as the stream of magical flames beat against his counter-spell, trying to punch through to consume him utterly. He willed the flames to extinguish, flooding them with wave after wave of smothering magic, pouring an ocean of Chaos onto the descending column of fire until it was completely drowned out.

The entire ordeal had taken less than a second, but it left Keegan exhausted. The seemingly infinite pool of Chaos he had drawn into himself from the Ring was gone, spent in an instant against a single attack by the dragon. He suddenly became aware that he had shrunk back down to his normal size, the spell of transformation broken when he had poured all his energy into deflecting the deadly flames.

The beast was slowly veering around again, preparing another assault. Its great bulk forced it to turn in a wide, lazy arc, giving Keegan the time he needed to prepare his defenses.

He gathered the Chaos once again, drawing upon the Ring to replenish his fading power. But the river of power running through him had dwindled to a faint trickle. Even as he felt the magic gathering inside him, he knew it would never be enough to protect him from another deadly blast of fire.

He cast his mind back to his studies, desperately trying to recall anything he had ever read about dragons during his study and research under Rexol. But the Chaos Spawn were long extinct; it had been centuries since a great wyrm had last taken to the air. There was little he could draw on.

The beast had circled the castle on Ferlhame's western edge and was now flying in low over the city. It gathered itself for another attack, its head rearing back as it prepared to unleash another gout of flame. The great green wings flapped in a powerful, steady rhythm as it glided swiftly toward him.

From the deepest recess of his mind a half-forgotten memory surfaced. Dragons were beasts of fire and flame. It was their greatest strength, but also a weakness that could be exploited—they were extremely vulnerable to cold.

With several quick, complicated motions of his hands and a rapid-fire series of arcane words, Keegan unleashed what little Chaos he was still able to call upon. It was a mere fraction of what had filled him before, but it was still more than any other mortal wizard could have conjured.

The beast's wings were instantly encased in sheets of solid blue ice as his spell took effect. Unable to maneuver, the great wyrm veered off course. The flames that would have incinerated Keegan shot over his head, the beast's aim completely thrown off. The fire slammed into one of the tall towers a block away, and the entire building was instantly alight.

The dragon careened down into the cityscape, the momentum of its flight sending it smashing into towers and buildings, leveling an entire block of the Danaan capital with a great crash before the enormous scaled body finally came to rest beneath tons of lumber and wooden rubble.

They were a mile from the city when they heard the dragon's cry. Their horses reared in response, their fore-hooves churning and kicking at the air as they whinnied in terror. Vaaler and Scythe managed to hold their seats, but Jerrod and Norr were thrown from the saddle. The monk rolled nimbly with the fall and sprang quickly to his feet, but the barbarian landed heavily on the ground. By the time he scrambled back up the horses had run off in the other direction.

"What was that?" Scythe screamed out, struggling to maintain control over her skittish mount.

Jerrod reached out and grabbed the reins, and the animal immediately stopped its struggles.

"Chaos Spawn," Jerrod replied after a moment's thought. "A creature of pure destruction."

"It came from the city," Vaaler said, keeping his voice low while rubbing his mount's neck in an effort to calm the wild-eyed animal.

"The beast must have awoken in response to the power of the Ring," the monk explained. "Keegan must have felt it. He must have known it would attack the city."

"That's why he came back!" Norr exclaimed with a broad smile. "He wanted to stop it! He really is the champion who will stand against them!"

Scythe was about to say something scathing, but the words died on her lips when Vaaler spurred his horse into a gallop.

"Keegan might need our help!" he called out over his shoulder as he rode off.

Leaving Norr and Jerrod to follow along once they recaptured their mounts, she charged off after him.

After only a few seconds, she broke through the trees and pulled up short, reining in so that her horse stood beside Vaaler's own. The prince was staring in stunned horror at the scene before them.

The city was a smoking ruin. Buildings had collapsed and hundreds—perhaps thousands—of bodies lay scattered about the streets. But it wasn't the devastation that drew Scythe's attention. Flying in from the western edge of the city was a glowing green monster, a great winged beast that even Scythe recognized as a dragon.

The dragon was homing in on a single lonely figure: Keegan, shrunk once more to his normal size. There was a flash of magic and the beast veered away, a blast of fire erupting from its jaws but missing its target. It slammed into a row of buildings in full flight, its enormous scaled body vanishing beneath the collapsing structures.

A second later, to Scythe's horror and utter disbelief, the dragon rose up from the rubble.

– – – –

For a moment the beast lay still, but then it shook itself free of the debris. It turned its head first to one side then the other, shooting short bursts of flame at its ice-bound wings then flapping them to dislodge the last shards still clinging to the glittering scales. It took a few lumbering steps on its massive legs, preparing to launch itself to the sky once more.

Keegan lashed out again, throwing every remaining ounce of energy into the hastily conjured spell. Shards of jagged ice flew from his raised fists, ripping through the leathery skin of the dragon's outstretched wings. Great holes tore into the hide, huge rifts in the flesh and sinew of the bat-like appendages, and the dragon screamed as its steaming blood gushed forth from the wounds and burst into flames as it hit the street.

The mage collapsed face-first onto the ground, too weak from the effort to even try to cushion his fall. For a second he just lay there, then with a great effort he managed to roll onto his side to bring his enemy into view once more.

The beast was crippled, but not beaten. No longer able to fly it began a slow, clumsy advance. Its massive, clawed feet crushed everything in its path as it crawled its way through the ruined debris that had once been the great wooden towers of the glorious forest city.

As soon as the creature was close enough, Keegan knew, it would incinerate him. He tried to summon the Chaos again, but his will was drained. He could still sense the power of Old Magic pulsing within the Ring, but he could no longer draw it out.

And yet he could release it all at once. He had managed to cage the fury of the Chaos within the Talisman; if he hadn't done so the magic would have overwhelmed him as it had Rexol when he had tried to use the Crown. If he released that magic now it would consume him utterly . . . but it might destroy his enemy as well.

He struggled to his feet and thrust his left hand up high above him in a clenched fist. The Ring glowed brightly, responding to the presence of the mystical beast that was inching ever closer. The dragon's steaming jaws yawned open. With his last conscious act, Keegan released the full power of the Ring.

Neither Scythe nor Vaaler had moved since emerging from the forest. The scene before them held them rapt, fascinated and horrified by what was unfolding. Their stupor was only broken when Jerrod's horse exploded out of the woods behind them, racing at a full gallop toward the young wizard and the dragon.

Jerrod crouched low in the saddle as he thundered toward the city, the world rushing by in a blur of shadows. His horse's hooves churned up great chunks of earth as he spurred it on. The animal raced across the field separating Ferlhame from the surrounding trees with unnatural speed, sure-footed in the darkness as the monk channeled his own energy and mystical second sight through the animal he rode.

Five hundred yards away from him Keegan unleashed a spell that ripped through the dragon's wings, then collapsed to the ground.

Three hundred yards away the Child of Chaos crawled forward while the wizard lay motionless on his side.

Two hundred yards away Keegan struggled to his feet.

One hundred and fifty yards away he thrust his hand up into the air, fingers clenched in a tight fist.

One hundred yards away the wyrm opened its jaws to reduce his foe to ashes. The Chaos burst forth from the Ring in a single glorious beam of pure white. It arced from Keegan's palm and plunged down the beast's gaping maw.

Fifty yards away the dragon exploded into a thousand chunks.

The force of the blast sent Jerrod and his horse hurtling through the air. The monk threw himself clear as his mount's body slammed into the ground, rolling to absorb the force of the impact. A spray of boiling blood splashed over him, searing his flesh and melting the fabric of his Danaan robe.

He ignored the pain of his burned skin and the screams of his dying horse as he sprang to his feet and crossed the last fifty yards at a run that was only slightly slower than the stallion's charge.

Keegan was still standing with his hand raised to the heavens, though he was no longer conscious. His body was as rigid as steel, frozen in place by the Chaos surging through him, devouring him from the inside. Great arcing beams of white light shot out from the Ring to lash at the city in a wild, random pattern, obliterating everything they touched.

Twenty feet from Keegan, Jerrod scooped up the sword of a fallen soldier without breaking stride. Smoke began to curl up from the wizard's skin.

Ten feet away a beam of deadly white light hurtled toward his chest. He ducked and somersaulted beneath it without losing any momentum, coming out of the roll five feet from the wizard's frozen form.

He leapt high into the air, flipping over as he did so. The Danaan blade flickered out, slashing at Keegan's upraised fist. Jerrod's forward momentum allowed the thin blade to slice cleanly through skin, tendon, and bone.

The arcing white beams vanished as the link between Talisman and wizard was broken, instantly terminating the spell. Keegan crumpled limp and unconscious to the ground, his cleanly severed hand—finger still wearing the Ring—landing beside him a moment later.

Epilogue

THREE DAYS HAD passed since the battle at Ferlhame, but Scythe knew it would take far, far longer for them all to recover from what had happened.

Jerrod had emerged from the wreckage that had once been the Danaan capital carrying Keegan's unconscious body, the young wizard's left arm wrapped in torn bandages to stem the bleeding from the cleaved stump that had once connected to his hand. Scythe had also noticed that the Ring dangled from a chain around the monk's neck, though she hadn't mentioned it at the time.

With their small group reunited, they had retreated into the forest where the monk had done his best to tend to Keegan's wounds. Within a few hours the young man had regained consciousness, though he was so weak he couldn't even stand. Despite this, Jerrod had insisted they move on, claiming it wasn't safe to linger so near the city.

Scythe had half expected Vaaler to abandon them at that point. She thought he might go back to try to help his people in the aftermath of the destruction, but the prince had simply saddled up and ridden off with them. Obviously he felt his place was at Keegan's side now.

Jerrod's horse had been killed during his mad rush into the battle, meaning they had only four mounts for the five of them. Since

Keegan was in no condition to ride alone this hardly mattered. They had placed him and Scythe on the same horse: Between them they were far less of a burden than Norr was to the unfortunate animal bearing his massive girth. The wizard rode in front with Scythe behind so she could help support him in the saddle whenever his exhausted body began to droop to one side or the other.

Since then they had moved at a slow but steady pace. Vaaler had assured them they didn't need to worry about the patrols anymore: All the Danaan would have been recalled to help with the rebuilding of Ferlhame and to care for the city's many wounded. He had said little else as he rode at the head of the group, leading them through the forest.

Scythe could understand his silence; he was struggling to cope with the destruction of his city and the guilt of knowing he had played a part in it. To make matters worse, there was the constant reminder of all the dead Danaan they passed. Several times in the first two days they had come across the gruesome remains of a patrol, their bodies impaled or hung from the branches of the trees and their throats stuffed with brown and withered leaves. But now they were nearing the eastern edge of the forest, and they seemed to have left the disturbing scenes behind them.

It had been Norr's idea to head east. There was really nowhere else for them to go. In the Southlands the remains of the Order would be hunting for them. By now news of Torian's fate would have all of the Free Cities up in arms. And the idea of traveling farther north into Danaan territory was unthinkable. Even so, Scythe had been surprised when Norr suggested they head for the lands of his people.

She supposed that was why he was so quiet during the journey. Her lover had never spoken of his homeland, or why he had left. She had long suspected the story was a painful one, and his somber mood now seemed to confirm that. He had chosen to ride at the head of the group beside Vaaler, and she had taken the hint and left him alone with his thoughts.

Jerrod rode at the back of the group. The monk had little to say, and Scythe couldn't help but wonder if he was suffering through a crisis of faith. His great champion had dared to use the power of the Ring and had survived . . . but only after being maimed so badly that even the monk's healing powers couldn't restore his lost hand.

He had defeated a dragon, but thousands of innocents had died in the process, and she wondered if the terrible destruction Keegan had unleashed might be enough to make even a religious zealot question the value of his beliefs.

As for the young wizard himself, he drifted in and out of consciousness as they rode. Most of the time he seemed to be unaware of where he was even when his eyes were open, which worried Scythe.

She had seen his power; she could only imagine what he might be capable of in his unbalanced state. Jerrod had tried to reassure her, swearing that without the Ring, Keegan was no threat to any of them. She only partly believed him.

But even though she was afraid of him, she also sensed how helpless and vulnerable he was. Keegan was physically weak, drained by his ordeal. He could easily succumb to sickness or infection in his severed stump. Despite her reservations about him and his supposed destiny, she didn't want him to die.

Surprisingly, Jerrod didn't seem concerned. He was convinced Keegan only needed time to rest and recover his strength. But for the first two days he had seemed perpetually trapped between a waking daze and a state of fitful, restless slumber. It was only last night that he had finally settled into a true sleep. He had woken up briefly when they had lifted him into the saddle, but within minutes he was snoring softly again, lulled by the steady rhythm of the horses' plodding hooves.

Their shared mount stumbled briefly, a jarring step. In the saddle in front of her the young man jerked awake with a sudden start, his head snapping from side to side in confusion as he tried to piece together his surroundings.

"Hush, hush," she whispered, placing a soothing hand on his shoulder. "You're safe. We're still riding. There's nothing to fear here."

"How long have I been asleep?" he mumbled. It was the first time he had spoken anything coherent since the Ring had nearly killed him. Scythe took it as a good sign.

"It's been three days," she said carefully, not sure how much he would remember.

"Three days since . . . since the dragon." His voice was stronger now, but he didn't seem upset.

"That's right." She spoke quietly enough that the others wouldn't overhear their conversation. If they realized Keegan was awake they might all want to speak with him at once, and she wasn't sure he was up to it. "Do you remember anything else?"

"The Ring . . . I couldn't control it anymore," he muttered, taking a cue from the tone of her voice. He held up his wounded arm and stared at where his missing hand should be.

"Jerrod . . . saved me."

"I guess he figured a savior missing a hand was better than a dead one," she said, trying to lighten the mood.

As soon as the words were out of her mouth she regretted them; the joke was in poor taste.

Fortunately, Keegan seemed to appreciate the effort. He glanced back over his shoulder at her with a faint smile.

"I thought you didn't believe in saviors and prophecies."

She didn't answer right away.

"I didn't used to," she finally said. "But with everything we've seen, I might be having a change of heart."

"I . . . I don't understand."

"I was convinced you had gone back to Ferlhame to destroy it," she admitted. "I thought you were acting out of revenge. But when I saw you fighting the dragon I realized I was wrong about you. The Danaan tried to kill you, yet you risked your life to go back and try to save them. Obviously, I misjudged you."

Keegan shifted uncomfortably. After a long silence he whispered, "I did go back for revenge. The dragon just happened to get there first."

Scythe didn't know how to respond to that. On the one hand his confession confirmed what she had first feared, but on the other hand he could easily have lied about his true motivations. His honesty had to count for something.

"I guess you were right all along," he said, his voice filled with self-loathing. "I'm not the savior after all."

"Maybe, maybe not," Scythe offered. "Whatever the reason you went back, you actually ended up doing the right thing. You stood against one of the Chaos Spawn and defeated it."

"And destroyed half of Ferlhame in the process."

"The dragon would have destroyed the entire city if you hadn't come along," she countered, aware of how much she was sounding like Jerrod. Was she trying to convince Keegan, or herself?

"Why are you suddenly on my side?" he asked.

She didn't know, exactly.

"I've seen things I wouldn't have believed were even possible a month ago," she said. "I don't know if you truly are the savior Jerrod thinks, but I'd be pretty damn stupid if I didn't realize there was something special about you.

"I'm not sure exactly what I've gotten myself caught up in, but it's something big. And I like to be part of the action."

"This is not some grand adventure," Jerrod said, abruptly joining the conversation.

He had ridden up silently behind them while she had been talking with Keegan, and Scythe wondered how much he had heard.

"The fate of the world hangs in the balance," the monk continued. "Keegan is our only hope, and we must all be willing to do whatever is necessary to see that he fulfills his destiny."

Scythe didn't say anything, but glared at him with burning hatred in her eyes. She was glad she'd had a chance to talk to Keegan alone before he had interrupted. Her feelings toward the young mage might be changing, but her dislike of the monk was as strong as ever.

"The Ring," Keegan said, suddenly noticing the chain dangling from Jerrod's neck. He reached out slowly with his mutilated arm, oblivious to the fact that he couldn't have grasped the Talisman without his missing hand.

Jerrod leaned back and tucked the Ring beneath his cloak, hiding it from sight.

"I'll keep this for a while, Keegan," he said softly. "You are weak; the Talisman's power is more than you can handle right now."

The young man snatched his phantom hand back, as if it had extended of its own accord and he had only now just become aware of it.

"Yes, keep it for now," he said, though his words didn't sound convincing. "Wait until my strength has returned."

The monk frowned. "Even then using the Ring will be very dangerous," he cautioned. "The Old Magic is the power of the True Gods. Whenever you unleash it you run the risk of waking any Chaos Spawn that might be entombed nearby."

Scythe laughed despite herself.

"So after all we went through to get this Ring, now we can't even use it?"

"Chaos is dangerous," Jerrod told her. "Whenever it is set free in the mortal world there are unforeseen consequences."

"Backlash," Keegan whispered.

The monk nodded. "You unleashed enough Chaos to fell a dragon and level an entire city. I shudder to think what the backlash of that might be."

On that note he spurred his horse to a brisk trot and rode on up ahead to let the others know that Keegan's state had improved. Norr and Vaaler pulled up their horses and dropped back to greet the wizard and express their relief at his recovery. And then they continued on in silence once more, each of them lost in his or her own thoughts as they headed for the plains of the Frozen East.

"You have a visitor, my Queen."

Rianna Avareen pulled her eyes away from the rubble that had once been her city. The Monarch's castle, bolstered by the Old Magic of her ancestor builders, had survived the destruction despite the battle against the dragon just beyond the gates. But of the rest of the Danaan capital—fully half the buildings—had been utterly destroyed.

For days she had stared from her window at the devastation, remembering the night the unquenchable fires had spread unchecked through the streets despite the efforts of her mages and sorcerers. Hourly she received casualty updates; just this morning the numbers of the dead had surpassed five thousand. And there were many bodies yet to come.

The grim air of death hung over the city like a pall. Not a single citizen had escaped the horror without losing a cherished loved one. Even the Queen had suffered. Drake's body had been recovered from the forest, along with that of his patrol. Vaaler, the son who had betrayed her people, was nowhere to be found. She had never felt so powerless, or so alone.

"You have a visitor, my Queen. He requests an audience." Andar's voice was louder this time, demanding a response from his silent liege.

The High Sorcerer had lost his wife, a captain of the guard, in the attack. His eldest son, a mage like his father, was still unaccounted for. Yet he performed the duties of his position with grace and honor. This was the bravery of a sort her people needed now, the courage to simply go on.

"I cannot give an individual audience to one of our people no matter the scope of his tragedy," the Queen said wearily. "We have all suffered beyond what we can bear, and I am not strong enough to shoulder the burden of others."

The truth shamed her, but she knew it must be so. She had to conserve her strength and her energy. The Danaan would rebuild Ferlhame, and they would turn to Rianna to lead them. She had to be ready for the ordeal.

"It is not a citizen, my Queen. Nor an emissary from one of the other cities in the kingdom. He is not a Danaan."

Rianna drew her breath in sharply. "A human dares come to us now, after one of their kind brought this upon us?"

"N-no, my Queen," Andar stammered. "He is definitely not human."

Only now did Rianna see the terror the High Sorcerer was struggling to keep in check.

"His name is Orath. He calls himself a . . . a Minion. He brings us a gift."

"What gift?" she asked, her throat suddenly dry.

"Revenge."

Acknowledgments

CHILDREN OF FIRE is the culmination of many, many years of sweat and toil—a project I've been working on in one form or another for over twenty years. The seeds were planted in my youth by the works of Tolkien, Terry Brooks, and David Eddings, authors I discovered because my parents—Ron and Viv—always encouraged me to read. Later, they opened up our home to me and my friends as we spent countless hours in the basement, lost in the fantasy worlds of Dungeons and Dragons. They bought me an electric typewriter in high school so I could start banging out the little bits and pieces spilling from my mind—pieces that over the years would evolve and coalesce into the foundation of my own original fantasy world.

When I dropped out of the business program at university, they supported me, even if they didn't fully understand why I did it at the time. Along with my wife, Jennifer, my parents always stood by me as I stumbled through a number of unappealing jobs and ill-suited careers, slowly finding my way to my true calling. They never once told me to give up on my dreams; they were always there for me when I needed them.

Ron and Viv—Mom and Dad—I've come a long, long way since those late nights in my room banging out those first few typewritten pages. But I'm here now, and it wouldn't have happened without you. Thank you, and I love you both.

ABOUT THE AUTHOR

DREW KARPYSHYN is the bestselling author of *Star Wars: The Old Republic: Revan* and the *Star Wars: Darth Bane* trilogy: *Path of Destruction, Rule of Two,* and *Dynasty of Evil.* He also wrote the acclaimed Mass Effect series of novels and worked as a writer/designer on numerous award-winning videogames. After spending most of his life in Canada, he finally grew tired of the long, cold winters and headed south in search of a climate more conducive to year-round golf. Drew Karpyshyn now lives in Texas with his wife, Jennifer, and their cat.

ABOUT THE TYPE

This book was set in Bembo, a typeface based on an old-style Roman face that was used for Cardinal Bembo's tract *De Aetna* in 1495. Bembo was cut by Francisco Griffo in the early sixteenth century. The Lanston Monotype Company of Philadelphia brought the well-proportioned letterforms of Bembo to the Untied States in the 1930s.